IT'S A KIND OF MAGIC

IT'S A KIND OF MAGIC

Carole Matthews

headline
review

First published in Great Britain in 2008
by Headline Review
An imprint of Headline Publishing Group

1

Cataloguing in Publication Data is
available from the British Library

ISBN 978 0 7553 2765 2 (hardback)
ISBN 978 0 7553 2766 9 (trade paperback)

Typeset in Bembo by
Palimpsest Book Production Limited, Grangemouth, Stirlingshire

Printed and bound in Great Britain by
Mackays of Chatham plc, Chatham, Kent

Headline's policy is to use papers that are natural, renewable and
recyclable products and made from wood grown in sustainable
forests. The logging and manufacturing processes are expected
to conform to the environmental regulations of the country of origin.

HEADLINE BOOK PUBLISHING
An Hachette Livre UK Company
338 Euston Road
London NW1 3BH

www.reviewbooks.co.uk
www.hodderheadline.com

I'm going to dedicate this book to all my lovely readers. Thanks for all the kind emails and notes that you've sent me over the years to keep me going. They make my fingers type just that little bit faster. I really appreciate your support over the years – some of you have been reading the books as long as I've been writing them! That's what I call dedication. Thank you so much.

Chapter One

Leo Harper's all-time favourite karaoke number was Madonna's 'Material Girl'. Which he was currently performing with a certain amount of panache. 'Material!' he crooned.

'Go, Leo! Go, Leo!' his audience chanted.

Leo's good friends, Grant and Lard, were always very encouraging of his vocal talents. This evening, they'd been plying him with strong alcohol since six o'clock to ensure that he was in fine voice.

'Do "I'm Every Woman" next!'

Leo held up his hand in modest salute. 'Can't. Can't.'

As well as being a thirty-two-year-old white, heterosexual male – which may or may not be relevant – his only other attribute was that he was generally known as unreliable. Leo worked in the City, but other than that he wasn't entirely sure what the purpose of his job was, other than to make huge sums of money for other people while making a reasonable amount of it for himself. Grant and Lard worked with him, although they were both considerably better at whatever they did than Leo was. They had earnest discussions about bear markets and bull markets and, quite frankly, Leo didn't really understand any of it. Because they were such good friends they covered up for all manner of his shortcomings and Leo loved them for it. He loved them very much. Leo felt he'd be more suited to being a . . . well, a something else. A singer, perhaps.

Leo turned his attention back to his performance. 'Material!' He considered himself exceptionally good at doing the high-pitched bits and waggled his imaginary breasts in the style of Madonna. 'Material!'

A look of concern crossed Grant's face and he shouted up at Leo through the cacophony, 'Mind you don't fall off the table, mate.'

Oh. And Leo was on a table. In an unspeakably trendy wine bar somewhere in the depths of the City of London. He had no idea where, as he'd been brought here totally against his will. The bar was very

Moulin Rouge. All chandeliers, red paint and gold-leaf mirrors. But no Nicole Kidman on a swing. Leo was at a leaving do – he couldn't remember whose. Fenella. Francine. Fiona. Something like that. Anyway, Leo thought she was a lovely lass. J-Lo arse and unfeasibly short skirts. Wonderful combination. Brain the size of a planet. Bit scary. And she was leaving. As soon as she removed her tongue from the boss's throat, if Leo wasn't mistaken. If she wasn't leaving she'd probably be sacked after her behaviour tonight so it was just as well.

Leo had to leave too as he was late. Extraordinarily late. Winding himself up for a big finale, he gave 'Material Girl' all he'd got. The audience cheered – Leo loved a cheering audience – even though most of them were marginally more drunk than he was. At this time in the evening, the bar at which torture ended and entertainment began had been lowered somewhat. Easily satisfied, they howled for more. Leo bowed gracefully as he prepared to take his leave. Someone else's tonsils would have to take the place of his.

A shout went up. 'Do "I Will Survive"!'

Next to 'Material Girl', this was Leo's best number. He also did a refreshingly original interpretation of 'My Way' – somewhere between Frank Sinatra and Sid Vicious. His 'Tainted Love' wasn't half bad either – even though he usually had to say it himself. Leo shook his head in a self-deprecating way even as he basked in his own glory. 'No. No. No.'

He certainly wouldn't survive if he didn't get a move on. Besides, he didn't do requests. Elvis didn't. So neither did Leo.

'Can't. Can't. Have to go. Emma'sh birthday.' Was that his voice slurring?

Emma was Leo's girlfriend. For years. And years. On and off. More off than on. He had no idea why she put up with him. Leo wouldn't, if he were her. But then he knew that Emma didn't know why she put up with him either. He couldn't remember quite how they met but he was sure it involved him being wonderfully suave and sophisticated and sweeping Emma off her feet. She'd been the only lady in his life ever since. And he loved her, loved her, loved her. Even the 'off' periods had been very brief, therefore, not necessitating the finding of a suitable replacement. Which was nice. During the 'on' periods, however, Leo was a constant source of irritation to her. His darling Emma didn't appreciate his singing talents. Nor his tardiness.

Leo's watch was very blurred, but he knew, instinctively, that it was telling him a bad thing. The hands should be pointing very differently if it was good, he was sure. 'Shit. Shit. Late. Late.'

In his haste to depart, Leo fell head-long off the table and landed in the arms of his true and trusted friends. His limbs were feeling very lovely. 'Emma will kill me,' he gasped before floating off to oblivion on a fluffy cloud.

From faraway Leo heard his friends sigh patiently. Grant looked over his head at Lard and said, 'She might not need to.'

Chapter Two

'Emma, darling, is that Vivaldi?' My mother cocks her head towards the direction of some unseen sound system.

'Yes.' I take a sip of my champagne and try to smile at her.

'How lovely.'

'Yes.'

'Very soothing. Relaxing.'

'Yes,' I say tightly. If I grip the stem of my glass any harder it will break. Already my knuckles bear an unhealthy white pallor.

This is a fabulous restaurant. There's no denying that. A firm family favourite. Whatever the celebration – anniversaries, the announcement of a new grandchild, the traditional Christmas gathering – a table is booked at Ranolfs. Thirtieth birthdays are no exception. And this is mine.

Ranolfs has a hushed, genteel atmosphere that panders perfectly to my parents' idea of having a good time. No rowdy pubs for the Chambers clan. No chain pizza places. No *faux* Mexican cantinas. No standing in line for buffet food. My father would rather saw off his own arm than queue up for a slice of roast beef. At Ranolfs a surfeit of waiters bustle about, unobtrusively catering to their patrons' every whim. The *maître d'hôtel* – a starched and black-suited cadaver of a man – has been the same person for around a hundred years. Look back at the historical photographs on the walls and you can see that he features in all of them – in the same way that Jack Nicholson did in *The Shining*. Oak panelling lines the walls, the like of which you'll never see in a Happy Eater. The starched white linen of each table bears an exquisite arrangement of highly-scented pastel roses. It's rather like an exclusive gentlemen's club – except that they grudgingly allow women in too. The lighting is subdued. Conversation is muted, quite probably frowned upon. Only the regular popping of expensive corks punctuates the light classical music.

4

Next to my mother is my father. 'I'm going to stop doing face-lifts,' he announces to no one in particular. 'The last woman I did ended up with a face like a smacked arse.' He shakes his head in bewilderment. 'Why they want to do it, I've no idea.'

My father, Charles Chambers, is 'old school' – bluff, bigoted and bombastic. He's a cosmetic surgeon of some note – if one acquires a reputation by giving eye-lifts to ageing soap stars and fading rock singers and daytime television presenters in the last desperate throes of their careers. Daddy might wonder why they all avail themselves of his services, but he doesn't mind charging them rather handsomely for the privilege.

'I'll stick to Botox.' He confirms this with a hearty swig of his champagne. 'Better just to paralyse someone's chops than cut bits out completely. You can be sued at the drop of a hat these days. There's no fun in being a surgeon any more.' Daddy, morosely, seeks succour in his alcohol.

'How lovely,' my mother says, patting her exquisitely coiffured and honey-coloured hair. She turns to me and places a hand on my arm. 'What do you think, darling?'

'Yes,' I reply automatically, not taking in the question. I glance towards the door again. This is torture. And extreme humiliation. Leo should have been here two hours ago. And he wasn't. As a consequence, my thirtieth birthday celebration dinner has been eaten in a tense silence. My unruly elfin haircut has been glammed up – though I feel like tearing chunks of it out. I'm wearing a fairytale floaty dress. And it has all been a pointless effort.

'Emma,' my father sighs theatrically. 'Do stop looking at the door. It's not going to make him get here any quicker.'

I pull out my mobile phone. 'Maybe I'll just give him a ring.'

Mobile phones are banned in Ranolfs and there's a collective gasp around the table which would have been more suited to me having pulled down the top of my gown to expose my breasts.

'You'll do no such thing,' my father says, snatching the phone from me.

'He may have had an accident.'

'I'll make bally sure he does one of these days.'

'Daddy!'

'Face it, darling,' Mr Chambers, cosmetic surgeon to the wannabe stars continues unabashed. 'He's let you down again.'

5

'You don't know that.'

'I do.' My father glances conspicuously at the one empty space at the table. The myriad of cutlery lies untouched, as does the neatly folded napkin in the shape of a fan. 'He always does.'

'Charles,' my mother intervenes – as she does so often in our frequent father-daughter spats. 'It's Emma's birthday. Don't upset her.'

'I'm not upsetting her,' he protests, his voice drowning out the delicate strains of Vivaldi. 'It's the lovely Leo who's not here. *Again*.'

'Charles. Please.'

'Why can't you find a nice man?' My father sweeps his arm expansively across the table. 'A man like Dicky or Austin?'

Dicky and Austin – the nice men in question – smile in a self-satisfied and distinctly unpleasant way. Dicky and Austin are, unfortunately in my view, married to my older sisters. The sisters who toed the line and found themselves suitable husbands and settled down early to produce the required number of grandchildren. While I, instead, found Leo.

Chinless wonders – that's the best way of describing my two brothers-in-law. Austin is a farmer; a gentleman farmer, possessed of acres of rolling farmland, fat, special breed sheep and his own brand of dairy ice-cream sold in theatres throughout the country. Arabelle, my eldest sister, is deemed to have married well. Even though she has to sleep with someone who is ruddy, rotund and sports an excess of nasal hair. Her three children range from angelic to the spawn from hell.

Dicky imports antique carpets and sells them out of a quaintly over-priced shop in a pretty little town in the heart of the Cotswolds – the sort of place that is lined with similar shops but where you can't buy a fresh vegetable or a newspaper. My brother-in-law spends a lot of his time in the third world, probably being extraordinarily obnoxious to people less fortunate than himself and ripping them off with unfair prices. 'Fair Trade' is not a term Dicky is familiar with. All his carpets are probably woven by the callused hands of small children for a few rupees and aren't antique at all. But Dicky is loaded and that counts for a lot in my father's world. Dicky is moderately passable in the looks department, if you discount the burgeoning businessman's paunch, but he's crushingly boring on every other level. Unless you're interested in the intricacies of carpets, of course. My brother-in-law also has a problem with self-esteem. Far too much of it. The middle sister of the Chambers' clan is Clara and, despite having two hyper-active school-age children, she still manages to conduct a long-term affair with their gardener – Darren – whenever Dicky sets foot on another continent. And, to be honest, I can't say that I blame her.

I, however, have been dating Leo for the last five years. Dating is the right term. I never know with Leo whether he'll be around for the next week or not. It isn't that he's a womaniser or anything like that – Leo would have absolutely no idea where to start when it comes to seducing a woman. I'm never going to find him locked in the under-stairs cupboard at a party with my best friend. He doesn't have it in him. Leo might well lock *himself* in the understairs cupboard at a party – but that would be as far as it went. He's clueless when it comes to women – and most other things. Utterly clueless. Which is extraordin-ary because he really is staggeringly good-looking and has cheekbones that most supermodels would kill for. Leo possesses an easy charm that he's completely unaware of, and that's his biggest asset. Women fall for it in droves. Why do we do that?

I – for better, for worse – am no exception. I met Leo through a mutual friend on a day out to the coast. Leo was trying to windsurf and had nearly drowned himself after getting tangled up in the sail. I swam out from the beach to rescue him. Even though he was coughing and spluttering and had seaweed strewn in his hair, within minutes, I'd fallen for him big time. Five years later it seems as if I'm still rescuing him from himself.

It was me that did all the initial running in this relationship. And me that's still doing it. Leo is physically incapable of planning ahead. That includes grocery shopping as much as relationships. The less inter-ested Leo was in being pinned down, the more I pursued him. It's prob-ably down to the fact that I'm the youngest and most spoiled daughter and am, therefore, used to getting everything that I want. All I've ever desired has been handed to me on a plate by my doting parents. A lovely position to be in – but not one that accustoms you to someone saying no. Even the men I've dated pre-Leo have doted on me and, subsequently, have bored me to tears. And how many modern women want a doormat as a boyfriend? With Leo it has been an entirely different matter from day one. He hasn't doted on me. He certainly hasn't bored me to tears. He was, from the start, elusive and frustrating. I saw Leo as a challenge. For the first three months of our relationship, he never once returned one of my telephone calls. He just knew that I'd continue to phone him and I often wonder what would have happened if I'd simply stopped calling.

Leo is not a natural hunter gatherer. The caveman gene has passed him by completely. There isn't a bone in his body that compels him to barbecue raw meat. He's never going to grab me by the hair and drag me into a cave, much as I may secretly have a fantasy that he might. It's an attitude that serves him in all other areas of his life. My dearly-beloved is reasonably successful in his chosen career but it couldn't be said that he pursues promotion with a vengeance. Casual, is the best way to describe Leo's approach to work – and to life and to love. Casual. *Very* casual. I can't help believing that Leo would be absolutely wonderful if only he'd apply himself to the real world.

He comes from very good stock, to use Dicky's phraseology. Nothing wrong with his pedigree and he could certainly give Awful Austin and Dreadful Dicky a run for their money. I look round the table and can see why Leo might not be keen to spend time with my delightful family. The men treat him like something of a leper because he doesn't have an opinion on politics, cricket or rugby. My sisters nag him, at every opportunity, about when he'll 'make an honest woman' of me.

Though, I have to say, his own family don't fare much better. It isn't entirely Leo's fault that none of his relatives are speaking to him at the moment. If you fall drunkenly into your grandma's grave at her funeral it tends to stretch the filial bonds to breaking point. I'm sure they will, in time, forgive him. After all, it was his beloved grandmother who taught him most of the drinking games he knows. She would have found it very amusing – God rest her soul. It's a shame the rest of his family don't. Which is unfair. Leo is Leo. They smashed the mould to smithereens after they made him. Some will say with just cause. But if you take the time to look, he has a lot of qualities. Amazing qualities. They're just hard to put your finger on.

'Leo is a nice man,' I insist. Everyone around the table avoids looking at me. My mother pats my hand sympathetically, which makes me want to cry. Out of all of them, only I can see Leo's good points. 'He is. He's just . . . He's just very good at hiding it.'

I grip my champagne glass even more tightly while smiling sweetly at the rest of the white-lipped gathering at the table. And when he finally shows up, I'll kill him.

Chapter Three

'See you tomorrow, Leo.' Grant and Lard were leaving. Reluctantly. They were clearly worried that they were abandoning Leo to the mercy of the night. Which they were. 'Will you be okay?'

'Fine. Fine.' Leo managed a wave. 'Night, night, chaps.' His best friends in the whole wide world were going off in search of a taxi, a woman or a kebab. Leo couldn't remember which. Instead of joining them, he was crawling along the pavement on all fours. Remaining upright had proved just too difficult. Strangely, Grant and Lard seemed to be coping much better with vertical.

The pavement was very cold and hard. Leo thought that pavements should be made in a much softer material, especially for moments like these. Then he noticed what a lovely night it was – the stars, moon, sky, that sort of thing – and he wished that Emma was there. But he didn't know why. Love, probably. Love, love, love. All you need is love. In one hand, he had a bottle of champagne. In the other, his car keys. Somewhere near was his car. A lovely car that he'd christened Ethel.

But all the cars looked the same. All the bloody same.

'Ah. Looks likely.' Leo ran his hands over Ethel's curvy flanks. Very likely. 'Hello, my shpeshial girl,' he slurred.

The keyhole didn't appear to be big enough. The key was all bendy too. Leo's mind wandered to kebabs – they seemed like a nice idea, but it was late. Late, late, late. Horribly late. No sex for a fortnight late. The key was still bendy, bendy, bendy. Leo couldn't get it to do the right thing.

'Open. Open. Open.' Leo shook the door handle in case the car was playing hard to get. 'Open, you bastard.'

A loud siren started. Beep. Beep. Beep. Too many decibels. 'Not bloody deaf,' Leo shouted and shook the handle some more. 'Come on, you bloody stubborn blue . . .'

Then it hit him. Not his car. His car was red. Yes, red. A battered

VW Beetle. Unlike its owner – young and flakey – Ethel was loyal, reliable. And not blue. 'Sorry. Sorry.' Leo gave the car an apologetic pat. 'Sorry, old chap.'

He crawled a bit more. His head and his knees throbbed. 'Ah!'

Then he saw Ethel. He leaned towards her, kissing her red bonnet. She was there all the time. Waiting nicely. The key fitted smoothly into the lock, the door swung open and he climbed in. 'That's more like it.'

Now all he had to do was negotiate the pedals. Up, down. Up, down. The gears were next. Wiggle, waggle. Giggle.

'Start, start, start.' His key fell to the floor. 'Start, start, start.'

Eventually the car started. He found first gear and eased out the clutch. With a few more revs he was off jumping, jumping down the road. But not too fast. The window was open and the champagne bottle was dangling out.

'Hello, cyclist.' Leo waved the champagne in what he hoped was a friendly gesture. But he was a bit too close.

The cyclist wobbled and fell off as Ethel continued to jump along. 'Sorry. Awfully sorry.'

Leo waved the champagne apologetically and the cyclist shook his fist. But Leo had no time to stop. He could see the restaurant ahead of him.

It was a posh restaurant. Stuffy. And Emma's party was taking place inside. Hours ago. Leo was well and truly stuffed.

As he stumbled out of car and tripped over on the pavement, Leo took some deep breaths. He straightened his tie. Straightened his hair. Straightened his eyes.

Emma, he thought smugly, would never guess that he'd been drinking.

Chapter Four

'Oh,' my mother cries. 'A lovely surprise!'

My family gathered at the table all look expectantly towards the door. My head shoots up and I try not to look too downhearted when there's still no sight of the errant Leo. Where the hell can he be at this time? Anything could have happened to him. He's a one-man disaster zone, a walking soap opera, not safe to be let out on his own. He could be anywhere – in a ditch, in a hospital, in the city centre naked and tied to a bollard – all of which have applied to Leo in the past. This better had be him and he'd better not be full of his usual Emmenthal excuses – stories with more holes in them than Swiss cheese.

But it isn't Leo. Instead, a rather grand waiter sweeps in bearing an equally grand birthday cake. It's white and iced with pink frills. Thirty candles flame exuberantly on the top and I hope that someone has a fire extinguisher to hand. Thirty bloody candles and what have I got to show for all these years?

Forcing a smile into place, I stand up as the waiter sets the cake on the table. My family start a tense and uncomfortable rendition of 'Happy Birthday' while I try to look deliriously happy, as the song requires, even though it's a truly terrible dirge. Halfway through, as my parents are running out of steam, there is a unearthly crashing noise from the adjoining hallway. 'Happy Birthday' is truncated. The gentle and civilised hum of conversation in the restaurant grinds to an abrupt halt.

A waiter appears, wearing what seems to be the contents of a soup tureen.

'Sorry. Sorry. Awfully sorry.' And following him is, of course, Leo. Carrying a bottle of champagne and weaving unsteadily. 'Sorry. Sorry.'

Two dozen stony faces turn towards him. Six of them from our table alone. Like a dinosaur experiencing pain, it takes a moment or two for Leo to realise the venom that's being directed towards him.

He gives me one of his heartbreakingly beautiful smiles. 'Sorry. Sorry. Late. Fuck. No. Sorry. Sorry. Not fuck. Bad language. Flip. Late. Oh flip. Very flip. Flipping heck. Late. Flipping office party. Bollocks.'

I want to die. I want to lie down and die. But first I want Leo to die. Painfully.

'Hello, Mrs . . . Mrs . . .'

'Chambers,' I supply tightly.

'Mother.' Leo gives her a cheesy smile.

My mother, never easily flustered, goes all girly. 'Oh.' She fans herself with her napkin.

'Mother.' Leo tries it again.

'Not while there's breath in my body,' my father mutters.

Leo, not realising that he should stop while he's on a roll, answers with, 'Dad' and a pantomime matey wink.

My father coughs out his drink.

Leo turns his gaze on me – a helpless puppy expression face-to-face with my best snarling werewolf look. 'Emma!' He holds up his bottle of champagne. 'Darling! Happy Birthday!' Leo swigs from his bottle. 'Happy Birthday to you . . .' He urges the crowd to join him. The crowd doesn't. 'Happy Birthday to you . . . Happy Birthday dear . . . dear . . .'

The pause goes on for too long.

'Emma,' I supply.

'I knew that! Happy Birthday, dear EMMA, Happy Birthday to you-hoo!'

Leo blows out all the candles on my cake. 'Marvellous,' he says. And then he passes out in it.

Chapter Five

The ladies' loo at Ranolfs is just as posh as the dining room. Deep marble sinks with individually folded fluffy hand towels stacked next to them grace one wall. A tray of complimentary perfumes and lotions await each customer. Plush velvet chairs grouped in one corner make sure that no one has to suffer the inconvenience of standing while waiting.

Leo sits in one now. Slumps, actually. All six gangly feet of him shoehorned into a delicate apricot velvet, fringed chair. There's a pink candle-holder from my birthday cake wedged behind his ear. I pick bits of sponge and jam from his dark, floppy hair and peel splatters of candle wax from his face more forcefully than is strictly necessary.

'Ow! Ow!'

'Shut up, Leo.' I hand him his cup of extra strong coffee which he obediently drinks in an attempt to sober himself up. 'You look dreadful. Everything's askew.' I take in his work suit. Clearly he hasn't even made it home from the office. 'You look like you've been crawling along the pavements.'

Leo looks shocked. 'Never.'

I resume my task with vigour. 'You're useless.'

'Yes, darling.'

'It's my birthday.'

He hangs his head. 'I know.'

'You should have been here hours ago.'

'I know.'

'You have humiliated me . . . mortified me . . . in front of my parents.' And my sisters' stupid, smug husbands, which probably hurts more. 'It's my birthday! Did you get me a present?'

Leo slaps his forehead. 'Fiddlesticks.'

'No.' I roll the ball of wax into one of the fluffy towels I've purloined for the purpose. 'You didn't last year either. Or the year before.'

'Sorry. Sorry,' Leo mumbles. 'Terrible er . . .'

'Memory,' I supply.

'Quite.'

'You have embarrassed me.'

'Again,' Leo adds.

'Yes, Leo. Again.'

'Sorry. Sorry. So bloody sorry.'

Standing up, I throw the soiled towel into the waiting hamper. How many times in the past has Leo let me down? My father is right. They're probably all out there now, eating my birthday cake, discussing what a loser Leo is and saying aren't I silly to have stayed with him all this time – particularly as I'm approaching my sell-by date. I can just hear the conversation. It's one that has played over in the Chambers' household many times. Usually when Leo fails to appear for something important at the pre-arranged time. Or turns up inappropriately dressed. The time he arrived in a pink tutu for a night of *Swan Lake* at the Royal Ballet singularly failed to amuse my father. Even though it was just a coincidence that it was a tutu and Leo was wearing it to raise money for Children in Need. A wonderful cause, I'm sure you'll agree. It wasn't my dear boyfriend's fault that it clashed with a night out with my parents. Both arrangements had been longstanding and Leo didn't want to lose the five hundred quid bet that he wouldn't last in it all day. My father offered him five hundred if he'd take it off. It was just a shame that Leo hadn't thought to bring any other clothes with him – otherwise they'd both have been happy. But that was one noble cause in a sea of less honourable ones. My mother occasionally rises to my loved one's defence, but she does sometimes wonder why she supports him. And even I'm getting fed up with explaining away all of Leo's failings.

I look at my boyfriend, pink icing in his hair, with dismay. He's ridiculously handsome and, when sober, charming and funny. It's just . . . it's just that it's rather like dating a fourteen year old. An irresponsible fourteen year old. Isn't it about time that I was in a relationship with someone who's my own mental age? I guess it is. But that doesn't make letting go any less painful. I love Leo. With all my heart. It's just that most of the time he drives me to distraction. Sometimes I feel more like his mother than his lover. I should have got hitched to one of the dullards I dated when I was nineteen – just like my sisters did. By now I would have been settled down with a barrister and a couple

14

of tousle-haired kids to keep my parents happy – or onto my first divorce. Finding a mate seems to become so much more complex as you hit thirty. Or perhaps I'm simply getting more fussy.

'This is it, Leo,' I say sadly. 'This is as far as it goes. It has to be. This is the end.'

'The end.' Leo looks up at me with bleary eyes. He appears to be going to sleep.

'You've gone too far, too often.'

'It was just a lickle-ickle leaving party, Ems.' He indicates 'lickle-ickle' with his fingers and flutters his eyelashes at me.

'One drink, you said, Leo. You said you would go for *one* drink.' I take the bottle of champagne that dangles from his hand and calmly pour the remaining contents over his head. Leo doesn't even flinch. 'Not several bottles.'

'I had a couple.'

'A couple? That usually means you've knocked it back like a man who's been stranded in the Sahara desert for six months with nothing to eat but salted peanuts.'

A woman with a fulsome matron's breast comes in and recoils in horror as she sees Leo in the corner. A man in the ladies' powder room is clearly an affront to her delicate sensibilities and it's quite obvious that she considers backing straight out again.

'Evening,' Leo says drunkenly, giving her a leery smile.

'He's with me,' I say. 'He's harmless. Mostly.'

The woman rushes by and, glaring at me, heads into one of the cubicles – thankfully not the one Leo has thrown up in. She locks the door behind her with feeling.

I lower my voice. 'We used to have fun, Leo.'

'I have fun.'

'Yes. With Grant and Lard. Not with me. Your idea of fun is getting drunk and dancing on tables.'

Leo looks at me, filled with indignation. 'It is not.'

'You're so unreliable these days.'

'I always have been.'

'And I've always hoped you'd grow out of it.'

Leo takes my hand. 'I'm trying to, Emma. Really I am.'

'You're not,' I insist. 'You're getting worse by the minute. And I've had enough. There's no magic any more.'

'Magic?'

'Yes, Leo. Magic.'

'Did there used to be?' he asks tentatively.

'Yes,' I say softly. 'Once upon a time.'

'I could buy a top hat and a white rabbit.' He shrugs his shoulders.

'It's suggestions like that which make me realise that you're a lost cause.'

'I might have the best of me hidden up my sleeve, ready to produce at an appropriate moment.'

'You might,' I sigh. 'But I doubt it.'

His lip droops sadly. 'I wish I could give you magic, Emma. Really I do.'

I shake my head. 'It's no good. It's gone. We could never get it back now. The magic has gone, Leo. Gone.'

'Gone.'

The woman emerges from her cubicle, hurriedly washes her hands, eschews the free toiletries and scurries out like a frightened rabbit rather than a white one, giving us both as wide a berth as possible.

'Nice meeting you,' Leo shouts after her. I'm sure in her panic the woman doesn't see my boyfriend's friendly wave. Perhaps he is losing his charm. I do hope so. Leo arranges his face to look suitably penitent.

'You never tell me that you love me,' I say.

'I do.'

'You don't.'

'I do.'

'What?'

'The L thing. I do. You know . . . L you.'

I sigh and rub my hands over my eyes. In the restaurant they'll be bringing in the coffee and the mints. I look at Leo's cup, the dregs inside going cold. 'You can't even bring yourself to say it.'

'I'm a bloke. An English bloke. We're appallingly bad at slushy stuff. Possibly the worst in the world. It's genetic. If I were French it would be a very different story. I'd be all *oui, oui, oui, ma chérie* and *je t'aime.* Kissy. Kissy. But I can't do that. Besides, you'd laugh at me if I tried to be romantic.'

'I think you'd better go now,' I tell him. ''Before I hold your head down a toilet and flush it. Probably the one you were heartily sick in.'

'Yes. You're right. Jolly good idea. Fine idea.' Leo stands up and retrieves his empty bottle of champagne. Still looking the worse for wear, he ambles towards the door. 'I'll give you a ring tomorrow. When you're feeling better.'

I stay where I am. Rooted to the spot. There's no way Leo is going to sweet-talk me round this time. I'm thirty years old. I have the birthday cards to prove it – with one notable exception. It's time I had a decent boyfriend. One who treats me properly. One who might even want to settle down and think about the future. One who, perish the thought, might even want to marry me. Can I ever imagine having children with Leo? Inwardly, I shudder. He'd be more badly behaved than any offspring we could produce. He'd be teaching them all how to do armpit farts before they could walk and putting vodka in their bedtime milk. My eyes follow Leo as he totters to the door and my heart contracts painfully. They'd be damn good-looking kids though. Is that enough to build a future on?

I look at him sadly. Leo has been a part of my life for a long time, maybe too long. Are we doing this out of habit now rather than love? It might well be a habit, but habits are notoriously difficult to break – even bad ones.

It's time to move on, start the next decade of my life with a clean sheet. They say life begins at forty, but I can't wait that long. My life is damn well going to have to get a move on at thirty. I just wish someone, anyone would come and sort Leo out for me. I wish it with all of my heart. I know that I want to be with Leo forever, but I'm tired of nagging him, cajoling him, bullying him. All I want is a nice, quiet relationship with him. It's frustrating when he has so much potential. I've tried everything and I'm at a loss. Isn't there a boyfriend makeover programme that could sort him out? Surely that Aggie woman off the television could clean his act up a bit. Can't someone take him away and bring him back refurbished as a proper, grown-up lover and save me all this trouble?

Suddenly, a warm breeze envelops me, but it makes me shiver nonetheless. I swing round, for some inexplicable reason expecting to see someone standing behind me. But there's no one there. I'm sure I hear the faintest peal of laughter. It's disconcerting, but not enough to distract me from my purpose.

'Tomorrow?' Leo says again, breaking into my reverie.

'There'll be no tomorrow, Leo. No ring. Not ever. It's over between us.'

Leo turns to me. There's a bleakness to his bleary eyes. 'Over?'

17

The tears spring to my eyes. 'Over.' I confirm it with a nod.

'Emma, I wish I could be what you want.' He looks unhappier than I've ever seen him.

'You mean not a deeply inadequate and crap boyfriend.'

'I've tried,' he says. 'I've tried to live up to your high standards, but I can't. This is me.' He holds out his hands.

'Me' has unkempt hair dotted with icing, a skew whiff tie, muddy knees, bits of birthday candle still stuck to his face and a heartbreaking smile.

'I do . . . thing . . . you,' he pleads. 'I do. And you know I do. I just can't do it the way you want me to.'

I exhale sadly. 'It isn't good enough any more.'

Leo echoes my sigh. 'No.'

We stare at each other without talking.

'So,' I say eventually. 'This is it.'

'Yes.'

'This could be the last time we meet,' I point out. In a ladies' loo in a ridiculously stuffy restaurant – even that is typically Leo.

'Yes.' Leo fiddles with his tie.

'Don't you want to say something?'

'I'm starving,' he blurts out. 'If it's any consolation I didn't go with Grant and Lard for a kebab. I don't suppose I could have some of your birthday cake for old times' sake?'

'Leo,' I snap. 'You are too pathetic for words.' And, without wanting to be overly dramatic, I burst into tears and bang out of the door.

Chapter Six

After Emma left, Leo looked at himself in the mirror. 'Wrong thing to say, old bean.' He tried to drink from the bottle of champagne but it was empty. 'Still, it looks like a great cake.' He pulled a bit of the icing from his hair and popped it into his mouth. 'Mmm.'

He'd looked for Emma at Ranolfs, but he couldn't find her. Though he had to admit that he didn't actually go back into the dining room as that would have meant facing her father and, quite frankly, Emma's father always looked far too keen to perform cosmetic surgery on him without the benefit of anaesthetic. And probably not on his face. So, there he was, out on the street – alone, cold and suddenly a lot more sober than he'd been a few minutes ago.

He had to throw a bit of light on this situation. Emma was a habitual dumper, thus making Leo a multiple dumpee. She dumped him, on average, three times a week for some real or imagined misdemeanour. And three times a week they then carried on as if nothing had ever happened. But even for Emma this sounded like a rather severe and final dumping. Leo had a horrible feeling that this time – perhaps for the first time – she was absolutely serious.

And he could see that she had a point. Really, he could. If he was Emma – a stunningly pretty and feisty young thing – he didn't think he'd put up with him either. He was always making her brown eyes blue – another favourite karaoke hit of his. But in his defence Leo had to confess that no matter how hard he tried, he just couldn't help it. The world, fate, his inability to keep a watch in working order, all conspired against him. From the age of five, he had tried to develop reliability as a character trait, but to no avail. There were people in life who were natural organisers – Emma, for one example. They ran their lives by diaries, BlackBerry computer whatsits and were perfectly capable of keeping appointments. And they were wonderful. Truly wonderful. Leo was filled with admiration for anyone who had that sort of brain capacity. He, on the other hand, was one of life's air-heads. If he could possibly miss a train, he would. If he could turn up at the wrong theatre/restaurant/wedding/address of any sort, he would. If he could arrive late – for anything – he would. The saying 'you'll be late for your own funeral' was invented just for Leo. He'd probably be at the wrong church too. Or the wrong body would be in the coffin and Leo would be in a hamper at a dry cleaners somewhere.

He blamed part of it on his English public school education – Leo was institutionalised from the moment he could walk. His parents were ridiculously wealthy and acrimoniously divorced, so during termtime he and his two older brothers had been nurtured by various house-masters with dubious tendencies. It was only the school holidays that had been a problem, for then his parents argued over who could and couldn't have their offspring in between trips to the yacht at St Tropez and the ski lodge in Gstaad. Leo, subsequently, spent a lot of time being herded about by chauffeurs and fed by housekeepers. He never would have said that he had it hard – on the contrary. He wasn't alone in being treated rather like an inconvenient parcel by his dear folks. In school he'd been surrounded by enormously privileged kids who had suffered abandonment and wealth-induced neglect far worse than he did. But everyone knew that boarding school was a hotbed of irrespon-sible and eccentric characters, that was why so many of their pupils turned out to be politicians. It also churned out a good few sexual deviants but Leo didn't think he was one of them – unless you count a mild shoe fetish inspired by a matron who had a penchant for white stilettos. They also, along the way, hammered out of you any inclina-tion you might have once harboured for forming intimate partnerships later in life. He might not have a clue what sort of people his parents really were or either of his brothers, for that matter, or have any sort of working relationship with them, but Leo was very self-sufficient in an annoyingly haphazard and blokey way. Really he was.

Even when he had bouts of trying to organise his life – keep a diary, buy vegetables and generally act like a grown up – he fared no better. Things happened to Leo without him even trying. Cars crashed into him unbidden. Baths overflowed into the downstairs flat with annoying regularity, particularly for the downstairs neighbours. Clothes became mysteriously stained without him even moving. And Emma just didn't fully understand that.

Leo's trusty car, Ethel, was waiting outside, but he'd had far too much booze — at the Last Chance Saloon, some might add — to consider driving all the way home. He couldn't actually find his car keys either, to be truthful. Leo searched his pockets again, but he hadn't got any cash for a cab — though he was sure he'd plenty when he set out for the night. Money vanished mysteriously from his pockets too.

Although there was a fresh breeze in the air, it was a fine night for a walk down by the Embankment of the River Thames — one of Leo's favourite spots in the whole of London and there were a lot of very charming spots to choose from these days.

He went over and gave his car a kiss. 'See you tomorrow. Be good.' Leo waved as he walked away and advised Ethel over his shoulder, 'Don't do anything I wouldn't do.'

Ethel stood there looking like a particularly guileless and well-behaved vehicle.

The stars were still twinkling, the moon was still a perfect crescent and it was amazing to think that life-changing events were going on all the time on the small planet called Earth, and yet the sky was unchanging. Well, Leo knew that it was changing all the time — he too watched *The Sky at Night* — but it didn't look any different to the untrained eye. Emma had dumped him. Permanently this time, it would seem, and yet none of the stars had gone out. The moon hadn't curled up and died. And you would think that they'd know that something awful had happened below them, wouldn't you? But they didn't. No one knew but Emma and Leo, and that made him feel close to her even though they'd parted. Leo turned up his collar and folded his jacket more tightly around him. No one berated him for coming out without a coat. And he knew already that life without Emma was going to be very strange.

Chapter Seven

I've found myself an elaborately-carved antique bench in a secluded corridor of the restaurant behind the kitchens and now sit curled up on it, knees hugged to my chest. Curling into a foetal ball is not far away. I sob into a tissue, sniffing loudly. Waiters bustle by, studiously ignoring me. But I don't care who sees my distress. One of the paintings on the wall opposite is skew whiff. A fault that I know only I will notice, despite my misery.

'Now, now, darling. What's all the fuss?' My mother comes along the corridor and sits down beside me. Always the picture of elegance, my dear Mummy, Catherine Chambers, straightens her silk skirt and crosses her legs. Now in her mid-sixties, she is still tall, slim and very beautiful. I hope that one day I'll age as gracefully. Whenever there is a crisis my father flies off the handle, while my mother stays steadfastly calm and unruffled.

Mummy pats my hand. 'I gather Leo has departed?'

I nod.

'You can always rely on Leo to make the party go with a swing,' she says, smiling.

'I could kill him,' I sniff. 'With my bare hands.'

'Oh, Emma.' My mother strokes my hair. 'Leo is Leo. Don't take him so seriously. That way holds nothing but constant pain and suffering. Let him be himself. You'll not change him.'

'I don't want to change him,' I insist, twisting my tissue into a tight spiral. 'I just want him to stop doing all the things that irritate me.'

Mummy gives me a knowing look.

'If only Leo would . . .' I start to cry again.

'Grow up? Start acting his age? Be more like someone else? Anyone else?' My mother shakes her head. 'It doesn't work like that. You can't change someone's basic character. I should know. Take your father. He's a dyed-in-the-wool insufferable bore.'

I look up, shocked.

'We all know that,' Mummy continues dismissively. 'Don't look so scandalised. He's been exactly the same since the day I met him. Some days he drives me to distraction. I could joyfully strangle him.' She looks at me with a warm smile and fine lines appear at the corner of her eyes under her flawless foundation. 'You wouldn't believe the number of times I've considered drugging his tea to make him more bearable. Or taping up his mouth so that he doesn't drone on and on about the same old thing. But I love him just the same. Always have.'

'That's different.'

'I think you'll find it isn't,' my mother advises.

'If Leo could just . . .'

'If you don't love him as he is, darling, then you must let him go. Leopards invariably stay spotted. And your Leo is definitely a leopard if ever I saw one. A very handsome one. If it's a domesticated lap cat that you want, then I'm afraid you're looking in the wrong place.'

'Why does he always have to be so annoying?'

'He's only annoying if you let him be. To some Leo is the life and soul of the party. He's handsome, funny, and – with the odd lapse – charming. Leo is always going to be a challenge. But then he's never going to be one to sit at home with his pipe and slippers. If that isn't what you want, then it might be time to move on. You can't spend your life trying to control him, darling.'

I sigh. 'Chance would be a fine thing.'

'That's not fair on either of you,' my mother warns. She puts her arm round me and I snuggle into her shoulder just as I did when I was a child. The strong, heady scent of her favourite Chanel No 5 perfume washes over me as unchanging and steadfast as my mother's love. 'You are my favourite daughter,' Catherine says. I make to protest but Mummy puts a finger to my lips. 'We both know that you are. But you take too much on your shoulders. You are a worrier like your father. Worrying doesn't change anything. It's very easy to spend your life in a complete dither about something that might never happen. All I want is that you are happy in your life. Think very carefully before you let Leo go. Are you sure you'd prefer to have a Dreadful Dicky or an Awful Austin?'

My eyes widen. I'd no idea that my mother and I have given them the same nicknames.

'I love your sisters too,' she continues. 'But their taste in men is abominable. I don't know how they can bear to be married to them. Leo might be a handful, but feisty men are so much more fun.'

I fail to look convinced.

'We're only on this little planet for a very brief time, darling. Don't spend it being miserable.' Catherine sits back on the hard bench. 'You need to relax. You're very uptight. Chill out. Let it all hang out, as they said in the sixties. You need to drink a little, dance a little. Maybe love a lot. That's my advice to you. Forget all about Leo for a few weeks. See where life takes you. Enjoy casual sex with a dangerous stranger.'

Now I do sit up and take notice. 'Mother!'

'You might see things very differently. Life is too short to spend it wracked with anxiety. Loosen up. You modern women can do whatever you like. Isn't that meant to be a benefit?'

'I suppose so.'

'Be thankful for that,' my mother says.

'You're probably right.' I pick at a fingernail. 'I love Leo so much. I want him to feel the same. I want him to show that he cares more, but he just seems to be completely incapable.'

'You'll worry yourself into an early grave.' Catherine hugs me. 'You girls have so many anxieties about your relationships. It seems as if you want the men in your life to be everything for you. That can't be right. Men are men. You can't take them and make them into another version of women, but with hairier chests.'

'It isn't that simple . . .'

'We are meant to be different, darling. Rejoice in that. *Vive la différence* as the French say. You'll sort it out, I'm sure you will.'

'Mummy? What's made you stay with Daddy all these years?'

'Why, he's an absolute animal in bed, darling. Grrr . . .'

I feel my jaw drop. An alarm goes off on my mother's watch. 'Oh. Time for Daddy's heart pills.'

She stands up and kisses my hair, ruffling it gently before she walks away.

I scratch my head. 'An animal in bed. My father?' I mutter to myself with a shudder. An unbidden image of my mother and father 'doing it' flashes inside my brain. Good heavens, no. I hang my head in my hands. 'I could do with a couple of those heart pills myself.'

24

Chapter Eight

The more sober he became, the more Leo decided that he couldn't give up on Emma quite so easily. He must explain to her that despite being a complete plonker he did, however, 'L' her a lot. In his own way. Why couldn't he just tell her that?

Instead of going home, he took himself down to the rather smart area of Shad Thames and headed towards Emma's apartment where he was planning to declare his undying 'L' for her. Using the whole word. That's the sort of thing she'd like. Trust him. After all this time together, Leo knew her so well.

Shad Thames was jam-packed with trendy flats – all converted dock-land warehouses and all outrageously expensive. Though they did have the most fabulous views of Tower Bridge and the turrets of the Tower of London. Needless to say, Emma couldn't afford to buy this pile by herself. It was one of her father's little investments and she had the benefit of it.

Leo ambled along the narrow, cobbled alleys. Funny how times changed. This place used to be full of stevedores, brigands, pirates and the like – of course, that was going back a while. It had been a noto-riously dangerous place. Now it was trendy and, therefore, overrun with City types and advertising executives and artists. The only mugging was carried out by estate agents.

Leo was almost completely nearly sober as he'd wandered round for some time, taking the circuitous route to Emma's place in an attempt to put some space between heavy drinking and declaring his undying wotsit. And, unfortunately, his champagne bottle was very empty. Also, it was now some ungodly hour in the morning. The only other problem was that Emma wasn't answering the buzzer to her flat, despite the fact he'd kept his finger on it for a good five minutes and he'd shouted up to her window a million times.

'Emma. Emma.' Leo tried again.

25

A window opened above his head. 'Clear off, Leo,' a disembodied voice said. That would be Mrs Canning. She'd never liked Leo since he let Emma's bath overflow and it caused a teeny bit of damage to her lounge ceiling. It wasn't only his own neighbours that he chose to temporarily inconvenience with his exuberant ablutions. You would have thought she would have enjoyed the three-month stay in a bed and breakfast hotel while her home was repaired, wouldn't you? But no. Emma had never heard the end of it. And Mrs Canning had given Leo a very wide berth ever since.

He could call Emma, but as well as his car keys, he seemed to have lost his mobile phone. This wasn't an unusual occurrence. Leo and his mobile phones were never together for long. He'd had quite a few one-night stands with them over the years. 'Emma!'

Still no reply. Leo decided there was only one thing for it.

I lie in bed, tossing and turning. My head is buzzing and I can't sleep. I'm too hot and then when I throw off the covers I'm too cold. My legs ache and my temples throb. A niggling tickle irritates my throat and I wonder if I'm coming down with a bug, so I sit up and sip at the glass of water on the bedside table. I fling myself back on the bed. If this is what love can do to you, then you can keep it. I rub at my eyes – they're gritty and have no desire to close in deep and peaceful sleep.

My mother's advice keeps playing round in my mind. Am I too harsh on Leo? He's the one who sails through life as if he doesn't have a care in the world, while I fret enough for two. I feel that my own body cells weigh me down when we go through yet another spat like this. My mother's right about one thing. I'm a born worrier. Why couldn't I have inherited my father's nose or toes or anything other than his personality? The worry gene is a very prevalent one in my make up. Even as a child I was always too frightened to play with my dolls for fear of damaging them, so I used to dress them and sit and look at them, while all my friends were tying fireworks to their Barbies' heads and trying to blow them up. I still blame the sudden disappearance of several of my favourite teddies on the ghoulish experiments of my sisters. Even now when I go to a cocktail party and have a great time, I'll be worrying the next day whether I've been too loud or that I've made a show of myself. I worry about the state of the planet, the state of my nails, the United States in general. Daylight Time Saving worries me tremendously: when I put my clocks back, does it mean that I lose that hour forever and, therefore, my life will be cut short? Or do I gain an hour when the clocks go forward, which means I outlive my expectancy? I never know where I am in the equation. But society isn't like that now – no one gives a damn about anyone any more. People go through life doing exactly what they like, when and where they like. I feel I care far too deeply about everything. The book *Stop Worrying and Start Living* was written for me, I'm sure. Except that I worry that I've never yet found time to read it. No one else in the family is like this. My mother is quietly confident, sure in her own skin, whereas my sisters are – and always have been – confident to the point of boorish. It's taken me years to realise that my father smothers a whole range of complex anxieties under his bombastic, professional façade.

Wide-eyed, I look at the clock. Leo could have phoned me. Except that he's probably parted company with his mobile phone once more. He loses them so regularly that he must easily be Vodaphone's best customer by now. Perhaps if we talk things through, he'll realise that changes need to be made . . . Oh. I pull myself up short. Hasn't my mother just warned me that danger lies in that way of thinking? I must accept Leo as he is. As he is and always will be. Could I really do that? It would take nothing short of a major miracle to make Leo change his ways. The thought doesn't make for a restful night.

Climbing drainpipes wasn't his forte, even Leo had to admit that. He was sure that he must have a forte – it had just lain undiscovered as yet.

'Right.' Leo put down his champagne bottle, ruing the fact that it was empty. *C'est la vie.* He briefly considered what burglars on television would do. Then he spat on his hands and took a run at the drainpipe, which made him dizzy. Maybe not a run, Leo, old son. Try a slow amble, that's more your style. Leo tried a slow amble. He gripped the drainpipe firmly and took a deep breath. Emma's flat was on the third floor. Which looked very high. Very high indeed.

Leo decided it would be a suitably romantic gesture though, shinning up twenty-five feet, maybe more. Especially as he had no head for heights. Best not to think about that. He let out a loud 'ouff' as he hoisted himself up.

Struggling up the narrow piping, trying to emulate the style of an ace commando, he scraped his knees on the wall. 'Ouch. Ouch.' A pause for quick shouting. 'Emma! Emma!'

27

Leo wished she'd answered the doorbell, thus making it unnecessary to put on an impromptu Spiderman performance. He now also wished he'd turned up to her party on time, thus eliminating altogether the necessity to shin up a drainpipe as an overtly romantic gesture. He only hoped that his dearly beloved would consider this superhuman effort as suitable recompense.

Leo looked down. 'Ooo.' He'd made it to the first floor. But had no idea how. Huffing and puffing, he heaved himself further up the drainpipe, realising that he wasn't as fit as he once was. Actually, Leo had never been fit. A window opened above him.

'Bugger off, Leo.' That wasn't Emma's voice. It was an old person's voice. 'Go on – bugger off.'

Leo risked looking up. There was, indeed, an old person in a hideous turquoise negligée with feather trim, looming above him. Mrs Canning again.

'Hello.' He tried to sound jolly while remembering not to let go of the drainpipe to wave.

'Aargh!' Leo was hit on the head by the irate old person wielding a fluffy slipper. 'Aargh!' And again.

'Why. Can't. You. Use. The. Door. Like. Everyone. Else?' More hitting.

'Emma won't open it.'

'Can't say I blame her,' Mrs Canning grunted. 'She could do so much better than you.'

At this point, Leo hoped that his darling girlfriend would open the window and come to his rescue, apologising profusely to the mad old bat and saving her romantic but possibly misguided boyfriend in the process. But, of course, she didn't.

Leo was hit on the head again. He thought he might have made an enemy of Mrs Canning and his grip on the drainpipe was slipping due to having to hold one hand on his head to stop major brain damage. 'Aargh!'

Then Leo lost his grip, completely. On his life and on the drainpipe. Leo to earth. Leo to earth. He landed in some sort of scratchy bush. Smashing the pot in which the scratchy bush had resided. 'Ouff.'

'I'll be sending you the bill for that pot too, young man.'

'Sorry. Sorry. Terribly sorry.'

The window banged shut above him.

'Goodnight, Mrs Canning. Sleep tight.' Leo waved affectionately at the closed window. The light snapped off.

With a sigh, Leo climbed out of the bush. 'Bugger.' He tidied up the pieces of broken pottery with his foot, sweeping them noisily into the gutter while checking for broken pieces of himself with his hands. Seemed okay. Possible extensive bruising. But all limbs, if not his brain, were functioning. Leo brushed himself down and picked up his champagne bottle. This was too depressing for words. Despite his valiant attempt to win her back it would seem that things really were over between Emma and him.

My mother opens the bedroom door. 'Can't you sleep, sweetheart?'

'No.' I sit up and switch on my bedside light.

'I could hear you tossing and turning.' My mother hands me a mug of hot chocolate. 'I thought this might help to settle you. It was always your favourite when you were small.'

'Thanks, Mummy.'

She strokes my hair while I sip at the hot, sweet and comforting drink. 'It's nice to have you back in your own bedroom.' I take in the frilly pink curtains and the gingham duvet. 'I've never been able to bring myself to change it.'

'It is a bit shrine-like.'

'Much nicer than going back to that pokey flat on your own while you were upset.'

'It isn't a pokey flat.' Strictly speaking, it is a pokey flat. If you're into cat swinging then it isn't the place to live. I prefer to call it 'bijou' which essentially is pokey with a great address. My flat is housed in a converted tobacco warehouse, but instead of a sweeping expanse of urban loft living space, I have – or, more accurately, my father has – bought one of the places whose main feature is being as short on space as it's high on price. 'And I like living alone,' I insist.

Do I? Wouldn't I really rather wake up snuggled down next to someone else? Leo perhaps. 'Maybe I should have gone straight home.' I chew at my lip. 'What if Leo went round there?'

'Then I'm sure he'll be sleeping in the gutter outside your flat,' my mother suggests. 'Don't worry about him. The state that Leo was in, he won't even know.'

'I do love him, Mummy,' I say. 'Even though he's a pain in the neck.'

'And the arse,' she adds.

We both laugh tiredly.

'If you really do love him, darling, then perhaps it's about time you started behaving as if you did.'

'I just want him to stop treating me like a pushover.'

'Well, be careful that you don't push him away completely.' My mother kisses me on the cheek. 'Goodnight, darling.'

As she leaves, I turn off the bedside light and slide down under the duvet. I look out of the window and over the rooftops of London and wonder where my maddeningly lovely, unstable and unpredictable Leo is now.

Chapter Nine

It was still a balmy night, but it was way past the time for Leo to be getting home. Already the sky was lightening. He had to go to work later this morning and already he was destined to get too few hours in bed to enable him to sleep off his hangover.

Heading back towards Tower Bridge, Leo resolved to pick up the pace of his stride – but it was such a wonderful night for wandering aimlessly. Leo adored this part of London, particularly at this time of night when it wasn't crowded with hordes of German and Japanese tourists weighed down with cameras. The skyline was a magnificent blend of old and new – the fine, crenellated turrets of the Tower of London standing proud against the enormous and newly-constructed glass gherkin-shaped office block of Swiss Re, the majestic pinnacle of St Paul's almost lost amongst the burgeoning tangle of buildings.

As he crossed the road, dodging a lone taxi, Leo glanced towards Tower Bridge. What he saw stopped him in his tracks. He couldn't believe it. There was a woman standing by one of the parapets. She was wearing a long velvet cloak and stood on tiptoe, teetering on the edge of the brightly-painted iron rail. With one hand she held onto one of the huge white stone pillars that supported the bridge. The other arm was outstretched towards the murky, swirling expanse of the River Thames. She was a tiny little thing – it looked as if one puff of wind would blow her away. Her face was pale in the moonlight.

What was she doing, he wondered. The woman leaned further forward. The breath in his lungs came to a rapid halt. And he had a horrible feeling that she was about to jump. He glanced round, searching for help, but there was no one else there. Anyone with any sense was tucked up in bed by now. There was only Leo. And the woman. A rush of adrenaline pumped through his body. The sort that turned normal, unin-spiring men into valiant knights on white chargers. Forcing a breath into his chest, he ran towards the railing. He had to save her.

31

'Don't! Don't.' He rushed onto the bridge and the woman turned to look at him.

Careful now. Smile nicely. Don't startle her. Crikey, why were there never any policemen around when you needed them? Leo wasn't the heroic sort. Anyone would tell you that. He passed out if he saw even a tiny drop of blood. Spiders? Terrified of them. Emma did all the stuff with the piece of paper and a glass if there were ever any lurking arachnids in the flat. Leo just screamed.

Omigod. Omigod. His breath caught in his throat. The woman leaned out even further and Leo gasped. She could do it any second. Just jump into oblivion.

'Don't do it! Don't.' Leo held out his arms. 'You'll smash yourself to death on the rocks below.' There weren't actually any rocks in the Thames, but Leo hoped that in her distressed state, the woman wouldn't see the flaw in his argument.

'There aren't any rocks below,' she said calmly.

Damn. You couldn't fool this one. 'The tide,' he offered. 'The tide is terribly dangerous. It'll drag you beneath the surface and sweep you out to sea and dreadful things like that. Crabs might eat you.'

She looked as if she didn't believe that either.

'Whatever,' Leo said, 'it would be a deeply unpleasant experience to have as your last one. I really, really would advise against it.'

She smiled at him and let him inch closer. He could nearly touch her. Despite the fact she'd perched on the edge of Tower Bridge hundreds of feet up in the air, he thought that she looked amazingly serene, almost unearthly. Leo noticed that there was a vague, translucent glow around her. Feeling the empty bottle of champagne knock against his thigh, he came to a conclusion. Ah. Maybe she wasn't really glowing. It could well be an optical illusion brought on by a surfeit of strong drink. That was more likely. People don't generally glow. Not unless they lived near a nuclear reactor, of course. There was a rumble of traffic and a lorry passed by, making the road across the bridge bounce unnervingly. Leo hoped that it wouldn't spook her. As was typical in London, the driver didn't even give them a second glance.

The woman looked at him and smiled again. Leo was relieved to see that she certainly didn't look startled. Amazingly, she looked very relaxed for a potential suicide committer – if that was the correct term. She was extraordinarily pretty. He was right next to her now and he leaned gratefully on the heavy, solid structure of the bridge, sighing with relief while trying to give off the most casual air he could manage. 'Don't jump,' he said. 'You're far too pretty to be fish food.'

The woman laughed at that.

Encouraged, Leo decided to continue in the same vein. 'You might be desperately unhappy now, but nothing is bad enough to be worth ending your life for. You'll get over it, whatever it is. Believe me – I know.'

Now she looked surprised.

'I've just been dumped by my girlfriend. Again.' He flicked his thumb back in the general direction of that awful restaurant and the débâcle that had been his true love's thirtieth birthday party. Leo cringed, thinking about it. 'And I'm hardly depressed at all.' He forced himself to grin widely just to prove it. The woman wasn't to know that the inside of his heart was like the image in a kaleidoscope, all in the right place, but fractured into hundreds of little pieces. 'In the morning I'll have forgotten all about her.' He sounded far too bright to be convincing; even Leo could tell that. 'If not in the morning, then fairly soon. A year or two, I expect.'

He gave the apparently suicidal woman a pathetic grin again, in the hope that she'd feel too guilty to kill herself. 'Come on. Come down.'

The woman laughed again. Not the unhinged laugh of someone on the verge of topping themselves, Leo noted. No, a tinkly happy laugh that made him think that she'd quite probably been at the fizz too. She came towards him and took the hand he offered to her, jumping down onto the pavement as light as a feather. Underneath the velvet cloak she was wearing something that looked suspiciously like lingerie to Leo. Something not nearly warm enough for the weather they were currently enjoying. But then women and their clothing choices had always been a mystery to him. Why would anyone sane choose to wear tights voluntarily? Though he'd always had a bit of a thing for bras.

'I wasn't going to jump,' she assured him. 'I can fly.'

'Oh. Me too. If I've had enough.' He held up the bottle of champagne.

'What are you celebrating?' she asked.

'Being a single man, I guess. Want some?' Leo shook the champagne.

She nodded. Leo thought he'd probably need a drink too if he was in her situation. He went to offer her the bottle and then remembered that it was empty. 'Oh. Empty. Sorry. Terribly sorry.'

'That's okay,' she said. And from the depths of her velvet cloak she

33

produced a champagne glass and handed it to Leo. Taking the bottle from him, she tipped it up . . . and champagne bubbled into the glass.

Leo's eyes widened. 'Bloody marvellous!' He took the bottle from her and shook it. It was empty. Definitely empty. 'This must be damn good stuff.'

The woman took the glass from him and sipped from it. 'It is.' She poured some more champagne.

Leo looked at her in amazement. 'That is a *seriously* good party trick.'

Her smile was utterly bewitching. Dazzling him. The woman looked very contented. 'I have lots of them.'

Leo and the woman leaned on the bridge looking down at the black maelstrom of water; the lights on the bridge swayed in the breeze and they shared the glass of champagne. The fleet of sightseeing boats were moored safely in their docks and the river was quiet. In the sky the moon was high, bright. Magical.

'So why did your girlfriend dump you?'

'Because I'm a shallow, emotionally retarded, commitment-phobe with a fear of intimacy and a love of strong drink.'

'Is that all?'

'And I snore.'

'Oh,' she said. 'That's awful.'

Leo puffed out his breath, not realising that he'd been holding it. 'I think Emma – my girlfriend – just wanted me to be all that I'm not and probably never will be.'

'Maybe you just haven't found the right woman.'

'Oh, she's the right woman,' he said. 'But maybe I'm not the right man. I love her so much but . . . well.' Leo seemed at a loss.

'Do you live near here?'

Leo nodded. 'Not far. Just around the corner. Well, two or three corners. You?'

'No. I come from a faraway place.'

'Bummer,' he commiserated. 'You've probably missed the last Tube. Were you planning to go back there tonight?' No, of course, she wasn't, Leo, you prat. She was planning to jump off a bridge – remember? 'I mean now. After you've decided not to . . .' He twitched his head towards the water.

'No,' she said with a wistful shake of her head. 'I'm not going back to where I'm from. Not just yet.' She wrapped her cloak around her. 'I thought you would like it if I came home with you.'

34

'With me?' Leo was rather surprised by the speed of the proceedings, but he wasn't one to look a gift horse in the mouth, if you'll pardon the expression. 'Oh. Absolutely.'

The woman took the champagne glass and threw it towards the river. Then she took Leo's hand, which he thought must feel big and clumsy and hot beneath her delicate touch. But she smiled at him as if nothing mattered. As if nothing mattered at all. As they headed off, hand-in-hand towards his flat, Leo noticed that his heart was pounding. And his heart would have pounded even more if he'd noticed that as the champagne glass soared through the air it transformed into a tiny silver butterfly which flew away into the dark, forbidding night.

Chapter Ten

Leo lived in a typical London street. In Bermondsey. A street with tightly-packed terraced houses, lots of them. Georgian affairs, that had mostly been converted to provide a couple of one- or two-bedroomed flats on each floor. Leo shared the top floor of one. It was small, but rather nice. The cute, perfectly-proportioned Eva Longoria of apartments. He'd got a bit of a roof terrace, which would look lovely if he ever got round to doing anything with it. As it stood, there was a rusting old bike up there and not a lot else. Emma, who watched a lot of gardening programmes, kept threatening to turn it into a lush tropical hideaway with nothing more than a few tree ferns and a couple of terracotta pots from B&Q. Which would be truly marvellous. Might give the neighbours a fright to see Leo out there in his shorts though. But Emma probably wouldn't be doing that now.

The road was always jammed with parked cars. Nightmare. You had to get a resident's parking permit and, of course, Leo kept forgetting to do so. He could have bought a modest holiday home in the Bahamas for the amount he'd spent on paying parking fines to the London Borough of Southwark. Plus he was just inside the Congestion Zone – which sounded like a terminal illness to Leo – and he constantly forgot to pay for that too. Unintentionally, Leo Harper was a one-man civil disorder.

The beauty of this street was that it was lined with magnificent purply-coloured trees – loads of them, all tall and proud. They were a sight to behold, even if it did mean that Leo's car was permanently covered in bird poo. He could forgive them that though, as the birds indiscriminately plopped on the parking wardens too.

Leo was feeling slightly awkward as he wasn't used to having a strange woman attached to his arm. He didn't know if this was a good idea and the organ that he called his brain was refusing to go into thinking mode. Its cells were probably still sodden with champagne and were having a lie-down. Leo didn't blame them. All the time he was desperately trying to think, to reason this through, yet they just kept getting inextricably nearer to his flat without him really having any idea of what was going on.

It wasn't a terribly long walk from Tower Bridge to Leo's place – something he'd worried inordinately about when Emma first moved into Shad Thames. Even though they'd been together for three years by then. Leo thought it might be a tad too close for comfort, but his fears were unfounded. He and his girlfriend had co-existed in near neighbourly companionship for over two years now. Emma had her space; Leo had his. And they'd both have a lot more of it after tonight.

Surprisingly, despite the longevity of their relationship, Emma and Leo had never discussed living together. He thought it was more than likely something Emma dreaded him raising, and as he completely avoided all difficult conversations, he had never dared to raise it. Besides, Leo probably would have very soon found himself swiftly murdered if Emma had ever moved in with him. His girlfriend was the tidiest person on this small planet, whereas Leo was not. Emma went to bed early so that she could enjoy eight hours of sleep. Leo stayed up all hours of the night watching rubbish on the telly as he largely viewed sleep as a waste of time. Sometimes he wondered if Emma was right when she stated, time and time again, that they weren't compatible.

Leo and his newly-acquired companion walked down Tooley Street which was dead at this time of night, save for a few hopeful taxis, and then carried on past the scrubby green expanse of Potters Fields. The woman didn't talk to him at all. She somehow seemed to know that he was deep in thought. Or as deep as Leo managed to get. He felt as if he should chat to her, find out her reasons for wanting to jump off a bridge, but – for once – he had no idea what to say.

The woman pulled her cloak around her and shivered slightly. The trees responded by rustling in the breeze as they walked under them. Leo thought that her cloak wasn't a great look. It gave her the air of a left-over from the worst sartorial excesses of the 1960s. Emma wouldn't be seen dead wearing something like that. Leo was sure. Which meant, if things ran true to form, she'd probably turn up at his flat next week wearing one because it was the latest thing. Except Emma wouldn't turn up at his flat next week because she didn't love him any more. And, although Leo didn't yet realise this, things weren't going to run true to form for quite some time.

Because they hadn't talked much, Leo decided that the woman was in a state of shock after her abandoned suicide attempt. He hoped that it wasn't every day that she tried to throw herself off a bridge – otherwise she was seriously unhinged and Leo was in big trouble. The truth was that he rather liked to be walking along with this quiet woman. Emma would have been moaning like mad by now. About everything. Leo would be top of a very long list, followed by the Labour government, uneven pavements (for which the Labour government would be blamed), speed cameras (Labour government), the litter everywhere (Labour government) and the price of fish (definitely Labour government).

'Well.' Leo stopped outside his humble abode. 'Here we are.'

Leo usually left a spare key under a plant pot outside the front door in case he ever lost his own key. As he *had* lost his own key, he now hoped that he'd remembered to put his spare key under the pot. Leo had keys cut in bulk at Lose Your Key? – key-cutters to the terminally forgetful. He got a great discount for buying two dozen at a time and a Christmas card from the buxom lady behind the counter who had developed a soft spot for him.

Leo reached down and, thank heavens, his spare key was there. All of Leo's neighbours held keys to his house, but they tended to get upset if he knocked on their doors in the wee small hours begging to be let in. Although he did have the sense to realise that it wasn't a good security measure to dish out the keys to your flat to all your neighbours, and it was especially not a good idea to also put them under a plant pot at your front door. This was the sort of thing that was popular in the 1950s in Britain when burglary was a remote possibility, but now it should have been eschewed as sheer madness. It was the very first place a burglar would look – unless they were particularly stupid. But if you were a particularly stupid householder, as Leo was, then you had to resort to desperate measures. Leo had never been burgled but expected to be any day now. It was long overdue. When all of his emergency key resources had been exhausted, Leo was often forced to sleep in dear old Ethel, except for the times when he had abandoned his car at an unknown location. Somewhere in London there were two other cars that belonged to Leo, but he'd never been able to find them, despite extensive searches when sober.

'That's my flat.' They both looked up at his window.

'So it is.'

'Look,' Leo said with a sigh, 'are you sure you want to do this?'

'I'm sure.'

'I can call you a taxi and we can say goodnight here.'

She smiled at him and Leo thought that it was a very pretty little smile. His toes suddenly felt very warm and Leo wasn't normally a person who was overly aware of his extremities. 'I don't think that will be necessary.'

'I could be an axe murderer.' Leo seemed to think it was best to point this out.

'But you're not.'

'No.'

The trees trembled deliciously above them. 'Take me inside,' the woman said with a shiver, even though it was a balmy night. 'I'm cold.'

Leo took her hand and they went inside.

Chapter Eleven

Leo felt that his apartment was looking rather too much like the bachelor pad it was. Although he hadn't actually planned on bringing anyone back here, in his defence. Not even Emma.

'This is nice,' the woman said.

It wasn't. Quite categorically, it wasn't. Pizza had been consumed for last night's supper and the box was still on the floor. Not good. Especially when combined with the plates, cups and lager cans from earlier in the week. Leo had been terribly busy. No time to tidy up the mags or books or DVDs either. Perhaps, he hoped, it would make him look like an intellectual. And then he spied *Becky's Big Night Out* on the coffee-table. The page three model's breasts were, as usual, bared. Perhaps not. With a few ill-placed mammaries, Leo kissed his intellectual aspirations goodbye. 'Well,' he said. 'It's home.'

Kicking the empty pizza box under the sofa, he hoped the woman hadn't noticed and might think him charming and urbane. Actually, in spite of the mess, Leo's flat was very nice. Mainly because Emma had made him have it all decorated professionally. He'd been given a great bonus last year – due entirely to work done by Grant and Lard and not his good self – but, at least, he was aware of that. Leo always made sure that he split his annual bonus with his friends three ways because, to be honest, they were the only reason Leo managed to get one in the first place. And if he didn't get a bonus every year, he would be out on his ear before you could say 'surplus to requirements'. Thornton Jones had no concept of loyalty, whereas Leo considered it to be one of the very few virtues he had. The remaining third of Leo's bonus share-out, of course, had gone to Emma's designated interior designer.

He had found it a very weird experience to have a woman ask him whether he would prefer florals or checks. Leo had no idea. Leo, to be honest, simply didn't care. He had told her, with a winning smile, to do whatever she liked. And she had.

He'd ended up with black, grey, steel and some red. Not much in the way of florals or checks. But it had all been very acceptable to him. Blown-up images from comic books hung on the walls. Leo couldn't imagine why she'd chosen those for him – Emma made him hide his comics – but they looked fab. With his unexpected guest standing there, he vowed to try to keep the place more tidy in future. Squalor was a bad, bad bloke thing.

The woman shrugged off the hood of her cloak, revealing hair that was the colour of raven's feathers, all black and glossy. It tumbled freely over her shoulders. Leo, for some reason, felt breathless.

'My word.' She was quite enchanting. Her face was tiny, perfectly-shaped and pale. Leo started to feel flustered. And then he worried that it might not have been a good idea to bring this strange, suicidal, 1960s' throwback woman to his flat without a formal introduction, even though the aforementioned woman was utterly gorgeous.

'Look,' he said uncomfortably, 'I might seem like a bit of a man about town, a bit of a Jack the lad . . . a bit of a guy . . . ' he punched her lightly and playfully on the arm, 'but you see . . . I haven't done this sort of thing for ages. I've been with my girlfriend, Emma, for years. Years and years. I don't do other women. Always been rubbish at it. Since a teenager. Desperately shy with the opposite sex. I'm hopelessly out of practice. I've only been single for an hour or so. No time to sharpen up my social skills yet.'

'Shall I go and make myself comfortable?'

'Oh. Yes. Comfortable. Yes. That's fine.' He knew he was babbling like someone's mother. His mother probably. 'Bathroom-type comfortable?'

Now it was the woman's turn for confusion. 'Is there any other type?' she asked.

Leo shrugged, nonplussed. He had no idea what a woman needed to make herself comfortable. Emma was the only woman of whom Leo had had recent intimate knowledge, and comfort for Emma generally meant a hot-water bottle, those dreadful baggy socks that you only ever saw in re-runs of *Fame* and copious amounts of chocolate. Perhaps he should offer this woman a Mars Bar?

'The bathroom's through there,' he said, running a hand through his ruffled hair. Leo hoped that he hadn't left the seat up and that there were no unpleasant 'survivors' in the loo. That would be too dreadful to contemplate. For him and for the woman. He promised himself that he must get a cleaning person as soon as humanly possible. The woman went towards the door.

Leo suddenly laughed out loud at what he saw as the absurdity of this situation. 'This is madness,' he said. 'I don't know anything about you. Other than that you have a great line in party tricks.'

She turned and he blinked at her. Her eyes were stunning and they twinkled with mischief. Despite the cloak, she was quite the most beautiful woman Leo had seen in a long time. And he did sometimes buy magazines with very beautiful women in them.

'What do you want to know?'

Leo shrugged. 'I don't know your name, your age . . .'

'I'm Isobel and I'm four hundred and sixty-three.'

He laughed again. 'Four hundred and sixty-three?'

She nodded.

Quite mad, he decided. 'Well,' he said, 'you look very good on it.'

'Thank you.'

'I'm Leo, by the way.' He nearly held out his hand for her to shake it, but quickly figured that they were past that stage.

'I know.' She turned away and left the room, heading into the bathroom.

Leo gave her a tentative wave and tried to look nonchalant but thought, quite rightly, that he failed. As soon as Isobel was out of the room, he ran round in a panic. Plumping cushions. Pushing dirty plates, cups, beer cans under handy plumped cushions. Turning on side lamps for more seductive lighting. Hiding dubious DVDs. Rifling through his CD collection. Which were all dodgy. Leo threw the unsatisfactory ones on the floor. Meatloaf. Bon Jovi. Queen. Bruce Springsteen. Air Guitar Greatest Hits. Although he did stop and briefly consider this one. Everyone likes air guitar, he reasoned, and practised a stroke with his own air guitar. Kerrang!

'No. No.' He threw it to the floor with the other CDs. 'No. No. No.' Kaiser Chiefs' CD? More Kerrang, but reasonably modern Kerrang. 'No.'

Leo consigned it to the floor with the rest of the noisy tunes. He continued his search. 'Whitney Houston. Flipping awful. Must be Emma's.' Leo rubbed his hands in glee. 'This will do nicely.'

He put Whitney in the CD player. 'I Believe in You and Me'. 'Shit,' he muttered. 'Emma's favourite.' Even Leo realised that this was a bad time to be thinking about his girlfriend. He tried to blank his memory

– something he usually had no trouble with at all. He leaned on the wall trying to look casual. 'No. All wrong.' Leo tried the sofa. 'Too forward.' It would make him look like he was expecting a shag, so he tried a different pose. One hand on head. One hand on hip. 'Too gay.'

Isobel came out of the bathroom and Leo shot upright in surprise as if he hadn't expected to see her standing there. He was glad that her Gandalf cloak had gone but was worried when he saw that she was, indeed, just wearing her lingerie. It looked all sort of shimmery and transparent. Even though it worried him, he also rather liked it.

'Oh, my word.'

'Shall we go to bed?' she said.

'Er . . .' Leo held up Whitney Houston. 'Whitney?'

Isobel smiled and held out her hand. 'Come, Leo.'

And Leo thought he just might.

Chapter Twelve

I allow my mother to fuss around me, force-feeding me an enormous, yet health-giving breakfast of fresh strawberries, yoghurt and wholemeal toast. Mummy has even squeezed me some fresh orange juice instead of just pouring out the carton variety. It's nice being spoiled again. And it's infinitely better than the polystyrene cup of Starbucks coffee that I usually drink on the hoof as I totter from my flat across a few cobbled courtyards to the rather pretentious and, naturally, overpriced art gallery where I work.

Now I feel rather over-dressed and slightly seedy in last night's silk party dress and strappy shoes. It's a long time since I've stayed overnight at my parents' house and the stash of clothes I used to keep there for emergencies such as this has long since dripped into my own flat. I'd taken the hint about moving out of home when my parents had eventually bought the flat in Shad Thames, encouraged me to use it as my own and had enthusiastically helped me to pack. After that amazing conversation with my mother last night about my father's sexual prowess, I now know that the real reason why they wanted me out was that they're still keen to be at it like teenagers all over the house. The thought makes me sigh inwardly. Is there anyone out there who might want to live with me out of choice?

I stare out of the window at the vast expanse of my parents' garden – an oasis in the middle of the city. The bright, plastic swings and slides of my childhood are long gone, replaced by terracotta urns and weathered teak furniture. The borders are fit to burst with a profusion of flowers – all my mother's work. Take away the ambulance sirens, the overhead planes and the general thrum of traffic and you could be anywhere in rural Britain. The washed-out clouds hang gloomily over the garden and I shiver at the thought of the chilly morning temperature that will, no doubt, be waiting outside despite it being the height of our supposed summer.

'Will you be all right, darling?'

'I'm fine, Mummy.' I phoned Leo's flat first thing – primarily to remind him to get up for work – but the call went straight to answerphone. Which either means that Leo has, miraculously, heard his alarm clock and is already at work or, more likely, he's slept through it again and is still snuggled down in his bed.

'Do let Daddy drive you home.'

'No, I'm fine. I'll get the bus. It will give me time to think.' If I'm stuck in the car with my father it will give him far too good an opportunity to lecture me about Leo's shortcomings, yet again.

It's depressing that all of my relatives – with the possible exception of my mother – regard Leo as something of a clown, albeit an affable one. What has gone wrong in my world? I've always been such a high achiever in every area, yet when it comes to love I've managed to fall for the least reliable and least romantic man that God created. Life seldom turns out as you expect. I can hear myself grinding my teeth on my toast.

My mother looks at me from over the top of the newspaper and frowns. 'Do some yoga or something before you go into work, darling. Relax a bit before you speak to Leo.'

'Am I really so tense?'

'Nothing that a good massage wouldn't soothe.'

'Or a good man?'

'Make it up with Leo,' Mummy urges. 'You know you're not happy without him to moan about.'

Is that what our relationship has been reduced to – a series of spats to entertain our families? Perhaps Leo isn't a worthy adversary any more. Recently he's accepted all of my criticisms without complaint, when previously he used to be so feisty. Maybe I've gone too far this time. What if Leo feels that he can no longer do right for doing wrong and simply gives up? I need to talk to him. But if there's one thing that Leo hates more than staying sober on important occasions, it's talking about anything difficult – or anything at all, really.

Finishing my toast, I slosh down the rest of my coffee and then kiss my mother goodbye. 'Thanks for looking after me last night. I do appreciate it.'

'What are mothers for?'

'Thanks for the advice too.'

'But will you take it, darling?'

I give her a rueful smile. 'Better go. Stuff to do.' Sorting out my love-life, for one thing.

Chapter Thirteen

There's no one at the bus stop who is remotely attractive, even though there are about ten guys of assorted age, shape and size in the queue. And there's no one on the bus who makes me catch my breath either. London is definitely suffering from a dearth of delicious men these days. Maybe the World Wildlife Fund should put them on their list of endangered species.

I sit back in my seat, sink down into my lightweight summer jacket to try to elicit a bit of warmth and let the bus bounce me along. Plus, very depressingly, none of the men – not even the really ugly ones with pot bellies – have given me a second glance. This does not bode well if I decide that I really do want to move on from Leo.

This is ridiculous. I look at my watch. It's not yet nine o'clock and already I'm softening towards Leo even though he hasn't even phoned to apologise – as he should have done. I check my phone for messages once more. Nothing. Damn. All over the bus women are chatting on mobile phones and the men are busily texting. I might be starting my first day in my thirtieth decade but I can still remember that bygone age when communication involved real dialogue. Today everyone seems to talk so much and yet say so little.

Reluctantly, I run with the crowd – if you can't beat them join them, I say – and punch in a rather curt text message enquiring as to Leo's whereabouts. Then, equally reluctantly, I delete the message without sending it. I have to make a stand. Leo was horrid last night. He was drunk and late and idiotic. All the things my boyfriend does so well. And, despite my mother's advice, I've decided that this time, I'm going to let Leo come back, tail between his legs, to me.

And, flying in the face of my good intentions, as soon as I open the door of my flat, I check the answerphone. The red message light blinks maniacally. Feeling my heart lift, I clap my hands together. I throw off my coat, tossing it over the back of the sofa with a well-practised aim as I hit the play button on the machine.

'Hi!' My friend Jo-Jo's voice booms out, filling the tiny lounge. 'Happy Birthday, sweetie. Hope your party wasn't too dull.'

No, it certainly wasn't that.

'Catch you later tonight,' she says, and the message cuts off.

The next offering is from a man trying to sell me a loyalty card for one of the local restaurants. Then there's the obligatory 'Congratulations! You have won a holiday . . .' scam – yadda, yadda.

The last message is a birthday greeting from my maternal grand-mother who is still alive and just about kicking, but who was deemed too fragile to attend the family party. If she'd seen the state of Leo, my poor old granny would possibly have expired on the spot, so it was probably just as well. My grandmother is very elegant if a little shrunken with age rather like a headhunter's trophy, but is at that time of life where her speech is punctuated by the rhythmic clack of dentures. She'd been happily married from the tender age of nineteen until my grand-father died unexpectedly of a heart-attack a few years ago, having just celebrated their sixtieth wedding anniversary. Sixty years married. I doubt that I'll even live that much longer, let alone be married to someone for all those years. If the trend for getting married much later in life continues, then the greetings card manufacturers are going to have a surfeit of Golden Anniversary cards on their hands in years to come. And, bizarrely, I do think I'd like to see one sitting on my mantel-piece at some point. Maybe if Leo gets a move on and proposes – like tomorrow – we might just about make it. But the odds aren't good. Particularly when I realise that these are my only messages and that one from Leo is definitely noticeable by its absence.

Kicking off my shoes, I pad through to my bedroom. Leo calls it my princess palace and he's probably right. When I started my deco-rating, I went out and bought every issue of *House Beautiful* and then faithfully replicated a magical pink bedroom complete with flower fairy stencils on the wall and a daisy-strewn duvet intended by the designer for eight-year-old girls. Perhaps at the age of thirty I should have encompassed something more minimalist or, at least, more adult. Do you think this is a subconscious attempt to inject some fantasy or a little magic into my life? If it is, it doesn't appear to be working.

Slipping off my party dress, I look sadly at how crumpled it is. I bought it especially for my birthday and for Leo, because I know he would have liked it. The same goes for the ridiculous wisp of Agent Provocateur underwear that's now rolled up and stuffed in the bottom of my handbag while I sport a pair of new white Marks & Spencers' big girls' pants that my mother thankfully found hidden away in the back of her dressing-table drawer. Admittedly, it isn't often that I put myself out in the underwear department for Leo and look what happens when I do. Said boyfriend was too drunk to enjoy the benefit of it. I can assure you, it will be a long, long time before minuscule lace graces my backside again.

Lying down on the bed, I stretch out, staring at the delicate fairies which flutter across the ceiling. Wouldn't it be nice to be weightless like that, floating free, not tethered to the earth? I have never been delicate. I've always been as tough as old boots. Maybe I shouldn't be quite so dominating with Leo – women of my age seem to have lost the ability to be feminine. I'm too strident with him. I know it. Equality nowadays seems to be all out of kilter and we think it's preferable to have a subservient male in tow rather than a strong partner. But I've spent so long controlling our relationship that it would be a hard habit to break. And if I don't control our relationship it will go completely to pot. If I left Leo in charge, our whole life would be complete chaos.

I take it as a bad sign that my closest friend, Caron, bought me a relaxation CD – *Let Go of Your Stress* with Felicity Frank – and some lavender de-stressing oil as my birthday present. It's very nice oil, but I'm not so stupid that I can't take the hint in that either. What sort of world do we live in where we've forgotten how to relax? Or need CDs to tell us how to do it? I find myself half-listening to conversations these days as I don't feel I have the time to give them my full attention. How terrible is that? Glancing at the clock – my favourite inanimate object – I realise that I've still got two hours before I have to go to work at the little art gallery which I help to run with Caron. If I hurry up I can just about fit in some relaxation along with all the other stuff I have to do between now and then. This could be another part of my 'life begins at thirty' programme. The new, relaxed me. I have a great job, reasonable pay and Caron and I, largely, have free-run of the place. It certainly isn't my career that's causing my stress. Oh no. That can be laid squarely at one person's door. And one person's door alone.

I slot the CD into the player that doubles as an alarm clock by my bed. Lying back, I close my eyes, adopting what might well be a yoga pose if I'd ever got round to doing yoga. All that lounging around, chanting has never really appealed. Pushing myself until I'm utterly exhausted is generally the best way of falling into bed for a sound night's sleep, I've found.

The voice on the CD is well-modulated, soothing, almost robotic. And spouts on for far too long about the benefits of relaxation.

'Yes, yes. We all know that,' I mutter at it.

'Exercise one,' the voice intones. 'Repeat these affirmations after me.'

I wiggle my toes in preparation.

'*Serenity* is my watchword . . .'

I take a deep breath. 'Serenity is my watchword.' Too tense, I think, and puff out another breath. Perhaps I can persuade Caron to start going to yoga classes with me. There are a million cranky places that do it round here. Although the only exercise Caron likes is propping up the bars of various nightclubs. Perhaps it's time she became a new woman too.

'*Serenity* is my watchword . . .'

Making a conscious effort to unclench my fists, I start to repeat again, '*Serenity* is my . . .' I sit up and stare at the CD-player. 'I've just said that! Get on with it.'

'*Patience* and *love* are my playmates . . .'

I look at the CD in disbelief. 'Say what?'

'*Patience* and *love* are my playmates . . .'

'Oh, for heaven's sake!' Picking up one of my Flower Fairies cushions, I aim it at the CD-player, then let it fly.

'*Anger* is my enemy . . .' The voice sounds slightly more slurred than previously. '*Anger* is my enemy . . .'

I jump off the bed. 'Yes,' I snap. 'And you're mine.' Ejecting the CD from the player, I whiz it like a Frisbee out of the window, where it soars across the rooftops. This is hardly going to bring Leo back to me, is it?

'Relaxation is very over-rated,' I shout after it before bursting into tears.

Chapter Fourteen

Leo was lying in bed and he was grinning. He knew he was. In fact, his cheeks were aching with the effort. His life-size David Beckham poster grinned down from the wall back at him. A person whom Emma hated with an irrational vengeance. What could Leo say about his bedroom? Probably the least said the better actually. There was a wardrobe. Not much used. Leo preferred to hang his clothes on the floor as they were much more accessible. He felt it must have been a woman who invented wardrobes. He had a bed. A double. With black sheets. Leo thought that they were kinky. Emma hated them. There was a selection of cartoons and some lurid comic strips, all put there by the interior designer and very trendy. Leo thought they added some much-needed class. What else? Oh, the bed was also empty. Apart from Leo. Which he viewed as strange. He couldn't believe that his unexpected overnight guest had simply vanished.

'Flip.'

Leo checked under the duvet. No. She'd definitely vamoosed, he concluded. There was, however, silver glittery stuff everywhere. Very strange.

Leo sat up. Which was a bad idea. He had a terrible hangover and it felt as if his brain had been replaced by a small cabbage that vibrated with the ferocity of a road drill. He lay down again. The full horror of last night came back. Had he really turned up pissed at Emma's thirtieth birthday party? Yes, he had. Had he really passed out in her cake? Yes, he had. Had he really brought a strange woman home, and had he done extremely naughty things with her for most of the remaining hours of darkness? Yes, he had.

'Oh flip!' he said to no one in particular.

Leo knew that he did some very stupid things; it was his speciality. But this was high on the stupidity scale even for him. He massaged his eyes and hoped it would all go away. He opened his eyes. It didn't. It was a good job that Emma didn't have the ability to become a fly on his wall, otherwise he'd be in deep trouble. But then he realised he was in deep trouble anyway.

He gave a glance at the clock. 'Flip. Late.' V. late.

Maybe, he thought, his overnight guest was currently in the kitchen making bacon and eggs, and he brightened up at the thought. He struggled out of bed, heaving his heavy limbs from under the duvet. Glitter was stuck to his chest and other body parts that really shouldn't come into contact with glitter. There was also a sprinkling of glitter in his hair. Which he shook. Now there was glitter on floor. Severe dandruff quantities.

Leo plodded into the lounge. There was still no sign of the elusive Isobel. There was, however, a Whitney Houston CD case open on the coffee-table. And a Whitney Houston CD on the stereo. 'Hell's Bells,' he muttered in alarm. 'This is worse than I thought.'

The kitchen wasn't a pretty sight either. Actually, it was a very nice kitchen, all chrome and steel with a marble work surface – or stuff that looked like marble. However, it was all cunningly camouflaged by dirty dishes so that instead it resembled the working end of a busy night in a Chinese restaurant. One condemned by environmental health inspectors. There was no smell of succulent sizzling bacon. Probably because Leo didn't have any bacon. And there was no Isobel either. Leo stared around in a perplexed manner. 'Not even a note.'

He picked up the least dirty dish after a swift perusal of his crockery. Taking care to choose one with no bacteria growing in it, he licked his finger and ran it round the inside of the bowl. Which was not very hygienic, he appreciated, but at least he knew they were his own germs. He found the cereal and tipped it into the bowl.

Leo clamped his hands to his ears. 'Too much snapping, crackling and popping, friends.' This must be a disease, he thought, where all the nerve-endings in his head had become very sensitive to loud sounds.

He filled the kettle with water, plugged it in carefully, avoiding sudden movements, and opened the cupboard in slow time. Slow, slow time. Taking out a cup, he tried to avoid clanging it against the next cup. His teeth hurt. The kettle was boiling too loud, so he turned it off and opened the fridge.

He was blinded by bright light, plus there was no milk. 'Flip.' Dry cereal would have to do. Again. Probably too much pain for teeth anyway. Leo gave up. Breakfast, he decided, was too complicated.

★

Dressing proved to be a painful experience, but Leo was, at least, ready to face the day now. Well, almost. He'd shaved. Not too many cuts. He'd combed the glitter from his hair. Well, mostly. He felt fragile. But no one would know. He checked in the mirror to see that he was looking great. No one would believe that he'd had a wild night on the tiles. He checked the mirror again. Yeah, right. Those bloodshot eyes would fool no one.

What he couldn't believe was that Isobel had just upped and left. Without saying goodbye. Did girls do that? Leo thought only blokes did the proverbial runner. He realised that he knew nothing about the mysterious world of dating or casual sex. But he must learn quickly. And would ask Grant and Lard for some superb advice. Superb advice as opposed to their usual advice. Which was deeply dodgy. Leo smiled to himself. It had been a very nice night though. Unusual. For many reasons.

He knew he should phone Emma but felt deeply guilty and, anyway, she currently hated him. A phone call would only antagonise her. It would probably be best to avoid all contact until her present homicidal rage passed.

Leo felt weird. Not in a drunk sense. Just weird. Disappointed. He liked Isobel. Even though she was strange. And four hundred and sixty-three. She was, however, very athletic for her age. He'd thought she might still be there in the morning. Leo shrugged and it hurt his shoulders and his brain. 'Women.'

Never mind. He'd better get himself off to work before he was sacked. Again. Although he couldn't really rush – he was far too wobbly. Leo left the flat, taking great care not to slam the door. And, in doing so, he failed to notice the silver butterfly fluttering on top of the Whitney Houston CD.

Chapter Fifteen

Isobel walked down Threadneedle Street, swinging her hips as the traffic thundered by. In a less politically correct age, she would have been hooted at by several men driving white vans. The velvet cloak and wisp of a dress had been replaced by a smart, but very sexy black business suit. She carried a black leather Birkin bag – a 'must have', it had said in the glossy magazine that she'd studied so carefully on her arrival in London. So, she had one. As she walked, she swished her hair, aware that she turned heads as she did. It was a nice feeling and she smiled at the guys who passed, taking delight as their mouths hung limply, their eyes popped and they walked, distracted, into lamp posts, bollards and traffic signs.

Outside one of the tall, glass-fronted office blocks a trade exhibition for Japan was advertised. Colourful oriental kites hung from flag-poles. Red and black wooden pergolas decorated with elaborate windchimes were displayed on the forecourt. A gaggle of businessmen drank green tea in untidy clusters. As Isobel passed, the kites fluttered wildly as if buffeted by a playful breeze. The windchimes struck up, ringing out a beautiful tune. She fluttered her eyelashes at the businessmen, who all stopped with their cups halfway to their gaping mouths. Isobel giggled. This was so much more fun than she'd ever imagined.

Stopping outside the offices of Reliable Temporary Staff, she admired herself in the window and adjusted her jacket. Slinging the Birkin bag jauntily over her shoulder just as she'd seen in the fashion spread, she went inside.

The office was chilly with the blast of air-conditioning and painted the most bland shade of beige imaginable. A woman at the first desk eyed Isobel coolly. Isobel smiled and sat down in front of her.

The woman's expression didn't change. 'How can I help?'

Isobel met her gaze. 'I'm looking for a job.'

'Well, you've certainly come to the right place.' The woman smiled tightly. 'Do you have an appointment?'

Isobel looked at the other desks. There were three other women all sitting alone at them. 'No.'

There was an audible sigh and the woman turned to her keyboard. 'Name?'

'Isobel.'

The woman paused, and when there was nothing more forthcoming: 'Surname?'

Isobel stared at her blankly.

'Surname,' she repeated. 'Or are you a celebrity? Like Jordan or Madonna or Cher? Do you have a last name?'

Isobel scanned the office. Her eyes fell on the computer printer. 'Hewlett-Packard,' she said.

The woman raised her eyebrows. 'Isobel Hewlett-Packard.'

'Yes.' Isobel thought that sounded nice. 'What's your name?'

'Patience,' the woman said sarcastically, and indicated her displeasure with another, more pronounced, sigh. 'Previous experience?'

'None.'

'None?' Patience repeated.

'None.'

Another sigh. This time even more heartfelt. 'Qualifications?'

Isobel's smile widened. 'None.'

'None?'

'Whatsoever.'

Patience pushed her keyboard away from her and fixed Isobel with a stare. 'Ms . . . Hewlett-Packard,' she said. 'I'm afraid that . . .'

'I don't just want *a* job,' Isobel told her as she took a small glittery wand from her Birkin bag. She waved it at Patience, who went into a dazed trance. 'I want *this* job.'

Isobel pointed her wand at Patience's computer. The screen scrolled wildly until it flashed up the name Thornton Jones. Isobel tapped the screen with her wand.

Patience blinked amiably. 'I'll arrange an interview for you.'

'Today,' Isobel said sweetly. 'At three o'clock.'

'Fine,' Patience replied.

Isobel zapped the woman again, stood up and returned the wand to the depths of her bag. Patience looked completely dazed and grinned at Isobel inanely.

'Thank you,' Isobel said politely. She reached out and shook her hand. 'You've been so very helpful.'

Patience smiled. 'It's my pleasure.'

'No,' Isobel smiled back. 'I think you'll find the pleasure's all mine.'

Chapter Sixteen

This was Leo's office. Thornton Jones Associates. A big glass monstrosity shaped rather like a phallic symbol plonk in the middle of the City of London. It was very fitting for the type of well-heeled financial firm that Leo worked for. Leo wasn't very fitting for them though, that was the mystery.

Hanging around with all the other suits in the huge, glass reception area, Leo was waiting for the lift to the tenth floor. The tenth floor was cool. Not high enough to have a great panoramic view, but low enough for it not to take twenty minutes to get out of the place in the evening. It meant that Leo looked at other people's rooftops all day – although there were a few remaining spires from ancient churches to break the monotony. When the lift arrived, Shania Twain serenaded him rather nicely on his ascent.

Quite frankly, Leo thought that his office let the place down a bit. It was open-plan, strewn with screwed-up bits of paper amid the closely-packed desks stacked with plastic coffee cups. Colleagues with hang-overs abounded. Speaking before ten o'clock unless strictly necessary was considered bad form. They were known as a heavy drinking depart-ment and, culturally, in this world it was socially acceptable to be a leery piss-head. Most of his colleagues were resolutely single or multi-divorced. Strange, that.

Occasionally Leo's boss, Old Baldy Baldwin – a sure sign that their humour wasn't very sophisticated either – was instructed by *his* bosses to have a clamp-down on political incorrectness. Out went the swearing, boozing, lap-dancing clubs and fondling junior staff at inappropriate times and in inappropriate places. And that was just for the women. Being PC made the office a very boring place and, generally, the effort lasted for about a week before they were all fucking off down to the local bar to get pissed and watch naked ladies. The one difference that Thornton Jones embraced in regard to sexual equality was that they paid all the women much higher bonuses than the men so that they'd put up with the rubbish they had to deal with on a daily basis and wouldn't be in a rush to sue them for sexual discrimination for that particular version of it. Which, in Leo's mind, was only fair.

Needless to say, Emma didn't understand that weekly bonding in a lap-dancing club was a requirement of the job and that it would seriously undermine his chance of promotion if Leo were to fail to appear on an embarrassingly regular basis. They didn't do team bonding at the art gallery in which she worked. It was too upper class to embrace such commercialism – even though they didn't mind charging forty grand for two blue blobs on a white canvas by someone considered an 'upcoming' artist. Con artist, more like. They weren't so different from the grubby world of finance – Emma just chose not to see it. Leo turned on his mobile. One that he'd retrieved from his dwindling spare stash in his desk drawer. Must stock up. He couldn't be the only person who bought phones in bulk, surely?

Leo was rather worried that Emma hadn't phoned to harangue him yet. He normally would have expected ten bollocky calls by now. At least. Given the cake incident. Perhaps he'd call her. Then he remembered, guiltily, what else went on *after* the cake incident and thought that maybe he'd leave it a while longer.

Grant and Lard were already at their desks. This wasn't unusual. Not only were they gifted in the mysterious ways of the world of high finance – something Leo had never quite come to grips with himself – but they were also punctual. Ditto the coming to grips bit.

Perhaps it was time for some further introductions. Grant's proper title was Mr Grant Fielding. Leo and Grant had worked together for several years now – well, Grant worked and Leo turned up at the same place daily – but you get the drift. They shared the same taste in music, television programmes, films and comics – old Batman collectibles being their favourites. And they both thought that there was no finer food on earth than a botty-burning Chicken Vindaloo.

Frankly, no one had any idea what Lard's real name was now because no one ever used it. Leo was sure that he used to know it once, but his memory wasn't all that it might be. He suspected it was something effeminate like Clive or Jason, because Lard always went very shifty when someone tried to quiz him about it. Everyone at work knew him as Lard, even his clients, and he was so named because he was a bit on the lardy side due to his severe chocolate fetish. Lard was a bit of a loner and his colleagues didn't have a clue about what went on in his life outside office hours. They all thought he'd gone over to the dark side, rather like Darth Vader. Or perhaps he lived with his ageing mother and didn't want to admit it to them. Leo liked him nevertheless and he was one of the club, one of the boys – even though he had the beginnings of comely man-breasts.

Lard was eating his way slowly through a pile of Danish pastries.

'You look particularly awful today, Leo,' he remarked.

'Thanks,' Leo said. 'I feel it.' And he went to the coffee machine to top up with some chemicals to help him through the day. Leo was feeling very weak and was convinced it must be the lack of breakfast – on top of a monumental hangover and no sleep, of course.

Sitting on the edge of Lard's desk, Leo helped himself to one of his pastries. 'Uum.' Lard slapped his hand, but only in a playful way. There was no way he could have eaten that lot. He just liked to play hard to get. Maybe, Leo thought, it was something he should try.

'No wonder they call it the demon drink,' Grant said as he joined them. 'You look like the arse end of hell.'

'Thanks.'

'Is there a particular reason why you're covered in glitter?' Grant too got the slapping treatment when he helped himself to Lard's breakfast.

'I had a very weird night,' Leo told them between mouthfuls.

'Didn't we all,' Grant noted.

'When I say weird, I mean really weird.' Leo beckoned them into a manly huddle. 'I met *the* most amazing woman last night.'

They all checked to see if Baldy Baldwin was well out of earshot and then reconvened.

'She was about to throw herself off Tower Bridge.' Leo paused to allow his colleagues to look suitably horrified. 'Somehow I managed to talk her out of it.'

'You usually make people want to throw themselves off bridges,' Grant said.

'I know. I know.' Leo gave them a perplexed shrug. 'She came back to my flat. Spent the night. We had the most incredible sex. Fantastic. Fantastic I-can't-believe-it's-happening-to-me sex. Six times.'

'Never!'

Lard let some of his Danish pastry fall out of his mouth.

'Really.' Leo lowered his voice. 'I woke up covered in glitter with all my hair standing on end.'

'It seems as if it wasn't the only thing standing on end,' Grant observed.

'And she'd gone. Vamoosed. Not a trace of her.'

'Sounds perfect.'

'Yeah,' Leo said thoughtfully. 'Except I sort of would have liked her to stay around.'

'Ooo,' Grant and Lard said in unison.

'Told you it was weird.'

'You were very lashed last night, Leo. Even by your standards.'

'I know. I could have imagined the whole thing, I suppose.'

'Except for the glitter.' Lard might be a fat bastard, but he was also very sharp.

Leo shook his head and some more silver dust fell from his hair onto his desk, despite the fact that he had washed it twice with extra strength Head & Shoulders. 'Except for the glitter,' he agreed.

Just then, Baldy Baldwin came out of the lift. He looked very hungover and bad-tempered as he strode up to them. 'Haven't you lot got any work to do?' he snapped.

Grant and Leo stood up. Baldy slammed into his office.

'Have we got any work to do?' Leo asked.

'Nothing that can't wait,' Grant assured him and they returned their bottoms to Lard's desk again.

'What happened to Emma?' Lard gathered his remaining pastries to himself protectively. 'I thought you were going to her birthday party.'

'I did.'

They waited expectantly. Leo would have liked to disappoint them and tell them that it was all completely uneventful, but given his previous discourse they wouldn't have believed him. 'I fell in her cake,' he admitted. 'Well, more sort of passed out.' He grimaced.

His friends grimaced in support.

'She dumped me.'

'Again?' Grant frequently voiced the opinion that he believed the course of true love should run infinitely more smoothly than the lumpy route that Emma and Leo decided to take.

'Yeah.' Leo tried to look downcast, but it was very hard when he began to remember the full outcome of last night's indiscretions. 'I think she means it this time though.'

'You say that every time,' Lard pointed out.

'Yeah.'

59

Grant gave him a sage look. Leo's friend was younger than him and, irritatingly, was saner and more sensible – though he wasn't as devilishly handsome, Leo consoled himself. 'Though she might be a bit more serious if she ever finds out about Miss Glitter Knickers.'

'True.' Leo and Grant stood up and prepared themselves for the rigours of the day ahead by stealing the rest of Lard's pastry stash.

'Oi!' Lard complained.

And as they hurried away, Leo said to Grant, 'You're right about Emma. She'd do her pieces. I'll just have to make sure she doesn't ever find out.'

Chapter Seventeen

The gallery where I work is in a tiny cobbled courtyard amid the winding, narrow back streets of old tobacco warehouses which have all now been converted into trendy flats. It's in a world of its own, a quiet, restful sanctuary, cut off from the hurly-burly of London at its worst. The surrounding shops are made up of exclusive jewellers, high-end estate agents, boutiques selling handbags with price tags that start at two thousand pounds, and ritzy art galleries galore.

Art For Art's Sake has the type of intimidating frontage that puts off all but the most dedicated of art collector – and that's exactly how the owner, Gregory, likes it. We are currently exhibiting sculptures by up-and-coming artist Earl Van Klug – which means that we're displaying life-size naked torsos fashioned from wire mesh, complete with 'men's furniture' as my mother would call it.

We have only a few regular clients at the gallery, but those who do visit tend to spend vast sums of money in one fell swoop. Which is rather nice as Caron and I are paid partly on commission. Going for quality rather than quantity of customers does tend to make the days drag somewhat, but ever since we had a bungled ram-raid last year, Gregory has been forced to employ increased security measures, which mean that now my friend and I work together on the same shift instead of just crossing briefly when we change over. Gregory deems it too unsafe for one person to be entrusted with the safekeeping of the artworks in the gallery and, secretly, I'm rather glad of it. Gossiping with my friend at least makes the slow hours enjoyable.

Caron and I get on very well. We share the same taste in scandal, were educated to the same standard in the same sort of high-security, elitist public school for 'gels', prefer Starbucks to Coffee Republic, both think the art we sell is over-priced and pretend to despise *Hello!* magazine while devouring it each week.

My friend is tall and blonde and looks like a man-eater although she always complains that there's too much of a time-lapse between infrequent dates. Caron shares a flat with her brother and makes it a rule never to go out with any of his mates, mainly so that they can't regale her sibling with salacious tales when the relationship invariably goes wrong. It means that she lives in constant torment, as a selection of half-naked rugby players, firemen and stockbrokers trail through their abode. I think it's a bit of a waste and that she should consider lowering her standards.

In our cash rich, time poor society there seems to be very little spare time left to devote to nurturing relationships. Women, it is said, are having less sex than women in the 1950s. I certainly am, and even Caron insists that it's better to be celibate than have her sex-life discussed by her brother down at the pub. At least she doesn't have a boyfriend like Leo to contend with. Having listened to me relate tales of Leo's adventures, Caron has said on more than one occasion that she's glad she is single. She's never said it with a lot of enthusiasm though.

The rooms in the gallery are all white, brightly-lit and, beyond the main reception and the naked torsos, are hung with a small selection of canary-yellow paintings done by yet another upcoming artist from East London with multiple piercings and a retro bright pink Mohawk hairdo. Today, the paintings are giving me a headache. I'm chewing at my fingernails while trying not to really bite them, but already my nails have gone soggy. It's now nearly lunchtime and I'm still complaining about Leo and his latest escapade.

Caron suddenly looks up from her magazine and says, 'Didn't you dump Leo just last week?'

'Yes,' I reply tetchily. Caron isn't being particularly sympathetic to my plight. When I told her about the cake incident, she actually laughed. Aren't we girls supposed to stick together? 'But not for real. This is for real.'

'Does Leo realise that?'

I pull at my hair. 'Do you think I should phone him and tell him again?' Picking up the phone, I toy with it.

Caron closes the latest copy of *Hello!* and folds it on her lap. 'Isn't that how you always get back together?'

I put down the phone. 'So you don't think I should ring him?'

'What is *wrong* with people these days?' Caron sighs. 'Take our cosy little gang. We're all the wrong side of thirty. Only just in your case, admittedly. But none of us are even near settling down. It's not just Leo who seems to be stretching out his teenage years – we're guilty too. We should have mortgages and pension plans and children. I can't even get a man. Or, at least, not one that doesn't just want convenient sex for a few weeks. You've landed yourself with the most resolutely juvenile commitment-phobe imaginable and yet you can't let go. You're hanging on there in the unlikely event that Leo will suddenly grow up and become the perfect boyfriend.'

'Leo isn't that bad.'

'You've been slagging him off all morning, Emma,' my friend points out. 'Every morning for the last five years, in fact.'

I open my mouth but don't speak.

'There are a lot worse than Leo out there,' Caron says. 'He's handsome, he's rich and you could have a great laugh with him, if you weren't so concerned about your image. Perhaps if you weren't so down on him all the time then he wouldn't feel the need to live up to his reputation. If you don't want him any more then move on and let some of us poor unfortunate cows have a go.'

'I love Leo,' I insist. 'I'm simply trying to . . . mould him. A little bit.' Isn't that what love is all about? You find someone nearly perfect and then chip away at their rough edges until they eventually become the person you want them to be.

'You're going to "mould" him into the arms of someone else if you're not very careful.'

'There are very few people who wouldn't benefit from some improvement.'

Caron rolls her eyes. 'You included?'

'Well . . .' I falter.

'You could be the perfect couple if only Leo wasn't such a twit and you weren't so anal. Meet him halfway.'

Good advice possibly, but I have no idea where halfway between twit and anal might be.

Caron extracts her emery board from the corner of the desk drawer that is its permanent home. She's very proud of her nails, which are long and always painted even though they aren't acrylic, they're all her own. With a flick of the emery board, she points at the window. 'Ditch Leo and you could end up with someone like that.'

There's a man lurking on the street, staring at the naked torsos. It looks like something he might do a lot – as a hobby. He's short with thinning hair and is wearing a grey mackintosh even though it isn't raining, and he probably isn't yet forty. The sort of man who wears Y-fronts – and not in an ironic way.

'So what do you think I should do?' I say.

The man sidles into the gallery. 'I wonder if you could tell me something about the sculptures in the window?'

Caron goes to answer him, but I cut her off in her prime.

I sigh. There's no way this guy is a serious art lover. He has *time-waster* – and possibly *pervert* – stamped all over him. 'Can't you see that we're busy?'

The man looks affronted.

'Do you think we're here – in this gallery and on this planet – so that you can treat us exactly as you like?'

Terror springs to his eyes and, before I can get into full flow, he scuttles out again.

'So you haven't tried the relaxation CD I bought you for your birthday?' Caron says over her nail-file.

'Yes, I have,' I say with a huff. 'This is me being relaxed.'

The man in the grey mac is fleeing down the street. 'Bloody men!' I shout after him.

Chapter Eighteen

L eo was with Grant and Lard and they were sitting at their favourite table in their favourite lunchtime haunt – Cash. Aptly named, as this place always managed to relieve them of plenty of it. The bar was a hop, skip and a jump from their office and was busier than usual today, so they were all huddled together at their small table, but in a blokey sort of way. Music was blaring out – Amy Winehouse or someone – and they were finding it hard to hear each other talk. So they'd kind of given up while they concentrated on their over-priced but freshly made ciabatta sandwiches.

'You are looking very romantically-inclined,' Grant said between bites of his bread, and Leo realised that he was staring wistfully out of the window.

'She was very nice,' he replied.

'Miss Glitter Knickers?' Lard didn't appreciate that speaking with his mouth full wasn't polite.

Nodding in response, Leo sighed in the manner of a romantic poet – Percy Bysshe Shelley or Byron or the one with the daffodils perhaps. 'I can't believe she just used me, abused me and then disappeared.'

'I can't believe you're so bloody lucky,' Lard muttered.

Grant scratched his head. 'I thought you were in love with Emma?'

Leo couldn't admit this out loud – he was a man, after all – and men had enough trouble admitting that sort of stuff to themselves, let alone to others. But this woman, Isobel. He had no idea what she'd done to him, but . . . well, she'd simply turned his world upside down. And his world hadn't been turned upside down for a long time.

Leo had been with Emma for years. He knew nothing else. Not really. She'd been the only person he'd ever had a long-term relationship with – unless you counted his parents, which was fairly disastrous and not something you'd want to use as a blueprint. Anyway, that wasn't quite the same, was it? And, the sad fact was that this new woman had

65

walked into his life out of nowhere and, quite frankly, Leo was starting to feel a little different about things.

Take sex, for example. Leo would have said that his sex-life with Emma was good. Very good. Regular. Now he wasn't so sure. When Isobel made love to him it was a revelation. And he chose those words very carefully, which he wasn't prone to do. Isobel didn't just have sex with him, she definitely made love to him – all night! Leo still couldn't believe that. He hadn't been so energetic since he was about nineteen. And, if he was honest, Isobel had been very much in charge. But not in a kinky way. In a soft and gentle way. Emma was always in charge during their lovemaking, but then weren't most women? And Leo didn't want to go into too much detail, because he was pretty hopeless at talking about this sort of thing, but Emma could be bossy. Very bossy. And not in a kinky way. Even between the sheets there was no 'off' button for her in-built bossiness – it was always 'Leo, do this', 'Leo, do that', 'Leo, harder/faster/slower'. 'Leo, any way but the way you were doing it', really. And though Leo thought that it was wonderful that women were now men's equals and they had the vote and could drive racing cars or play rugby and demand what they wanted in bed, he also thought: Sometimes, ladies, it would be nice if you'd pretend that men are in control; just every now and again. Faking it could be good. Really it could. Men were very simple souls – a bit of praise once in a while worked wonders. Leo didn't think that Isobel was faking it, but she certainly didn't have any complaints. And Leo didn't mean that in a wink, wink way. He meant that she didn't complain all the way through. And it was a revelation to Leo that someone could find him wonderful without him having to pretend not to be him.

Leo did the romantic sigh again. 'I thought I was in love with Emma.'

'But not any more?'

'I have absolutely no idea.'

'Well, here's your chance to find out. Emma alert!'

Leo glanced up and Grant was right: Emma was walking past the window and peering in. She knew that Leo was there, regular as clock-work, virtually every day of the week. 'Oh no.' He gave Grant and Lard an impassioned look. 'I can't do this now. Really I can't.'

Emma's shoes were circling the table slowly. Leo knew it was her from the determination of her step rather than recognising her choice of footwear. He was ashamed he had to admit this, but to avoid Emma,

Grant and Lard and Leo all slid under the table. They sat with their knees up round their ears and their heads bent down which made them look like leprechauns – but without the green clothes. It was a frightfully grubby little space and you wouldn't believe how much chewing gum was stuck to the underside of the table – none of it theirs, of course. People these days were very dirty. And cowardly. Leo clutched his beer to his chest and dreaded the fact that at any moment Emma could look under the table and he would be sprung. The shoes tippy-tapped around with a menacing air and then they disappeared.

'She's gone,' Lard said.

'Check,' Leo advised. Emma was very devious and could just be lurking ready to pounce.

Lard peeped his head out. 'She's definitely gone. The coast's clear.'

They unfolded their knees, realising that they might have benefited from a few years of hatha yoga before adopting this extreme position. 'Did she have any blunt instruments with her?'

Lard shook his head.

'Sharp ones?'

'Not that I could see.'

'Emotional torture then,' Leo said. This was the worst form of punishment and the one at which Emma was most effective. She was like the love-child of Freddie Kruger when cheesed off. They crawled out from under the table, trying not to spill valuable droplets of their beer.

'You could just talk to her,' Lard suggested, picking bits of fluff from his trousers with a scowl on his face.

Grant and Leo stared at him open-mouthed. Leo couldn't even begin to locate the power of speech.

'What?' Lard said, when they remained silent.

'Are you mad?' Grant asked eventually. 'Completely mad?'

'We're guys,' Leo pointed out. 'Talking is an alien concept to us.'

'Sorry,' Lard said sheepishly. 'I don't know what I was thinking of.'

There was a pink Post-It note stuck to the top of the table amid the white rings and bits of stale peanut. As they resumed their places, Leo picked up the note as, quite rightly, he expected that it would be for him. *Grow up*, it said and was signed, *Emma*.

Chapter Nineteen

Isobel stood and regarded the towering offices of Thornton Jones, before hitching her bag onto her shoulder and stepping purposefully inside. The building was all shiny and hard-edged, very different from the type of place she was used to. Her eyes widened in wonder. There were tall trees growing inside and she'd never seen that before. Where she came from, trees grew outside in woods. Amazing. She was learning so much. Thrilled rather than daunted by the strangeness of her surroundings, Isobel checked through the list of companies displayed on a stainless-steel noticeboard in the foyer until she found the floor she wanted.

Following the steady stream of men and women in smart suits, she stepped into a small glass room that took them up, up, up on the outside of the building. Isobel pressed her face against the glass and watched as the pedestrians scuttling by on the streets below her grew smaller until they were tiny, tiny people that made her think of home. She was pleased that she'd done her homework well and looked just like the other women in her neat black suit and kitten heels. She'd twisted her long flowing hair into a tidy bun and had produced some horn-rimmed glasses to complete the look. Isobel smiled to herself. Fitting in here would be seamless. She couldn't wait.

There was a small reception area with another tight-lipped woman behind a desk. Perhaps it was a requirement here for women behind desks to be unpleasant.

'Yes,' the woman said without looking up.

'I have an interview,' Isobel told the top of her head. 'With a Mr Baldwin.'

'Name?'

'Isobel Hewlett-Packard.'

'Take a seat, please.' When the woman finally looked up, she glowered at Isobel who smiled politely back.

Isobel sat down and leafed through the magazines on the coffee-table. If there was anything destined to make her feel like an outsider it was the fashions. She'd have to get a grip on those. Her outfit today was a success, but it was difficult when so few of the women on the street looked like the women in the fashion spreads. Women here were all shapes and sizes and yet there appeared to be a separate long, thin race of women without blemishes who were the only ones allowed to feature in magazines.

'Mr Baldwin will see you now,' the woman informed her crisply. 'Third door on the left.'

Isobel walked down the hall, aware that from the open–plan office many heads had swivelled in her direction and a phalanx of popping eyes were watching her progress. She turned and gave the men in the office a dazzling smile, before disappearing into Mr Baldwin's private office.

Mr Baldwin was hurriedly swallowing two tablets as she went in and clearly looked unwell. He stood up and walked from behind his desk to greet her. Mr Baldwin, too, looked taken aback by her appearance and Isobel wondered if all women had this effect on men. If they did, it was rather nice.

'Good afternoon, Ms ... er ...'

'Isobel.' She shook his hand.

'Isobel.' He smiled and rolled the word around as if savouring it on his tongue. 'Please sit down.'

Isobel sat down opposite him while Mr Baldwin rifled through the piles of paperwork on his desk. It was a terribly untidy office. There were mountains of documents that looked as if they should have been filed away, and the potted plants drooped listlessly. This man definitely needed her help.

'I don't seem to have a CV here for you,' he said at length, then abandoned his search. 'I must have mislaid it. Have you brought one with you?'

'Yes.' Isobel opened her handbag and pulled out her wand again. She zapped Mr Baldwin.

'Oh, my word,' Mr Baldwin said.

'I'd like to start tomorrow.'

Her future boss shook himself, like a dog shaking off water. 'Yes, yes. That's fine. It all seems to be in order.'

Isobel tucked her wand away.

'Welcome on board.' Mr Baldwin shook her hand, starting as if he'd touched an electrical socket by mistake. 'We'll see you at nine o'clock prompt.'

'Prompt?'

'If that suits you, of course,' Mr Baldwin said.

Isobel stood up and went over and kissed Mr Baldwin on the cheek. 'That suits me just fine.'

'Good, good.' Mr Baldwin stroked his cheek.

'I'll see you in the morning.'

'Yes, yes. Wonderful. Marvellous.'

'You should start to feel better now,' Isobel said, and she went out to survey her new empire.

'I'm fine,' Mr Baldwin said, dazed. 'Absolutely fine.' And he picked up the packet of tablets to check exactly what it was he'd taken.

Chapter Twenty

Leo hadn't chosen this particular career path, it had chosen him. Basically, Leo was doing this job because his father had secured it for him through one of his old cronies. A terrible admission, Leo knew. But when he'd left university, after he'd enjoyed three very nice years of drunken debauchery and yet somehow managed to blag a passable 2.2, he still had no firm idea of where his life was headed. His father took over and within weeks Leo was in the City, in finance, in this office.

And all these years later, having managed to hang onto his job by the skin of his teeth, he still really had no idea what he was actually doing or why, indeed, he was doing it. Throughout the morning, he'd been crunching numbers for a purpose that steadfastly eluded him. If he were saving lives by curing cancer or teaching children with learning difficulties or something that had a tangible end product other than simply making more money, then he might have felt it was worthwhile. Grant and Lard had no such compunction – they loved making money for the sake of it. In fact, they loved it so much that they excelled at it and, therefore, had time to cover Leo's arse when he fell woefully short of expectations. And for this, he thanked them regularly.

Before Leo could lament this further, his eye made an involuntary glance up at the clock – not for the first time today – to check the time and see how much longer this interminable afternoon had left to run. And – double-take! Flip. Flip. It was her. Ms Glitter Knickers!

She was grinning at him and mouthed, 'See you later,' before she disappeared round the corner towards the bank of elevators.

'Flip. Flip.' Leo tried to log off from his computer and in the process pressed all the wrong bastardy buttons. 'Flip. Flip.' And then he knocked his coffee into the keyboard which meant he had to use his suit jacket to mop it up. And then his jacket knocked all his papers to the floor. 'Flip. Flip.'

Finally, he managed by some miracle to disentangle himself from his desk, leaving a trail of devastation behind him. As he arrived at the lift, he saw the doors close with Isobel inside. She lifted her hand in a delicate wave.

'Isobel! Isobel!' Oh bollocks. The only thing for it was the stairs. If Leo took them two at a time, he could head off the lift by the time it got to the bottom. Even at this point, Leo realised that he was failing to take into account that he was on the tenth floor and was, basically, an unfit bastard. All those hours he could have spent in the gym rather than wasting his money in seedy bars would have come in very handy now.

What was he thinking of? They did it in films all the time. Heading off villains and departing romantic heroines with consummate ease. Leo sprinted to the Emergency Exit door which led to the stairs. What Thornton Jones had lavished on marble and chrome for the public areas of the offices they had saved by making the back staircase the most dingy place on earth. It was a dimly lit underbelly of unpainted concrete and it echoed eerily. The sort of place that any self-respecting serial killer would be happy to call home.

As Leo had promised himself, he took the steps two at a time, sprinting athletically while still clinging to the black iron handrail for balance. His feet clattered on the concrete steps. Leo hadn't run like this since . . . probably since the egg and spoon race in primary school. Generally, he tried to avoid exerting himself at all costs. But these were extreme circumstances. Whatever it took, Leo had to find her before she walked out of his life again. If nothing else, he needed to know what on earth was going on. In times of crisis it was well-known that humans are capable of producing superhuman effort. That was all that was required here.

One floor later. 'Ouff. Ouff.'

Not. That. Fit. At. All. Puff. Puff. Deep unpleasantness. Two floors later.

'Shit.' Pant. Pant. Stop for minute. Breathe. Breathe. Hot air in lungs. Give up smoking. Again. Go to gym.

Three floors later. Superhuman effort not yet kicking in. Bollocks. Can't speak. Wheezing. Asthma attack surely.

Four floors. Dying. Seriously. Barely alive. Collapse on stairs. Lie here and let vultures peck out eyes. Breathing heavily. Knackered. Like fat Labrador. Major depression. Will never catch her now. Probably halfway to Outer Mongolia.

'Bugger.' Gasp. Gasp.

Stand up. Amble down rest of stairs. Carefully.

Chapter Twenty-One

In the blazing summer sunshine, Grant and Lard were sitting on one of the granite walls that surrounded the flowerbeds outside the Thornton Jones building – originally installed to soften the hard edges of the brash architecture, but in effect, a great refuge for the hardened smokers among the largely nicotine-encrusted staff. They were just the perfect height for the perching of a bottom, and a regular prayer of thanks was said to the man who designed them for that fact. Otherwise, they'd all be forced to stand up with their fags. Terrible hardship.

Lard was merely a social smoker, but he chain-ate Mars Bars which also made him something of a leper in the offices where carb-free seemed to be king. He alternated puffs of his low tar whatever with gargantuan gobblings of chocolate and toffee. Grant, however, was dragging deeply on his outsize, full hit ciggie. A tiny silver butterfly flitted past Leo's eye, brushing his hair, and he wafted it away with his hand – but in a nice way, not irritably. Mainly because he was too exhausted to do irritable and it was a very pretty butterfly. It was depressing that they had such short life-spans, so Leo tried not to think about butterflies too often. The butterfly eschewed the fragrant flowers and fluttered off into the congestion of cars.

Leo wandered over to Grant and Lard and sat down next to them. The traffic on Leadenhall Road trundled slowly past, horns blaring, filling the warm summer air with the acrid smell of petrol fumes that won the battle with the scent of roses struggling up from the flowerbeds. Leo breathed in the toxic mix of pollution until he got his breath back.

'I'm on the cadge,' he said when he could speak again.

'Cancer or calories?' Lard enquired.

'Er . . . cancer.'

Grant handed him a cigarette and Leo went through the blessed ritual of lighting up which, actually, he preferred to the process of smoking. Leo loved all that fiddling about with the packet and the cigarette and the lighter. After the first inhalation he could take it or leave it.

'I thought you'd given up?'

Though leaving it was actually a bit harder in practice. 'So did I.'

They all sat in a row like the three wise monkeys and dragged on their cigarettes in unison. After observing a suitable period of silence while they took in the traffic noise and watched the motorbike couriers weave in and out of the cars indulging in a spot of extreme parcel delivery, and they'd admired a few young women in short, flippy skirts, Leo then said, 'You didn't happen to see an extraordinarily beautiful girl pass by a few minutes ago, did you?'

'How beautiful?' Grant wanted to know.

'One look would be enough to melt the elastic on your underpants.'

Grant and Lard looked impressed and then somewhere the penny dropped. Grant's mouth fell slightly agog. 'Not Ms Glitter Knickers again?'

Leo nodded in confirmation. 'I'm sure I saw her in the office. Just now. She came out of Old Baldy's office, waved to me and then disappeared into the lift. I ran down the stairs . . .'

'You did what?'

'I ran down the stairs after her.'

They looked at Leo in disbelief.

'But you're terminally unfit,' coughed Lard.

'And you had six shags last night,' Grant reminded him. 'Even Kelly Holmes would be hard pushed to summon up a run after that.'

'True,' Leo conceded. Then, as they all contemplated this turn of events over another drag, 'But neither of you two saw her leave the building?'

His friends shook their heads and looked rather disappointed that they hadn't.

'She's utterly gorgeous,' Leo said flatly. 'And now I'm not sure if the whole thing was a hallucination.' Instead of the translucent underwear and velvet cloak, she had been wearing a very fetching business suit, but Leo would have known her anywhere. He was sure he would. 'There are odd things happening to me. And I don't know why.'

'When did you last have a holiday, mate?' Grant asked. 'Even for you, you're acting very strangely.'

'Yeah,' Leo agreed. 'I'd be the first to admit that I'm feeling decidedly unhinged at the moment.'

'What you need is a few glasses of fizz inside you. Hair of the dog and all that. We must head straight to the nearest and seediest bar as soon as we are released from our daily toil.'

But − and this was really strange − Leo couldn't summon up the necessary enthusiasm for heavy drinking. Very strange, indeed. 'I think I'll give it a miss, boys.'

Stubbing out his cigarette, Leo turned to wander back into the office. As he left, he heard Grant and Lard mutter, 'That is not a well man!'

Chapter Twenty-Two

L eo went home early. Which, along with him refusing a drink, was also unheard of. You could be sacked from Thornton Jones for simply going home on time. And he took a cab as he was feeling far too peculiar to face a long walk or be squashed on the Tube – even though it was only a couple of stops.

Sitting in the back of the cab, Leo thought about recent events as the driver played dodge the traffic, swerving in and out of lanes so that his progress wouldn't be hampered. He should phone Emma, he knew he should. But, basically, he was frightened of her. If he even spoke to her she would know that he'd been having carnal knowledge of another woman. Leo would bet that she could even spot a few lustful thoughts from a mile off. She would, no doubt, be deeply suspicious of the silver glitter that was still sprouting forth from his hair. He looked like someone who had spent too long at a glam-rock fancy dress party. Actually, that would be a rather good excuse should he need one.

Leo's phone had been turned off all day and he didn't dare check it for messages. He wasn't trying to avoid reality. Not really. He just wasn't ready to visit it at the moment. Leo was also thinking of having an early night and wondered with something approaching alarm if the Peter Pan phase of his life was suddenly coming to an end. That would be too hideous to contemplate. One night of athletic lust and he was totally knackered. Very soon, he could be forced to consider a pension fund and health insurance and all manner of responsible things. He might start buying slippers. It made Leo shudder just thinking about it, so he stopped immediately. And he thought about Emma instead.

Leo paid the taxi driver, and glad to still be in possession of his latest door key, let himself into the house. He high-fived his neighbour Dominic as they passed each other on the stairs.

'Mate,' Leo said.

'Mate,' Dominic said back.

Leo liked Dominic. He was a great neighbour. He was uncomplicated, rather like himself. Dominic lived with his girlfriend Lydia next door to Leo. She was as complicated as they come. But she did have great legs.

'We must catch up some time,' Dominic said.

'Yeah. Yeah,' Leo agreed. They always said this when they met, but they never did. Busy people. Busy lives. They were lucky if they got together once or twice every summer for a few beers on Dominic's and Lydia's posh roof terrace, and then they'd always vow to do it more regularly. Needless to say, Leo never invited them back to his place. He couldn't bear the humiliation. His rusting bike couldn't compete with their stainless-steel planters. Leo wasn't a terribly competitive person, but he did appreciate there were standards that must be maintained and, in this case, his were very low. Leo decided he must get Emma to spend his next bonus on a roof terrace designer and then he remembered with a sharp jolt that his darling Emma wasn't going to be doing anything for him ever again. His heart sank. It wasn't the fact that he wasn't perfectly capable of organising a roof terrace designer all by himself, he just rather liked Emma organising everything for him, if the truth were known. And, if that wasn't going to happen, then he knew that he'd never get round to doing it. The rusting bike and Leo were destined to live in untidy harmony for some considerable time yet.

Climbing the remaining stairs, Leo felt quite low, as if he was coming down with a cold. But when he opened the door to the flat, he heard the sound of music coming from the kitchen – not the Julie Andrews *Sound of Music* we all know and love. No. The sound of this music was produced by James Brown's dulcet tones screeching out 'Get Up Offa That Thing'.

Assuming that a burglar wouldn't be so bold or have such great taste in music, Leo pushed open the kitchen door. Isobel – Ms Glitter Knickers – was dancing round his kitchen. His uninvited guest was barefoot and was dressed only in a brief slip of silk kimono which Leo found very appealing. She was also brandishing a small silver wand. Oh. And the dirty dishes were washing themselves. They were jumping in and out of the sink all of their own accord. Very much in time to the music. And Isobel was conducting them. She was quite a mover. So were Leo's plates. It wasn't a quality he'd previously considered necessary in a dinner plate. His knives and forks weren't too shabby either as they performed a passable disco routine.

'Hello,' Leo said.

'Ooo.'

The music stopped abruptly and Isobel spun round, clutching her wand to her chest. Her kimono was gaping attractively, but that was by the by. Leo's dishes ground to a halt, some huddled together nervously as if discovered *in flagrante delicto* rather than just doing a bit of disco dancing. Some toppled into the sink in surprise.

'Relax,' Isobel said to the dishes. They all fell back onto the draining board and there was a noise that sounded remarkably like a plate sighing.

'Another interesting party trick,' Leo felt moved to say. Even though he was amazed that he still had the power of speech.

'I can explain,' Isobel said, hanging her head, chewing her lip and doing all sorts of cute 'I'm embarrassed' type stuff.

Walking over to the fridge and opening it rather gingerly just in case the carton of milk was doing a tango, Leo helped himself to a beer. 'This I can't wait to hear.'

Leo then opened a kitchen cupboard and tried to find some peanuts or something to go with the beer. This was a definite snack-attack moment. Leo thought that he must be turning into Lard, who always advised an excess of calories in times of crisis. It wasn't just girls who liked chocolate. Once he'd found some comfort food and a modicum of equilibrium, he turned his attention back to Isobel.

Meeting his eyes, she made a huffing sound. 'I'm not like other women,' she said.

'I've managed to work out that much.'

'I'm a fairy.'

Blame it on shock, but somehow Leo managed to hit his head on the open cupboard door, and the next thing he saw was the floor coming up to meet him.

Chapter Twenty-Three

Isobel was dabbing at a cut on Leo's forehead with a damp and very smelly J-cloth. None too tenderly. Leo was propped upright on a kitchen chair, but the universe still seemed rather skewed. He was bleeding profusely and was convinced that he wasn't long for this world.

'Ow! Ow!' He cringed away from her.

'For heaven's sake,' Isobel tutted, scowling at him as she did. Despite the pain, Leo thought she looked very cute.

With an insouciant stare, she pulled out her wand and, even though Leo shrank back into his chair, she waved it over him. Leo was expecting something horrid to happen, but it didn't. The bloodflow from the cut arrested immediately and when he touched his forehead there was no sign that it had ever existed. He went to say something, but unusually, nothing would come out.

Isobel gazed at him evenly. 'I'm a fairy.'

Ah, so he hadn't been hearing things. 'A fairy,' Leo managed when this had eventually started to sink in. He tried to eat some peanuts. Because if this was a dream, peanut-eating would be impossible. Wouldn't it?

Isobel waited patiently. The peanuts tasted exactly like peanuts.

'So?' Leo asked eventually. 'A fairy? Is that like being a lesbian?'

'No,' Isobel said. She sat down on the chair next to him and pulled it close. Her beautiful, glowy face was frowning with concern. 'I'm a magical being, Leo. A nymph.'

Leo gave himself time to digest this. 'I've been out with a nympho-maniac before, but I don't think I've ever had the pleasure of dating a plain old nymph.'

'And I've never had a boyfriend who wasn't a fairy,' Isobel countered.

'Are we really having this conversation?'

Isobel nodded at him.

'And you haven't been drinking?'

She shook her head.

'Me neither.' But Leo rather wished he had. Perhaps, he thought, he was going to come round at any moment and would still be up to his eyeballs in cake at Emma's birthday party because everything since then was shaping up to be one humdinger of a nightmare.

'Fairies have co-existed with humans for hundreds of years.'

'Four hundred and sixty-three in your case. If I remember rightly.'

Isobel looked at him beseechingly. 'Is it so difficult to believe?'

'Oh, no. No. Not at all. I get mightily pissed, dumped by my girl-friend and bump into a fairy trying to top herself on Tower Bridge.' Leo was starting to get a headache and he didn't think it was from the bang on his head. 'An everyday story of ordinary folk.'

'I can't "top myself",' Isobel pointed out. 'I'm immortal.'

'Yeah. You and David Beckham.'

In the background Leo noted that his dirty dishes were now quietly popping themselves in and out of the sink, trying hard not to attract his attention. Leo didn't tell them that they'd been rumbled. He closed his eyes momentarily and then opened them again. Yes, they were still washing themselves.

'Isobel?' Leo suddenly felt very weary. 'What are you doing here? Why are you in this flat? Why me?'

Isobel took his hands in hers. They were as cool as a mountain spring. 'You are my mortal soulmate, Leo,' she told him earnestly. 'I have come across time to find you.'

'Right.' This could be too much information. 'You did say *time* and not *town*?'

Isobel nodded in a very sombre way and he knew that she wasn't joking.

'Thought so.'

'We are meant to be together.'

'Isobel, you are an extraordinarily beautiful woman . . . fairy. Look at you, you're all shimmery and shiny and vaguely see-through. Even though you're knocking on for five hundred. Joan Collins doesn't look that good and she's bloody marvellous for her age.' Leo stood up and went to get his beer because, as I'm sure you'll appreciate, he damn well needed one. This also gave him the chance to pace about as sitting still wasn't really an option in this situation either. 'And I'm really flat-tered that you've come all the way across time to find me, but I'm not worth it. I'm a crap boyfriend. Really I am. And I already have a girl-friend.' Leo pulled himself up sharply. 'Wait! Emma hasn't set this all up as a joke, has she? Because I'll bloody kill her if she has. I'll dump her back.'

'No, Leo. It isn't a joke.'

For a moment Leo thought that Isobel looked very shifty. Her eyelashes were firmly lowered over her eyes. Could Emma be involved in this? Could she possibly have drummed this up with Isobel to teach him a lesson? Women of any species probably stick together. Then he remembered the self-washing dishes and realised that even Emma wasn't that resourceful.

'And, actually, you don't have a girlfriend,' Isobel continued, avoiding his eyes.

Leo's newfound little fairy friend zapped the answerphone with her wand. Emma's voice flooded through the flat.

'Leo! You are a crap boyfriend,' she shouted.

Leo gave Isobel an I-told-you-so look.

Emma ranted on. *'It's still over between us. I thought I'd better confirm it just in case you were too pissed to remember that I dumped you. For ever, this time.'*

She never dumped Leo for ever. It was a week, max.

'And even if you ring or come round here, I won't talk to you. You're not going to charm your way back into my affections – or my bed – ever again, Leo Harper.'

Isobel had folded her arms and was listening intently. Leo felt that she might be learning too much. There was a beeping noise and the line went dead.

'Phew,' he said.

'There's more.' Isobel waved her wand again.

Emma's voice fast-forwarded to the next message. *'There's no point in buying a massive, belated birthday present,'* she yelled. *'It's too late. Too, too late! Even if it was a ring. A special kind of ring. There's no way that would work. I wouldn't even consider it. I saw you hiding under the table from me!'*

Leo cringed. That was a very childish thing to do.

'That was a very childish thing to do,' Emma shouted.

Then there was the heartfelt slam of a phone and the line went dead again.

'Bugger.' That was a fulsome rant even for Emma.

81

Isobel gave him another knowing look and waved that blasted wand again. Leo was growing to dislike it by the moment.

'I'm not going to be sitting here at home tonight, moping and waiting for the phone to ring,' his very ex-girlfriend said. 'I'm going to be out having fun. Fun with someone you don't know.'

Leo didn't like the sound of this.

'I'm going out at eight o'clock, well about quarter past. And I won't be home until way after midnight. Way, way after midnight. And then I might not be alone. Or I might not come home at all.'

Alarm bells were ringing. Where would she go? And who with?

'And I won't have my mobile phone switched on because I won't want to be disturbed. So even if you were thinking of ringing me to apologise – profusely – then you probably couldn't even get me until tomorrow morning anyway.'

The line went dead again and all that was left was the empty whirring sound of the answerphone.

'Shit.' This was terrible. A bleak feeling stole over Leo. 'It's really over this time.'

'I think so,' Isobel said confidently.

'Emma never really dumps me,' Leo explained. 'It's like a sport for her. She sees me as a challenge.' At least he thought she did. She certainly used to. 'After she's cooled down – which can sometimes take days – we just get together again as if nothing's ever happened.' Leo felt worry wiggle across his brow. 'She sounds serious.'

'Don't look downcast.' Isobel came and wrapped her arms round him. 'This is meant to be, Leo. Your soul called to me.'

'I don't think it did, Isobel. I'm pretty sure I would have known.'

'Leo, you are meant to be a part of me.' She pulled away from him slightly and her beautiful face looked troubled. 'How much do you know about fairies?'

'Surprisingly little,' he admitted. 'I studied English at university. Chaucer. Shakespeare. Dead poets. They're my speciality. The fairy course was all full up.'

'Fairies don't have souls,' Isobel continued unabashed. 'We need human men to give us what we most desire.'

'And what's that?'

'All in good time, Leo. You'll learn. All in good time.'

'This sounds very spooky.'

'You won't feel a thing.' His scary fairy friend smiled at him re-assuringly. 'I promise you.'

'Right.' He let the word drag, but his lack of knowledge re fairies also extended to not knowing if they got irony – a bit like Americans. Call him suspicious, but it sounded to Leo as if there might be a catch to all this. He was going to take rather a lot of convincing on this – glitter or no glitter. In Leo's book, if something sounded too good to be true then you could be sure that it damn well was. 'And what do I get out of this deal? Apart from free champagne and an unusual, but undeniably effective dishwasher?'

'More than you will ever know, Leo,' she assured him. 'I'll show you how to love in ways you never thought possible.'

'Really?' This perked Leo up no end. Over the years, he had been forced, on occasions, to watch several of Grant's more adventurous Swedish films and, you'd better believe it, if the Swedes were anything to go by then there were an awful lot of ways to love. 'Do you fancy going to bed again to test this theory?'

'I don't mean that kind of love, Leo.'

'Oh.'

'I will show you shades of human love that you never thought possible.'

'Still sounds kinky to me.'

Isobel smiled sweetly. Leo took her hand and she led him towards the bedroom. 'I have to warn you,' he said. 'One way and another, it's been a very taxing day. I don't think I can manage it six times again.'

Isobel's smile widened. 'I'd like to bet you can.'

And Leo noted, with some relief, that she had brought her wand along with her, secreted discreetly behind her back.

Chapter Twenty-Four

I pour out three brimming glasses of Rioja – for the third time. My good friends, Caron and Jo, swig deeply and gratefully. Something truly mournful is playing on the stereo – I just can't remember what. Something suitable for the death of a relationship. Morrissey, Bob Dylan, Nick Drake – that sort of thing. They all work equally well. No cheery humming required. Music to slit your wrists by. It captures my mood perfectly. And, anyway, I've left all my decent girly CDs at Leo's flat – Whitney Houston, Norah Jones and Alicia Keyes will all lie unplayed in his CD rack, gathering dust. The minute my back is turned, the Kaiser Chiefs and Keane will be shaking the pictures off the walls.

Caron and Jo put their glasses on the coffee-table and they sit in silence as whoever warbles on about disaster.

'This is fun,' Jo says, with more than a touch of sarcasm.

'Ssh!' Caron shushes.

'I've been to happier wakes.'

'This *is* a wake,' I announce dramatically. 'We are mourning the demise of my relationship with Leo.'

Jo sighs. 'I bet he's not sitting at home mourning anything.'

'Be sympathetic,' Caron admonishes her. 'Emma was very caring towards you when Archie dumped you.'

'Yes, but Archie dumped me for my sister. My entire family knew he was shagging her, but not one of them told me. It caused a massive rift and even to this day none of us are on speaking terms.'

It *was* a fairly terrible time, I remember.

'Emma dumps Leo frequently for the slightest reason,' Jo says. 'Is coming home drunk with a traffic cone on your head every now and again just cause to end a relationship?'

'The last time he came home with a traffic cone on his head, he'd also lost his underpants,' I feel moved to point out.

'Yes, but you did find them hanging from the aerial of his car a few days later.'

'When he eventually found his car,' I add.

'I'd go out with Leo,' Jo says. 'He's lush.'

'He is *a* lush,' Caron says with a nod.

'Well, no one's asking you. Thank you, Joanna.' I fold my arms. It's desperate being single again. You are forced to hang around with your mates because you have no choice rather than because you want to — and that's a very different feeling. How many days has it been now? Two? I have a heart-sink moment. It already seems like an eternity.

'Remember the boy who cried wolf?' Jo asks. 'His mates all disappeared off to the nightclub and left him to it. Girls who cry wolf get the same treatment.'

I look around at the bare brick walls of my lovely flat which suddenly seems to be closing in on me. I can see myself dying here alone and friendless, surrounded by my IKEA furniture with statement pieces from the Conran shop — that's if I don't get a move on and get a decent relationship.

'I was reading *SHE* magazine on the Tube this morning,' Caron says, 'and scientists have identified three types of perfectionist. There are those who set impossibly high standards for themselves, those who set impossibly high standards for others and those who are desperate to be seen as perfectionists in order to gain peer-group approval.'

'And?' I say.

'I think you might be all of them, Emma.'

'Oh, that's charming!'

'I'm trying to be helpful. They say it's a form of mental illness — like depression or . . . or . . . insanity.'

'I can't help it if I like everything to be just so.' I refuse to look at my books and CDs, which are all set at the exact same angle, arranged alphabetically. And I won't even think about my wardrobe where everything is colour-coded and has to be hanging in the same direction on the same type of coat hanger. Doesn't everyone else worry if the handles on their mugs don't line up the right way in the cupboards? Is it possible for your life to be too ordered? Doesn't it simply mean that I'm very, very organised?

'It might be a good idea if you went to see a therapist,' Caron suggests, using her kind voice.

I sag. 'That would feel like giving in to life.'

'Or it might salvage your relationship.' Caron hugs me. 'We want what's best for you and it would help if you knew what that was yourself.'

I've never heard a truer statement and, unfortunately, I don't have an answer off pat for my friend. I want Leo and I don't. I want to be independent and married. I want my freedom and a shedload of children. I want to eat exactly what I like and stay rake thin. Even to me, it seems as if I might want rather a lot. But isn't that the way of the world now? Am I really any different to any other women of my age?

We all sit and stare at the walls.

Jo is the first to break the silence. 'So what are we going to do?' she wants to know.

'Do?' I say. 'We're doing *this.*'

'Can't we go to a wine bar and do it?'

'I can't face socialising. What if I accidentally bump into Leo?' I hold a hand to my forehead. 'I might never go out again.'

'Attention seeker,' Jo mouths silently at Caron.

'I saw that,' I say.

'The thing with Leo,' Jo goes on, 'is that you can rely on him for a laugh.'

'It's the only thing you can rely on him for.'

'And what's wrong with that?' Jo winds her legs into the sofa, clearly becoming resigned to the fact that we aren't destined to be going out on the town tonight. 'Leo's always up for some fun. He's usually gone along with exactly what you wanted, Em. How many blokes would go salsa dancing without the threat of reduced sexual activity? Not many. Most blokes are too self-conscious or selfish to go. At least Leo doesn't mind making an arse of himself.'

'He does it at every possible opportunity,' I protest. 'It's embarrassing to have a boyfriend who behaves like a three year old.'

'The trouble with you, Emma,' Jo says, replenishing her wine and settling in for the night, 'is that you've never had a proper crisis to deal with. Your life has been a bed of roses. Therefore, you blow every little misdemeanour of Leo's out of all proportion. Life can never run as smoothly as you want it to. He's a great bloke, if only you'd relax a bit and see him for what he is.'

'Why does everyone say that? You don't have to live with him.'

'As I said at the start of this conversation, I wouldn't mind a chance. But it's you he adores – in his own Leo-ish way.' Jo looks round the flat. 'Besides, you're not living with him.'

And maybe that was part of the problem too. It would be my dream to settle down and live with Leo permanently, but I don't know if I could stand having him around on a daily basis. Or anyone else, for that matter. I've always been fiercely independent and it will be hard to give up some of that to live in constant compromise with someone else. I don't relish the thought at all. Isn't that the quandary of all feisty young women today? We all complain about men being commitment-phobes, but aren't we as bad? There's a distinct reluctance among my friends to pitch in their lot with a man.

Once upon a time, all the romance books peddled the fairy story that all your problems would be solved if only you could find a strong, capable man. But strong, capable men are thin on the ground and today when you find a man it's likely to signal the start of a whole new raft of problems. I slug back my wine. But the option of being without Leo suddenly seems less appealing. He's so irritating, but Jo's right, there's a certain something about him – the lovable rogue, the Peter Pan approach to life, the untameable streak. Maybe a touch of the old romantic hero in him. Whatever it is, there's something that keeps me coming back for more.

The phone rings and all three of us jump. I shoot out of my chair. 'Oh good grief. Oh good grief. It might be him. What shall I say? What shall I say?'

'Be yourself,' my friend advises. 'He doesn't have to know you're missing him already.'

'You answer it. You answer it.'

'Emma,' Caron says calmly, 'Pick it up. Be cool.'

'Cool?'

'Chill. Chill.'

'Chill?'

'Very chill.' Caron shivers.

I copy her. 'Chill. Chill. Chill.' I jump up and down, unable to help a thrill of excitement as I pick up the phone.

'You're a useless bastard,' I shout as soon as the receiver is near my mouth, 'and I'd never go out with you again even if you crawled over broken glass to beg me!' I smile and stick up a thumb at Jo and Caron, looking for approval.

Caron turns to Jo. 'Maybe too chill.'

I slither to the floor, still clutching the phone and I can't help the look of disappointment that I feel spreading over my face. 'Hi, Mummy.'

Caron and Jo slump back into their chairs.

'No. No.' I shake my head. 'Of course I didn't think you were Leo.'

'Are we going to go through this every time the phone rings?' Jo wants to know.

'Probably,' Caron says.

Jo tops up her wine again. 'Marvellous. The sooner she starts her therapy the better.'

Chapter Twenty-Five

L eo was lying in bed and he feared that there might well be a stupid grin on his face again. This wasn't an unusual occurrence these days. When he finally managed to find the wherewithal to move himself, he looked at the clock.

'Flip. Late.' Leo glanced over at the other side of the bed. Isobel had gone again. 'Flip. Gone.'

Forcing himself to sit up, he shook the now obligatory glitter from his hair and swung his legs out of the bed. He was starting to get used to the glittery dandruff, but Isobel's regular disappearing act was proving a little more difficult to contend with. Wasn't it blokes who were supposed to do that to women?

Leo padded into the bathroom and was surprised to see his overnight guest, as large as life, in there.

'Whoah!' Leo offered in the way of a greeting as he recoiled in surprise.

Isobel was already dressed and was wearing a sexy, silver-grey business suit. Her hair was piled up neatly on her head in an equally foxy fashion.

'Good morning,' Isobel said, patting a few recalcitrant strands of her hair into place.

'You look great.' She had a very kissable neck and Leo just couldn't resist it.

'Thank you.'

'Hey,' he continued as he slipped his arms round her, 'last night was wonderful. I thought you'd skipped out on me again.'

Isobel turned and kissed him. 'No.'

'One tiny thing.' Leo shook his hair again, covering his bath mat with a deluge of sparkly stuff. 'Any chance of doing it without the glitter?'

Isobel smiled at him. 'We need the glitter for the magic to work.'

'Oh. Okay. Just checking. Glitter's good.'

Turning, she showed him her finished look. It took Leo's breath away. She was quite simply the most stunning woman he'd ever seen. If a little more transparent than most. And he didn't mean transparent as in . . . you know . . . he meant *really* transparent. 'You look fantastic.'

'I've got a job,' she announced proudly.

'Great.' Leo hesitated. 'It isn't washing dishes, by any chance?'

'No.' Isobel laughed and it was like a cool waterfall on hot skin.

'You have a natural flair for it.'

'I have to go,' she stated. 'Better not be late on my first day. I'll see you later.'

Standing on her tiptoes, she kissed him again. Leo felt that he could be persuaded never to leave his bed ever again if Isobel was in it. 'Isobel, this is hard for me to say, but . . . there's no hurry to look for anywhere else to stay. If you need to. There's plenty of room here. Oodles of it. If you want to stay . . .'

She breezed past him. 'I'm planning to.'

'Oh.'

She wafted out and, while Leo stood and contemplated this new development, he heard the front door slam.

'Fine,' Leo said as he turned on the shower. 'That's fine.' He had a permanent housemate. Something that he'd successfully managed to avoid until now. But, do you know, the strange thing was it did feel fine.

However, when Leo looked at himself in the mirror, he was brought back down to earth. It was not a pretty sight. Isobel was quite clearly using up his hideously inadequate energy reserves at breakneck speed. His cheeks were puffy – even puffier when he pulled them out sideways. He tugged the rims of his reddened, bleary eyes downwards. His tongue was the colour of wet cement. Not good.

'Flip.' Leo puffed at himself. 'I'd better buy some vitamins. Fast.'

Chapter Twenty-Six

I took Leo's car keys from his pocket on the night of my birthday celebration to prevent him from driving. And, in typical Leo fashion, he hasn't even phoned to find out if I have them. He's so sure that I'll always be there to protect him or if I can't do that, to pick up the pieces afterwards. Still, it's unusual that I haven't yet heard from him. And worrying.

His long-suffering car, Ethel, had been parked directly outside the restaurant, so at least I knew where it was this time instead of having to trawl the streets for hours to see where Leo might have left it. There was a parking ticket on it, of course. Leo, quite possibly, has the largest collection in London. But at least it hadn't been clamped or towed away. Although that's a familiar drill now. I'm on first-names terms with the guys at every car pound in town. The London Wide Vehicle Tracing Service is on my phone's Friends and Family list. Some of them even call me to let me know when Ethel turns up. If there was a *Guinness Book of Records* category for the most clamped car, Leo would be the record-holder. He treats his transport with the same indifference as he treats me.

Today I simply had to go straight to Ethel and now I'm driving my dearly-beloved's abandoned vehicle safely back to his front door. That man doesn't deserve her. Or me. Really he doesn't. Despite what my friends say.

Leo lives in a lovely leafy street, but it isn't a trendy address like mine and it's further away from the river. However, his flat is much bigger and I wonder if we do ever bite the bullet and move in together whether we would live at my place or his. Or maybe we should sell both and start all over again with a new place, possibly even a house. A home. Even the thought of it makes me nervous.

I've been thinking about Leo a lot. In fact, I've thought about little else. He does have a lot of good qualities. He's generous, fun-loving and not too shabby between the sheets. Perhaps it's inevitable when you've been together as long as we have that you start to see past the qualities that first attracted you and start to take each other for granted. How much effort has either of us put into our relationship over the last few years? Perhaps we've both become complacent in the way we've let things slide.

Following Caron's advice, I mustered all of my courage and phoned a shrink this morning. It's not very British to admit that you need help, but the woman I picked at random out of the *Yellow Pages* seemed – over the phone – to be a very normal sort of shrink and not the type of woman who might be moved to wear kaftans and eat her own placenta. She sounded suitably down-to-earth and businesslike. So I've made an appointment for later in the day and I'll tell Leo sometime soon in the hope that he might come along with me and we can have counselling for our relationship. The shrink might well tell him he has to pull his socks up if he wants to stay as my boyfriend. I smile to myself at the thought. Yes. This could be a good move. Getting an impartial third party to confirm that currently he isn't ideal life-partner material might make him buck up his ideas. This could be a *very* good move. I slap my hands on the steering wheel in delight and wonder why I haven't thought of it earlier.

I manoeuvre Leo's car into the only available space outside his flat, muttering to myself. Why on earth does he still insist on driving this old heap of a Beetle when everyone else's boyfriends have Mercedes and BMWs and Porsches. It isn't as if he doesn't have the money to exchange it – he simply can't be bothered and he has an unhealthily loyal attachment to the damn thing despite his shameful neglect of it. He insists it would be like selling his granny – even though he leaves it lying abandoned all over London at the drop of a hat for me to recover. That's another thing we can address in our counselling sessions.

As I turn off the engine and get out of the car, a woman comes out of the front door of Leo's building. And not just an ordinary woman. She stops and looks directly across at me, an enigmatic but rather self-satisfied smile on her lips. I feel myself reeling. My eyes pop. What a stunner! She's tiny with elfin features and masses of glossy black hair that tumbles down her back. I've always gone for neat and tidy cropped styles – boyish rather than vampish. There isn't enough time in my life for curling tongs and straightening irons. Functional – that's the approach I've always taken. It's sensible hair, not the type that would be used in

L'Oreal adverts. Whereas this woman is a walking commercial for expensive conditioner. Swish, swish, it goes but her gaze never flickers. Do I know her? I feel that somehow I should recognise her. Bizarrely, I hear the sound of gentle laughter inside my head. It takes me back to the night that Leo and I parted. Is it the same laughter as I heard then? Am I going completely mad?

There's no sign of Leo, but it starts me wondering. Exactly which flat has this hottie come out of? There are only four flats in the converted house. The downstairs two are occupied by a gay couple – Frank and Phil – and the other by a forty-two-year-old divorcée – Jenny – who entertains a string of different men, in all shapes, sizes and colours. The rumour is that she might have a professional interest in them – unfounded – but in all the years I've been with Leo I've never seen another woman coming out of her apartment. Makes you think, doesn't it? On the top floor there's Dominic and Lydia, Leo's immediate neighbours and a nauseatingly lovey-dovey couple if ever there was one. It is, of course, quite possible that the woman could have been visiting any of Leo's neighbours, but that doesn't stop my eyebrows from coming together in a scowl. I feel myself staring and then, can you believe it, the woman winks at me, turns on her high heels and waltzes off down the street. And it isn't just a casual wink, it's a *knowing* wink. A wink that acknowledges that there's some sort of connection between us. That's it. Now I'm sure. This woman has come out of Leo's flat.

My breath is high in my chest and shallow to the point of hyperventilation. I couldn't be more sure of Leo's infidelity if I'd caught him with his bare bottom bobbing up and down. As a woman, sometimes you know. You just *know*! And I bloody well know. 'You bastard,' I hiss.

Then my gaze falls on the rather large builders' skip directly in front of me. You can always find a skip on any of the streets round here due to the current British fever for renovating dilapidated properties. Well, it will serve my purpose rather nicely. Jumping back into the car, I gun the engine. Slipping Ethel into gear, I say, 'Take this!'

Slamming the accelerator down, I drive headlong straight into the skip. I brace myself for the impact. There's a horrible crunching noise. The bonnet crumples and there's the satisfying tinkle of shattering headlights. Things groan underneath the bonnet and, when the noise stops, a delicate plume of smoke curls up from the engine.

I get out, slightly dazed from the collision, and look at the damage. It's a shame I haven't done more. Although, in the cold light of day, I think it's a terrible thing to do to such an old girl. Poor Ethel. If I wasn't so incensed about Leo's betrayal, I might feel even more guilty. Let's see what he thinks about *that*!

I stagger along the pavement. What to do now? If I knock on the door of Leo's flat and find him there in nothing but his boxer shorts there's no telling what kind of damage I might inflict on him. He might well end up with more than a crumpled bonnet and smashed head-lights. This isn't how the scenario is supposed to progress. He's supposed to be missing me. He's supposed to be begging me to take him back. He always does. That's the usual routine. What's gone wrong this time?

A red mist descends in front of my eyes. It's that woman. That bloody, bloody woman. I'm sure. That's why Leo hasn't been on the phone to me apologising. I rub my hands over my face. But how long has this been going on? Why haven't I seen the signs? What signs were there? Leo has been Leo – no better, no worse. He hasn't taken to wearing more aftershave or going to the gym or making excuses not to see me. I've had no inkling that there's a rival for Leo's affections in my life. This puts a whole new slant on things. I've always been in control of the relationship, the dominant one. Leo can't manage without me. He knows that. I know that. He'll go to pieces. He's completely dependent on me. It's a shock to find out that now that might not be the case at all. My knees feel ridiculously weak. I should follow this woman – this woman who's trying to take my Leo from me. Except I'm not sure that my feet will move in the required manner.

I look down the street in the direction the woman has taken, and it's weird, but there's no sign of her at all. None. But I hear that bloody laughter again. It's soft and sugary and very irritating.

Glancing up at Leo's flat, I see him flit by the window. I chew my nails for a bit, but before I've decided what to do, Leo emerges from the front door. He looks a mess – which isn't unusual, particularly first thing in the morning. But even for Leo, he looks . . . dazed. As if he's barely slept at all. And happy. Happy without me.

Blood rushes to my brain and, thankfully, all the rest of my limbs, galvanising me into action. Slipping behind the skip, I try to duck out of sight but I needn't have bothered. Leo, grinning to himself, is in his own sweet world and fails to notice either me or his lightly smoking car. He wanders down the road, seemingly oblivious to everything that life has to offer.

I frown. How could he do this? How could he do this to *me*? It isn't in Leo's nature to be duplicitous. He probably doesn't even know what it means. All that rubbish about men being born to spread their seed over as wide a range of the female population as possible – it simply doesn't apply to Leo. He's just too damn lazy. If there's one thing he isn't, it's a skilled seducer. So how on earth has this turn of events come to pass?

Well, there's no way this woman is going to have him. Leo might be a crap boyfriend, but he's *my* crap boyfriend. Not someone else's! A strategy needs to be planned. I kick Ethel's hub-cab, twice for good luck – and something niggling in my brain tells me that I might need it. Something has happened to Leo and I'm not sure what. But I will find out. I will *definitely* find out. But not yet. Not just yet. I watch my dear lover amble away from me, smiling wistfully. First I need to calm down. I need to do that bloody relaxation CD. Perhaps it's still lying in the street outside my flat. Or maybe I'll have to invest in another one. Whatever, I need my wits about me for this. So, I storm off down the road in the opposite direction before I'm tempted to kill Leo first and ask questions later.

Chapter Twenty-Seven

When Leo finally arrived at the office, everyone was jumping up and down. This was an unusual sight, as normally everyone was slumped over their desks. There was a particularly dense line of people jumping up and down near Old Baldy's office, Grant and Lard among them. Lard jumped for very little, so Leo was more than a tad surprised.

Once he'd availed himself of a wonderful cup of the brown goo that posed as coffee in this place, he wandered over to see what was going on. Leo gulped the coffee down gratefully and waited for it to kick in. If he was going to keep up with Isobel in the bedroom department, then he would have to seriously increase his caffeine intake. He might have to start injecting it rather than just drinking it.

'Am I missing something?' Leo hated to think he was missing anything as he was naturally very nosy.

Grant turned round. 'Baldy Baldwin has got the most amazing assistant,' he told his friend slightly breathlessly. His pupils were dilated with joy. 'She started work this morning.'

'Really?'

Grant gave another few sprightly springs. 'You can't see much.'

Leo put down his coffee and jumped up and down too, trying to get a glimpse.

'You have to jump high,' his friend advised. He puffed again. 'To see over the filing cabinets.'

'Can't you just walk past the office?'

'We tried that,' Grant said. 'The door was closed. We didn't want her to think we were spying on her.'

'Even though you are?' Leo braced himself for a big jump. The coffee sloshed unpleasantly in his stomach. 'Ouff.' His knees definitely weren't what they used to be. 'I can't see anything.' Putting his hands on Lard's shoulder, he tried to get a bit more leverage.

'Stop that,' Lard snapped. 'It's my turn to get a look. Give me a leg up, Leo.'

Grant looked vaguely bewildered, all agog, and Leo was sure he'd seen that expression somewhere before. 'She's unbelievable,' Grant panted excitedly. 'Enough to make grown men weep.'

Leo stopped mid-bounce. He didn't need to know any more. 'Oh no. Oh bloody hell, no!'

'What?' Grant and Lard shouted behind him.

Leo rushed into Baldy Baldwin's office. And sure enough, Isobel was sitting behind Mr Baldwin's desk; she had her feet up and in one hand was a cup of coffee. And Leo would have liked to bet that it didn't taste like the manky machine stuff he'd just quaffed. In her other hand she was holding her wand. She was waving it at the piles of papers waiting for filing, which in turn danced along the desk and the windowsill and efficiently popped themselves into the filing cabinets or shuffled themselves cheerily into tidier piles. And they were doing it to the tune of 'Mambo No 5'.

Leo realised that he knew very little about women. After all, he was used to good old Emma who was reliable to a fault. She didn't do anything out of character. There were no surprises with Emma. No shocks. Even the regular dumping had just become a ripple in the tranquil lake of their lives. Leo thought that was why it was very difficult trying to cope with Isobel, who kept disappearing and popping up in strange places doing strange things. He was actually beginning to appreciate what Emma had to endure while with him. But even Leo, at his least reliable, wasn't a patch on Isobel.

'Isobel,' he gasped, barely able to speak.

She gave him one of her loveliest smiles. 'Hello, Leo.'

'What are you doing here?'

'Working,' she said.

'Working?'

'In my own way.'

Own *unique* way. 'Why here?'

His frustrating fairy friend simply shrugged. 'I thought it would make it possible for us to spend all day together.'

'Oh.' Leo had to get his head round this one and it was very hard to think in the middle of dancing filing. 'Stop. Stop that,' he shouted at the papers before he realised what he was doing.

'Mambo No 5' ground to an abrupt halt, as did all the papers. Rather reminiscent of his jigging crockery, they all bumped into each other and then slithered into untidy heaps.

'This is insane.' Leo could hear himself shrieking. 'What would you do if Old Baldy came in?'

And, of course, at that very moment, Mr Baldwin – Old Baldy himself – appeared in the doorway. Leo could feel his mouth and his eyes widen in a silent scream.

'Leo?' Old Baldy said, a dark and thunderous look crossing his countenance.

An involuntary gasp of terror escaped from Leo. In the nick of time Isobel waved her wand and Old Baldy froze.

'I'd probably do that,' Isobel informed Leo, casting a glance at her immobilised victim.

Leo's shoulders sagged with relief. Old Baldy looked like a waxwork from Madame Tussaud's – one of the better ones. Circling him cautiously, Leo was mesmerised. Even though it grossed him out completely, he touched the end of Old Baldy's nose tentatively, cagey in case the currently catatonic boss should suddenly move. But no. He pulled at his boss's bottom lip and let it twang back to his mouth. Nothing. Mr Baldwin, thankfully, remained totally inert. Leo could have drawn all over him with a felt-tipped pen and Old Baldy would be none the wiser. The idea was very tempting. Leo's breathing was slowly returning to normal. All this excitement was going to knock years off his life.

He looked over at Isobel and sighed. 'Do you know that you're a truly amazing woman?'

'Yes.'

Leo went to sit on the edge of her desk. Clearly she was going to be in control here from now on. Leo's life, even in the office, was no longer his own.

'The guys can't wait to meet you,' he said. They glanced at the window. Grant and Lard were still pogo-ing up and down beyond it like demented punk rockers.

'You can't tell them, Leo.'

If Leo hadn't felt confused enough before, he was now thrown into a complete tailspin. 'Tell them what?'

'You can't tell them that I'm a fairy.'

'Oh, but they'll love it!'

Isobel shook her head. 'No. You mustn't.'

'Why? They're my best mates. They'll think it's really cool.'

'They won't. They won't believe you, Leo. And if people don't believe in me, it weakens my powers. I won't be able to stay here.'

'At Thornton Jones?'

'No, Leo. I won't be able to stay here on earth, with you.'

'Bugger.' Leo jumped off the desk and paced a bit. He was sure that neither Grant nor Lard had ever been out with a fairy. This was a great one to have up on them. They had to know. 'Can't I tell them just a tiny bit? It would help considerably if I could explain my glitter problem.' Leo gave his hair a shake to elicit some sympathy.

'No. It has to be our secret.'

'Oh.'

Isobel got up from behind Old Baldy's desk and took up a notebook. She sat in the chair more commonly assigned to an assistant. Keeping up appearances, clearly. 'We have work to do, Leo.'

'Oh, yes.' And Leo had to stop the guys jumping up and down before they all had a heart-attack and had to be rushed off to Casualty – then he'd be left to manage on his own in the department and everyone would realise that he knew nothing about his job and millions of people would go broke all over the world and it would all be Leo's fault.

The top of Grant's head appeared in the window. Lard would have to eat chocolate all day to replace his expended calories. 'Yes. Better get on,' Leo said with some urgency.

Isobel swished that damn wand again.

'Hurry up, boys,' she urged the filing. And there was a mad scramble of papers as they all dived for the filing cabinets.

Leo couldn't help but smile. 'Wicked.'

'This has to be between me and you, Leo,' she stressed. 'You do understand that?'

'Of course.' Leo was going to add that he wasn't an idiot, but sometimes even he wondered.

Isobel zapped Old Baldy who sort of melted immediately and continued to stride into the office as if nothing had happened.

'Leo,' he barked. 'You're late again!'

'I know. I . . . er, I . . . er . . .'

He gave Isobel a pleading look. She glanced up from her notebook and her poised-to-take-notes pose. With a tut she swished her wand again.

'I see I'm going to have to give you a pay rise,' Mr Baldwin said.

'A p . . . p . . . pay rise?'

'Yes.' Baldy took up his rightful place behind his desk. 'Was there anything else?'

'No. N . . . no,' Leo stammered. 'Absolutely not. No. I'll just go. Go back to work. Shall I? Lots to do. Lots and lots.' He started to back out of the door before the spell broke and something truly dreadful happened.

Mr Baldwin smiled benignly at him. Not something he did often.

Turning to Isobel, Leo said, 'I'll see you later.' He hoped his voice held a note of warning.

And Isobel smiled and looked at him as if butter wouldn't melt in her mouth. Leo backed into the wall in the corridor. Grant and Lard looked at him expectantly, but he was too stunned to speak. His brain was busy with troubling thoughts. What was happening? And what the hell was he going to do with this woman?

Chapter Twenty-Eight

Leo followed Grant and Lard back into their own part of the office. Everyone had now given up on trying to catch a glimpse of the new assistant and they'd returned instead to their desks and the dire state of the foreign markets.

Sitting down and slumping in front of his computer screen, Leo was exhausted and overwhelmed by several different emotions. His friends were behaving like two excitable schoolboys. They clearly weren't in control of their emotions either. Grant was beside himself with glee. 'Is she not worth considering the "I do" words for?'

'Yes,' Leo mumbled. His head got nearer to his desk and he raked his fingers through his very dishevelled hair, trying to massage his very dishevelled brain.

Grant and Lard stopped and stared at him questioningly.

'That's Isobel,' Leo offered.

'Isobel?' Lard said.

Both of his friends looked at him blankly and then Lard had a moment of revelation, not dissimilar to Moses and the burning bush. He gasped out loud. Any minute now he'd be rushing to the nearest Twix for succour. 'Not six-time-a-night woman?'

Leo nodded.

'Oh my good grief,' Grant breathed. 'That's her?' His face took on an unhealthy flush of redness. 'Let me have her. When you've finished with her, please let me have her.'

'No. I want her,' Lard said petulantly.

'We'll share,' Grant suggested to him while Leo looked on bemused. 'You can have her on Monday, Wednesday and Friday. Given her reputation, I'm not sure that I could cope with her all week anyway.'

Lard glanced Leo's way. 'I'm not sure that Leo can either.'

He might have a point. Leo sank further into his chair. Going to work used to be such a simple affair.

'You're looking decidedly peaky, mate.' Lard sat on Leo's desk and frowned at him with concern.

'I do feel rather peaky,' Leo squeaked. Living with Isobel was like being on an emotional rollercoaster. In the dark. With a blindfold on. And your hands tied behind your back. Leo was feeling so disorientated that he'd no idea what might happen next.

Lard pulled open his desk drawer. 'Walnut Whip or Twix?'

Leo had managed to predict that with only a modicum of thought. If only Isobel was as easy to analyse.

'No.' He shook his head, releasing another shower of glitter dandruff. 'No thanks.'

Grant rubbed his chin and looked rather shifty. 'You might feel a bit more peaky when you find out what we've done.'

Leo's senses were suddenly alert. 'What?' Grabbing the Twix from Lard's meaty hands, he bit into it. Believe it, he needed endorphins.

'Emma phoned,' Grant told him. 'We agreed that you'd meet her for lunch at Bertorini's.'

Leo heard himself groan.

'At twelve o'clock,' Lard admitted.

They all glanced at the clock. It was just before twelve. Leo groaned a bit louder.

'Phone her. Tell her I'm ill,' he suggested.

'She'd never believe us.'

'Dead,' he said brightly. 'Tell her I'm dead.'

'Leo, if you don't meet Emma for lunch, you will be.'

Leo forced himself to his feet. 'I thought you two were supposed to be my friends.'

Grant and Lard swivelled their gaze to Old Baldy's office. 'What shall we tell Isobel?'

'Nothing,' he said with a shake of his head. 'She'll know. She'll know all about it already.'

'We could look after her for you,' Lard suggested. He licked some melted chocolate from his lower lip in a very lascivious manner.

'Don't even think about it,' Leo warned him. 'She'll chew you up and spit you out.' And, not noticing that his friends looked quite interested in being chewed up and spat out by Isobel, he proceeded, like Daniel going into the lion's den, to keep his lunch appointment with Emma.

Chapter Twenty-Nine

Bertorini's is one of my favourite restaurants. And not just because it's the haunt of celebrities who are trying to convince the world that they're just 'ordinary' people, or even because it has featured in several trendy films and television series. It isn't far from where I work or live, down by the side of the Thames near St Saviour's Dock and, as such, is one of my local haunts.

Leo and I came here on one of our first dates – that's also why it's so special for me and also why I've chosen it today. Not that Leo will ever remember the romantic significance of the venue. I sigh to myself. I'm going to be very calm and grown up about this. Discuss rationally with Leo where we have gone wrong in our relationship. Even though it's mostly his fault, I'm feeling magnanimous enough to concede that it's never a show without Punch.

The restaurant is busy, even this early, with lunchtime diners. There's a terrace that borders the river, but it's far too cold to sit out there today, even with the patio heaters on full blast. The umbrellas are out, but they're being buffeted by the strong breeze that's invariably present along the water's edge and look as if they could topple over at any moment. Oh, the joys of a British summer.

I stare out of the window, toying with the stem of my wine glass. Sipping my Chardonnay, I pretend that I don't mind being alone, although I desperately wish I'd thought to buy a newspaper to read or a trashy magazine. It's already 12.15 p.m. and Leo is late. The pitying glances from the staff will start soon. Staff who are used to me spending hours in here alone waiting for Leo. But before I work myself up into a lather, I'm going to try to convince myself that it's the fault of his dunderheaded friends for failing to pass on a message properly and not down to Leo's usual tardiness. I'm maniacally punctual. If I'm fifteen minutes early for something, I'm always convinced I'm late. Poor punctuality is, to me, one of the worst forms of arrogance. It says to someone that you feel your time is more important than theirs. I'd rather chew off one of my own ears than be late. At this rate I'm going to chew off both of Leo's ears — and possibly something else — if he's any later.

At that moment, just as my shoulders can reach no higher up my neck, Leo walks in. And it is a walk. Not a rush. Not a dash. Just a walk. But, at least, it isn't a saunter.

'Hi.' He looks bashful and it's a look that can melt my heart. Leo does very good bashful. Pulling up a chair, he sits down opposite me. 'How are you?'

All the calm, measured sentences I have rehearsed fly out of my brain like a flock of scattering birds.

'Leo,' I say, without preamble, 'when we were together, were you seeing someone else?'

'Er . . .'

The waitress comes over. I feel like kicking her in the leg. This is very bad timing. I've gone for Leo's jugular and now she has given him an excuse to duck.

Oblivious to my irritation, the waitress hands Leo a menu — in a very leisurely manner it seems from my side of the table. 'Can I get you a drink, sir?'

'Vodka, please.'

The waitress smiles at *my boyfriend* as she walks away. An overly familiar smile, if you ask me. Leo grins back. I clutch at my knife.

'Is that why you were unable to commit to me?' I ask.

'Make that a double, please,' Leo calls after the waitress. He looks back at me. 'No and no, are the answers to those questions.'

'I brought your car back this morning,' I tell him. 'The one you abandoned outside the restaurant without another thought.'

'Ah. Good old girl.'

I'm not entirely sure whether he's referring to me or the car.

'Wondered where she was. Fine example of modern motoring.'

'It's a heap,' I say dismissively. 'You were far too drunk to drive. I took the keys off you.'

'I remember,' Leo says. 'It's all coming back to me now.'

'I saw her, Leo.' I blink back a tear. 'I saw her. Coming out of your flat. This morning.'

'Ah.' Leo's face has guilty written all over it.

So I'm right. I always am. Nevertheless, it's like a body blow. Nothing can ever prepare you for this moment. Leo is a lot of things, but I don't think he's ever been unfaithful before.

The waitress returns with two shot glasses of ice-cold vodka for Leo. He knocks them both back in one.

'You couldn't just bring me the bottle, please?'

'How long has it been going on?' I persist.

Leo looks with desperation at his empty glasses. 'Not long.'

'How long is not long?' I want to know. I *need* to know. 'Two weeks? Six weeks? Six months?'

'I didn't meet her until after you'd dumped me.'

'That was the night before last, Leo! You've been single for one day. One whole day.'

Leo hangs his head. 'I met her on the way home from your birthday party.'

'The birthday party that you largely missed? Except for the bit where you passed out in my cake, of course.'

'Yes,' Leo says. 'That would be the one.'

I feel as if I'm going into meltdown. Is this what a panic attack feels like? My palms are clammy and I can feel all my insides shaking like they do on those exercise machines that wobble you about. 'You certainly didn't waste your time.'

Leo's shoulders slump and he reaches out to take my hand. 'Emma.' He uses his soft, sugary voice, the one that he normally reserves for when I'm sick. 'I never meant for any of this to happen.'

I snatch my hand away. 'That is just the most typical thing for a man to say.'

'I am a man.'

Finding a tissue, I sniff into it. I feel on the verge of tears and this isn't how I'd wanted it to go at all. I hate tearful, clingy women and Leo does too. Or does he? I've got to the point where I'm not sure what Leo likes or doesn't like any more. Have I ever really taken the time to find out? 'Tell me, Leo,' I say. 'And I want you to be perfectly honest about this. What does she have that I haven't got?'

'Er . . .' Leo looks round the dining room, clearly hoping that some sort of International Rescue for the emotionally retarded might swoop in and help him out.

'Do you think she's prettier than me?'

'Yes,' Leo says. 'She's all sort of sparkly and gorgeous.'

I feel my face crumple.

'Emma.' Leo takes my hand again. 'You said you wanted me to be honest.'

'I know what I said,' I snap. 'But there's *honest* and there's *honest*, Leo. Why couldn't you have lied? You normally do.'

'Perhaps this is the new me.'

'Well, perhaps I don't like it any better than the old one.' Rummaging for another tissue in my bag, I try to compose myself. I don't want some bit-part soap starlet who happens to be in the restaurant seeing me like this. 'Is she younger than me?'

'Er . . . Are we going for honesty again?'

I shake my head. 'Not too much honesty.'

'Not necessarily.'

The waitress returns with the bottle of vodka and puts it down next to Leo, along with a large wine glass. 'Thank you,' he says gratefully and proceeds to pour himself an unhealthy measure.

'It doesn't have to be like this,' I say. 'I'm quite prepared to overlook your . . . mistakes. All of them. And give you one more chance. Just one more.'

Leo downs half of the vodka. 'Emma,' he says. 'I don't know what to say.'

I smile at him. This is like old times. It *could* be like old times. Just me and Leo. The hand-holding. The looking sincerely into my eyes. He can be so sweet when he wants to be. We've had some good times together. Some very good times.

'I don't want another chance,' Leo says, breaking into my reverie with another hammer blow. He sighs and swigs at his drink. 'You said yourself, the magic has gone. It's over for us. And I've met the most magical being I've ever encountered. She has bewitched me and there's no going back. I've never been able to make you happy, Emma. You've always wanted me to change. To be someone else. *Anyone* else. She wants me just as I am. Goodness only knows why. She doesn't want me sober, punctual and in a strait-jacket. She wants me. Just me. And I want her. She's fun to be with.'

'And I'm not?'

'We want different things from life.'

'You want fun and I don't?'

'It isn't that simple, Emma. I feel that you constantly disapprove of me. You might have loved me, but I'm not sure that you ever really liked me.'

I can hear the dull thud of my heart. It fills my ears, my brain. The worst thing about it is that Leo is right. And he's never right. I'm the one who's right in this relationship.

'I'm in love, Emma,' Leo carries on hammering away. 'I'm in love with someone else.'

Everything in my world stops. They're the words that no one ever wants to hear. Now Leo is saying them to me. I summon every ounce of dignity that I can muster and dress it with a tight smile. 'Then there's really nothing more to say.'

'No,' Leo whispers. 'I'm sorry. Flip. I'm so really, really sorry.'

I make myself stand up even though my legs feel strangely wobbly as if I'm just getting off a boat after several days on a rough sea.

'I loved you,' Leo says. 'I loved you very much.'

'Until yesterday?'

Leo can't meet my eye.

'You had a funny way of showing it.'

'I had *my* way of showing it,' Leo counters.

'So this is it?'

Leo nods sadly.

'It's been very nice knowing you,' I say.

'Emma . . .'

I don't want to hear anything else Leo has to say, so I walk calmly away, even though the other diners seem suddenly to be blurred.

Leo looks upset. I can tell that it isn't coming easy to him to do this. He doesn't hurt deliberately – he isn't that type. Leo only hurts people by accident. Surely he'll realise that soon.

I still keep a watchful eye on him as he refills his glass again and sits alone at the table looking miserable. How could he do this to me? He must be mistaken, surely? Leo has never, ever wanted to end our relationship. He's always been happy with the way things were. And it hurts me to admit that Leo's right, I've been the one to do all the complaining. Any minute now he'll call me back. He'll laugh and say that he was giving me a taste of my own medicine. But it doesn't happen. I keep on walking and Leo keeps on letting me go, saying nothing, until I'm nearly out of the restaurant. I've lost him, I think desolately. I've lost him to someone else. Through both of us being too stupid to see how good our relationship was.

The waitress, bearing a tray with plates of steaming pasta, tries to squeeze her way past me. 'Excuse me,' she says with a smile.

'Wait,' I say, staying her with my hand on her arm. To the waitress's evident surprise, I take one of the plates of pasta and turn to head back to Leo. 'I'll deliver this.'

'He didn't order that,' the waitress says hurriedly after me.

'It doesn't matter,' I assure her. The pasta in question is a creamy combination laden with bacon, mushrooms and layered with cheese. It smells divine.

I walk towards Leo and, when I reach him, put the plate of pasta down in front of him. Leo looks up with an uncertain smile.

I tip the plate and the hot pasta slides off and lands in Leo's lap. Revenge, I think, is a dish best tipped over someone hot. To his credit, Leo doesn't jump up or make a fuss or try to avoid his punishment. He sits there and endures it stoically. I love him all the more for it.

'Bastard,' I say softly and then turn on my heel, leaving Leo, the waitress and the other diners speechless.

And I appreciate that this might be an inappropriate emotional response to my sorrow, but it feels very good. Very good, indeed.

Chapter Thirty

Leo was in his local hostelry – the nearest within stumbling distance of the office – and he was propping up the bar with Grant and Lard. The place was full of people who were dressed exactly like them in the uniform of the City; in recent years double-breasted pinstripes had given way to single-breasted, three-button designer-label suits now, but you could still spot them a mile away. And they were all talking in loud voices and not listening. The early-evening crowd letting off steam before heading home or to their favourite restaurant or takeaway. Leo's so-called best friends were sniggering into their beer at his plight.

'It's all right for you two to laugh,' he complained. 'That was the longest lunch-hour of my life.'

'Emma took it badly?' Lard said.

'I should say so,' Leo confirmed. They all looked down at his lap which was still covered in the creamy remnants of Emma's pasta punishment. It looked vaguely obscene.

'It could have been worse,' Grant told him.

'How?'

Grant studied the froth on his beer. 'I'll get back to you on that one.'

Leo didn't understand Emma. She'd spent years telling him how useless he was and how she'd be better off without him, then when he finally obliged and found someone else – or someone else found him – she wasn't happy about that either. Leo decided that he would never grasp the intricacies of the female mind – they were all mystical, magical, unfathomable beings. Not just the one with fairy wings and a lethal wand. Emma could wreak just as much havoc without one.

'Emma saw Isobel coming out of my flat. This morning. She put two and two together . . .'

'And came up with four,' Grant noted with a wise nod.

'Yes.'

'Not good,' Lard said. 'But at least it means that Emma can't fail to see how you were a goner in the face of such beauty. A mere, defence-less snowflake to an avalanche of blatant raw sex.'

'Quite,' Leo agreed. 'I'm just not sure my girlfriend views it like that.'

'Ex-girlfriend,' Lard reminded him.

'Oh. Of course.' It was so easy to forget. You couldn't simply disen-tangle yourself from your previous life overnight. He was going to miss Emma. Despite the fact that she didn't think he loved her enough, Leo really did love her more than anything. He just might not have been able to do it or say it the way she wanted him to. And that saddened him.

From now on, this would be his advice to anyone who might be struggling with a relationship – if anyone told you that they loved you, just say it right back. Don't even think about it. Certainly don't leave one of those uncomfortable pauses. Just spit it out. It would save an awful lot of trouble in the long run, really it would. Leo wished that he'd had the sort of parents who'd told him that they loved him on a regular basis, but he could acknowledge now that not once in his life had they ever said those crucial three words to him. And Leo had never said it to them. That was probably why the L-word was such a big deal to him and why he had trouble wrangling with emotions in general, although Leo wasn't one to over-analyse these things or to blame his shortcomings entirely on his parents. Basically, he thought that he was far too shallow to warrant an in-depth probe. Children could safely have paddled in him.

'Emma's gorgeous too,' Grant said in a rather clipped way.

'Yes, Emma's beautiful. But she's not all glittery and girly,' Leo pointed out. 'Isobel's so feminine and floaty. She looks as if she'd break if you touched her.' Looks, however, were deceiving. 'You, my friend, are speaking as a man who has never been thwacked by the full force of Emma's handbag.'

'Does Isobel have any sisters?' Lard asked. Lard found it very hard to get girlfriends, that was why he ate so much chocolate. And because he ate so much chocolate, he found it hard to get girlfriends.

Sighing, Leo said, 'I have to tell you something. But it's a big secret. A big, big secret.'

'Get a life,' Grant advised him.

'No,' he said. 'This is serious. You might be shocked.' Leo huddled closer to them.

'Wait,' Lard said. 'Wait, wait. This doesn't involve bedroom gymnastics again, does it? You've not managed seven times a night? She's not kinky, is she? I don't think I could look at Isobel without spontaneously combusting if you told me she'd got her own set of pink, fur-lined handcuffs.'

'No. No.' Leo tried not to sound irritated by the fact that it was his sex-life and not his welfare which preoccupied his seedy friends' minds. Then he paused. If Isobel *had* produced pink, fur-lined handcuffs it wouldn't have surprised him in the least. Actually, he felt quite cheered up by the thought. 'Though she may have.'

His friends were all ears now. 'This is serious,' Leo repeated. 'Very serious. And you are *seriously* not going to believe me.'

Grant and Lard shuffled closer to him. Leo cleared his throat. Having made this announcement, he didn't then know quite where to begin. So he went for some more throat-clearing. His furtive friends glanced round to check that no one was listening, then nodded for him to proceed.

'The thing is . . .' Leo began. He took a deep breath. 'Isobel can do strange things.'

'I knew it,' Lard puffed. 'I just knew this was going to be about sex!'

'Ssh. Ssh,' Leo urged him. 'It's not about sex. Really it isn't. She can do strange things.' They looked unconvinced. 'Magic things.'

Grant frowned. 'She's a magician?'

He was usually considered the more intelligent of the two. 'No, no,' Leo said. 'She's not a bloody magician!'

They both stared at Leo blankly.

'She's a fairy,' he said.

They continued to stare at him blankly.

Then, after some considerable time had passed, Lard was the first to speak. 'A fairy?'

Leo nodded at them in an earnest fashion.

'And how do you know this?' Lard asked, now that he'd found his voice.

'Isobel told me.'

'And you believe her?'

'Of course I do.' Leo took a steadying drink of his beer. 'It may seem a bit weird . . .'

'A bit weird!' Grant said. 'You really believe this, don't you?'

'Yes. I think she's telling the truth.'

'She might think she is, but have you considered checking with any of the local lunatic asylums to see if they've got any of their inmates missing?'

'She isn't crazy,' he insisted. 'Well, she is . . .' It had to be said that some of Isobel's behaviour could not be classed as normal. 'Completely crazy.'

'Particularly in bed?' Lard was dribbling.

'Will you shut up about sex,' Leo snapped. This was not going well. 'This is not about sex.'

'If she's not crazy,' Grant observed, 'then perhaps you are.'

Leo slumped towards the bar and, for once, it wasn't because of the amount of strong alcohol he'd consumed. 'I've seen things, Grant. Things that forty-eight hours ago I wouldn't have believed either.'

'Leo,' Grant said with a sigh, 'you haven't been smoking those strange-smelling cigarettes again?'

'I know she's telling the truth. You have to believe me. You have to.'

Grant and Lard exchanged a glance and Leo knew that he was wasting his time. Isobel was right – they didn't believe him. It was time for Leo to leave. 'I'd better be off.'

'Yeah,' Lard said. 'Alice in Wonderland might be having a tea-party in your front room.'

'Shit!' Leo bolted down the flat remains of his drink. 'You're right. See you tomorrow.'

As he rushed to the door, he saw his friends shaking their heads. 'That is one very sick man,' he heard Grant say.

'Love-sick?'

'Yes,' Grant answered, 'And that's something I wouldn't have believed if I hadn't seen it with my own eyes.'

As he pushed his way out of the door, Leo had to concede that they were right. So very right.

Chapter Thirty-One

I bustle round trying to keep myself busy. If I stop for one minute, the events of this morning and the disastrous lunch with Leo keep playing in my head. Only the feverish dusting of a row of modern glass sculptures is keeping me from picking up the phone and speaking to him. Only the fact that the glass sculptures are worth in excess of a hundred thousand pounds is stopping me from throwing one against the wall.

It's nearly time to go home. Time to go home to an empty flat and face hours stretching ahead alone. We're the generation who have it all – everything except enduring love, it seems.

Caron has left early from the gallery to get ready for a hot date tonight. Her last three hot dates in as many weeks have all proved to be lukewarm endurance tests. I hope that tonight will be better for my friend. But then if Caron hooks up with a smokin' new boyfriend, what on earth will I then do for company? In fact, what are all the resolutely single women of thirty going to do in the long years ahead when we have no family, no friends, no children and no husband to care for us? It's great to be with friends, but how many friendships survive for a lifetime? A handful? Less than that? How many good friends will suddenly disappear when you not only need them for the odd bout of tea and sympathy but start to rely on them for the daily needs of life if you're ill or incapacitated in some way? Being single at thirty might be great fun, but I'd like to bet that it's less of a giggle when you're knocking on sixty. Instead of women being the nurturers, we seem to be hell-bent on creating a whole raft of lonely people. Are we, the Germaine Greer generation, by setting ourselves impossibly high standards, simply failing to achieve anything of worth?

I flick my duster harder. Today, I can't think about these things, my brain hurts too much. And that is the least injured of my bodily parts. A knock on the window surprises me. Spinning round, I see Leo's friend, Grant, staring back. It's pouring down with rain and he's getting very wet. He grins cheesily at me. Despite my black mood, I find myself smiling back. Grant and Leo could have been chipped from the same block.

I've always had a strained relationship with Leo's friends. It isn't often that we all socialise these days. Grant and Lard, I think, tend to view me as a necessary nuisance. Whereas I tend to see Grant and Lard as just nuisances. Unnecessary ones. Whenever Leo is in trouble – frequently – they are always behind it somewhere. Usually egging him on. And I hate to sound so petty, but I also see them as rivals for his affection.

Grant sidles into the gallery.

I carry on dusting. 'I'm just closing up.'

Sitting himself down on the edge of the desk, Grant pulls his soaking mackintosh around him. 'I'm not here to buy.'

'Don't drip on my desk,' I say. I'm in no mood to play games with Leo's envoy – which is what I assume Grant is here for.

Grant avoids my eyes. 'Leo told me what's been going on,' he says quietly. 'With the two of you.'

'With the *three* of us,' I correct. 'And if you've come here on a plea-bargaining mission for that feckless bastard you call your best friend, you needn't bother.'

Grant looks hurt. 'That bad?'

I sink down next to him on the desk, heedless of the puddle forming around him. 'Yes.'

'Leo doesn't know that I'm here,' he tells me.

'Oh.'

'I'm just extending the hand of friendship.' He waggles his fingers at me. 'Come and have a drink of Australian grape juice with your Uncle Grant.' He slips a damp arm round me and I don't have the energy to shrug it off. 'I thought you might need an ear to bend.'

'I'm not very good company at the moment,' I say.

'You're always good company,' Grant insists. 'It might make you feel better.'

'I doubt it.'

'What else had you got planned for this evening?'

'Nothing,' I admit with a weary exhalation. Jo and Caron are getting fed up with my constant ear-bending, so it's nice to be offered a fresh pair. And if I'm doing nothing else, I might as well go out with Grant and drink myself silly as stay at home alone and do it.

Grant nudges me. He has a very cheeky expression on his face. 'Come on, then.'

'Okay.' I jump down off the desk and force a smile to my lips. 'And I promise I'm not going to mention that bastard once.'

Chapter Thirty-Two

Emma was right. She did leave his car outside the flat this morning. 'Hello, lovely car,' he said, and kissed Ethel on her roof.

What he didn't realise, however, was that Emma had left his cherished vehicle in a rather crumpled state and that Isobel had been at it with her witchy little wand and Ethel was now fully repaired. He gave his car a friendly pat. 'Welcome home, old girl.'

Going in through the front door of the flat, Leo noticed that everything was very tidy — nay, positively gleaming. It had a magical air about it. Something he would have scoffed at just a few short days ago and now look how sensitive he'd become. Emma's Whitney Houston CD was playing again. The soft, sultry music drifted over him.

Ducking back out of the door, Leo checked the number. Yep. It was the right flat. Clearly, Isobel was at home.

Leo went back inside and, with a deep breath, headed through to the kitchen. Isobel was at the sink. Wearing an apron. And rubber gloves. Washing dishes in the more traditional manner. Which Leo knew was purely for his benefit. The whole kitchen had an unearthly sparkle. His chrome accessories — kettle, toaster, microwave — all glinted as they did in adverts for new, improved cleaning products. Little star-shaped spangles twinkled off them in the light. It was as if Isobel had read a manual on how to be the ideal housewife — which, Leo guessed, she probably had — and was putting it all into practice. She'd already confessed that most of her knowledge of humans had been gleaned from glossy magazines — which was a truly terrifying thought.

Throwing down his laptop, Leo instantly felt guilty for making the place look untidy. 'I take it Mr Sheen didn't do this?'

Isobel turned to him with an enigmatic smile. Leo had never seen anyone but the Mona Lisa do a smile more enigmatic. 'Who?'

'Never mind.' Leo went to the fridge and when he opened it, he found it crammed full of beer. 'Phoar!' He gave the cans a squeeze to check that they were real.

Isobel gave him a reproving look. 'I went to Sainsbury's,' she said with a tut.

'Oh.' But he'd like to bet she blasted the cashier with her wand so she didn't have to pay for them.

'And I used the spare key under the plant pot to let myself in,' she said. 'Just in case you were wondering.'

Leo hadn't wondered and it just went to show how his levels of acceptance had changed in recent days. He helped himself to a beer and then went over to Isobel and wrapped his arms round her. He realised that this was not the natural order – it should have been cuddle first, beer later – and resolved to be better in future. Even fairy women would probably get the arse if you did that sort of thing regularly, he reckoned. 'How did you enjoy your first day at work?'

'It was great,' Isobel said animatedly. 'I typed up some documents.' She looked sheepish. 'In a manner of speaking.'

'I can imagine.'

She shrugged. 'How was your lunch with Emma?'

'Great,' Leo said, looking at his feet. 'We had a nice time. "In a manner of speaking".' He held out his beer and Isobel twitched her head. The top obediently snapped off and Leo took a slurp. 'I am well and truly a single man.'

Isobel looked at him quizzically. 'Oh really?'

'Well. In a manner of speaking.' Leo pulled her to him tightly. His conscience was still struggling with finally breaking up with Emma. But it had to be better for both of them. Didn't it? Emma was now free to find someone who would treat her as she deserved and Leo must learn from his mistakes and not make a complete bollocks of the new chance he'd been given. Leo vowed that he was going to be more attentive in this relationship. In a grown-up way.

'I was going to buy you flowers,' he told Isobel. 'But . . . this is a terrible admission – I've never done it before. I got as far as the florist's doorway and I . . . well . . . I just couldn't go in. I came out in a cold sweat. Flowers are a very female thing. I've never quite got the hang of them. I paced up and down, but eventually had to walk away empty-handed. I know that lots of men buy flowers for their other halves, but I simply couldn't do it. In my mind I can rationalise that it's a good thing to do, but in reality . . .' Leo held up his hands in a gesture of surrender. 'To be honest, I felt a bit of a prat.'

'What type of flowers did you have in mind?'

'Red roses,' he confessed.

'The flower of love.'

'What else?'

Isobel produced her wand from her apron and waved it at the table. And, of course, a beautiful bouquet of red roses appeared in a vase. Leo's fabulous, fairy friend kissed him on the nose. 'Thank you, darling,' she said. 'You're so thoughtful.'

Leo was quite amazed and felt deeply ashamed by his years of ingrained inadequacy. 'You make all this stuff so easy.'

'That's my job.'

Pulling up a chair, Leo sat down. 'What's this all about, Isobel?' he asked. His head was whirring. 'Why me?'

'I heard that mortal men were great in bed,' she said flippantly.

'Oh really?'

'Yes,' she teased. 'I thought I'd come and see for myself.'

'And?'

'They are.' She grinned. '*You* are.'

Isobel came to sit on his knee and Leo held her close. She felt so small and fragile compared to him. Emma was much more compact and sturdy. More like a real woman and less like a fairy, Leo supposed.

Isobel gazed up at him. Her skin was luminescent and Leo had never really known what that word meant until now. Her eyes were the colour of the night sky and they shimmered with stars of light.

'I want a child, Leo,' she breathed.

Leo felt his face fall.

'A human child. Your child.'

He held her away from him. 'Oh no,' he said. 'No. No. No. I don't do babies. I have a fatal allergy to Pampers. Like people do with peanuts but much, much worse.'

She took his hand. 'This is what I came for,' she told him. 'This is what it's all about.'

'No. *No.* If I'm so useless with flowers, just imagine what I'd be like with a baby.' Leo gave that some time to sink in.

But it was no good, Isobel's chin took on a determined set. 'I want a baby, Leo.'

Leo shook his head vehemently, starting a glitter snowstorm. 'This

118

is not what happens on my planet.' He spoke slowly as you would to a foreigner. Which, essentially, Isobel was. 'First we date. With no commitment. Maybe for a couple of years. Then we spend a long time skirting round the dance floor of marriage. Eventually – after a long, long time – we bow to peer pressure, get married, settle down, buy gardening and home make-over DVDs for a while and then when we are well and truly bored with that, we think – just *think* – about starting a family. It's a very long – *hideously* long – and involved process. We don't rush into these things. We used to, but not any more. They have to be very carefully considered and then invariably we leave it too late, so we have to scrabble round desperately as we approach the twilight of our years. Families cost an absolute fortune too. There's the nannies and the private education and the top-of-the-range buggy with disc brakes and GPS systems to buy. We much prefer foreign holidays to having kids these days. This is how it is. You need to read more glossies. Perhaps your information is out of date.'

Isobel regarded him levelly. Leo could tell that he was talking to an immovable object. 'What happened here? You've skipped a couple of chapters in the book of life,' he pointed out. 'We should still be on fumbling foreplay.'

Isobel twisted his hair between her fingers. 'The truth is, Leo, I don't know how much time I've got.'

'You're a spring chicken!' he said magnanimously. And she was. 'You're barely half a millennium old. Probably not even near the peak of your fertility. Do fairies go through the menopause?'

'That wasn't what I meant.' Isobel looked sad. 'I only have so much time here.'

'So do we all!' Leo threw up his hands. 'One minute we're learning to walk, the next – but a blink of an eye later – and we're driving round on motability scooters. I'm barely halfway between the two. I'm still clinging wildly to my youth. I can't even consider moving onto responsibility yet. The closest I've ever come to it was looking after my next-door neighbour's goldfish while they were on holiday. It died.' Glancing towards Dominic and Lydia's flat, he wondered if they'd ever really forgiven him for that. 'I went in one day and it was all white and floating on the surface of its little bowl. If I can't look after a fish for a week, doesn't it prove that I'm not ready for the next level? I'd need to practise on cats – or maybe a hamster. What about a dog? They're a real tie. But a baby? That's a whole new ball game.' And one that Leo hadn't even previously considered. He sort of assumed it would happen with Emma. One day. But not yet. And certainly not with a fairy.

'I'm really not ready for this. Don't you want a career? Earth women put having children on hold for years – years and years – virtually until the point where it's a real struggle to have them and they have to get eggs and stuff from much younger and fitter women. They all want careers much more than babies. Much, much more. Don't you want a career? You'd look terrible with stretchmarks. Although you'd probably be able to sort them out with that thing.' He pointed at her wand. 'We need to discuss this thoroughly. At a later date.' Leo didn't tell her that human men and British ones in particular avoid discussing anything. 'This is not the right time. This is definitely not the right time.'

'It is. And you'll come to know that it is, Leo. Men on earth seem to have been conditioned to think that entering into a loving partnership means that they have to give up something of themselves. But it doesn't have to be like that.'

Leo raised a sceptical eyebrow.

'Trust me.'

'I'm learning that fairies are not to be trusted. At all.'

Isobel kissed him. Leo's brain was spinning. But she kissed him a lot and nearly succeeded in kissing his worries away. Her kisses were truly potent things. They left his head reeling and his lips tingling – very probably there was some kind of spell involved. But this conversation had introduced something into the equation that Leo hadn't even wanted to think about. Men's sperm stayed wriggly for years, they didn't need to think about children until they were ready to draw their pension. They could have a James Bond lifestyle until they were well into their seventies – just look at Sean Connery – and then think about giving up the good things in life. Leo must vet the sort of magazines that Isobel was reading; she was obviously getting her hands on all these trendy ones that had a downer on men. Perhaps she could find herself a proper career, one that she couldn't do by waving her magic little wand, so she'd come home all tired and stressed and wouldn't be interested in jumping his bones every night, all night, let alone the by-products of reproduction.

'Why are you frightened of love?'

'Who says that I'm frightened?' Leo could feel his hands trembling.

'If you're in love you should be happy to share your life with that person.'

'Now you're talking about marriage,' he said. 'And that's an entirely different kettle of fish.'

Isobel waited for him to continue.

Leo could feel a cold sweat breaking out under his arms which was deeply unpleasant. 'Marriage is essentially about taking two great people and turning them into one boring fart.'

'Is that why you never married Emma?'

Even trying to think of an answer to that question made Leo's head whirl.

'Are you scared to love fully in case that person leaves you?'

It was fair to say that Leo had never wanted to suffer the bitter agonies of a divorce. He watched his parents go through it and couldn't bear to go through that himself. Or to put anyone else through it. 'Not at all,' he stated instead, showing that he was truly comfortable with expressing his feelings. The only thing Leo liked to express was his right to be too drunk to stand up. 'But that's what happens here. No one stays together any more. Splitting up is the new getting married. We're all jaded cynics who don't believe in happy ever after. That's the way of our world.'

'It doesn't have to be like that.' Isobel shook her head. 'People still can be together for ever. All they need is a little bit of help, some good luck and perhaps a smattering of magic.'

'And you'd contribute that part?'

She gave him an unfathomable look. Leo hated that. He even struggled with her fathomable looks. 'I could do,' she said. 'But there are times when it's better if people make their own magic.'

'Ah.' He spotted a fatal flaw in her argument. 'That's the part we have a bit of trouble with.'

'Sometimes you have to throw caution to the wind and jump in with both feet otherwise some of the best experiences of your life could pass you by.'

Leo couldn't take this in. He needed more time – and more beer – to recover from this shock.

'Men are much more sensitive than women, or fairies,' he said. 'You only have to see how much more we suffer when we catch a common cold. We need to be eased gently into these things. Over many, many years.'

'Then let's not discuss it any more tonight,' Isobel wisely suggested. She could probably tell from the pale colour of his face that this was too much for Leo to absorb.

'No,' he said. 'Let's not. That's a very good idea.'

She kissed him on the nose. 'What do you want for dinner?' she said brightly.

'Dinner?' Leo couldn't even concentrate on the mundane. 'You have completely and utterly ruined my appetite with all that talk of the little folk.'

'Don't you like babies?'

'Yes,' he said, 'but I couldn't eat a whole one.'

She laughed and wrapped her arms round him. 'You always say the funniest things.'

Leo felt everything inside him dissolve. His will was no longer his own. And it frightened him that he could agree to anything this woman . . . fairy . . . required of him.

'Tonight is traditionally my curry night,' he admitted. 'I usually go out with the boys.' A rather lame male-bonding ritual, Leo knew, but one he enjoyed and rarely remembered afterwards.

Isobel pouted at him with lips that he was sure must have formed the concept of strawberries. 'You don't mind staying at home instead?'

'What do you think?'

'I'll make you glad that you did,' she said, running the tips of her fingers down his neck.

Leo shivered. 'Oh really?'

'Where do you normally go for your curry?'

'The Bombay Plaza.' Not terribly salubrious, but it was cheap and the manager didn't mind the singing which they invariably indulged in. Leo's rendition of 'Walking on Sunshine' enjoyed a degree of renown in certain local eateries.

There was a sudden and blinding flash in the kitchen. Leo was catapulted from his chair and Isobel, instead of falling to the floor with a hefty bump as she should, simply floated away. 'Flip!'

In times of crisis Leo's extensive vocabulary usually deserted him. All his hair was standing on end and he felt as if his face had been scorched. On the table was a wonderful Indian feast, comprising all of his favourite dishes. Isobel, it seemed, was also telepathic when it came to curry-house menus. Indian music was playing – some sort of Ravi Shankar plinky-plonky stuff involving a sitar – and there was a very bemused waiter standing at the head of the table with a white cloth over his arm.

'Hi.' Leo gave him a tentative wave.

Recovering his composure remarkably quickly, the waiter just sort of assumed that he was supposed to be here in the middle of Leo's kitchen, in his flat, and gave him a formal nod. 'Good evening, sir.'

'You can serve dinner now,' Isobel said. The apron had gone and she was wearing some sort of silky, Indian pyjama thing. Very nice. Very themed.

The waiter stepped forward. Leo was so shocked that even the previous shock Isobel had given him did recede into the background somewhat.

'Isobel. Remind me never to ask you for shark's fin soup for dinner.' Leo shuffled his chair into place at the table. And he had to say this looked like a damn fine curry.

Chapter Thirty-Three

Grant takes me to a small Italian restaurant in Soho, well away from any of our usual haunts. Not that I've mixed with Grant very often and certainly not alone on any previous occasion. If Leo can be unbearable on his own, he's normally twice as bad when let loose with Grant and Lard. They all regress fifteen years. Yet, so far this evening, Grant has been charm personified. If he normally chooses to keep this side of himself hidden, I wonder why.

It's a cosy restaurant, with red gingham cloths on tables that are all squashed together, and there's a mist of condensation on the windows. This is the sort of place that people come to for a pre-theatre meal and it's quiet now that everyone else has rushed off to see *Mamma Mia!* or *Chicago* or whatever else 'must-see' show is playing these days. It's years since I've been to the theatre, mainly because Leo finds it impossible to sit still for three hours. Actually, he finds it impossible to sit still for ten minutes. My appreciation of the arts is lost on him. Leo's favourite film is *Alien versus Predator* – which speaks volumes.

I'm on my fourth or fifth glass of house plonk – I've stopped counting – and I'm feeling a great warmth in my toes. I never drink like this, not on a work night. Not even at the weekend. The ladette culture of binge-drinking has firmly passed me by. Although I do seem to be making up for lost time now. Well, one of us had to stay sober and I was normally looking after Leo to make sure he didn't make a fool of himself – without much success, usually.

Tonight I'm feeling mellow and chatty. Grant has proved to be good company and a very good listener. 'And you'll never guess what he did next. Never.' I prod Grant. 'Never! Never in a million, trillion years.'

Grant stifles a yawn. 'He was sick in the potted plant.'

I shriek. 'He was sick in the . . .' I stop abruptly. 'How did you know that?'

My dinner companion sighs. 'I have heard, several times, every Leo story known to man. And you have mentioned "that bastard" approx-imately two hundred and ten times in the last hour.'

I feel myself deflate. 'Oh. Have I?'

Grant nods.

I pick at the melted candle wax congealed in colourful stalagmites coming down from the top of the wine bottle in the middle of the table. I thought that I'd hardly mentioned Leo at all. I thought we were having fun, not talking about Leo. It seems that I'm wrong. 'I've talked non-stop about him?'

Grant nods again.

'Are you sure?'

'I'm sure.' Grant sounds a lot more sober than I do.

Sighing out loud, I say, 'How is he then?'

'He's fine,' Grant tells me.

'I'd rather he was suicidal and missing me.'

Grant shrugs. 'You know Leo.'

'Only too well.' I slug down my wine and pour out some more. 'Have you met my rival for his affections?'

'Yes.'

'What does she have that I don't?'

'Apart from Leo, you mean?'

'Point taken,' I say. Toying with a breadstick, I avoid looking at my companion. 'Leo thinks she's the sun and stars all wrapped up together.'

'Well,' Grant pauses over his wine. 'She's certainly . . . different.'

'Different?'

'Different.'

Clearly Grant isn't going to be drawn into comparing me to Leo's new woman. It's probably a good decision to choose the safe, neutral ground. 'Did he ever feel like that about me, Grant? Did he used to talk about me the way he talks about her?'

'Yes.' Grant puffs out loud. 'He did. All the time.'

'Oh,' I say. 'I didn't know that.' My eyes start to prick with tears.

'He loved you a lot,' Grant says. 'Adored you. He might not always have shown it in the way you wanted, but – well, you know Leo.'

I wonder if I did at all.

'Let's get you home,' Grant says, standing up. 'I can't cope with any more of playing gooseberry to Lovely Leo.' He gives a strained laugh. 'Especially when Leo isn't even here.'

★

125

The taxi pulls up outside my flat. Grant pays and then helps me out as my legs seem to have gone very watery during the journey. He escorts me to my building.

I put my hand on Grant's arm. 'I'm sorry,' I say. 'I've spoiled the evening now and we were having such fun.' Fumbling in my handbag, I eventually find my key. 'I don't normally drink so much.'

'It doesn't hurt once in a while,' Grant assures me as I totter towards the front door.

'And you're an expert, are you?'

'Unfortunately, I am.'

I slump against him, misery and booze making it hard to be upright. 'How am I going to stop feeling like this? How am I going to get over him, Grant?'

'You'll be all right,' he says, propping me up. 'It takes time, but you'll be fine.'

'And what if I'm not?' I burp and lurch inside, bashing the automatic light en route which bathes us in the floodlight of a dozen bare bulbs from the overhead spotlights. I wince against the glare. I've never noticed the brightness of these lights before. 'Ooo.'

Grant follows me up the stairs and to my flat.

'My mother said I should have casual sex with a dangerous stranger,' I say over my shoulder. My voice catches on the words. Despite being emboldened by drink, I still know what I'm insinuating.

'Well, that rules me out on both counts,' Grant says lightly. 'I'm not dangerous and I'm not a stranger.'

I peer at him with my bleary and probably bloodshot eyes. 'No.' But he's very attractive in a Leo's friend-ish sort of way. It's funny that I haven't noticed that before. He's tall and dark and rather lovely. Not a bag of bones like Leo, more thickset. Sturdy. Reliable. Well, he looks reliable – but looks, as I know to my cost, can be deceptive. I swing the door open more exuberantly than I intend, and it crashes against the wall. 'Welcome to my humble abode.'

'I'm glad you're home safely and in more or less one piece,' Grant says. 'It's been a really nice evening. We should do it again.'

'It's been terrible,' I say. 'I whined about Leo all night. Next time I'll stay sober and won't moan.'

'I might hold you to that.' Grant grins. He has nice teeth. Lots of them. Straight ones. 'I'd better be going.'

'Don't you want to come in?'

Grant shakes his head. 'It's probably not wise.'

'Just for coffee?'

'I've got an early start tomorrow. The cut and thrust of the money markets waits for no one.'

'I promise not to pounce on you.'

'Thank you,' Grant says. 'I respect your considerable restraint.'

I giggle. Should I pounce on him? Would it be a good way to get Leo out of my system? I've hardly had any lovers. Should I be thinking about adding another one to the meagre list?

'It wouldn't solve anything.'

'No. Probably not.' I smile lopsidedy at him. 'Sure I can't tempt you with a chocolate digestive then?'

'Positive. If it was Lard, that would be a different matter. He'd be putty in your hands.'

'You're more resistant to my charms.'

'No,' Grant sighs. 'Not really.'

I lean on the doorpost. 'You've never brought the same girlfriend twice when we've been out together as a group.'

'Ah, well. They say variety is the spice of life.'

'Has there never been anyone special, Grant?'

'No.' He jams his hands into his pockets. 'I work too hard. I play too hard . . .' He shrugs.

'But?'

'But it would be nice to have someone who loved me as much as you love Leo.'

'*Loved*,' I say, emphasising the past tense. '*Loved*.'

'You know you don't mean that.'

I huff. 'I love him so much and yet most of the time I could kill him. Does that make any sense?'

'Probably to another woman,' Grant admits.

'My last offer of a choccy biccy?'

The timer on the automatic light clicks and then plunges us into darkness, apart from the moon shining through the window in the hall. Could this be considered romantic?

'I think that's my cue to leave.' Grant kisses me on the cheek. 'Sleep tight.'

'I'm sorry, Grant.'

Even in the darkness I can see that he looks regretful. 'Me too,' he says and then he walks away.

I watch him as he lets himself out of the building. He gives me a wave without looking back at me. Grant is nice. He's very nice. A genuine guy with an occasionally unleashed wild streak. I thought he was a prat. How could I have read him so wrong? It seems as if I've been doing that a lot lately. And now I'm alone. I let myself into the flat. It's going to be hell getting up in time for work in the morning. I'm so, so tired and all I want to do is sleep for ever with someone's arms around me. I close my eyes and feel sleep rush in. And, with that, I slither slowly and drunkenly to the floor.

Chapter Thirty-Four

Grant and Lard were sitting on Leo's desk when he finally arrived in the office, amid the remnants of some rather tasty-looking pastries. Needless to say there had been another lovemaking and glitter frenzy last night after the sumptuous Indian extravaganza, and Leo wasn't sure how long he'd be able to keep this up. Keep *anything* up! But that was strictly confidential. Leo didn't want to ruin his reputation. And Isobel didn't even complain about his curry breath. There were times, Leo thought, when you could tell that she was definitely not a proper woman.

Isobel was still fast asleep in bed and, for a fairy, she seemed to need a lot of sleep. The difference with Isobel was that she'd waltz in here about eleven o'clock, wave her wand and no one would be any the wiser. It was only some strange sense of loyalty that had made Leo come here under his own steam. He must be mad.

Isobel's conversation with him last night had left Leo feeling very unsettled. He 'L'd' Isobel – he was sure he did. But babies? Marriage? Still scared the poo out of him. Nothing would convince Leo that they weren't a really bad idea. He couldn't even make it compute – he could almost hear the separate bits of his brain clicking round trying to find sense in it. To Leo, it was like a Rubik's Cube and the little coloured squares just wouldn't line up and slot into place for him no matter how hard he tried.

It was almost a relief to get to work so that he could think about other rubbish – stocks, shares, blah, blah, blah. No, he hadn't lost it completely – he did say *almost*.

'How does he do it?' he heard Grant say as he approached his dear friends, hoping to immerse his worries in the slurry of office gossip. 'He's got two gorgeous women hopelessly in love with him and I can't even get one. I'm beginning to dislike him intensely.'

Leo wandered up and snatched the only remaining chocolate croissant.

'I spat on that,' Lard said.

'A bit of bodily fluid shared between brothers doesn't bother me.' Leo bit into it regardless. He knew that Lard would never abuse an innocent pastry so. 'Who do you dislike intensely?'

'You,' Grant snapped.

'Oh. I thought it was someone interesting you were dissing.'

'You're not being fair to Emma.'

'I'm not doing anything to Emma.'

'That's why she's so bloody miserable.'

'She wanted me out of her life,' Leo pointed out, perhaps a little too crisply. 'I'm out. I thought she'd be happy about that.'

Grant rent his hair in frustration and Leo didn't understand why his friend was getting so het up about his love-life. 'You know nothing about women.'

'No.' Leo would have been the first to admit that. 'Do you?'

Grant slumped. 'No.'

Lard covetously moved the last of the pastries out of Leo's reach and addressed him from beneath his fringe. 'How would you feel if Emma was seeing someone else?'

'Emma is wonderful,' Leo pronounced magnanimously. 'She deserves to meet someone equally wonderful.' But perhaps not too much more wonderful than him or that would show Leo up in a very bad light. 'And I sincerely hope she does meet someone else,' he continued. 'One day.'

Grant and Lard exchanged a surreptitious glance.

'What?' he said. 'What am I missing here?'

Chapter Thirty-Five

I scurry along by the side of the Thames heading for the Hay's Galleria. The best thing for a broken heart is a spot of retail therapy – according to the glossy magazines, anyway. I've run out of wine which, after last night, is just as well because my liver is beginning to suffer. All the little cells must be curling up in a toxic haze after the battering they've had. I'm sure I've consumed my entire annual alcohol quota in the last few days. I'll have to start a detox programme before my body turns into a landfill site. And this is from a woman who previously considered Quorn an appetising foodstuff. So, in order to avoid the booze route to repair a broken heart – which hasn't worked – it's worth giving the shops a try. I'm still sane enough to know that a bout of excessive and unnecessary purchasing won't bring me happiness, but it might help to numb the pain for a while.

It's a bright, sunny day – cold but not bitterly so. 'Cardigan weather', my mother would call it. The sky is blue. Cottonwool clouds are billowing just as they should do. It's the sort of day that makes you glad to be alive. I don't feel glad to be alive exactly, but I don't feel too skanky either. A few well-aimed Nurofen have restored some of my equilibrium.

I swing into the Galleria – a trendy spot more like a theme park than a shopping mall. It has been made to look like an old London dockside alley, even down to the cobbled street. In the centre, a metal galleon in full sail disports itself as a fountain under an arched glass roof. The shops are largely of the tourist variety – who, as it's summer, are present in abundance. There's also a spattering of trendy art galleries, boutiques and jewellers. But within a short space of time, I've still managed to make a few useful purchases – tights, make-up, nail polish – and a few totally pointless ones too. A white top that has cost a lot of money that I don't have and that I'm never, ever going to be able to wear in case I spill something on it. And if I was still with Leo I'd

131

never, ever be able to wear it because he always managed to spill something on me. I know there must be a moral in there somewhere, but it's currently eluding me. My hangover is receding – this, I conclude, is due to the fact that the body can cope with only one pain at a time and the pain of flexing my credit card is taking my mind off my headache.

Stopping for a much-needed refill of coffee at Starbucks, I enjoy it sitting outside at a scattering of tables and chairs on the pavement. And I feel okay about sitting here alone, surrounded by my purchases. I can do this. Being alone is different from being lonely. Some experiences are still as rewarding when they're completed as a single person rather than as part of a couple. Drinking coffee is one of them. Renewed with vigour and caffeine, I set off on my 'Forget Leo' shopping mission once more.

An hour later and my assessment is that everything is going rather well – the carrier bags are accumulating nicely, my feet are beginning to hurt, my purse is emptying fast. All the ingredients of a successful retail experience. Everything is going rather too well, perhaps. You know how you get this niggling feeling that something untoward is about to happen? Call it women's intuition. Call it what you will. I was half-expecting something awful to occur. But not this. I never expected this. Leo and his new woman are coming along the pavement towards me. 'Oh no,' I whimper. 'Please no.'

The happy couple are arm-in-arm, browsing in shop windows and looking very lovey-dovey. And Leo is laughing. Leo never laughs when he's shopping – it's one of the few times in his life when he could be guaranteed to be terminally miserable. Like most blokes he would choose to have all his toenails removed without anaesthetic rather than go shopping. I had to drag him out once a year – usually with days to go before his jeans and shoes fell apart completely. Then I had to herd him into a changing room and coerce him into staying in there by confiscating all his clothes until he'd tried on everything I'd picked out for him. But then, I suppose, there are few guys who view shopping as a hobby – that remains a peculiarly female trait. Leo thinks it is something to be endured on as few occasions as humanly possible – not conducted arm-in-arm whilst laughing. And yet here he is, giggling away like a man without a care in the world. I feel as if I've wandered into a parallel universe.

★

'Why do mortal women value these trinkets, Leo?' Isobel asked him.

A forced, tinkling laugh escaped Leo's lips. It could so nearly have been a scream.

They were looking in the window of a terribly trendy jewellers and, of course, like the female of any species, Isobel's eyes had gravitated straight towards the diamond rings. The expensive ones. Huge solitaires with equally huge price tags.

Leo shook his head. 'I've no idea. Absolutely no idea.'

'Do they have a symbolic meaning?'

'Er . . . no. No.' He pretended to contemplate this matter deeply. 'Don't think so.'

But Leo did think that it was time to hustle her away from the window and towards a less emotionally-loaded shop, if there was such a thing. Isobel seemed intrigued by shopping, but not dedicated to it. Leo wondered if they embraced retail therapy with a vengeance in fairyland as they did here. Did they have purveyors of fine wings or toadstools? Leo realised that he knew so little about his new love. What sort of needs did she have when she was back in her real home? Here, if Isobel needed new clothes, she just seemed to wave her wand and they appeared. Maybe, Leo wondered, he could persuade her to turn this into a business concept, thus making their fortunes and enabling him to retire at a very youthful age from the binding world of high finance.

Bizarrely, it had been Leo's suggestion to come here and shop, so he only had himself to blame. Wild horses wouldn't have dragged him here a few weeks ago. Leo hated the thought of parting with money for things that you didn't really need – unless, of course, those things were computer games, blokey-type gadgets, comics or booze. Perhaps he was mellowing in his old age. Though it would be a sad day when Leo considered a visit to B&Q, Homebase or Wickes. It came as a bit of a shock to him that he could even name three DIY retailers.

He took Isobel's arm, laughed gaily again, and briskly steered her away from the jeweller's window.

I look round, panic gripping me. There's no way I want to be forced into a situation where I have to confront a maniacally giggling Leo and his new girlfriend. This is terrible. It isn't that I'm having a bad hair day or anything – definitely a time when you don't want to run into your love rival and your ex. I grind to a halt. It still takes some adjusting of my mindset to think of Leo in that way and that's why I don't want to bump into him like this. I need more time to get used to the situation – about fifty years should do it.

What on earth am I going to do? Any minute now they'll see me. Alone. Shopping alone. Because I have no man and no mates. Because I'm a sad, sexless spinster. It can't happen. It simply can't happen. The Galleria is a small enclosed space and they're gaining on me rapidly; the gap between us is shrinking by the minute. I look around, terror looming large. If I act quickly, I might just be able to make a quick getaway. But no, it's too late. They're nearly upon me. As I turn to bolt, I see a gorgeous young man bearing down on me. He's carrying a charity collecting tin in his hand which he's rattling at me. I grab him by the hand.

'Come on,' I bark at him. 'You'll do.'

'What?' The man looks terrified.

I snatch his tin from him – he's collecting for an animal charity. A predisposition to be nice to furry creatures, eh? Always a good thing in a man. Leo hates animals, but that's usually because they somehow manage to wee on him – even an elephant when we went to London Zoo together once. It would have been quite funny, if it hadn't been for the smell on the Tube on the way home. I toss the charity tin into a very pretty display of geraniums outside the nearby florists.

'But . . . but . . .'

'Don't say anything,' I order. 'I'll make it worth your while.'

When Leo looked up, Emma was standing there. In his haste to get Isobel away from the engagement rings, Leo hadn't even noticed his ex-girlfriend. She was clutching the arm of a very tall man and was looking nervous. The man looked a bit twitchy too.

'Hi,' Emma said. 'Leo!' She sounded very happy and perky.

'Oh. Hi.' He tried to sound perky too. Leo wondered who the hell this guy was. They looked very friendly. Emma was clinging onto his arm as if she was never going to let him go. Leo felt a twinge of pain and guilt. Perhaps she was hanging onto him for grim death because she was afraid he might bolt like he himself had. He glanced down and noticed that Isobel was clinging onto him in the same way.

Leo looked at the guy and felt perplexed for some reason. The other guy looked back at Leo in exactly the same way. He appeared to be slightly more blank than Leo – if that was humanly possible.

'Oh,' Emma said into the awkward silence. 'Let me introduce you. This is Stefan. My boyfriend . . . My *fiancé*.'

'Fiancé?' Leo sounded put out even to his own ears.

'You were right, Leo. It was time for us both to move on.'

'Yes. Yes. Absolutely.' Why was his mind crying out, 'Oh no!'? He eyed Emma's fiancé – good grief, he was bloody handsome, the bastard! Without knowing what he was doing, Leo held out his hand and pumped Emma's fiancé's hand enthusiastically.

'Leo,' he said to the twat on Emma's arm. He looked loaded too. Fucker.

The fiancé gaped at Leo open-mouthed.

'Stefan's foreign,' Emma interjected. 'Bulgarian. He doesn't speak very much English.'

He shook Leo's hand and nodded vigorously. No glitter fell out of his hair. Arsehole.

His darling ex-Emma looked at Isobel and smiled sweetly. My word, she really had moved on. Leo had thought that she'd be wanting to scratch Isobel's eyes out. Grant was right. He'd never understand women. 'And this must be . . . ?'

'Isobel,' Leo said. 'This is Isobel.'

'Charmed to meet you, I'm sure,' Emma said pleasantly.

Isobel also did her sweetest smile. But thankfully, she said nothing and she didn't whip out her wand to create untold havoc either.

They all stood and grinned at each other inanely. Leo was surprised at the ferocity of his emotion, but he really would have liked to punch that dickhead.

'Well, this is very nice,' Emma said with a happy little jump. 'I'm so glad that we bumped into you.' She gave Stefan the fuckwit's arm a loving squeeze. 'Can't stand chatting though,' she babbled on. 'Stefan and I are going to choose a ring.'

'A ring?'

'Engagement ring,' Emma said, confirming Leo's worst fears.

'*Engagement* ring.' He could feel himself going purple. '*Engagement* ring?'

Emma's eyes shone with love for this wanker. 'It's wonderful, isn't it?'

Leo could quite honestly say that he couldn't find any words to describe what he felt. He stood there, mouth gaping like the Blackwall Tunnel.

'Take care, Leo,' Emma said brightly.

135

'And you.' Leo felt that he should wish her well in her new life or something like that, but it wouldn't come out. Nothing would.

'Isobel.' Emma nodded at his fairy friend. 'Nice to meet you. Perhaps you could both come to the wedding.'

Wedding!

And then Emma was gone. Bouncing happily away, Bulgarian Git Face in tow.

Leo grabbed Isobel's hand and dragged her down the street as fast as her legs could carry her.

'What's wrong, Leo?' she asked breathlessly.

'Nothing.'

'Is it Emma?'

'No.'

'Is it those rings? There is a significance to them, isn't there?'

'No.'

The only significance was that all the years they were together, Emma and Leo had never got engaged and now five minutes later – FIVE MINUTES! – she was slipping her finger into for ever. Flip. Leo could have kicked something. Flip. Double, double flip. He wondered if Isobel could magic him up a cat to kick.

I laugh as gaily and as loudly as I can manage without appearing insane. Glancing over my shoulder, I see that Leo is striding off in the other direction. Good. He's out of harm's way now. I feel like lying down and weeping – he's so happy. They look perfect together and Isobel – her name is like dust in my mouth – is all tiny and girly and horribly nice. I really, really want to hate her. And, thankfully, I do.

I turn to my newly-acquired fiancé. 'Well,' I say briskly, 'thanks for that.' Reaching into my purse, I peel out a twenty-pound note. 'For the sick animals.' I hand it to the guy. 'Bye.'

'Wait. Wait,' he says. 'Actually, my name's Jacob.'

'Then thanks, Jacob,' I say. 'Sorry about the Stefan bit. It was the first thing that came to me.'

Jacob grins. 'I'm not from Bulgaria either. I'm from Barnsley.'

'I'm sorry,' I repeat. 'I was desperate.'

'I quite enjoyed it. I don't get much chance for subterfuge.'

'Believe me, it's vastly over-rated.' I turn to go.

'Hey,' he calls softly. 'Seeing as we're engaged, I wondered if you'd like to have dinner with me tonight?'

I spin on my heels. 'Are you mad?' I ask. 'Didn't you see the agony I just went through. He's left me – for her! That twinkly little gorgeous person. Can't you see I'm nursing a broken heart?'

Jacob stands open-mouthed. 'I thought it might help you to forget him.'

'How typical! We have been together for years,' I tell him. 'How am I ever going to forget him? Are all men so shallow?'

'Does this mean the engagement's off?' Jacob wants to know.

'I wouldn't marry you if you were the last man on earth!'

And I stomp off down the high street, leaving Jacob clutching his twenty-pound note and looking very confused.

Chapter Thirty-Six

It was late and Leo couldn't sleep. He'd tossed and turned for hours, to no avail. Leo had been thinking about babies and Emma and how, five minutes after having dumped him, she'd found someone else she wanted to marry. Leo decided that he was too naive for the ways of this world and his heart felt bruised by this latest turn of events.

A few short days ago he was such a happy soul with not a care to call his own. Now Leo had grey hairs sprouting amidst his glitter and a permanent frown on his brow. Isobel was making his life truly wonderful – albeit in a chaotic kind of way – and yet Leo felt so sad about all that Emma and he had missed out on. He thought about the things they could have done together, achieved together, if only they'd tried a little bit harder. *He'd* tried a little bit harder.

Beside him, his fairy friend was slumbering deeply. Leo passed his hand gently over her cheek, fretting that she was so delicate and vulnerable. Eventually, he decided that he might as well be up and worrying as lying down and doing it.

As he pottered into the kitchen, Leo noticed a pile of dishes sitting on the draining board.

'Hi, guys.'

He opened the fridge to get a beer, purely for medicinal purposes. 'Oh bollocks.' Leo stopped in his own tracks. 'I'm talking to my crockery.'

Isobel, drowsy and rubbing her eyes, came in behind him a few minutes later looking thoughtful. Leo waved a tin of beer at her, but she shook her head.

'I was talking to the dishes,' Leo said with a laugh.

'I don't think they speak English,' Isobel replied. And Leo didn't think that she was joking.

She sat down at the table and then picked at the grooves in the wood. 'Couldn't you sleep?'

Leo shook his head.

'What are you thinking about?'

'This and that,' he answered dismissively.

'She loves you a lot, doesn't she?'

'Emma?' This was a surprise.

Isobel nodded. Leo sat down next to her and opened the beer. 'I suppose so.'

'And you love her very much too.'

'I did,' he said. 'In my own way.'

'So why didn't it work out?' She leaned sleepily against him.

Leo tasted the froth from the can as he contemplated his reply. 'I could never live up to Emma's ideals.'

'Ideals?'

'Emma's pretty much a perfect human being. She's got everything sorted. Well, she thinks so,' he said without malice. 'I'm not like that. I bumble my way through life, messing it up as I go. That wasn't enough for her and I couldn't change.'

'Did you try?'

'No,' he admitted. Leo registered the note of sadness in his voice. 'Not enough. It seemed too hard. Whatever I did was wrong, so I stopped trying. She expected too much from me.'

'Like what?'

Leo sighed and slid down onto the table. 'Like one of those sparkly rings.'

'So they *are* important?' Isobel's eyes brightened. 'I knew it.'

'Yeah, well, they sort of mean that you'll be together for ever. Well, not so much for ever these days, but that's the gist.'

'And you couldn't promise Emma for ever?'

'No,' he confessed. It pained Leo to admit it, so he added flippantly, 'It's something that human blokes resist at all costs.'

'Except for her new . . . *fiancé*,' Isobel noted. 'He offered for ever very quickly.'

'Yes. A bit too bloody quick, if you ask me.'

'I don't think anyone did, Leo.'

'No.'

She reached across and took Leo's hand. 'What does human love feel like?'

'What does it feel like?' Leo laughed. What a question! Describe love in less than one hundred words. 'It makes your heart soar. It makes you feel all warm and tingly inside. It makes you laugh at the silliest little thing. It makes you want to fly. And it makes you think of the other person before yourself.'

'And that's how Emma made you feel?'

Leo thought about it for a minute, replaying the highlights of their time together – the times when they soared and flew and were warm and tingly together. And there had been lots of them. 'Yes.' He laughed again, this time sadly. 'Yes, she did. I just didn't realise it at the time. The other thing that you have to understand about humans is that we have a tendency to take all our good fortune for granted.' Leo wanted to talk to Emma about these things, to explain to her how he felt. But it was too late. The time for talking, Leo guessed, had long since passed.

Isobel interrupted his thoughts. There was an anxious look marring her pretty face. 'Is that how you feel about me?'

Leo reached out and took both of her hands. 'I think it is.'

'I love you, Leo,' she said.

He took a deep breath, felt the thump of his heart and then said, 'I love you too.'

The kitchen lights started to flash on and off. Glitter floated down from the ceiling. The dishes started to jump up and down. Then, of course, the romantic music kicked in. Whitney Houston again, Leo believed. It seemed to be a favourite of Isobel's.

'Darling,' he said as he took her in his arms and buried his face in her neck. 'We need to talk about some of your worst excesses.'

Chapter Thirty-Seven

I sit on the toilet seat while Jo and Caron squash themselves into the cubicle with me. I'm very drunk and crying loudly. My friends look at each other in alarm.

'We've come out for some fun,' Jo says crisply. 'Remember?'

I wail again. 'I don't want fun. I want Leo.'

Caron crouches down next to me. 'You can't spend all night at a great club like this locked in the loo.'

'We've paid a fortune to get in, Em.'

I wail again.

'Emma, he's a bastard,' Caron reminds me. 'You have said so yourself on many occasions. He's given you the run around for too long.'

'But I love him,' I wail. I don't want to be in a trendy nightclub with lots of noise and ridiculous-sounding drinks and women with indecently low-cut trousers and indecently low-cut tops. Joni Mitchell was right – or was it Melanie? You don't know what you've got until it's gone. I want to be at home with Leo, curled up on the sofa and watching crap on telly. And I know that I moaned when we did that, but I hadn't realised how nice it was at the time.

'He's not good enough for you,' Jo chips in. She doesn't say it with any great sense of conviction.

'But I love him!' I pull some more loo roll from the holder and blow my nose fiercely into it. And now he's with someone else. Someone lovelier than me. And they're probably curled up on Leo's sofa right now watching *Wife Swap Saved My Marriage* or some other dross, feeding each other Maltesers.

'You could have anyone, Emma.' Caron continues her cajoling. 'You're beautiful.'

I don't look it at the moment. My lipstick is smeared. My hair is birds-nesting of its own accord and there are two tracks of wet mascara down my face. Men are just like mascara – running at the first sign of any emotion. I've bought a new 'going-out' dress especially for the occasion on another retail therapy expedition. It looked great in the shop – dangling its promises of sexiness alluringly in front of me. My credit card was handed over in a greedy blur and maxed once more. And now it looks dreadful – tarty – as if I'm a desperate single person out on the pull for a boyfriend. Which I am.

'You could have anyone,' Caron continues gently. 'Leo's not even that good-looking.' She looks to Jo for support.

'He is,' Jo mouths. 'He's bloody gorgeous!'

Caron scowls at her.

'But I love him,' I wail.

Jo also kneels down beside Caron. 'Emma. Sweetheart. He's found someone else. Someone who you say looks like a million movie stars rolled into one.'

I wail louder. 'But I love him!'

'Come on. Come on.' Caron and Jo hoist me from the toilet. 'Be a brave girl. Let's put our party face back on and go out and get a new man!'

'But . . .'

'No buts,' Caron says firmly. 'You can do it.' She pulls off some more loo roll and hands it to me. 'Now. Good girl. Dry your eyes.' She dabs at me with the loo roll. 'Right, big blow. No one will want to dance with you if you're all snotty.'

I unwind some more and blow my nose again, smiling weakly at my friends.

'That's my big brave girl,' Caron says. 'Now – let's go and drive the men wild.'

I'm getting too old for dancing, I decide. I'd like to go back to the time when it was more genteel. A time of perky bopping with the girls round a pile of great, sack-like handbags. Now you can't take out a handbag because it's likely to be stolen, so everyone has those silly little purses that hold nothing. And the perky boppings are now obscene gyrations, grinding your hips in time with men that you don't know and are never destined to see again.

'This is great,' Caron shouts encouragingly. 'Isn't it?'

I nod and widen my smile. It's terrible. More than terrible. It's sheer torture.

The music is at a level that's making my ears want to bleed and I wish that more people who were determined to end comfy long-term relationships to regain their youthful freedom spent a few nights in clubs like this. It's better therapy than Relate could ever offer. It has certainly made me realise in a flash that the singles scene is a hugely over-rated phenomenon.

All the women look tarty and hard. They laugh too loudly and toss back lurid-coloured drinks at an alarming rate while eyeing up lurching, drunken men with predatory stares. Is this what I want to turn into? Once upon a time men used to come up and ask you to dance and even engage in conversation before they tried to grope your bum. Didn't they? I'm sure I can remember back that far. Well, gone are those days. Now the men come up and either prod you in the chest as some sort of basic mating ritual or just stand there and twitch in front of you, not giving you the choice to say yes or no. And most of them are definite nos. They only manage to get halfway through a dance track before their hands are trying to locate your underwear. Leo could never be classed as gallant, but even at his worst he'd never been this bad. My boyfriend – ex-boyfriend – has a certain charm, which is more than can be said for this lot of single-cell amoebas.

Caron and Jo surround me on the dance floor. They look like a pair of sheepdogs guarding a particularly skittish ewe, scared that it's going to bolt at any moment. And they're probably right. It will take very little encouragement for me to be heading back to the loo for another cry or to jump in a taxi and dash for the sanctuary of my home. I'm grateful that my friends are trying to jolt me out of my misery, but this clearly isn't the way to do it. How am I going to find someone caring and sensitive in a place like this? Where on earth is the magic of romance to be found for the woman of the new millennium?

A handsome young guy sidles up to me. He's already jigging. I brace myself.

He places his face close to mine and I try not to recoil. 'Would you like to dance?' he yells.

I burst into tears. It's all too much. The noise, the crowd, the gaping hole in my heart.

The young man looks terrified. 'I take it that's a no?'

'I'll dance with you,' Jo says. Caron glares at her, but the young man shrugs his shoulders and, without the need for any further persuasion, gets jiggy with Jo instead.

I see my escape opportunity and rush out. The loo, it seems, is my only refuge.

Chapter Thirty-Eight

L eo was at his desk and it looked as if a tornado had recently hit. Even by Leo's levels of untidiness it was bad. Half-empty coffee cups nestled amidst a mountain of discarded chocolate wrappers from bars all cadged from Lard's never-ending stash. He wished he could smoke a cigarette. Leo was desperate. And he was having to work. Really work. Things in the unfathomable world of finance were going horribly wrong and Leo didn't know what to do. He needed Grant or Lard to sort it out, but they were both in a meeting and Leo didn't dare go in to admit defeat. He'd be out on his ear as soon as you could say 'hopeless failure'. He'd hit the phones but none of his deals were showing any hope of saving the day. Leo punched at the keys on his computer in the vain hope that something he did would make a difference. But he was drowning. Slow, painful glugs that were sending him further and further into deep water.

Isobel came in. 'Coming for lunch?'

She held up a brown paper bag, clearly stuffed with all manner of goodies. Leo couldn't bear to ask whether she'd been out to buy this impromptu picnic or whether it was something she'd conjured up herself. In fact, he hardly needed to ask. Leo wondered if there were any calories in food created by fairies? This could well be another huge business opportunity. And he felt that he might be looking for a new job very shortly.

'Can't. Can't.' Leo shook his head furiously and gave Isobel his most stressed look. This was serious. 'Mega, mega problems. Market's crashing. Dollar's buggered. I'm buggered. Flipping awful.'

Isobel leaned over his shoulder and frowned. 'Let me see,' she said and then eased Leo off his chair to take his place. That bloody wand appeared from nowhere.

'Isobel!' Leo hissed.

'Sssh!' she said.

Isobel checked that no one was watching – so she must have learned some discretion – and then wafted her wand over his computer. The numbers on the screen started to flash and go crazy. It all scrolled up and down and sideways and goodness only knows what else.

'Oh heavens to Betsy,' Leo breathed, wanting to sink to his knees and disappear into the carpet. However, he was careful not to voice this.

The only other thing he saw flashing before him was his career, such as it was. The dole queue, Leo feared, was looming large. And not a chirpy dole queue where they were all dancing, like that scene in *The Full Monty*, but a serious dole queue where they're all in grey suits and manacled to the floor. If it wasn't beckoning before, then Leo was absolutely sure it was now. Any minute his computer was going to start smoking and then quietly explode into a thousand smithereens. Leo could hardly bear to watch. So he didn't. Instead he covered his eyes and pretended that he was lounging on a Bahamian beach.

Eventually, Leo peeped through his fingers. The screen had finally calmed down and all the figures had come to a halt. 'Oh my word.'

Isobel smiled. 'Is that better?'

Leo edged her out of his seat and gazed at the screen, trying to take in the full enormity of what she'd done. This woman should have come with a health warning. 'Better?' he squeaked.

'I can do it again. If you like.'

'I don't like,' he said. 'Keep that damn thing to yourself.' He pushed her wand away from him. It was like being next to a loaded gun. A smoking loaded gun in this case.

He ran his eyes over the figures just in case he was mistaken – but he wasn't. The evidence was right there before him. Leo's breathing was very shallow. 'Do you realise you have just made an awful lot of people instant millionaires?'

'But that's good, isn't it?'

Leo flopped back into his chair. He felt very pale. The computer screen flickered away innocently. No worse for its experience – unlike Leo. Who had just aged ten years. 'It's very good.'

Leo had no idea how he was going to explain away this sudden streak of brilliance that had befallen him.

'Can we go to lunch now?'

Even though it would be several hours before his heart-rate returned to normal, Leo managed to shrug. 'Why not?'

As they headed for the office door to escape into the fresh air and a rare spot of seasonal sunshine, Grant and Lard appeared looking ragged after their meeting. They both looked towards Leo and Isobel, mimicking the motions of drinking. Leo shook his head – more glitter – and gestured towards Isobel, who in turn showed them the picnic bag. Speaking or any form of coherent explanation was beyond Leo – most of the time – but particularly now.

He saw Grant and Lard exchange another one of their glances, but Leo couldn't worry about them now. He had just narrowly avoided the sack and a heart-attack in the last five minutes, and that was more than one man should have to bear. A nice sit-down and a sandwich was about the most strenuous thing Leo could cope with right now.

Chapter Thirty-Nine

'We're losing him, aren't we?' Lard said as they watched Leo depart with Isobel.

Grant nodded thoughtfully.

'What will happen to the Curry Monsters' Club?'

'I think you'll find that its current membership will be cut by a third.'

The friends wandered over to the window, just in time to see Leo and Isobel emerging from the office and running across the road, dodging the traffic, to the small, scrubby haven of green across the street that masqueraded as a park in this part of the City.

The grass was littered with relaxing bodies – businessmen and women, stretched out for an hour, jackets removed and enjoying the rare window of sunshine. Seemingly unaware that they were being monitored, Isobel and Leo opened the wrought-iron gate and found the nearest bench. They were cuddling and laughing, teasing each other.

'They're very much in love,' Lard said, a vaguely wistful note in his voice.

'That is truly nauseating to watch,' Grant said, pretending to turn away. 'I'm going to be sick. Really I am. I can feel all that vomity stuff coming up in my throat.'

'You need comfort food.' Lard produced a Mars Bar from his pocket.

'You're like a magician. The David Blane of the chocolate world. Cheers, mate.' Grant bit into the sweet, sticky chocolate appreciatively. 'Not a moment too soon.'

In the park, Isobel stretched out and rested her head on Leo's lap, gazing at him adoringly.

'I think I liked him better when he was with Emma,' Lard said thoughtfully.

'Yeah,' Grant agreed. 'You knew where you where with him when he was an inconsiderate twit all the time.'

Lard delved in his pockets and pulled out a Snickers for himself. 'Do you think we're simply jealous because we haven't got anyone as wonderful as Isobel in our sad little lives?'

'No way!'

A pretty young colleague walked past to get to the coffee machine. She smiled flirtatiously at them both. Grant and Lard grinned back. As she went on her way, both Grant and Lard's faces fell.

'It's just not the same, is it?'

'No,' Grant admitted. 'Somehow she's not so shiny and shimmery.'

They both glanced down at Isobel and Leo mooning over each other on the park bench – in a romantic, not a bare-bottomed way as was Leo's usual penchant for mooning – and nibbled at their chocolate in quiet contemplation.

'Do you believe it?'

'What?' Grant asked. 'That she's one of the little folk? Of course I don't! She's unutterably beautiful – of that there's no doubt. I do, however, believe that she's quite probably barking mad. But, in spite of that, our friend Leo has fallen for her hook, line and sinker.'

'She must have something special.'

'Yes,' Grant agreed. 'And I would vow never to look at Christina Aguilera in a lascivious manner again to find out exactly what.' He paused and looked pensive. 'Can I tell you something?'

'You haven't got a deadly disease?'

'No.' Grant shook his head. 'But I think I've something that may be catching.'

Lard moved away from him and Grant looked sheepish.

'I feel really . . . *sorry* . . . for Emma.'

'How . . . *sorry*?'

'Quite a bit . . . *sorry*.'

'Sorry enough to consider a mutually satisfying exchange of bodily fluids?'

'Yes.'

'Ooo,' Lard said, wide-eyed. 'I don't think you can get any cream for that.'

'I suspect not.'

'Leo will go bonkers.'

'Emma isn't his girlfriend any more.'

'Are you sure? Miss Glitter Knickers here might have his attention for the moment, but he and Emma go back a long way. Bonds like that aren't easily broken.'

'Leo's blown it,' Grant said flatly. 'I just have to wait until Emma realises that.'

'It would be much better if Leo and Emma got back together, Grant. This woman is completely messing with his head.' They both glanced out of the window and Lard put his hand on Grant's arm. 'There are plenty more fish in the sea. Fish that haven't spent five years with Leo. I'd suggest that you cast Emma from your mind.'

'If only it were that easy.'

'Do you think we should try to split Leo and Tinkerbell up? That would restore the status quo. Emma and Leo would get back together, as they always do, and you never know, Tinkerbell might fancy one of us.' Lard brightened. 'Or both of us. Together.'

'Don't be revolting.'

'It wouldn't take much to put a spanner in the works.'

'I beg to differ with you. She might look all floaty and insubstantial, but mark my words, that woman is a ball breaker.'

Grant and Lard turned away from the window and, as they did, suddenly banged their heads together with a painful thunk of skull on skull. 'Ow. Ow!'

They rubbed their heads. 'Jeez, mate.' Grant looked accusingly at Lard. 'Watch what you're doing.'

'It wasn't my fault.'

'Well, it certainly wasn't mine. I hardly moved.'

On the breeze – a breeze which hadn't been there a minute ago – there was the bright tinkle of faint laughter.

'It's cold in here.' They both shivered.

The laugh came again and they turned back towards the window. Isobel was looking up from the park bench, eyes directed straight back at them and she had a self-satisfied smirk on her face.

'That woman is trouble,' Grant said sagely.

'I still bet we could split them up.'

'Really?' Grant said. 'Personally, I vote for retaining my testicles.'

Chapter Forty

Tonight, I'm going to get an early night. My head has been pounding all day as an aftermath of the noise and humiliation that was my nightclub experience. A quiet night in with a romantic comedy DVD – *Sleepless in Seattle* is always a good standby – and a cup of herbal tea is much more my thing. Followed by a long, hot bath, it has almost been the perfect evening. *Almost.* It would be nice – like Meg and Tom – to be heading to my bed to cuddle up to someone. A sigh escapes into the silence.

I'm thirty years old. I don't want to be single any more. I want to be married. I want lilies in my bouquet. I want a three-tier cake and a diamond-set platinum wedding ring. I want children. Three of them. And I want breast-pads and leaking nipples and stretchmarks. All of the things I have previously spurned. I want a house – roses round the door are an optional extra – but it has to be somewhere that I can put down roots, somewhere to build a future. I'm sure of it. But how to get it? Instead of making the most of my chance while I had it, up to now I've been going through life rudderless, letting the current trends of singledom and childlessness buffet my true feelings about until I'm not even sure what they are any more and, even worse, I'm frightened to admit it. Why are we women so keen to suppress our natural instincts these days?

I'm padding round my bedroom in my oldest, comfiest pyjamas. The ones that Leo loves – and only Leo could love me in fleecy nightwear adorned with snoring sheep. I try not to look too many times at his photograph on my bedside table. Strangely, you might say, life without Leo is proving considerably more traumatic than life with Leo. Contrary to all popular beliefs.

I pull my favourite cuddly toy to me. My entire array of fluffy animals – and there are quite a few of them – have been purchased by Leo. He's of the opinion that a woman can never have too much cute fur

150

fabric. In the early days of our relationship, he even remembered to buy them on my birthdays too. This particular toy was acquired on a visit to Thorpe Park a couple of years ago. I know many women whose boyfriends take them to Paris, Rome, Prague. I'm not in this smug club. Leo was more likely to take me to Blackpool or Alton Towers or, in this case, Thorpe Park. He prefers theme parks to museums. Many men pride themselves on their ability to choose fine wines or champagne. My man was an aficionado of the greasy hot-dog stand and knew which was the best log flume to get utterly soaked on. I sigh and shake the toy. It's a bright red fluffy devil with black horns and an evil smile. Rather like Leo's. When shaken, it giggles and says wickedly, 'I'm a little devil.' It's Leo, all over. Other men buy their loved ones flowers – roses, lilies, even bloody daffodils. Leo buys stuffed toys that chortle or fart or say, 'Fuck off' in maniacal tones. I slide into the bed and hug the giggling ball of fluff to me. 'Oh Leo,' I sob.

Isobel and Leo were sharing the mirror in the bathroom. Leo was cleaning his teeth and Isobel was smiling mysteriously. Fairies, Leo decided – and this one in particular – made him very nervous.

'What?' he said.

'Nothing.'

'I find that look very disturbing, Fairy Isobel.'

'You have a very suspicious nature,' she told him.

'I didn't until I met you.' He'd never have previously considered his life with Emma uncomplicated, but he realised now that it was.

Kissing Leo, she skipped out of the bathroom. He had never before in his life considered an early night to be a good thing either, but Isobel left him feeling permanently exhausted. Quite frankly, he was a shadow of his former self. Leo looked at his haggard face in the mirror. Ghastly. 'Mirror, mirror on the wall, have I got more grey hair since a fairy came to call?'

'Yes,' a disembodied voice came back from the mirror. Now his bathroom accessories were answering back.

'Flip.' Leo briskly finished cleaning his teeth and scuttled after Isobel and into bed. She was lying there looking far too innocent.

'I don't want any funny business,' he warned her as he cuddled up next to her.

'Not any?'

'Well,' Leo relented. 'Just a bit.'

Isobel wrapped her arms round him and suddenly he felt very, very sleepy.

'Iso . . .' But Leo couldn't even finish the word before he was out for the count.

I toss and turn. I'm too hot. Then too cold. I kick the covers off. Then pull them back on. I'm dreaming of Leo. An action replay of some of our happiest times together – punting on the River Cam when Leo fell in, making love in a hay field when Leo got hayfever and sneezed non-stop for five days, renting a tandem in the Lake District when we took a corner too fast and Leo ended up in a ditch. Suddenly I wake. Throwing back the duvet, I go to the window. There's a strange mist outside and I'm not sure if I'm actually awake or still dreaming.

The London skyline looks like a cardboard cut-out in the background. I rub at the window panes with the sleeve of my pyjamas, but they're misty too and no matter how much I rub, they just won't clear. There's a figure outside, watching me, I'm sure. I peer into the mist. It looks like Leo's new girlfriend, Isobel. It can't be. I try to look at the clock, but the face of that is misty too and the numbers are blurred. Isobel seems to be wearing a trenchcoat and sunglasses and looks like some cheap private detective. The faint sound of laughter seeps into my room. I strain to get a proper look. This is bizarre. Isobel appears to be leaning on the lamp post across the street, but it looks like she's hovering above the ground. It's a dream, I decide. Possibly a nightmare. And I resent that Leo's new love is in it. I open the window and a swirl of warm mist envelops me, twining itself round my arms and legs. Suddenly, I feel sleepy again. I try to stare at Isobel, but she's blurring. I'm struggling to keep my eyes open. Isobel starts to laugh and I'd recognise that sound anywhere. I have *definitely* heard it before.

'What are you doing in our lives?' I ask, but sleep is overcoming me. 'Who are you? Where have you come from?'

She says something, but it's too faint for me to hear. It sounded as if she said she was helping me. Helping me by stealing Leo away from me? What is she talking about?

'Get lost,' I shout into the street in a final attempt at defiance, though my limbs feel as if they're made of lead. 'Go away. Go on. And give me my boyfriend back!'

★

Leo had no idea what he was doing on the Embankment down by the River Thames in the middle of the night. Or how he got there. But he was absolutely sure that Isobel had something to do with it. The fact that he was wearing a rather smart top hat and tails reinforced his view. 'Isobel,' Leo shouted into the air, 'what are you playing at?'

But there was no answer. Like policemen, fairies seemed miraculously to disappear when you really needed them. London looked fabulous at night. Particularly this slice of London. There was a shimmer of water on the pavements, even though Leo didn't remember it raining. All along the riverside, the street lamps were reflected in it and the hoops of lights which were strung between them swung gently in the breeze, making the whole area look like stars on a stage set. The stunning backdrop of the Houses of Parliament, Big Ben and Tower Bridge gave it a magical air. A full moon was out in force and sparkled – rather like the glitter in Leo's hair – across the inky black of the river. It was a marvellous night for a walk. Leo's heart skipped a beat . . . or for dancing.

Without warning, Emma appeared in front of him. Leo wondered where she came from and why she looked remarkably like Ginger Rogers to his Fred Astaire. Her hair was pinned up in what his mother might have called 'bangs' and looked fabulously glamorous. She was wearing a long, white floaty dress nipped in at her waist and she had a white feather boa draped round her shoulders. And this was a good look for her. A very good look.

Leo somehow acquired a cane and behind him on the Embankment, out of a rolling cloud of fine mist, an orchestra materialised. A big one. Complete with violins and cellos – all that sort of stuff. The musicians were all wearing white tail suits and loads of brilliantine on their slicked-back hair. If this was a dream, it was a lovely one, Leo thought. Emma had never seemed more beautiful. She smiled and moved towards him.

Despite the glamour, she was slightly hesitant, awkward, maybe a bit uptight. The sounds of the opening to Irving Berlin's 'Let's Face the Music and Dance' floated on the breeze. She started to move more gracefully and floated into Leo's arms. He caught hold of her waist and twirled her, making her gasp. It seemed like the right thing to do. And, surprising as it might be, Leo had never been considered much of a dancer. He was kicked out of the country dancing lessons at prep school for trying to look up the girls' skirts. Nor did he ever manage to crack the Argentinian Tango despite his desire to fling Emma about in the style of Gomez Addams and despite the number of lessons they had. Eventually, Leo had been invited to leave that class too. The instructor seemed to feel that simply turning up with a rose between his teeth each week wasn't taking his tuition seriously enough. But Leo had always wished that he could be considered to be a dancer, rather than emulating a twitching idiot with his finger in an electrical socket, which was his current style. Apart from tonight . . .

Emma, unlike Leo, was as light as a feather on her feet. She melted into his arms, their bodies merged. They tapdanced in complete unison up and down the steps to the river and threw in a bit of the quick-step for good measure. Leo handled his cane with all the skill of a first-rate baton-twirler. A ray of moonlight followed them like a spotlight in a 1940s' movie. Leo twirled and whirled her again and they danced through the streets of London, their feet tap, tap, tapping on the empty pavements, serenaded by their own players. A silver butterfly and a stream of dancing stardust shadowed their every move.

'I love you,' Emma murmured. She had tears in her eyes. 'I dream of us being together again.'

'I love you too,' Leo said. His heart surged with joy. It made him think that if Isobel was truly behind all this – and it certainly had her mark on it – why was she doing it? Did Emma, he wondered, have any idea what was happening to them? When Leo made up his own dreams they were about him scoring for England or shagging Kylie Minogue and Cameron Diaz both at once. He didn't dream up tapdancing and fabulous music – Leo only wished that he did. This had been a most marvellous experience. Even if it wasn't real. He tapped at the pavement with his cane to check it out. It had a very real ring to it, it must be said.

Then they stopped, just the two of them – Emma and Leo – alone on the Embankment in the dead of the night. The music lifted them, exalted them, the moon swelled with joy and filled the sky. The stars exploded like fireworks. Their lips met and the sparkling taste of cham-pagne flooded Leo's brain. And, to be honest, that was the last thing he remembered.

Chapter Forty-One

I struggle to open my eyes. The daylight seems more harsh than usual and I put my hands over my eyes, but shafts of sunlight still pierce through them. I feel as if I've been hit over the head, drugged and am waking from a deep sleep, verging on the border of a coma. Conversely, I also feel like I haven't slept a wink, as if I've tossed and turned all night. My eyelids scrape over my eyeballs as I rub my eyes and force them open.

'Ahh!' I close them again. This can't be happening to me. I open them again and look down at myself. Yes. I'm still wearing my pyjamas and yet I'm not in my bed. I very definitely am not in my bed. 'Ahh!'

I've never been fond of heights. This isn't somewhere I'd normally choose to be. Particularly not in my nightwear. I force myself to look up. The view hasn't changed. And I have no idea why I'm waking up in one of the glass capsules on the giant ferris-wheel of the London Eye, high – very, very high – above the River Thames, clad only in ancient pyjamas bearing cartoon sheep.

'Fuckfuckfuck,' I mutter to myself. I'm alone in my pod, but all the other pods are filled with inquisitive people. In the one above me, a group of Japanese tourists take photographs of me.

I huddle by the bench in the centre of the floor. My only hiding place. The capsule moves interminably slowly, inching its way to the ground – it will be a good twenty minutes more before my humiliation is over. How the hell did I get here? It slowly comes back to me about the wonderful dream in which Leo took me in his arms and danced with me along the Embankment. I must have been sleepwalking. Add a propensity towards somnambulance to the growing list of other things that I've got to worry about. The people in the next pod are waving to me. I try to ignore them and when that fails, I wave back meekly.

'Please let this end,' I whimper. 'Please let this end.'

★

By the time Leo woke up, Isobel was already in the bathroom. He could hear her splashing away in the shower, so he dragged himself up and plodded through into the bathroom.

She was wrapping herself in a towel – considerably more fluffy since she'd arrived and Leo didn't think it was to do with a change of fabric conditioner – as he squeezed in behind her.

'Good morning.' Isobel kissed him. 'Sleep well?'

'I dreamed that I could tapdance last night.'

'That's nice.'

'Yes.' Leo flicked open the lid of the wicker washing basket next to him, so that Isobel could throw in her towel. Inside was a top hat – remarkably like the one he was wearing last night, in fact. Leo glanced down at it and gave Isobel a querying look which she blatantly ignored. 'I'm sure it wasn't anything to do with you.'

Isobel pouted. 'Of course not.'

'Of course not.'

She finished towelling herself and left the bathroom – grinning to herself if he wasn't mistaken.

Leo stood in front of the mirror and, once again, took in the wreckage that had become his face. It looked as if he'd been up tapdancing all night. This cannot go on, Leo thought; he was ageing in dog years since he'd met Isobel. He definitely had greying hair now. He wasn't sure that it wasn't starting to thin too. Horrors upon horrors. Leo examined his pate just in case. No imminent signs of balding, but if things carried on like this then he suspected it wouldn't be long before the shower would look as if a badger had died in it every time he washed his hair. Still, it had been very nice last night with Emma – more than worth the resulting exhaustion. It had brought back memories of old times. Good times. Maybe for a brief moment, Leo understood what sort of magic Emma longed for in their lives. As far as Leo was concerned, he seemed to have a surfeit of it at the moment. He sighed a melancholy little sigh and wondered where this would all end.

'I look like doggydoo,' he said to the mirror. Then he wagged his finger at it. 'And I don't want a word out of you.'

The capsule in which I'm entrapped finally circles around to the ground, by which time a crowd has gathered. As it comes to the platform for me to disembark, the London Eye staff look very bemused as to how I've managed to get in here in my nightwear without them noticing, and I hope they won't arrest me or ask me for a ticket because it appears that I don't have one of those either. It has been a very nice trip and it's only a shame that I was too terrified and humiliated to fully appreciate it.

The steward, open-mouthed, lets me out of the pod.

I call on all my reserves of dignity. 'Thank you,' I say politely. I'm grateful that the steward is too speechless to ask any searching questions.

Pulling my pyjamas tightly around me, I walk serenely through the gawping crowd. Will this trauma never end? I'm going to have to hail a taxi or blag my way onto a bus looking like this. Do I really have the bottle to pretend that fleecy jim-jams are the latest look? Somehow I'm sure that Leo is tied up in this, but I have to admit that I have no idea how. Even when I simply dream about him, he still manages to get me into a heap of trouble! There's definitely something going on.

I'm going to have to up the number of sessions I have with my psychiatrist. It's clear that the benefits of therapy haven't yet kicked in and there's no way I can carry on like this. They'll be locking me up and throwing away the key. What sort of woman, other than a mad one, wears her pyjamas in public?

I endure it as long as I can, holding my head high, smiling tightly – until I can bear it no longer and I break into a frantic run, scattering the crowd and trying to hang onto what is left of my fragile sanity.

Chapter Forty-Two

Grant made the assessment that Leo was enjoying a pleasant snooze while the world's money markets did exactly what they liked around him.

His friend's head was resting on his desk and there were gentle purring noises coming from his general direction. Grant went over and gave him a nudge. Leo snorted, then looked up and rubbed his eyes.

'A six-shag night?' Grant asked.

'No,' Leo said, shaking his head. They were now all used to the shower of glitter that accompanied it. 'Tapdancing.'

Grant shrugged as if it was an everyday thing. Nothing his unhinged little buddy did now surprised him.

'I'm knackered though,' Leo mumbled. 'I didn't know all that shuffle ball-change stuff was so exhausting.' He pushed himself upright and rubbed his hands together. 'Fancy the pub?'

'Sorry, mate. I can't,' Grant said, avoiding his friend's eyes. 'I'm taking someone out to lunch.'

'A client?'

'Something like that.'

'Oh.' Leo slumped back towards his desk. 'Catch you later then.'

'Later,' Grant agreed and headed towards the door. 'Make sure you get some beauty sleep before tonight.'

'Why?' Leo was suddenly alert. 'What's happening tonight?'

'For goodness sake, Leo! How can you forget?' His friend looked as if he had forgotten. Completely.

'The Thornton Jones annual bash,' Grant reminded him with a sigh.

'Oh no,' Leo groaned. 'Oh no. Four hours of boredom and back-stabbing.'

'You know you love it,' Grant said. 'Taking Isobel?'

'Oh no,' Leo groaned again. They both glanced over at Isobel who was talking to Old Baldy in his office. On cue, she winked at them.

'I don't suppose I've got any choice.' Leo looked visibly shaken. 'She's not the company party sort of girl. I dread to think what she'll get up to.'

'She might liven it up,' Grant said.

'That's what I'm extremely worried about.'

'I'm going to be late,' Grant said. 'I'll have to leave you to think about that.'

'Thanks.' Leo gingerly lowered his head back to his desk. 'You're all heart.'

Grant rushed for the elevator, but Lard headed him off at the pass. 'I hope you know what you're doing,' he said. 'Leo won't be a happy bunny if he finds out.'

'I know,' Grant admitted, glancing nervously over his shoulder to where his friend was fast asleep again at his desk. 'But it's a risk I'm prepared to take.'

Grant was actually taking Emma out to lunch, not a client, and he wasn't sure why he couldn't be absolutely straight with Leo about it. Was it because there was the sneaking suspicion that it wasn't really over between them? Or that it ever would be?

He'd taken a leaf out of Isobel's book and had arranged for them to have a picnic lunch together in the park. He hoped it would have them giggling and laughing together like a pair of schoolkids. Love and laughter hadn't figured in his life for quite a while and he wondered why. Maybe he was always so busy 'achieving' things that he never took the time to cultivate serious relationships and had been content to fill a few lonely hours with whoever happened to be passing.

It was difficult to know as a modern man when the right time was to settle down and load yourself up with responsibilities. Now you could get away with living the bachelor lifestyle until you were in your forties or even fifties, before you took yourself a much younger wife and started to produce replicas of yourself. It was the sort of thing men used to do in their twenties. But if you spent too long living the bachelor life it was hard to give that up once it became the norm. Even if he had someone to stay over for the weekend now, he began to feel claustrophobic. It was a trend that he wanted to address and, hopefully, reverse. Emma, of course, featured heavily in this plan.

He'd swung out of the Thornton Jones offices, collected the picnic bag from the local deli – hoping that Emma would be ecstatic over his choice of carefully-selected sandwiches and goodies – then he hailed a cab to take him to the gallery where Emma worked. Grant knew so little about her, except the stuff that he'd learned about her second-hand from Leo, and that wasn't nearly enough. He wanted to take time to get to know her better and he hoped that she'd feel the same.

Now they were sitting in Potter's Fields Square, a stone's throw from the gallery and, thankfully, the weather had been kind again. A defiant summer sunshine, determined to make London feel positively Mediterranean, warmed the air, took the chill from the damp ground and played with the leaves so that they formed a dappled shade. On the surface it appeared to be quite a romantic spot – the area bordered the Thames and was rich with history. It had a wonderful view of Tower Bridge and the trees were lush and green. But on closer inspection, the grass was scrubby and there was too much litter and every other person was a dosser sprawled out fast asleep for the day. It was very hard to be any kind of romantic hero these days.

He was sweating inside his suit and it might have been the sun or it might have been nerves. Grant slipped off his jacket. Emma sat primly on the grass, skirt tucked around her legs. She looked beautiful.

Tucking into a sandwich, she said, 'This is very thoughtful of you, Grant.'

'I'm a thoughtful kind of guy.' He wished he'd been thoughtful enough to bring a rug, but maybe that was going a bit too far. If he was very chivalrous he could have spread out his suit jacket on the ground for Emma to sit on, but then he'd have to wear it at work this afternoon stained with grass and dirt. And Emma might well drop mayonnaise or something on it. Not that it would be her fault, but it wouldn't look great. The practicalities of being a gentleman weren't a small consideration – no wonder so many of his peer group had chosen to abandon any attempt at it.

'I know. And I can't believe that I used to think you were such a ...' Emma stumbled to a halt.

'A tosser?'

'No, no, no. Such a Leo clone.'

'Still an insult?'

'You're very much your own person,' Emma assured him with a pat on his arm. 'And all the lovelier for it.'

This was going better than he expected, Grant thought. He'd always liked Emma, but she had often been brittle and controlling when she was with Leo. He preferred this softer side to her.

'I know that I'm one of Leo's friends . . .'

'His best friend,' Emma pointed out in between bites of sandwich.

Grant shrugged his acceptance. 'But do you think you could see me any other way?'

Emma looked puzzled. 'No. Of course not.'

'Not ever?'

'No,' Emma said, her frown deepening. 'What other way would I want to see you?'

Grant rolled over onto his stomach. Perhaps his best intentions had been just too subtle. Shouldn't a picnic automatically be viewed as a romantic overture? It was also very hard to be a romantic hero when women were so unused to being 'wooed' – for want of a better word. They might think they liked all that hearts and flowers stuff, but they actually wouldn't recognise it unless they were hit over the head with it. Or maybe it was because he turned down Emma's invitation to go into her flat the other night? Whatever way, she clearly didn't feel the same way about him as he was feeling about her. He was going to have to have a serious re-think of his strategy. 'It doesn't matter,' he said.

Emma picked at the olives he'd chosen. 'So how is Leo?' She pouted at him and it was heartbreakingly cute. 'Still in love?'

Grant nodded at her. 'And you?'

Emma nodded too.

'Thought so.' Grant smiled sadly and concentrated on his food.

'I dreamed about him last night,' she said with a sigh and stretched out on the grass.

'You weren't tapdancing?'

Emma turned to him. 'How did you know that?'

'A wild guess.' There was definitely something weird going on here and perhaps it was best not to get embroiled in it.

'We danced all along the Embankment,' she told him. 'It was very romantic.'

More romantic than a picnic in a scrotty park, it would seem.

Emma lowered her eyelashes. They were long and dark and Grant thought that he'd love to feel them brushing his cheeks. The cheeks on his face, he should make that thought clear, before he did sound too much like Leo.

'I woke up in one of the capsules on the London Eye,' Emma said. She looked up to see Grant register his surprise. 'Mad, eh?'

'How did you get there?'

161

'I've no idea,' Emma confessed. 'But it's not the action of a sane woman, is it?'

Grant shook his head, a worried expression on his face. There was *definitely* something weird going on.

'It made me realise how much I miss him,' Emma said. 'I thought he was driving me nuts when I was with him, but I'm going nuts even quicker without him.'

'Bummer,' Grant said, but his mind was racing. Did Isobel really have some sort of magical powers? Was she behind all these strange happenings?

'My mother thinks I shouldn't worry about the more usual qualities for a life partner; she thinks I should marry a man who's an animal in bed.'

Grant choked on his sandwich. Emma patted him on the back while he coughed. 'And Leo is?' he managed to ask when he finally found his voice.

'What?'

'An animal in bed?'

'Yes,' Emma said.

Grant cleared his throat. 'What kind of animal?'

'A sloth.'

Grant perked up. 'Really?'

'No.' Emma sighed with disappointment.

Chapter Forty-Three

L eo was in the lounge. He was wearing a rather natty dinner suit and having a terrible time with his bow tie. So far he'd managed to get himself into a half-nelson and bind himself to a potted plant. You could tell why he wasn't into bondage in a big way. Eventually, he gave up.

'This is a really big deal tonight, Isobel.' Leo was shouting to her because she was still in the bathroom. She'd been in there for hours. She might have been a fairy, but in some ways she was a typical woman. Fairy leg hair in his razor, fairy tights drying over the bath, fairy hair dye staining his towels. No. Not really. That was just a joke. Isobel didn't seem to have to worry about the normal sort of ablutions that human women did. One of the many benefits of being a magical creature was saving a fortune on leg-waxing and manicures. But something was causing the wand-waving to take an inordinate amount of time tonight.

'It's going to be full of stuffed shirts,' he went on. '*Important* stuffed shirts. The members of the board will be there. Top management. All the people who could stop my career dead in its tracks. Everyone will be on their best behaviour.' Leo was hoping for some sort of response here, but there wasn't one forthcoming. 'You included, I hope.' Still nothing. 'Promise me there'll be no funny stuff?'

While he was still straining to hear a reply, Isobel came into the room. She was wearing an old sack and was looking very scruffy. Her hair looked as if it had been back-combed by a combine harvester. Dirt smears emphasised her lovely cheekbones.

Leo stopped dead in his tracks. 'Interesting.'

'You think so?'

'Very retro,' he said. 'Somewhere around the Middle Ages.' Then he held out his bow tie. 'Do you do stuff with these?'

Isobel pulled out her wand.

163

'Of course you do.'

She waved her wand and, as if by magic, his bow tie twiddled itself into a perfect knot. His fantastic – and very useful – fairy friend smiled and said, 'You look wonderful.'

'Thank you.' Emma used to love Leo wearing a dinner suit. She'd said it made him look like George Clooney. Which had always made Leo feel on top of the world. But he wouldn't think about Emma now as that would be too, too sad and Leo was feeling happy – if more than a little apprehensive. Leo admired himself in the mirror and, without him even asking for its opinion, it whistled back at him.

'And me?' Isobel gave him a twirl.

Leo rubbed his hand over his chin. 'That is a really bad question to ask a man. In fact, the worst possible question.'

Isobel waited patiently.

'Your bum doesn't look big in it,' he said. 'That's the best I can manage.'

'I read the fairy story *Cinderella*,' Isobel told him. 'She looked just like this before she went to the ball.'

'Yes,' Leo agreed, 'but if you're going for the Cinderella look, then something a little less "before" and a little more "after" would be nice.'

Isobel giggled and twirled round again. There was a small explosion – something Leo was becoming more used to experiencing in his lounge room – and a shower of the ubiquitous glitter. Suddenly she'd transformed before his very eyes. Isobel was now wearing a shimmering, gossamer evening gown and her hair was swept up revealing her long, slender neck. She looked . . . well . . . extraordinarily shagable. Sorry. He was a bloke. It was the best he could come up with at short notice.

'Better?' she asked.

Leo was filled with all sorts of conflicting emotions. His voice came out as a squeak again, as it was prone to do these days. 'I think so.'

'Now we can go to the ball.' Isobel took his arm.

'I've booked a taxi,' he told her. Then he stopped short. 'The poor bastard isn't sitting outside in a pumpkin overrun by bloody mice, is he?'

Isobel laughed. 'I think you're getting to know me too well.'

Leo turned to her and held her close. 'I'd never know all there is to know about you,' he said. 'Not if I lived to be a thousand years old.'

'That can be arranged too,' she said, and kissed him on the nose. They headed for the door while the night was still young and while Leo still had a career.

164

'Be good tonight, will you?' he pleaded.

'I'll be *awesome,*' Isobel assured him.

And that's what worried Leo. That's what worried him a lot.

Chapter Forty-Four

The Thornton Jones annual bash was always held at somewhere terribly swizzy in one of the most fashionable areas of London – no cheap jaunts on some scraggy old tub on the River Thames for them. Oh no. Champagne flowed, canapés were consumed with gusto. This time the destination was a large white, double-fronted Georgian mansion – the type where you could imagine a horse and carriage pulling up outside. Instead, Isobel and Leo clattered up in their smoking diesel London cab and Leo wished that he'd booked a big white limo, but he decided to keep quiet about it. There was no knowing what would happen if he voiced that thought to Isobel. Actually, he knew *exactly* what would happen – and explaining the sudden appearance of a limo in the middle of the street to his work colleagues might prove a bit tricky.

The lights were blazing in all the windows and there was a bustle of people arriving at the same time – immaculately dinner-suited men and slender ballgowned women. Unfortunately, they were Leo's toffee-nosed colleagues – but then at an office party that was hardly surprising. White ribbons fluttered from rows of standard bay trees at the entrance and there were huge bunches of silver and white balloons tied to the wrought-iron railings outside.

Leo paid the cab driver and they stepped out into the fray. This was a very grand affair and Isobel's eyes were out on stalks. Clearly they didn't throw pretentious parties like this where she came from. This might have been a sweeping generalisation but Leo wouldn't mind betting that in fairyland they all sat around on toadstools and sang folk songs to the accompaniment of hand-carved pipes. Isobel wouldn't know what had hit her – and Leo was rather frightened that Thornton Jones would come to feel the same.

All the company's top nobs – and he chose that word advisedly – were in attendance. The reception area was draped with white chiffon and thousands of tiny twinkling lights. It looked like a fairy grotto. Or what Leo would assume a fairy grotto looked like. Groups of people were having their official photographs taken by a woodland setting that the photographer had created – frondy ferns, trees laden with fairy-lights, some sort of waterfall painting in the background. Obligingly Isobel and Leo stood in line and were duly snapped by the harassed-looking photographer. Leo saw tears filling Isobel's eyes.

'Okay?' he asked.

She nodded quietly.

'Homesick?'

'It seems so very far away,' she said, and Leo squeezed her hand.

'Is that what it's like?' He flicked a look at the fake woods behind them.

'Yes,' she said. 'But not so tacky.'

In the resulting photograph, Leo looked rather cheesy and as if he should be playing the piano in a down-market cocktail bar. Isobel, of course, looked like a cover model – except she was air-brushed in real life. So many heads had snapped round as she'd passed by that Leo thought that there'd be a lot of stiff necks in the office tomorrow. He felt as if he was on the arm of Liv Tyler or Kate Beckinsale or Keira Knightley or someone equally famous and gorgeous.

Isobel also stood out a mile because she was the only female there whose skin was the colour of pure, driven snow.

'Why are some human women orange?' she whispered to him as they watched two women a deep shade of Dale Winton drift by in their tight, strapless evening gowns.

'It's fake tan,' he told her. 'They get themselves sprayed.'

'Why?'

'It's the fashion.'

She gave him a puzzled look.

'To make them look more attractive.'

'And do they?'

'No,' Leo said. 'They just look more orange.'

'Should I do it to myself?' She fished in her evening bag for her wand. 'It wouldn't take a moment.'

'No. No.' He gripped her hand. Damn. Leo hoped that she'd left that bloody thing behind. 'I like you just the way you are.'

Before she had any more time to think about giving herself a new paint job, Leo tugged her towards the main reception. The champagne

167

was already flowing. White-coated waiters were delivering it to eager, waiting hands. There was a string quartet in the corner and, for a moment, he was overwhelmed by a flashback to last night and his superb dance routine with Emma. A pang of something indefinable hit his heart. Leo used to bring Emma to this party – and she used to hate it. All of it.

Isobel squeezed his arm and looked at him tenderly. 'Okay?'

'I'm fine,' he said. But he didn't sound fine.

Grant and Lard were lurking in the corner looking furtive. Both guys stared slightly goggle-eyed at Isobel as the couple approached them. At least Leo assumed it was Isobel they were smitten with and that his tuxedo wasn't responsible for turning their heads.

'What are you two reprobates up to?' he asked genially.

'Nothing,' Grant said miserably.

'In a *big* way,' Lard agreed. They both looked down at their drinks.

'Is that really just orange juice?'

'Career prospects damage limitation plan. We are both going to stay as sober as judges.'

'Bugger.' A waiter appeared at Leo's elbow with a tray of drinks. He took the orange juice too. If all of his *compadres* were planning on staying upright, then he felt he should too. How dull! The only fun at these parties was to get absolutely bladdered.

'Have you ever had strong drink?' he asked Isobel.

'Lavender-flower poteen,' she told him in all seriousness.

'Have this.' He handed a glass of orange juice to her too. 'I've never seen you drunk and I don't really want to start tonight.'

'Leo,' she sighed. 'You worry too much.' She took her glass of orange juice and swapped it for a flute of champagne, fluttering her eyelashes at the waiter as she did. Seeing her with a glass in her hand like that reminded him of the night they first met on Tower Bridge – and didn't that seem like a million lifetimes ago?

Isobel grinned at him as she sipped it, her nose wrinkling as the bubbles tickled it. 'Ooo. That's nice.'

Leo's heart sank. 'I don't think I worry enough,' he said. And then Aulden Hinley-Smythe, the oldest and most crusty partner in Thornton Jones came towards them.

'Leo!' He clapped Leo on the back even though he had never before spoken to him in his entire life. To Mr Hinley-Smythe, Leo was one of the ranks of minions at Thornton Jones – an ever-present annoyance, but no one really wanted to acknowledge their existence. A bit like cold sores or athlete's foot.

Leo nodded in greeting and tried to look like a responsible member of staff. Seeing as he wasn't roaring drunk as usual this wasn't as hard as it might have been. 'Mr Hinley-Smythe.'

'Aulden,' he said magnanimously.

Leo would have liked to bet that if he addressed him as that in the corridor by the coffee machine tomorrow he'd be given the order of the boot.

'I hear you've been responsible for some pretty nifty footwork in the market recently.' Good old Aulden tapped the side of his nose.

'Er, well . . .' Leo tried not to look at Isobel. Who had on her butter-wouldn't-melt-in-my-mouth face. 'Teamwork.'

'Modesty,' the older man noted. 'I like that in a man. Thornton Jones needs fearless young blood like you.'

'Yes.' Leo didn't like to tell him that he was quaking in his boots and that if Aulden Hindley-Smythe really knew who – or what – was responsible for his clients' good fortune then he would have been fired on the spot. Either that or they'd have kidnapped Isobel and would have held her against her will, forcing her to perform international money market miracles at their evil instruction.

He clapped Leo on the back again – rather vigorously for an old bloke, if you asked Leo – and he coughed. 'I'm going to be keeping an eye on you from now on, young Leo.'

'Oh good,' Leo muttered.

Mr Hinley-Smythe gave him the wink of the ancient and lecherous and – thank heavens! – moved away.

'How exactly *did* you manage that little market manoeuvre, Leo?' Grant asked.

'It was not entirely of my doing,' Leo admitted.

Then the Master of Ceremonies came to his rescue before he was pressed to explain himself. 'Ladies and Gentlemen! Dinner is served!'

Leo took Isobel's arm. 'Come on. The next part of the ordeal is about to begin.'

As they passed yet another smiling waiter, Isobel grabbed yet another glass of champagne. Leo felt that this was going to be a rather long night.

Chapter Forty-Five

On the stage at the front of the ornately-decorated ballroom, one of Thornton Jones's most obnoxious and voluble managing partners, Joshua Hartnell, was coming to the end of a rambling speech. Instead of looking round at the wonderful flower arrangements, Leo tuned in for the last few seconds.

'. . . and it's teamwork that makes Thornton Jones the company it is today. The team that plays together, stays together . . .'

There was a smattering of assenting applause. Leo tugged at his shirt collar and noticed that Isobel was also bored to tears – there was probably not much in the way of corporate politics in the land of fairies – and, more alarmingly, she was also a bit squiffy.

Hartnell blathered on. 'So, raise your glass in a toast to Thornton Jones!'

Leo picked up his orange juice and looked at it in disgust. There were times in your life when being sober was simply not appropriate. And this was one of them. They all shuffled to their feet, raising their glasses. 'Thornton Jones!'

Isobel raised her glass a moment too late. 'Thornton Jones!' she slurred loudly and then hiccoughed. Oh dear. Leo forced her back into her chair.

Joshua Hartnell finally gave up his burgeoning stage career and sat down again. A rather middle-aged band in sombre dinner suits ambled on in his place and started to knock out a few watered-down middle-of-the-road pop standards.

Isobel stifled a yawn. Perhaps, Leo thought, he should get her another drink and see if it would send her to sleep completely. 'We can go home soon.'

'I wouldn't dream of it,' she said, forcing herself to perk up. 'Dance?'

'I can't think of anything I'd rather do,' he answered, hoping that fairies got irony.

The dance floor was slowly filling with couples dancing stiffly. As well as being unable to express emotion and remember birthdays, British men were entirely incapable of dancing properly – unless, of course, they became tapdancing maestros on the Embankment in their dreams. Leo noticed that his shortlived skill had departed and they shuffled round to a couple of old, and rather inexpertly played, Abba tunes.

Isobel yawned again. 'Leo? Is this what it's going to be like all night?'

'Oh, yes. All of it.'

She frowned. 'Maybe I can liven things up a bit.'

'Oh no,' he said. 'Oh no. Definitely not. This is how it always is. This is how we like it.'

But before he could forcibly restrain her, Isobel produced her wand.

'Not that thing,' Leo begged. 'Put it away, Isobel. Put it away *now*.'

Unfortunately for Leo, Isobel's face merely took on a mischievous expression. She waved her wand at the band – who instantly livened up. Their staid dinner suits became all sparkly and the music shifted up a tempo. Suddenly, they were all in time with each other. Everyone in the ballroom looked at them in surprise. Except for Leo.

Instead, he glared at Isobel. 'You promised me,' he said, wagging his finger at her. 'You said you'd behave. I remember it distinctly.'

Isobel giggled wildly. Oh flip. The band started to play 'Saturday Night Fever'. Oh very flip. 'Isobel.' Leo put on his stern voice. The voice that meant he would stand no nonsense. 'I'm warning you.'

And, of course, she zapped Leo with her wand. A jolt of electricity surged through his body and his limbs started to twitch. Against his will Leo headed towards the middle of the dance floor. 'I mean it, Isobel,' he heard himself say.

The music was taking him over. Last night Leo was Fred Astaire, tonight he was clearly destined to become John Travolta. His fingers were clicking of their own volition and his legs had developed a definite strut. 'This isn't funny, Isobel.'

The other dancers on the floor looked very bemused, but nevertheless parted for him. Leo wiggled his hips in the style of Travolta and he knew, instinctively, that this was going to be deeply humiliating. 'Now I'm very cross,' he shouted at Isobel.

She simply laughed at him and waved her wand at the gathered crowd, who started to clap in time with his gyrations.

'Oh no.' With a series of involuntary jerks, Leo whipped off his jacket and whirled it round his head before skimming it across the dance floor. This was too embarrassing for words. 'Now I'm very cross indeed!'

Starting to dance, Leo strutted his stuff up and down the floor. At least he had an appreciative audience who were cheering him on. He would, however, kill Isobel when he got her alone.

Grant and Lard were standing at the edge of the dance floor, faces fixed with expressions of utter bewilderment.

'Help me,' Leo gasped as he shimmied past them. 'Help me. This is all Isobel's doing.'

Grant turned to Lard and, while he was performing a few steps from The Hustle, Leo heard him say, 'Has Leo gone completely mad?'

'Yes,' Lard said, and they both looked at their orange juice, dumped their glasses and grabbed a bottle of champagne each from a passing waiter. None of which helped Leo.

The song was – thankfully – coming to an end. Leo finished his 1970s' disco routine with an exuberant twirl and the splits. Yes, really. The crowd cheered wildly. Even Grant and Lard clapped appreciatively. Bastards.

Leo bowed graciously, taking leave of his adoring audience, and then marched over to Isobel to give her what-for. Grabbing her elbow, he steered her out of harm's way. 'You and I need to talk, young lady.'

Isobel pouted. 'I'm just starting to have fun.'

'Yes, I know. That's what I'm afraid of.'

'Everyone else is too.'

They glanced back at the dance floor. The band were playing Lulu's 'Shout'. Everyone was on the dance floor, including the stuffy old partners and, most shocking of all, Grant and Lard. They were all strutting their funky stuff. Leo had never seen such slick movers – his good self excepted.

'Is this your fault too?'

'I just loosened them up a little,' she confessed.

'You are a terrible woman.'

'And you're a great dancer,' she said.

Isobel and Leo started to laugh. 'Come on.' He took her by the hand. 'I deserve a drink.'

Much, much later and they were sitting in the corner of the room on the floor. Isobel was cuddled up against Leo and they were both swigging from a bottle of champagne as they watched the mayhem continue on the dance floor. All decorum had flown out of the window and now everyone was doing a synchronised routine to the theme tune from *Men in Black*. Grant and Lard were leading from the front and they were definitely bouncing with it and letting it slide. There was the neck work. And the freeze. Leo shook his head in wonderment and deposited glitter in his champagne.

'I can quite categorically state, without fear of contradiction, that I've never been to a Thornton Jones ball quite like this.' He hugged his fabulous fairy friend to him. 'You're the only person I know who's more badly behaved than I am.'

Isobel grinned. 'I'll take that as a compliment.'

Leo tilted her chin towards him and kissed those delicious wild straw-berry lips. 'You are a lot of fun to be with, Fairy Isobel.' He pulled her to her feet. 'Come on,' he said. 'Let's go home.'

Chapter Forty-Six

L eo was standing at the edge of the pavement trying to hail a cab. It wasn't proving easy. Three had already sailed by without stopping. Another one approached. He gave his most shrill whistle. 'Taxi!'

It also went straight past. Leo was beginning to wonder if it was his aftershave. 'Bugger!'

Isobel was waiting patiently by the wrought-iron railings, fiddling with one of the huge bunches of balloons. Leo went back to her, head hung miserably, thwarted in his attempts to perform a manly task. 'I should have ordered one before we left.'

'It doesn't matter,' she said brightly.

'Can't you wave your wand and get us one?'

'There's another way.'

'I'm not walking,' Leo complained. 'It's too far. And I'm too pissed.'

Isobel grabbed him by the arm and started pulling him down the street. 'Come on.'

'I'm not walking.'

She hurried him along and Leo suddenly noticed that she had liberated one of the bunches of balloons and was trailing them in her wake. There must have been thirty of them and Isobel didn't look inconspicuous.

'You can't nick those.' Leo was aghast. A thieving fairy! 'Someone might notice.'

'Don't be an old stick-in-the-mud,' she said, hustling him into a secluded side street.

'I can't believe you.' And when Isobel started to cuddle up to him: 'Don't think you're going to win me round with that old ploy.'

'Put your arms round me,' Isobel instructed.

Leo sighed and did as he was told. 'Did I ever tell you that you're one of the bossiest women I know? Well, apart from Emma. Who was well known for her bossiness.'

Isobel wasn't listening. 'Hold tight,' she said.

Obligingly, Leo held tight.

And then he realised that he was floating. Off the ground. OFF THE GROUND! The balloons were carrying them upwards, past the windows in the ballroom where the party was still in full swing, past the roof of the building. Up, up and away.

Leo was clinging very tightly to Isobel. He realised that all that was between him and sudden death was a few festive balloons.

'This isn't funny either,' he said, on the point of hyperventilation.

'Ssh, Leo,' she cooed at him. 'Relax.'

Relax? Leo was rigid with terror. Or maybe excitement. 'Shag me sideways on a scooter,' he muttered under his breath.

The wind caught them and whisked them ever higher. 'Oh. Oh. Oh.'

Isobel laughed gaily and they soared above the streets, above London and, to Leo's horror, just below the stars.

Grant and Lard came out of the party a few minutes later and – having also failed in their quest to hail a cab – started to walk along the street.

Grant sighed heavily and flicked up the collar of his coat. It had been a strange night in many ways. 'You know that I've fallen hopelessly in love?'

'With me?' Lard asked.

'No. Even though you're a very nice mover,' Grant said. He sighed again. 'With Emma.'

'Ooo!' Lard exclaimed. 'That's a very bad place to be.'

'I know.' It would have been nice to have had someone with him tonight. Someone laughing and joking with him and loving him, like Leo had.

'Presumably the reason why you're sighing so much is that you are completely and utterly invisible to her.'

'Yep.'

'You have my heartfelt commiserations.'

'Thank you.'

'She's still utterly smitten with Leo?'

'Got it in one.' Grant scuffed the pavement with his shoe.

'What are you going to do about it?'

'I have no idea.'

High in the sky, a flash of white caught their eye and they both looked up. Amid the clouds, and lit up by the brilliant moon, Leo and

Isobel sailed past them, holding tightly to the strings of a bunch of helium balloons that it looked like they'd nicked from the party.

Lard was blinking rapidly. 'I didn't really just see that, did I?'

Grant blinked himself and took another look to make sure. 'No.'

'And you didn't see it either?'

'No.'

'Good. Good,' Lard said. He exhaled shakily. 'So we didn't see Leo flying across the sky on a bunch of balloons?'

'No.' Grant jammed his hands deep into his pockets. He didn't think this night could get any stranger.

Lard puffed expansively. 'I was quite worried there for a minute.'

Grant turned his gaze to the sky once more. Leo, legs dangling over the rooftops, was nearly out of view. 'Me too.'

They were still way, way too high for Leo's liking. And he'd always thought he'd like to go on a balloon ride, but he had imagined that he would do it in a basket or something rather more substantial than this. That was, of course, until this devilish little fairy dropped into his life from who knows where. Another thing Leo was beginning to realise about Isobel was that he knew so little about her. And this was an awful admission, but he sort of felt the same about Emma. They'd spent so long together and yet he now wondered if he had really made enough effort to get to know her. Leo now felt that they had somehow glossed over the surface of a relationship, never really talking about what made each of them tick, and he was sad that he'd missed that opportunity. But Leo couldn't dwell on it now, as he was too busy hanging onto a bunch of balloons and trying not to die. But in a bizarre way, he was actually starting to enjoy it. Floating free of all ties to the ground was a rather nice feeling. The moon was dazzling at this close proximity, the view of the rooftops of London like something out of *Mary Poppins*. Leo felt like breaking out into a corny song, but appreciated that it would completely and utterly spoil the mood.

I don't want to spend another night tapdancing with Leo, as wonderful as it was. Nor, even more importantly, do I want to wake up on the London Eye. So I stay up late, drink too much cheap wine and watch trashy television until my eyes roll with tiredness. I brush my teeth, snuggle into the sheep pyjamas, select my cuddly toy for the night and am just about to go to bed.

I stare out of the window at the view, thinking, Out there, some-where, is Leo. Leo doing things, having a life without me. Sitting on the edge of my windowsill, gazing into the clear, sharp night, I wonder where he might be. Reaching up to draw my curtains, I see Leo and Isobel float past on the breeze, clinging to a bunch of balloons. I blink. Am I asleep already? Is this another Leo-based dream? I'm sure I'm awake. Almost sure. Has an excess of wine made me hallucinate? I'll have to cut back on the booze if this is the effect it's going to have on me. I blink again. No. It's definitely Leo and his new woman in the sky. High in the sky. Beneath a bunch of ballons. I shudder. This is it – I've lost my marbles completely. All the counselling I've been having is far, far too late. I can feel myself starting to hyperventilate. Drawing the curtains briskly, I pull all my soft toys off the shelf and throw them into my bed. Jumping in beside them, I tug the duvet over my head and pray for morning.

Leo could see his flat in the distance and they were approaching it at a fair pace. The trees shivered as they passed. This had been, he had to concede, infinitely more interesting than getting a cab home. And some of the stories that cabbies told could be very amusing. They started to descend, slowly, gently and then landed on the pavement outside with not so much as a bump.

'Perfect landing,' Leo complimented his pilot and tried to ignore the surge of relief at being on terra firma once more.

Isobel smiled at him. Then she looked a little dizzy. Leo thought that the champagne had finally caught up with her. She sagged into his arms and he noticed that all the leaves on the trees had drooped too.

'Are you okay?'

'I'm very tired,' Isobel admitted.

She'd gone very pale and seemed so fragile that it tugged at his heart. She looked like a hologram that was fading. 'Let's get you inside.' He kept the concern from his voice. 'You've had far too much excitement for one night.'

Leo scooped her up into his arms and was frightened by how insub-stantial she felt.

Chapter Forty-Seven

I stand outside a splendid Georgian house in Harley Street. A small gold plate on the smart black door reads *Dr P. Sloane, Psychiatrist.* The P, I think, is for Pricey. Pressing the bell for the umpteenth time, I bash the brass knocker against its plate and hammer loudly at the solid door.

A milk-float pulls up and the milkman jumps out, passing me by to place two pints of red top on Dr P. Sloane's doorstep. He tips his hat to me and then jumps back in his cart and drives further down the road to continue gaily on his round, whistling tunelessly, seemingly unmoved by the crisis that is taking place in front of him. Perhaps there are frantic patients trying to beat down the psychiatrist's door every morning.

I check my watch. It's early, but not that early. Shouldn't a doctor be up and about by seven o'clock? Particularly when she has desperate patients. And I'm definitely desperate. A lone jogger puffs past, red-faced and sweating. Perhaps I should take up jogging. It's supposed to be good for improving both the physical and emotional state – and my emotional state could definitely do with some improvement.

I've left a dozen messages on my psychiatrist's answerphone since about five-thirty this morning, when I decided I couldn't bear lying in bed thinking about Leo whizzing across the sky for a moment longer. The woman said she'd be available 24/7 – her words, not mine – and that I should call whenever I need her. Well, I need her and I've been calling. So where the hell is she?

'Come on! Come on!' I yell into the letterbox. The morning's refuse collection is starting to take place. The men in their orange fluorescent jackets are giving me strange looks as they hoist the black refuse sacks into the waiting lorry. Pulling my coat around me, I lean nearer to the door.

'I haven't got all day,' I mutter to myself. At this rate, my sanity won't last until tea-time. Opening the letterbox again, I peer inside. *Nada.* All

I can see is the vast emptiness of the hall with its acres of black and white chequered floor tiles. 'I haven't got all day,' I shout into it.

I pace up and down outside on the pavement. 'I pay this woman a fortune,' I shout to the watching refuse collectors. 'An *absolute* fortune. You'd think she'd be available when my life is crashing around me.' They hurry about their work.

Eventually, a dishevelled-looking woman in a tired velour dressing-gown half-opens the door. I push my way inside. 'Emergency,' I bark. I know she'll agree when she hears this. She might even get a book out of it.

'Good morning, Emma,' the psychiatrist says sleepily, and bends to collect her milk from the doorstep before following me inside.

I'm lying on the psychiatrist's couch. The psychiatrist, nursing a cup of tea, is still in her dressing-gown. The room is supposed to be relaxing, but I find it oppressive. It looks like a gangster's office. All brown leather chairs with green glass reading lamps next to them and pictures of race-horses on the wall. It isn't what you could call feminine. What does that say about Dr Sloane?

I'm in full flow. 'Tapdancing,' I say. 'I spent all night tapdancing. And I thought it was a dream, but I woke up on the London Eye in nothing but my pyjamas. Do you have any idea how humiliating that is?'

Dr Sloane scribbles on her notepad.

'And now I think I've gone completely mad. They were floating across the bloody sky last night,' I prop myself up on one elbow and raise my voice, '*on balloons*. Leo and his gorgeous new girlfriend. I wasn't asleep, I was wide awake. There's no way that was a dream.'

Dr Sloane scribbles again.

'That's not normal, is it?' I say.

The psychiatrist stifles a yawn.

'I know there's something funny going on,' I continue, 'but I don't know what. I'm sure it's down to this new woman of his.'

More scribbling. 'You can't blame everything on Leo's new girlfriend,' Dr Sloane tells me. 'She's just an ordinary woman. She has no hold over Leo.'

This is not what I want to hear. I want to hear that Leo is under some sort of siren spell and that as soon as she releases him, he'll come back to me. But, of course, that isn't what you pay psychiatrists for.

'You can do what you like to me,' I say, flopping back down on the couch. I have a cup of tea too, but as yet it's untouched. 'Hypnotise me. Stick me with pins . . .'

'Acupuncture,' the psychiatrist interjects.

'Give me strong drugs. Lots of them. Or one of those useless sodding self-help CDs. I don't care.' I feel my eyes prick with tears. 'Do whatever you like. I just need to stop thinking about Leo.'

With a well-practised move, the psychiatrist hands me a tissue. On cue, I start to cry.

'You have an unhealthy attraction to bad boys,' Dr Sloane says in her most soothing voice.

'But Leo isn't bad, he's just . . .'

The psychiatrist flicks through her notes. 'Unreliable, untidy, infuriating, unpunctual and unusually irritating. We've discussed this before. Several times.'

'But I can't stop thinking about him.'

Dr Sloane gives me an ingratiating smile. 'That's what letting go of a bad boy is all about.'

I burst into a bout of fresh tears. 'I don't want to let go of him. I love him!'

Chapter Forty-Eight

The brashly-lit offices of Thornton Jones were filled with very peaky-looking staff. There was the low-key air of a corporate hangover and sales of Resolve in nearby chemist's shops had soared.

Leo, however, was full of beans. He wasn't sure if it was to do with surviving a near-death experience *à la* helium balloon, but he felt full of the joys of spring or summer or possibly all of the seasons rolled together. It seemed he was alone in this. Even Isobel looked sickly. Her skin was normally pale and porcelain-like, but today she looked as white as a ghost and even a bit transparent in parts.

They'd caught a taxi together to the office and she'd sat wanly in the back, gazing out of the window. Leo wondered if she had used up too many of her magic powers last night – if that was possible. He didn't have a clue how these things worked.

Leo gave her arm a gentle squeeze. 'Are you sure you're okay?'

Isobel nodded weakly.

'You could have thrown a sickie,' he said.

She looked at him blankly.

'A duvet day,' he elaborated. 'You could have stayed in bed.'

'I wanted to be with you,' she told him tiredly.

'Well,' Leo said, giving her a kiss on the nose, 'that's understandable.'

She smiled good-humouredly at him.

'I'll see you later then,' he said.

Isobel went off towards her office, listlessly, and didn't see Leo's frown.

Grant was sitting on Lard's desk with their traditional morning pile of pastries heaped in front of them. They must both have hangovers too, despite their flirtations with orange juice, as Lard was picking his way cautiously through a *pain au chocolat* and not demolishing it whole as was his usual modus operandi.

Leo sat on the other side of the desk and nicked a pastry too.

'Good party?' Grant said.

'Excellent!'

'Manage to get a taxi home?' Lard asked.

'Yeah.'

'Thought so,' Lard said, and he and Grant exchanged one of their looks.

Leo concentrated on the delicious custard in the middle of his pastry.

'You're a very nice dancer,' Grant said.

'Thank you. You two were giving it plenty as well.'

They both nodded in a considered manner.

'I need to talk to you.' Grant took Leo by the arm and steered him away from Lard's desk. This must be serious if Lard wasn't party to it. Those two were like the Marx Brothers – sharing everything in a slightly irritating, but comical manner.

They headed over to the coffee machine and Grant went through the palaver of getting two revolting cups of coffee for them whilst avoiding Leo's eyes.

'Leo,' he said, as he handed him a polystyrene cup, 'I've got a bit of a problem.'

'We aren't allowed to have problems,' Leo reminded him. 'Company directive. We can have issues or situations, but not problems.'

'This isn't a work matter,' Grant said, 'and I definitely have a problem.'

Leo shrugged, trying to make light of it as was his way. 'Haven't we all?'

'Well,' Grant ploughed on, 'this is a bit delicate.'

'A blokes' problem?'

'You could say that.'

'I just did.'

'Leo. Shut the fuck up and listen.'

As his friend looked like he might be inclined to hit him, Leo did as instructed.

'I've got a problem that I want to discuss with you. Seriously.'

Leo's mind was racing. 'Floppy todger?' He punched his friend playfully on the shoulder.

Grant sighed. 'No,' he said. 'A bit too perky, if anything.'

Leo waited for an explanation as he'd no idea what else Grant could want to discuss with him. His friend took a deep breath. 'I'm in love,' he said eventually.

Leo was taken aback. Grant wasn't normally moved to say such things. In all the time Leo had known him, he didn't think he'd ever come out with the 'L' word. He was more resolutely a bachelor than Leo ever was. 'This is a bit sudden.'

'Well, yeah.' Grant looked embarrassed. 'I suppose so.'

'Anyone I know?'

'Well.' Grant rubbed at his hair. 'As a matter of fact, yes.'

Leo waited again. And he ran through all the possible contenders he knew from the office. Slack Suzy from the third floor. Easy Elizabeth from Human Resources. Titanic Tania with Triple C tits on reception. They had discussed the charms of these women, and more, many a time. In a very politically correct way, of course.

Grant was chewing at his lip. 'Emma,' he said. 'I'm in love with Emma.'

Leo's brain trawled through the names of their female colleagues to no avail. 'Who's Emma?'

'Oh, Leo,' his friend sighed.

Leo was nearly rendered speechless, but managed to stammer, 'Em . . . Emma? *My* Emma?'

Grant nodded.

Leo leaned against the wall for support. 'You and Emma? Emma and you?' He felt breathless. 'I can't believe this. You're supposed to be my best friend.'

Leo's supposed best friend's jaw set. 'And?'

'And?' Leo ran a hand through his hair in exasperation. 'Emma's my girlfriend.'

'I'm not sure that Emma – or Isobel – would see it that way.'

'Ex-girlfriend, then,' he said. '*Barely* ex-girlfriend. My side of the bed's probably not had time to go cold yet.' A sudden thought hit him. 'You haven't, have you?'

'Don't be ridiculous.' Grant glowered at him. A very Heathcliff, slightly unhinged sort of glower.

This was extraordinary news. Grant and Emma! 'Anyway,' Leo said, struggling to regroup his scattered senses, 'you can't be with Emma. What about her new fiancé, Stephen or Stefan or whatever the hell he's called?' Due to the shock he'd almost forgotten that someone else was already warming up his side of the bed.

'New fiancé?'

Clearly Grant didn't know about this little development. Then his friend laughed out loud. 'New fiancé? Oh Leo. One day I would like to visit your planet. It must be wonderful.'

Leo had no idea what he was talking about.

'So,' Grant continued, 'you have a problem with me and Emma getting together?'

'Yes,' Leo said. 'I have a slight *issue* with it.' This possibly wasn't a rational response. Perhaps he should be clapping Grant on the back and wishing him well and telling him about all the cute little things Emma could do with her tongue if you begged long enough. Leo couldn't even contemplate that they might complete Full Docking Manoeuvres together! He closed his eyes. This couldn't be happening. 'Actually, I have a big *problem* with it.'

'Why?' Grant said. 'You didn't hesitate to dump her for Isobel.'

'She dumped me.'

'Oh for heaven's sake, Leo. Get into the real world. Neither of you are fifteen any more. Isn't it time you grew up and started behaving like an adult?'

'Presumably that would involve me being happy for you to get low down and dirty with Emma?' Leo started to pace the floor. If he wasn't very much mistaken, he'd say they were squaring up to each other. 'I've seen how you treat your women.'

'I think that's a fine statement coming from you.' Grant jabbed his finger at him. 'You never loved Emma.'

'I did,' Leo shouted. 'I *do*.' His breath was coming in ragged pants, he was so out of condition. Leo thought he'd die on the spot if Grant hit him. Don't get him wrong, he adored Isobel. How could he not be blown away by someone from another world with the magical powers that she had? Leo would be the first to admit that she had turned his head so much that it was still spinning. In one moment, his life was literally turned upside down by her. But that didn't mean he'd simply forgotten about Emma. On the contrary, he still felt far too much for her, if the truth was known. 'I *do*,' he repeated. Leo's voice was barely audible but he said, 'The problem is I do still love her.'

Grant's face looked sad and defeated. 'And – strange and foolish woman that she is – she's still very much in love with you.'

'I can't help that,' Leo said. The ridiculous thing was that it gave him a thrill just to hear Grant say it.

'I think you can, Leo. You could let her go. Don't you want to see Emma find someone else to love?'

'Yes. Eventually. But not you.'

'That's a very selfish attitude.'

184

It would be utter torture seeing Emma with Grant. Leo might have to socialise with them and stuff like that. It would be impossible. How could Leo tell him that? They were blokes – they didn't discuss such matters of the heart. 'I think you'll find that once women have worshipped at the altar of Leo, they have great difficulty accepting a "normal" man.'

'And now you're testiculating.' Office-speak for waving his arms and talking bollocks.

Grant was right. But Leo didn't really want to face this. He'd rather Emma *was* engaged to some dodgy Bulgarian chappy called Stefan than see her with Grant. 'I can't help it,' he said. 'There's very little I can do about it.'

'There is,' Grant said flatly. 'I want you to ask Isobel to help.'

'Isobel?'

'I've seen the things she's been doing, Leo.' Grant stared at him evenly. 'I witnessed your impromptu balloon flight.'

'Ah.'

'I know that she can do these things. This is a very small favour to ask,' he said, his voice rising. 'Can't she help me too?'

'Ssh,' Leo hissed. 'You're not meant to know that she's a ...' He glanced round in alarm '... a *thingy*.'

'Or is that because she isn't really a ...' now Grant looked round ... a *thingy* at all?'

'Ssh,' Leo hissed again. 'Don't say that! Of course she is. How else can you explain the things that she does?'

'But she just does them for you?'

'Well,' Leo admitted, 'as a matter of fact she does.'

'Sometimes, mate,' Grant spat back, 'you can be a right royal pain in the arse.'

'You're the one trying to steal my ex-girlfriend.'

'Get a life, Leo.'

'You are going the right way to be crossed off my Christmas card list,' Leo warned him.

'You don't send Christmas cards,' Grant said as he stormed off. 'Emma always did it.'

Leo stood and watched him stomp off down the corridor and thought about what he had said. And, among other things, it was true that he'd never ever written one of his own greetings cards.

185

Chapter Forty-Nine

Isobel was sorting some papers, lethargically and by hand, when Mr Baldwin came into the office behind her. He looked dreadful – pasty and sweating. So she wasn't the only one feeling terrible. Perhaps her own tiredness was down to the excesses of the party, after all. Mr Baldwin flopped down into the seat behind his desk.

'Morning, Isobel.' His voice was croaky and dry.

'Hello.'

'I think we need to break out the headache tablets,' he said. 'Too much of a good thing. Perhaps I had one glass of fizz too many.' He reached into his drawer and pulled out a packet of Nurofen and chased two down with some water, shuddering as they hit the spot.

'It looks as if all the team are feeling the same,' Old Baldy continued. 'They all go mad at the sight of a free bar. It certainly made the party go with a swing though. I know you'll find this hard to believe,' he gave a little laugh, 'but Thornton Jones's parties are normally quite staid affairs.'

She wondered if any of the staff realised how much of the evening's success had been down to her intervention. She also wondered how many would find it impossible to believe, even if she told them the truth.

'You look a little pale too. If you don't mind me saying.'

'I am a little tired,' she admitted. 'But I had a great time. Wasn't it a magical evening?'

'Magical?' Mr Baldwin laughed. 'My dear Isobel, what a funny thing to say. There's nothing very magical about drinking too much and making a fool of yourself. Even though it was fun at the time.'

'Is that all you think it was?' She stopped her work. 'You had such a great time simply because you'd had too much to drink?'

Her boss looked perplexed. 'Isn't that always the case?'

Isobel sat heavily in the nearest chair.

'Isn't that why you're feeling peaky too?'

'Peaky?' Isobel looked down at her trembling hands. 'Is that what this feeling is?'

'Well,' Mr Baldwin said, slightly flustered, 'I think "peaky" may be a touch understating the case. You do seem a little out of sorts.'

Isobel looked upset.

'Don't get upset, Isobel.' Mr Baldwin was floundering. 'What about a nice cup of tea? A bit of rehydration – that's what's needed. It's just a hangover.'

Was it just a hangover? Her limbs ached and she felt as if she was fading into the background. Could too much champagne make you feel like this? Or did it mean that her time here was coming to an end quicker than she'd imagined? She wondered if the disbelief and cynicism at large in the world was beginning to weaken her already. Her elders had warned her that this could be a hostile place, but she hadn't anticipated just how fast this would affect her. She hadn't anticipated either how funny, warm and lovely some humans could be. Isobel cast a glance over to where Leo sat. It would be hard to leave when the time came. She only hoped that it wasn't now. She still hadn't accomplished all that she'd come here for.

Mr Baldwin came round his desk and looked at her with concern. 'Is there anything else wrong, my dear? Something that I can help with?'

'No. No,' she insisted.

Her boss gave her a hearty, jocular smile, seemingly at a loss for words.

Isobel stood up. 'I'll go and get that tea,' she said.

'Don't worry yourself so.' He gave her arm a comforting squeeze. 'We'll live.'

But Isobel wasn't sure that she would.

Isobel joined the queue for the vending machine. There were four bubbly girls standing in line in front of her, regaling each other with tales of last night's misdemeanours and giggling loudly at their escapades. Leo's dancing, it seemed, was coming in for particular attention. If Isobel could have blushed, she would have. They smiled at her when she tagged on the end.

'You look like I feel,' one of them remarked.

'It was a good party,' Isobel ventured.

'You're telling me,' she said. The girl gestured at the machine. 'I need about ten cups of this stuff to get me going this morning.'

'I know,' her friend piped up. 'It was a blast. I've never seen Old Baldy boogie like that before. Fab. The booze must have really been flowing. Everyone was legless. Look at the state of the office this morning.' She flicked a thumb towards the rows of desks with people in various degrees of slump over them. The girl shook her head and smiled. 'We all must have had a skinful.'

'Don't you think it was more than that?' Isobel was feeling weaker by the moment.

They both looked at her blankly. 'You clearly haven't been to a Thornton Jones party when they're not all drunk,' one of them said.

'Isn't it possible to have a good time without everyone being drunk?' Isobel asked.

They stared at her as if she was from another planet. Which in some ways she supposed she was. Isobel turned and staggered away from the coffee machine, bumping into the wall and then knocking over the wastepaper bin as she did. She struggled to right it. The girls tittered behind her. A sharp pain pierced her head and she put her hands to her eyes as her vision blurred. She had to see Leo. He was the only one who truly believed in her. Perhaps he could make this terrible, terrible feeling go away.

Chapter Fifty

The staff canteen was generally somewhere to be avoided at all costs. The food was truly abysmal and you ate it on plastic seats under the glare of a million halogen light bulbs. If you didn't feel dreadful when you came in, you would by the time you went out. Isobel and Leo were sitting opposite each other. She looked absolutely miserable and her food was untouched.

'You're very quiet,' Leo said. 'Are the sandwiches so awful?'

Isobel pushed her plate away. 'No one believes in my magic, Leo.'

'They do!'

'They don't,' she insisted. Her eyes looked bleak and there was no colour at all in her cheeks. The beautiful red lips that entranced him so much, looked bloodless and tinged with blue. 'Everyone thinks they had a great time at the party last night because they had too much to drink.'

'Humans tend to equate that with having a good time. It's one of our cultural deficiencies. Don't ask me why.' Leo gave a shrug. 'I never touch a drop.'

Even that failed to raise a smile.

'Couldn't they feel the magic in the air?' she asked.

'Give us a chance.' Leo took her hand. 'We're a very repressed race. We handle our emotions very badly. Even if people did feel something in the air, it would make them feel more comfortable to explain it away on a few drinks too many. We wouldn't automatically think to credit it to something mystical. We've closed our mind to so much of that stuff that we can't see it when it's right in front of our noses. We have very little joy in our lives, Isobel. You can't blame us for that.'

Isobel forced a tired smile. 'No one believes in fairies.'

'Grant and Lard believe in you.'

'Leo! This is supposed to be a secret. Our secret.'

'I only told them a little bit,' he protested. 'And they didn't take any convincing at all. Hardly any.'

189

'Really?'

'Really. In fact, Grant has a little problem – an *issue* – at the moment that he wondered if you could help him out with.' Leo felt as if he was looking shifty. There was no way he should be doing this. Grant should find his own damn fairy, rather than using his one. 'He wants you to make Emma love him.' Everything in Leo screamed that this was a really bad idea, but perhaps Grant was right. Leo should let Emma go. It was just that he was surprised to learn that she still loved him so much. Why could neither of them admit how much they loved each other when it mattered? And now it had come to this. There was no way back for them, Leo was sure.

His friend, it seemed, had no such qualms. Grant loved Emma and wanted her to love him back. Grant – a young pretender – could stand at the coffee machine and admit that he loved Emma when Leo – her longtime lover – had never even been able to say it to her. What did that say about him? That he had indeed been a deeply inadequate and crap boyfriend all along, it would seem. And what of Emma? Did Leo have the right to stand in the way of her happiness? That pained him more than he dared to admit – but Grant was a mate and Leo had said that he would do it. 'My Emma,' he added, purely for clarity.

Leo tried to shrug nonchalantly, but couldn't. Inside, his heart was breaking. He didn't want Emma falling in love with Grant. He didn't want her falling in love with anyone else either. He wanted her to still be in love with him.

Isobel shook her head. 'I can't do that, Leo. The human heart can't be manipulated. Not by me. Not by anyone.'

You wouldn't believe how much Leo wanted to hear this, but still he ploughed on. 'What about Cupid? I thought he was well known for his wily ways. Isn't he a fairy?'

'He's the God of Love.'

'Is there any difference? Don't you know him? You're not on speaking terms with him? You haven't bumped into him recently down at the fairy pub?'

Leo would swear that his conversations with Isobel were getting more surreal by the minute and this one was fuelled by desperation. She shook her head.

'You couldn't text him? Ask him to shoot a few arrows?'

His fairy friend looked cross. 'Now you're just being silly, Leo.'

'I'm known for it,' he said. 'That and my John Travolta imperson-
ation now, thanks to you.'

Isobel looked at him earnestly. 'There are times in your life when
you must be serious.'

Leo went to speak but she ignored him.

'This is important. You must listen to me carefully, Leo.' She sighed
at him. 'Emma isn't destined to love Grant.'

'Not ever?'

'No.'

'Oh well.' Leo suddenly sounded very chirpy. He didn't want to
know why Isobel was so sure about this, but he was relieved to hear
that Emma wasn't in imminent danger of falling in love with Grant.
Phew. Leo felt that it gave him a reprieve and he was very grateful for
a reprieve, even though he had no idea what he was going to do with
it.

'Never mind,' he said with a happy huff. He had tried, hadn't he?
Not that hard, admittedly. But at least he could face Grant and explain,
with an element of truth, that Emma was a no-go area for him. Leo
could see that Isobel wanted to tell him something else, but – quite
frankly – he'd had enough of revelations for the moment. He was just
glad that he wouldn't be having to buy Emma and Grant a wedding
present.

Isobel smiled at Leo sadly. 'You seem to like making your relationships very complicated.'

'It's an art. We spend years perfecting it.'

'Humans are strange creatures.'

'You have to give us time,' he said. 'We're very stressed out. We've
forgotten how to enjoy magic. Or even where to look for it. Instead,
we all have crippling mortgages and dwindling pensions and plum-
meting share portfolios and heaps of commitments and spreading waist-
lines to worry about.'

'You must be very sad people.'

'I'm a lot happier since I met you.' And it was true. Leo didn't know
what had shifted in him since Isobel had arrived on the scene, but there
was a seed of contentment inside him that had never previously been
there before, and he felt that it was blossoming. There was a settling
inside of him. His days of drunken crooning in late-nite bars could
well be over. Leo could end up living in the country and raising chickens
if this carried on. If only he'd discovered this earlier, then Emma might

191

have liked him more and they wouldn't be in this mess now. He could never regret meeting Isobel – she was wonderful, if not a little surreal – but he sometimes wished that he could wind back the clock and that he and Emma could go back to exactly how they were. Except that now he'd be the new, improved version of himself and he wouldn't irritate her quite so much.

Just as Leo was pleased to be discovering new things about himself, Isobel, on the other hand, was looking more careworn as the days went by. It worried Leo that the pressures of this life were proving too much for her. He couldn't bear the thought of Isobel leaving him, as well as Emma.

He took her hand and kissed it. 'Hang on in there,' he begged. 'For me.'

Chapter Fifty-One

'I'm in a bad way, Mummy,' I admit miserably as we stare at Rodin's magnificent sculpture, *The Kiss*.

'It's *Le Baiser*, in French,' my mother informs me, rolling the name round her tongue. 'Why is it that everything sounds so much more romantic in that language? I love it when Daddy speaks French.'

The Kiss is certainly more to my mother's taste than some of the strange and eccentric collections that the gallery houses. Depicting the adulterous lovers, Paulo Malatesta and Francesca da Rimini, its gracious marble curves with their superb blend of eroticism and idealism make it one of the greatest images of sexual love. As if I care. It has also been described as 'three tons of pornography'.

'Here's a man who enjoyed – revelled in – the beauty of the female form,' Catherine Chambers says. 'Not like that Picasso with his arms and legs all over the jolly place. What's that supposed to be? To my mind, he had no appreciation of our grace whatsoever.'

My mother likes art to look like art. She doesn't think a pile of bricks or three bright pink lights in an otherwise empty room can be credited with any sort of merit or skill. Naked men and women are supposed to be pink, not blue. The National Portrait Gallery is more my mum's cup of tea. Fusty old farts that look like fusty old farts.

Today, we're at Tate Modern – a former power station transformed into a radical new art gallery gracing the South Bank of the Thames, a stone's throw from the beautiful stainless-steel lines of the Millennium Bridge. My choice of venue and a bit of a busman's holiday for me. We sit, side-by-side on a curved wooden bench in a stark, white cube of a room, enjoying the peace and quiet. Every so often, we try to have mother and daughter bonding days, taking in an art gallery, a new restaurant or some shopping in Town – or all three. Days when we can chat away without my father putting in his five-pence worth, as he's prone to do. This particular bonding day has been called in an emergency.

We are currently in the Nude/Action/Body gallery, which to my mind is far too sensual by half. The rooms are stuffed full of lurid paintings of naked men, phallic statues, writhing bodies, couples entwined. It makes me uncomfortably aware that I'm missing Leo in more ways than one. All those things that I took for granted in our relationship are suddenly standing out to me in sharp relief. Why is it that when you're in a permanent relationship, sex slips further and further down the list of 'things to do'? When you're single you suddenly become desperate for it. I sigh, turn to my mother and say, 'I'm seeing a shrink.'

'You don't need a psychiatrist,' my mother says dismissively. 'I've told you already, darling. You need a good dinner and some great sex. In fact, you don't really need the dinner.'

'Oh Mummy,' I huff. 'It isn't so straightforward these days.'

'It is, sweetheart,' my mother assures me. 'You young things make your lives so unnecessarily complicated. You think far too deeply about trivia and worry about all sorts of things that don't matter. In my day, we found someone passable – preferably from a good family if you could manage it – got married, gave up work and had babies. It was no more complicated than that. We had time to do our own housework, bake our own cakes and were never too tired to have sex. We didn't consider whether we actually wanted children or not. We just had them, because that's what everyone did. Now it's a lifestyle choice. So what if we didn't have careers that kept us in the office until midnight or business trips abroad so that we could get tiddly with the sales force, or be of independent means? It doesn't mean that we didn't have great lives. You think you have it all these days, but in reality you have so little. A rich and fulfilling life isn't found behind a desk.'

'No one gets *tiddly* these days, Mummy. We get lashed,' I say. 'You sound like some sort of terrible throwback from the Victorian era.'

'I'm not, darling. I'm simply saying that the so-called liberation of women has resulted in them being more oppressed than ever before. Superman might go out and save the world, but he doesn't come home to a pile of ironing, name tags to sew on and a list as long as your arm for Tescos.'

'Women have fought long and hard for their independence.'

'Independence is a myth,' my mother says, patting her hair. 'We are all totally dependent on others whether we like it or not. No one can operate entirely alone. We need people. And, you're right, women have *fought* for their rights, but they need to know when to stop fighting.

You've battled for a long time to achieve your status as strong, independent women, but then you all wonder why men don't want to settle down and commit to you. Relationships shouldn't be seen as war zones with battle-lines drawn. They should be a constant compromise. You shouldn't spend all your time trying to control the person in your life who you're supposed to love more than anyone.' My mother nods at the sculpture. 'Does Francesca look as if she's been having a ding-dong with Paulo about whose turn it is to unload the dishwasher?' She looks sideways at me. 'Of course not. She's using her power as a woman to draw him in. Look at him, poor thing – he's putty in her hands. Francesca is the powerful force. We girls have to control the relationship, but we have to do it in a way so that our men don't realise they're being controlled, darling.' My mother gives me a kindly look. 'Have you ever been held like that?'

'I don't have the time to sit around cuddling.' I scuff my shoes on the grey concrete floor.

'You should make time,' my mother advises. 'You always used to go on about how wonderful Leo was, but then I have a very good long-term memory.'

Is it a long time since I've had a good word for my ex-lover, when he wasn't an ex anything?

'Leo loved you just as you were. Could you say the same about him?'

I say nothing. Instead I try to lose myself in the statue again. It's certainly very sexy. I can positively feel Paulo and Francesca yearning for each other – a seething mass of sexual tension. Kissing – they say it's the most erotic of all sexual acts. The beginning of the journey, before disappointment has time to set in.

'The sexes aren't the same. Not even remotely. We should all draw on our strengths and weaknesses and not fight each other for supremacy.'

'So forty years of female emancipation didn't exist in our household?'

My mother turns to me. 'Are you worse off because of it? I was at home to look after you and your sisters. Your every need was pandered to – perhaps too much.' There's a sharp note in her voice and I feel myself blush. It isn't just only children who are spoiled. 'Your father has never been near a duster in our entire married life. He has no idea how to work the washing machine or the microwave. Even the kettle is somewhat of a mystery to him. But that doesn't mean we've had a bad marriage.'

'You've been lucky,' I say. 'You had a wealthy husband to look after you. Women these days have to work so that their families can have even the basics.'

'Nonsense. I've seen it at the Women's Institute – women who work their fingers to the bone so that they can afford a fortnight in Spain or a bigger car. The basics don't include foreign holidays and in-car multi-change CD-players or air-conditioning. Those aren't the priorities in life. Designer labels really don't matter. We never holidayed abroad. You loved your two weeks in Devon every year, didn't you?'

I nod in agreement. They were idyllic times spent on the beach eating cheese rolls gritty with sand and burying our father up to his neck in it too. I don't point out to my mother that it would probably cost considerably more to have two weeks in Devon now than it would two weeks in the Costa del Sol.

'And Daddy always had to be on call for the hospital. There was no question of us ever being more than a few hours' drive away from his work. In those days he didn't spend his time making insecure women feel better about themselves by smoothing out a few wrinkles or blemishes, his skills were employed on correcting serious facial disfigurements.' My mother shakes her head. 'I don't think cellulite had even been invented when I was your age. If it had, we certainly didn't worry about it. Sometimes, it seems as if our whole society has become so much more shallow.'

'So you think I'm wasting money on therapy?'

'Of course I do,' my mother sighs. 'There's nothing wrong with you. Or with Leo, for that matter. You're both human and, therefore, you're both fundamentally flawed. But it's nothing more sinister than that. You're just ordinary people trying to make the best of life. And you can either get on and do it together, riding the knocks and the bad times, or you can try to find someone else that you can rub along with instead.'

'I might not have any choice.'

'He's still with this other woman?'

'Yes,' I say. 'And it's all going swimmingly, by all accounts.'

'Don't give up hope just yet, dear,' my mother advises. 'Sometimes it's all we've got.'

Catherine brushes down her skirt and stands up, taking me by the hand. 'Unless you can kiss like that, you will never know true intimacy,' she warns. 'Paulo and Francesca were prepared to die for their love.'

'They did,' I say. 'Her husband killed them both.'

'A crime of passion.' As my mother stares at the statue, her eyes fill with emotion. 'Another very French concept.'

'Come on,' I say, linking my arm through hers. 'It's time we had some lunch. All this passion is very exhausting on an empty stomach.'

We take one last long look at the statue.

'Paulo has very inadequate genitals,' my mother murmurs. 'That's the only disappointment.'

Chapter Fifty-Two

Grant and Leo were sitting with their backs turned to each other and they were both sulking. Grant because Isobel wouldn't help him to snare Emma and Leo because he didn't think that Grant should even want to.

'You said she could do anything,' Grant said over his shoulder.

'She can't do this,' Leo snapped. 'I did try.'

'Perhaps not hard enough.'

'Perhaps you should find someone who isn't my ex-girlfriend.'

'You're an arsehole, Leo.'

'And you're a . . .' What was Grant? He was a mate, really. Leo didn't suppose that Grant could help falling for Emma – she was fabulous. Anyone in their right mind would be mad for her. *Just as he was.* Leo stopped and scratched his head. He wondered if he had ever told her that enough. No, he suspected not. 'You're a . . . You're a . . .' But hard as he tried, an insult wouldn't come.

Grant was Leo's friend and he didn't want to fall out with him. Leo hated arguing with people. Really he just wanted a quiet life. Which seemed nigh on impossible these days. Leo had always been useless at fighting, even in the playground. He'd never, ever hit anyone – he simply couldn't work himself up to get that angry. But Grant could go out with anyone. Anyone other than Emma. He was a great-looking bloke and, as such, should be perfectly capable of finding someone else. He'd got money, a flash car, all his own teeth and hair. He knew the lyrics to every Queen song ever written. He knew that Bruce Springsteen *was* The Boss. Despite all of these qualities, he wasn't right for Emma. They might well make a great couple – that thought made Leo go cold – but he didn't want Grant knowing the things he knew about Emma – unless he told him, of course. Leo didn't want his friend kissing her the way he did. And Leo certainly didn't want him doing anything more than that. How could Grant even consider it? 'You're a sad muppet,' Leo settled on.

'I hope you're both very happy,' Lard snapped. 'I'm having to comfort eat because of you two.' He stuffed a Mars Bar into his mouth, chomping it with indignant bites.

Leo had a suspicion that, in the privacy of his own home, Lard contented himself with plastic replicas of women, and there were some days – increasingly frequent – that he couldn't say he blamed him. If Saucy Suzy started to give you too much grief then you just let her go down on you. Leo didn't mean *that*. He meant you could simply deflate her.

Leo got up and walked out. He hated confrontation and 'atmospheres' and there was definitely an 'atmosphere' in the office today. Which was a shame because normally they all rubbed along so well. Grant and Lard were like brothers to him, partners in crime, The Three Musketeers – all for one and one for all, et cetera. Leo didn't like to think that there were cracks forming in their cosy threesome. Perhaps Isobel could wave her wand over them and make them all good friends once more. Speaking of which, Leo wandered through to her office knowing that her soothing voice would ease his troubled mind. Plus she might wave her wand over Old Baldy too and they could clear off early for lunch.

However, in Old Baldy's office, Isobel was nowhere in sight.

Mr Baldwin nodded at him. 'Nice mover, Leo.'

'Thanks,' he said. Leo would never, ever live down his *Saturday Night Fever* performance at the office party. He could just see that he was going to be asked to do it year in, year out. 'Where's Isobel?'

'Suffering from the company hangover, I think,' Old Baldy told him. 'Poor girl looked dreadful. She got steadily worse throughout the morning. Perhaps she ate something that didn't agree with her too.' He really did look quite concerned about her, which was not good as Old Baldy was normally concerned about nothing but departmental targets. 'I thought it was best for her to lie down, so I sent her home for the day.'

'Home?' And she didn't come to tell him?

'Some time ago,' his boss confirmed.

'Cheers,' Leo said, swinging out of the office.

He rushed back to his desk, logged off his computer – sod the foreign markets for today, it was only money – grabbed his jacket and dashed out.

'Leo!' He heard Lard shouting after him, but he didn't stop. 'Leo!'

Leo had to get home to Isobel. Nothing else mattered.

His palms were sweating as he pressed the button for the lift and it seemed like an interminable amount of time before it arrived. Leo even considered the stair option again, but dismissed that as too ridiculous. Instead he waited impatiently for the lift and then marked the time it took to travel to the ground floor. Isobel shouldn't be ill – she was a fairy. Like Captain Scarlet, shouldn't she be indestructible?

Leo hailed a cab and jumped in. The traffic everywhere was at a complete standstill. And the journey home was the longest Leo had ever had in his life.

Chapter Fifty-Three

Eventually the cab pulled up outside Leo's flat — it would have been a darn sight quicker to walk — and he paid the driver and dived across the road, heedless of the traffic. It was at times like these when he could join the Green Party and vote for stopping everyone from having cars — everyone except taxi drivers and himself, of course.

Oh my word. The breath caught in Leo's throat and his step faltered. All the magnificent purple trees outside the flat had drooped. Their beautiful leaves hung limply and the ground beneath them was covered with fallen leaves even though it was nowhere near autumn. And, even though Leo knew it in his gut, he hoped against hope that this wasn't anything to do with Isobel.

He sprinted up the stairs and rushed into the flat, breathless. Must take up jogging. Again.

Isobel was in the lounge. She was lying on the sofa looking terribly pale and wan. Crikey — Leo could almost see the cushions through her.

'Oh shit. Oh shit,' he said in lieu of a greeting. 'What's wrong?'

'I'm weak, Leo.' Isobel's breathing was even heavier than his. It was high in her chest and didn't seem anywhere near sufficient. She was gasping like a fish out of water. 'Is this what human illness feels like?'

'Is that what you think it is?'

'I don't know,' she admitted and, for the first time, he saw what he thought might be fear in her eyes. Leo's blood ran cold. He wanted her to be in control and naughty and not frightened. 'Everyone at work was complaining about the after-effects of too much champagne. Do you think that's what's wrong with me?'

Leo chewed his lip nervously. 'It might be.'

'I have no idea why humans touch the stuff, if it is.' Isobel coughed as if she'd suddenly contracted consumption and his heart lurched. 'They were all complaining of tiredness and headaches — which is what I have.

201

They seemed to bounce back to relative health after popping a few tablets and drinking a few cups of coffee. Is that right?'

'It can help,' Leo said, having been there many, many times before.

'But I didn't want to risk taking any,' she continued. 'I don't know what they would do to my system. They seemed to think it was good to feel like that, but I've been getting weaker and weaker all day.'

Tears filled Isobel's eyes and he pulled her to him. 'Don't worry.'

'I got a cab home,' Isobel said shakily. 'And when I got out, all the trees . . .' She choked back a sob.

'Ssh.' He held her close.

'All the trees wilted, Leo.' His beautiful fairy friend started to cry. 'I feel as if I'm fading away.' She took his hand. 'I think my time here might be coming to an end.'

'No,' he put a finger to her lips. 'Don't say that.'

'I can't help it.'

'What can I get you? Do you need a hot-water bottle? Aspirin? Brandy?' Leo jumped up and rushed over to the stash of bottles he kept on his sideboard and poured a huge glass of brandy.

Isobel shook her head. 'Not brandy.'

'This is for me.' He downed half of it quickly. 'I'll take you to the hospital.'

'No. No. I can't have anyone examine me. I'm not the same as you are. They'd know,' she said sadly. 'They'd know. And then what would happen to me?'

That didn't bear thinking about. Look what they tried to do to ET. 'What can I do? Just tell me.'

She merged into the pillow behind her. It looked as if she was slipping away from him. 'I don't know.'

'Think,' Leo said sharply. 'Think, I'll do anything. Anything. We can get married. I'll have your babies. Just don't leave me.'

She closed her eyes and he went back to holding her again.

'Please don't leave me.' Leo had no idea who to pray to at times like this – he'd never before had a time like this – but he offered silent supplications to whoever out there in the universe might be listening. He didn't want Isobel to go. He didn't want her to leave him. What would he do?

When Leo was six years old his grandma gave him a red cape for his birthday. She'd hand-stitched it herself, even though her eyesight wasn't what it might be and her fingers were misshapen with arthritis.

He'd truly believed he was Superman in that cape and that he could go around the world, righting wrongs, ridding the place of evil, making the universe a better place. Leo wished he still had that cape now. My God, he *needed* a cape like that now.

After a moment Isobel opened her eyes and there was a slight spark there, faint but still there. 'I need to be beneath an oak tree.'

'An oak tree?'

Isobel nodded. She pulled him to her and spoke softly. 'We don't have much time.'

'Right.' Leo could feel a gulp travel down his throat. 'What exactly does an oak tree look like?'

Chapter Fifty-Four

I sit at my desk in Art For Art's Sake, chin resting on my hands, sniffing back tears. I have a box of tissues at my fingertips and am pulling them out one at a time. After blowing my nose, I drop each sodden tissue into the wastepaper bin. 'He loves me.'

'Emma,' Caron begs. 'Don't do this.'

I pull out another tissue. 'I'm desperate.' I've spent the afternoon imagining being held in Leo's arms, twined together like Francesca and Paulo. When I could have spent time cuddling with Leo, I hadn't wanted to be bothered. Life really isn't fair. I sniffle into the tissue again and then throw it away. 'He loves me not.'

'What did the psychiatrist say?'

'She said I have an unhealthy attraction to bad boys.'

'And how much did she charge you for that pearl of wisdom?'

'Too much,' I snort. Then, shame-faced I say, 'A hundred and fifty quid.'

Caron nearly chokes on her coffee.

'But then I did knock her out of bed at some ungodly hour,' I admit.

'A hundred and fifty quid for her to tell you something we both already know?'

'She also said I need to move on.'

Caron nods sagely. 'That's very good advice.'

'Yes,' I agree. 'She just didn't tell me how.' Pulling another tissue from the box, I blow again. 'He loves me.' The tissue goes in the bin.

'Oh, Em,' Caron says. 'Don't torture yourself. Mark it down to bad luck and a bit of mismanagement. Learn from your mistakes. One day you'll meet another man who'll blow you away and you'll forget Leo ever existed.'

'Never!'

'What about Grant? He seems to like you. Dating his best friend is a very good revenge policy.'

'I couldn't.' I shake my head. 'I'd have to socialise with Leo and I

204

couldn't stand that. He looks so damn happy these days.' Now he hasn't got me to nag him, I think bitterly. 'Besides, Grant is Grant. He's nice as a friend, but anything more . . .' I wrinkle my nose. 'He's too close to home.'

'You can't mope around for ever.'

I pull the final tissue out of the box. My face crumples. I wave the tissue at my friend like a flag of surrender. 'He loves me not.'

'Oh, sweetie.' Caron puts her arm round me and I start to cry.

The gallery door opens and an extraordinarily handsome man pops his head inside. 'Is this a bad time?' he says with a disarming smile.

I stop crying abruptly. 'Absolutely not.' I throw my tissue into the bin.

The man edges further into the gallery. Somehow, even though I'm sure I've never seen him before, he looks vaguely familiar. He's tall with a dark mop of curly hair, a bit like the cute one from *Lord of the Rings*. And he has intelligent fingers – long, slender ones. He seems sophisticated, well-read and urbane. This looks like the sort of man who is a stranger to wearing road traffic cones on his head.

'My friend here is having a terrible time with her relationship,' I say, pointing at Caron. 'I was sympathising.'

Caron stares at me open-mouthed.

'Is there anything I can do for you?' I offer, sliding out from behind my desk.

The man grins at me. 'Perhaps we could discuss that over dinner,' he says.

I laugh in my best coquettish manner. Flirting, I find, is very good for a broken heart.

'*Corny,*' Caron mouths silently to me over his shoulder.

'*Smooth,*' I mouth back when he turns to admire the wire-mesh men.

'Perhaps you could show me round the gallery for now,' he says.

'Absolutely.' I start to lead him towards the other rooms of the gallery. 'My name's Emma.'

He shakes my hand. Letting it linger rather too long, I think. His touch is strong and warm. Of course. 'Alec,' he says.

'Well, Alec, what sort of art are you interested in?'

'I have a small private collection,' he tells me. 'I'm looking to add a few more pieces to it . . .'

As he rambles on, I turn back towards Caron with a self-satisfied smirk and mouth, '*Leo? Leo who?*'

Chapter Fifty-Five

Grant shifted uncomfortably on his chair. He hadn't planned to interrogate Emma's friend as to the possibility of her having any sort of affection for him, but when he'd casually dropped into the gallery he was disappointed to learn that Emma had already left for the day. He should have phoned. That was the sensible thing to do. No. The sensible thing to do was stop chasing Leo's ex-girlfriend.

'I think Emma's probably a lost cause as far as Leo is concerned,' Caron said.

If Grant had realised that she'd just left with the rather suave-looking guy called Alec for the evening, he would have been even more disappointed. Caron, however, had made him a cup of coffee and they'd sat and chatted amid the naked torsos.

Caron smiled at him sympathetically. 'I hate to be the bearer of bad tidings.'

Grant shrugged. 'I'd managed to work it out for myself,' he admitted. 'It's interesting to have a second opinion though.'

'We ought to hatch a plan to get them back together,' Caron suggested, while wondering whether Emma's impromptu date tonight would prove a suitable cure for her broken heart. 'I hate to see my friend suffering like this.'

'Leo is such a lucky bastard,' Grant said. 'Two women in love with him. What I wouldn't give . . .' He stopped suddenly, realising what he was about to say.

'You seem like a great guy,' Caron said, blushing. 'Emma says you're lovely.'

'But not quite lovely enough.'

'Not for Emma,' Caron said sadly. 'But there are plenty of other available women.' She flushed a deeper shade of red and lowered her eyelashes. 'I'd like to say that she'd get over him, eventually. But it may not be true. You could hang around waiting for her for years.'

It was a depressing thought and Grant wondered whether Emma was worth it – whether any woman was worth it. 'It's nothing more than a delayed schoolboy crush,' Grant said. 'I'll get over it quick enough.' And he hoped that was true. Caron was right. Emma and Leo were meant to be together. Isobel was all very well, but Leo had been acting very strangely since they'd been together. Even more strangely than normal.

Caron glanced at her watch. 'I have to close up the gallery.'

'Oh.' Grant got to his feet. 'I'm delaying you.'

'No,' Caron said. 'I didn't mean that. It would be nice to carry on talking about Emma and Leo. We just need to move on to a bar or get a bite to eat. If you haven't got anything else lined up.'

'No,' Grant said. 'Nothing.'

'I know a good place just round the corner.'

'Fine,' Grant said. 'That would be nice.' He and Caron smiled shyly at each other.

'I need to lock some things away,' she said. 'I'll be back in a minute.' She grabbed her handbag and then scuttled out into the back office of the gallery.

Grant kicked back on his chair while he waited. Love was bad enough, but unrequited love was really bad news. It would be nicer to go out rather than to go home to an empty flat. An unexpected buzz of anticipation was tingling inside him. Caron was a very attractive woman. She seemed very genuine – so concerned about Emma's well-being. With luck, she'd spare a little bit of that empathy for him too. Grant grinned to himself. Perhaps the evening wouldn't be a complete waste of time, after all.

Chapter Fifty-Six

'So,' Leo said. 'This is an oak tree?'

Isobel barely nodded in acknowledgement. Leo was sitting on a grassy mound which was slightly damp with the evening dew and he was cradling Isobel on his lap. She was wrapped in a blanket, but she was still shivering. There was nothing to her. A slight breeze could blow her away from him and Leo hung on tightly to her as the wind stirred the leaves of the majestic oak beneath which they were sheltering. The tree felt strong and sturdy and as if it knew what was going on – that this could be a matter of life and death.

'Will this make you feel better?'

She nodded again. 'Oak trees have ancient restorative powers.'

Leo reached down and pulled out the flask from the hastily-assembled picnic he'd thrown together. It consisted of a packet of Nurofen, some Venos cough remedy – well, you never knew when you might need it – some out-of-date Twiglets and this, the flask of tea.

He poured some out for Isobel. 'Drink this,' he told her. 'This has ancient restorative powers too.'

'What is it?'

'Good old, hairy-chested English tea. Typhoo.'

Isobel took a sip.

'Better?'

'Much,' she said with a weak smile.

'Good.' Leo felt completely and utterly helpless and he cursed his gender for being so pathetic. He wished he knew what else he could do for her. 'This is the cure for all human ills.' He spoke in his most reassuring voice as he urged her to take another sip. 'Emotional and physical.'

'Then I'm in very good hands.'

She closed her eyes and sank into his arms. The cup of tea fell to the ground, soaking away instantly as if it had never been there. Isobel's breathing was laboured. There was such a long gap between gasps, that Leo began to wonder after each one whether she would ever take another breath. Isobel was looking worse by the minute and Leo wished that this bloody oak would hurry up and do its stuff.

He wished, also, that he could have found an oak tree in a more salubrious location, but it was the closest he could find to the flat. Leo nursed Isobel to him and cradled her head, sheltering her from the noise. The rumbling of lorries and buses shook the roots of the oak tree and he hoped it didn't mind. A few car horns honked and, if he'd had the strength, he would have given them the finger. Leo wondered what the drivers who circled them on this busy traffic roundabout – right in the middle of a major intersection, in the height of the London rush hour – thought about their plight. Did they think of them at all? Did they perhaps assume they were lovers overcome with passion? Or could they tell that they were two frightened beings and that one of them might be dying?

It had grown dark and, after the rush hour passed, the traffic had thinned and the noise dropped to a gentle hum. There was a full moon peeping through the branches at them and, surely, that must be a good omen. Weren't full moons supposed to be auspicious or something? Leo regretted that he didn't know more about these things. Isobel was fast asleep in his arms and he'd got cramp in his knees and a very numb bum. He couldn't tell if she was any better or worse. Leo wished he had some useful caring skills or talents other than singing passable Karaoke renditions of 1980s' hit pop tunes. A working knowledge of alternative therapies would come in particularly handy just now.

Isobel shifted in his arms as he picked her up and carried her home. She weighed nothing, so he didn't even have to stagger up the stairs with her.

In the flat, he gently laid her listless body on the bed and pulled the duvet over her, tucking it in round her tiny frame. She stirred slightly and he kissed her on the lips, barely brushing them for fear of hurting her.

Leo then lit a lavender candle – a remnant from one of Emma's frequent overnight stays here. He had never thought it would come in useful, but it was relaxing and healing, he was sure. Something like that. Emma would know. Could he ring Emma and tell her his troubles? Would she come over and help him? She was a great woman, and he was sure she'd know what to do, but he thought that might be pushing it too far. He didn't know what to do and Emma was so good at sorting things out. She always had been – it was her forte. Even though she hadn't got a wand she could act like she had. Leo wondered how she'd fare with a fast–fading fairy.

It struck him that he couldn't phone his family. He wasn't close enough to them to confide in any of them about what was going on, and that saddened him more than he could say. Leo realised that he'd spent years being too busy and too lazy to return their calls or to visit them. He was emotionally detached from all the people who should matter the most in his life. They had no idea who he was as a person. No more, indeed, than he had any idea who they were. It scared him that he had no one other than Emma who understood him as a person. And he wasn't sure that she did, most of the time. He wasn't sure that *he* did. Leo had relied on Emma too much, and he knew that now. Without her, he was lost and without a lifeline.

Isobel tried to speak and Leo bent down next to her. 'Hush, sweetheart,' he said. 'Just rest now. Go to sleep.'

And her eyes fluttered closed once more. Leo pulled up the leather chair from the corner of his room, pushing all the clothes piled on it to the floor and sat down. He was going to try to stay awake and watch over Isobel. He needed a shower and a shave and certainly a change of clothes. His suit was crumpled and smelled of damp grass and diesel fumes. Leo hadn't eaten either, but he had no appetite. He'd go to get the bottle of brandy for succour, but he didn't dare to leave her, not even for a moment. She was too good at disappearing and Leo couldn't face coming back to find an empty bed. He let his head drop into his hands. The thought of Isobel leaving made him feel sick to his stomach. How would he carry on if she left him alone? Leo knew that whatever happened, he was going to have to try to sort this out himself. The thought terrified him. He was firmly ensconced in the generation that shirked their responsibilities – those who lived for today and didn't save for their old age, ignoring the fact that the population of the country as a whole owed over a trillion pounds in debt – to which Leo made a significant contribution. They squandered their fertility until they were too old to reproduce and they pretended that they could conquer all illnesses, avoid ageing and even cheat death. And Leo had bought into all of it – until now.

If he'd believed in God, he'd pray now and he'd promise to give up

210

all his wordly goods to save Isobel – but he didn't because, of course, like everyone else, he was spiritually bereft. The nearest Leo had ever come to being spiritual was wearing holey underpants. Now he wanted to face his responsibilities, taking them head on like a speeding train. All he desired was to be happy and to settle down and have 2.4 children. Although he had always wondered what point four of a child would look like.

Leo took a glance at the clock. This, in a very different way from the Thornton Jones party, was also going to be a very long night.

Chapter Fifty-Seven

This is proving to be a very long night. I gulp down my wine. It's as good an anaesthetic as any. The weird thing is that I've wanted to come to this restaurant for ages – it's the current 'in' place to go in London. Of course, that means it's packed and over-priced and the service is terrible. Their stick-thin surly waiters are as legendary as their small portions.

I pick my way through my *poussins*. Little chickens. Nothing more grand than that, despite the posh name. I look up at Alec. He has been talking for a very long time about investments. I try, and fail, to stifle a yawn.

'I find unit trusts so fascinating,' Alec says. 'Do you?'

'Fascinating,' I echo vaguely. For a man with great looks and a trendy name, Alec is proving to be a crashing bore. The only positive thing I can say about him is that he would fit in perfectly well at family parties that involve my sisters' tiresome husbands, Dreadful Dickie and Awful Austin. He could become Atrocious Alec. Does he have to sit so absolutely upright? Perhaps he isn't suave and sophisticated after all. Perhaps he's just starchy.

We exhaust his knowledge of art in about ten minutes. He looks as if he knows what he's talking about, but he's a bullshitter. And he's the worst type of bullshitter, because he doesn't think he is one; he actually thinks he knows what he's talking about. He didn't buy anything from the gallery either, which automatically puts a black mark against him.

Alec works in the City in one of the huge financial institutions, like Leo. But unlike Leo, he's enthralled by his work. And thinks everyone else should be. Whereas, the only head for figures that Leo has is for female ones.

I had a late and sleepless night last night, plus an early start at my shrink's. It's no wonder I'm exhausted. It isn't yet nine o'clock and already I can feel myself sliding down my chair with fatigue. I'm still trying to fight sleep, when the waiter comes to top up our glasses. Alec puts his hand over his wine glass. 'No. Goodness. Not for me thanks,' he says with a disapproving look. 'One glass is more than enough.'

'Slug it in,' I instruct the waiter. 'One glass isn't nearly enough.' Through a rapidly developing drunken haze, I grin cheesily at Alec.

My date looks faintly alarmed. 'I have an early start in the morning.'

I think Alec looks like the type who jogs. At six o'clock in the morning. He is a high maintenance boyfriend. The sort who wouldn't appreciate waking up next to ancient sheep-patterned pyjamas. He'd want something filmy from Agent Provocateur on his woman.

I stare at him through bleary eyes.

'I think I'll get the bill,' he says crisply, as if reading my thoughts. 'Shall we split it?'

Uptight and cheap, I think bitterly. No dessert, no coffee. And, after my measly main course, I'm still starving. Yet, I know in my heart of hearts that it is definitely time to go.

Outside, on the street, the fresh air hits me. Suddenly, I feel very tired and very alone. My limbs are heavy and aching.

Alec is shrugging on his coat. It isn't cold enough for a coat. My father will be the only other person in London who'll be wearing a coat tonight.

I put two fingers in my mouth and whistle for a cab that's passing – a very useful trick that Leo taught me. Alec doesn't look impressed by my skill. Obligingly, the driver pulls up in front of me. The end of this interminable evening is in sight.

'Well,' Alec says tightly. 'Thank you for a pleasant evening.'

'Yes,' I say politely. 'It's been very . . . very . . . Well. Thanks.' We both know that it has been perfectly awful. 'Come into the gallery some time.'

'I will,' he says. And we both know that he will never darken its door again.

He waves briskly and then marches off down the street – into the balmy summer night in his coat. If I'd turned round and looked again just a moment later, I would have seen that damn woman – that *Isobel* – in exactly the place where Alec had been, wearing a very oversized coat and a satisfied smile on her face. Then I would have realised that there is something very strange going on in my life. But I don't. I'm so grateful to have hailed a cab, I climb into it without a backward glance and collapse back in the seat.

'Where to, love?' the driver wants to know.

Before I know what I'm doing, I rattle off Leo's address – I blame the drink myself.

The cab swings out into the evening traffic.

'Oh Leo,' I wail loudly. 'Why do I still love you?'

The cab driver, I note, closes his dividing window.

In the end, I had the taxi driver drop me at the bottom of Leo's road when I see that the Doner Kebab takeaway is still open. I buy myself the biggest, greasiest kebab on the menu and it tastes a lot better than the scraggy *poussins* that I paid ten times the price for in the trendy, rip-off eaterie.

Now I'm sitting on the bonnet of Leo's manky old car, Ethel, opposite his flat. And really I have no idea why – except that I know it's another hundred and fifty quid of psychiatrist's fees up in smoke. I also need to feel close to Leo – in distance if nothing else. It's still relatively early and yet Leo's bedroom light is on and the curtains are closed. They're probably curled up in bed together having just made mad, passionate love, I think, and the chilli sauce from my kebab burns an acidic hole in my stomach. Thank goodness there aren't any shadows moving against the curtains. That would have been too hard to bear. I might have been tempted to brick in Leo's windows.

I seethe as I sit here. I want my boyfriend back and, make no mistake, I'm going to get him. By hook or by crook. All I have to do is come up with a foolproof strategy. How hard can that be? I'm an intelligent and resourceful woman. Intelligent and resourceful enough to know that it's time I was going home. The walk back to my own flat isn't too far even though it will be filled with only my lonely footsteps.

Jumping down from the bonnet, I brush the dirt from my skirt. It's a shame that Leo never washes his car, but then the grime is probably the only thing holding Ethel together. Leo, with his usual scant appreciation of security, has left his car window open. Screwing up the paper that my doner kebab has been wrapped in, I push it in through the window. Punishment for Leo making me sit outside his flat without him. The car will stink in the morning. No doubt Leo won't even notice.

Chapter Fifty-Eight

'How did you get on with Emma last night?' Lard asked. 'I didn't "get on" with Emma,' Grant admitted. 'I "got on" with her best friend, Caron.' He gave Lard a sheepish grin.

'What? Are you turning into Leo?' Lard wanted to know as he crammed another chocolate croissant into his mouth. All this emotional turmoil was doing his diet no good at all.

'I hope not,' Grant said. 'I just realised that it was a very bad idea to pursue his ex.' The fact that Caron had been great company had certainly helped to persuade him of the fact. But it was more than that. He didn't want anything to spoil his friendship with Leo. 'I want to be his mate again, not his enemy.'

Grant looked at the clock. 'Speaking of which,' he said, 'where is the Boy Wonder? This is very late, even for Leo.' It was nearly lunchtime and they'd still heard nothing from him.

'Perhaps he's going for a personal best?'

Grant craned his neck and checked in Old Baldy's office. A frown creased his forehead. 'Isobel isn't here either.' He suddenly felt a frisson of worry. 'Isn't that odd?'

'Seeing them fly across the sky on balloons is what I call odd,' Lard said flatly. 'This doesn't even register as a blip.'

Grant scratched at his ear. 'Something's not right.'

'He's probably still in bed,' Lard said. 'Ring him.'

'I can't ring him,' Grant puffed. 'He's still not talking to me. We need a bit of time to make our peace. You do it.'

Lard tutted. 'I hope you realise that all this falling out is giving me dyspepsia,' he complained as he reached for the phone with one hand and another croissant with the other.

Leo could hear the phone ringing in the hall and realised that he must, after all, have dropped off in the wee small hours. Glancing over at

Isobel, he was relieved to see that she was still here at least. But she didn't look good. She was fast asleep, but her breathing was troubled and her face was contorted with pain.

Leo's legs were numb where he'd been sleeping in the chair. Tiptoeing out to the hall, he closed the bedroom door so that he didn't disturb Isobel and picked up the phone. When Leo heard Lard's cheery, comforting voice he nearly passed out with relief.

'Mate,' Lard said. 'Where are you? There are cakes here for the eating.'

'Isobel's sick,' Leo replied. Even he could hear the panic and strain in his voice. 'She's very sick. I think she has to go back.' His throat was so clogged with emotion that he could hardly speak. This was the first time he'd voiced his fears. 'I don't know what to do.'

'Leave it to Uncle Lard,' his friend said and hung up.

As Lard hung up the phone he turned to Grant with a worried look. 'Isobel's sick,' he said. 'She has to go back.'

'Go back where?'

'I don't know,' Lard admitted with a grimace. 'To where she comes from, I presume.' He shrugged. 'Leo sounded really screwed up. I think he might need our help. He doesn't know what to do.'

'Do we?'

Grant and Lard both turned and looked at the computer together.

'Not yet,' Lard said, flexing his fingers and cracking them in a decisive manner.

'Thank goodness for the internet,' Grant said. 'Useful not only for nailing down the cheapest prices for Viagra and Russian brides, but also for finding out all you need to know about fairies.'

Grant pushed Lard out of the way and started tapping away at his computer. Feeling beads of sweat gathering on his forehead, he could only hope that he was right.

Lard sat down next to him. 'I feel an excess of calories coming on.'

Chapter Fifty-Nine

I decide to do something mad. Really mad. Leo-type mad. I want my man back and I'm going to shock him into noticing me again. He'll soon tire of that fluffy, fragile little woman he's with – she isn't robust enough to stand the rigours of Leo – but I'm not sure I can wait long enough for nature to take its course. I have to do something desperate.

I look at the huge cardboard box in my lounge. This certainly could be classed as desperate. One of the life-size wire-mesh figures was delivered in it to the gallery, so there's no doubt that it's fit for my purpose. As soon as my master-plan popped into my mind, I'd jumped out of bed, sprinted down to the gallery and struggled back with the box through the narrow cobbled streets of Shad Thames, just as the rest of London was emerging from sleep. I also left a note for Caron saying that I'd be late for work – although, with a bit of luck, I won't be turning up at all today. Explanations can come later.

Now to put phase two into action. Picking up the phone, I make a provisional booking with the specialist delivery company we regularly use at the gallery. They aren't too shocked by my request – perhaps they've seen it all before in the art world – and give me a price that won't break the bank. And they're used to handling fragile packages, which is a bonus. When that's done, I punch in Leo's work number. 'Can I speak to Grant Fielding, please?'

After a moment Grant comes on the line.

'It's Emma,' I say.

'Oh.' There's a slight pause. 'How are you?'

'Terrible,' I tell him. 'And you?'

'Fine. Fine.' His voice sounds strained.

'Look, Grant,' I say, 'can you do me a favour?'

'Anything.'

'Can you tell me if Leo is in work today?'

Another pause. 'Not yet.'

217

'Is he sick?'

'I don't think so.'

'Is he at home?'

'Er . . . yes.'

I sigh. 'This is like pulling teeth, Grant. I need to know if he's likely to be alone.' I can't imagine that he would have let that woman move in with him. Whatever else Leo is, he's resolutely a bachelor. We've been together for five years and yet he's managed to avoid any kind of formal commitment at all costs. His new woman is, hopefully, at work – whatever that might entail. 'Is he alone?'

'Er . . . yes,' Grant says.

I sag with relief. That will make life so much easier.

'Thanks, Grant. I owe you one,' I say, realising that I probably owe him several.

Hanging up, I eye my cardboard box again, taking a deep breath. This is a bold scheme. I'm going to get myself delivered to Leo. My plan is to spring out of the cardboard box and give him the surprise of his life. I smile at my own ingenuity. I'll make him realise what he's been missing! If I was going to be delivered to his office, I would have needed to remain suitably attired. As I'm going directly to his home I can opt for something considerably more risqué.

I pad through to my bedroom. More risqué involves the red silky thong that Leo bought me as a joke last Valentine's Day. It's emblazoned with the legend MISS FUNNY FANNY in white embroidery and giggles when you pressed a padded button in a strategic place. Perhaps Leo is right, I have lost my sense of fun. For some reason I didn't find it remotely amusing when he presented it to me. Perhaps it was because Jo had received a gold bracelet from her current squeeze and Caron had been bombarded with bouquets of red roses from several unidentified admirers.

Now I can see that it has its uses. Slipping off my clothes, I step into the red thong. It certainly isn't in keeping with my usual underwear style. You can tell the length of a relationship by the lingerie choices, I think. Comfy pants have generally replaced anything sexy or lacy – except on high days and holidays and birthdays, of course. Delving into the drawer once more, I find a big red ribbon that had been round the Easter egg that Leo bought me and I know now that I've been wise to save it for a special occasion. It's just long enough to wind round my ample breasts and tie in a bow at the front.

Risking a glance in the mirror, I gasp out loud. 'Oh my word.' I close my eyes in shock. I look like something that's wandered out of a Spearmint Rhino establishment. Leo will love it. And although it seems a very good theory, in practice I'm not quite sure that I'm up to this at all. I don't think I'm a natural temptress. Hasn't one of the main reasons for loving Leo been that he hasn't expected very much from me in that department? Well, that's about to change. I'm going to show him that I can be fun. FUN. FUN. FUN.

Back in the lounge, I call the delivery company to confirm my booking. They agree to pick me up in twenty minutes. Literally.

I try out the cardboard box for size. Perfect fit. Even though I have to curl up in a ball at the bottom to squeeze in. It does, however, feel a bit flimsy. Wire-mesh sculptures, it seems, weigh considerably less than a thirty-year-old flesh and blood woman. What to do? There's no way I want the humiliation of falling out of the bottom of the box when they pick it up. I ease myself out of the box and go into the kitchen. The seams clearly needed reinforcement and I might have some parcel tape lurking in one of the kitchen drawers.

I pull the blind in case any of my neighbours are at home during the day and wonder what I'm doing in nothing more than sleazy under-wear and a gift bow at my kitchen sink. Rummaging through the drawers, I fail in my quest to find parcel tape. I do, however, find a brand new tube of Superglue. That will do the job just as well. Doesn't it stick anything to anything?

I scuttle back to the lounge, superglue in hand. Time is running out – the delivery company will be here at any moment. One of the reasons why we keep using them is that they're ultra-punctual – something very rarely found these days, in humans or delivery companies. Snapping the top from the glue as instructed, I smear it along the bottom seam of the box, then along all the side seams, pressing the cardboard together. It oozes out of the seams, but I know better than to try to wipe it off. This stuff is lethal. Standing back, I admire my handiwork. That surely will hold my weight a bit better.

Quickly, I scribble on the top of my box: '*To Leo, with love.*' And, just as I've finished, my doorbell rings. The delivery company has arrived.

This is going to be the embarrassing bit. There's no way that I can avoid the delivery men seeing me like this. The box is too small for me to be able to put on some other clothes and then shrug out of them before I reveal myself – in more ways than one. I just hope it isn't Tom and Eric, the usual guys who collect items from the gallery – the young, fit ones – otherwise I'll never be able to face them again.

The doorbell rings again and I sidle towards it, covering as much of myself as possible with my arms. I hide behind the door as I open it. 'Hi.' A gulp travels down my throat. 'Tom. Eric.'

Their eyes are out on stalks.

'I need you both to close your eyes while I go and get in the box.'

They both nod, amazement having robbed them of speech.

I run to the cardboard box, not daring to look back to see if Tom and Eric have kept their side of the bargain, and jumping in, I settle myself down in the bottom, curled up in a neat ball. 'Okay,' I shout at the delivery guys.

A moment later, Tom and Eric peer over the top of the box. Their eyes shoot out further and I hear Tom clear his throat. 'Are you sure this is what you want?'

'Yes,' I insist. There'll be no bottling out now. 'It's a surprise for my boyfriend.'

'Well, I hope he's worth it,' Eric comments.

'I think so,' I say.

'Shall we carry you downstairs like this?' Tom asks. 'Then tape the top shut when we arrive at our destination?'

'No,' I say. 'It's not far. Ten minutes max, if the traffic behaves. Better to tape the lid up now. If Leo's looking out of the window, he might see you and wonder what's going on. I want you to drop me off, ring the bell and then zoom off quickly. I must be on his doorstep in my box before he knows what's happened. Surprise is the important element.'

Tom and Eric both look unconvinced. Eric sounds nervous. 'You won't sue us for this?'

'Of course not,' I snap. 'What could possibly go wrong?'

Another look passes between the guys. 'Can't say we've ever done this before.'

'It will be a breeze,' I reassure them.

Hesitantly, Tom pulls a roll of parcel tape from his back pocket. They both wave at me and I'm sure I can see a tear in Eric's eye. 'Bye,' they both say. 'Good luck.'

Tom closes the lid and suddenly everything goes very black. I've never experienced claustrophobia and it's something I'm now rather glad of. I hear the rasping noise as Tom tapes the top shut. Then it all goes quiet.

I can hear my own heart beat. Thank goodness I won't be in here for very long. Already I'm struggling to move. My knees are wedged under my chin and my feet are braced against the side of the box. The top presses down on my head.

Then there's a violent jolt as I feel Tom and Eric hoist me up.

'Careful,' Eric says, puffing heavily.

They stagger towards the door with me. This is a good idea, I tell myself. Really it is.

'Do you think we should have cut some air-holes in it?' I hear Tom lower his voice to a whisper. 'How long do you think she's got before she runs out of oxygen?'

It's only then that I start to worry.

Chapter Sixty

L eo was cradling Isobel and mopping her brow with a cold flannel.
He didn't know whether she was too hot or too cold – it seemed
to change by the minute. But he did know that, whatever was wrong
with her, it was much more serious than a touch of the company hangover. What was that old wives' tale? Feed a cold and starve a fever?
Where could you find an old wife when you needed one? Perhaps he
should be making Isobel something to eat, even though she didn't look
strong enough. Chicken soup – wasn't that what was called for?

Bits of Isobel were almost transparent and Leo didn't think that was
a good thing. She looked so weak he could weep. Then the doorbell
rang, which made him jump out of his skin, and he wondered who
the hell it was.

As Leo kissed Isobel, promising her that he'd be back in a minute,
it rang again – someone out there was rather impatient – and so he
plodded out of the bedroom to see what all the fuss was about.

When he opened the door, Grant and Lard were standing there. Lard
was carrying a large holdall. Leo hoped he wasn't planning to move in
with him. Grant and Leo eyed each other sheepishly.

'Stonehenge,' Grant said crisply.

'The same to you,' he replied.

'We've got to get there,' he told Leo. 'Fast.'

'And how exactly have you arrived at this conclusion?'

Grant held up a sheaf of papers. 'Internet. We Googled fairy legends.'

'Stonehenge is the gateway to the fairy underworld,' Lard explained
as if it was an everyday thing; as if he was telling Leo which bus to
catch to Marble Arch. 'The Land of Light.'

'And that's where Isobel is from?'

'It looks like it,' Grant confirmed.

Leo shrugged because he didn't know what else to do. 'Stonehenge
it is.'

They shuffled into the flat and Leo caught Grant's eye. 'You're a mate,' he said. Relief flooded Grant's features and Leo clasped his friend to him. 'You're a real mate.'

Grant nodded his acknowledgement. 'We'd better get moving.'

'I'll go and get Isobel.' Leo's eyes filled with unshed tears. 'I'll tell her that the cavalry is here.'

'I hope we're right about this,' Lard leaned in towards Grant and whispered confidentially. He chewed his lip anxiously.

'So do I,' Grant admitted, with a tense exhalation of breath. 'We're doing our best for Leo. We can't do any more than that. I just hope it's enough.'

'If Isobel has to go back to her home, does that mean that Emma will get back with Leo?'

'I haven't a clue,' Grant said. 'And I don't even want to think about that now. Or any other implications of the stuff we're planning to do.'

Lard flashed a commiserating look at him.

'This is all getting far too complicated for me. We used to have such a quiet life. You, me, Leo, lots of chocolate, some curry, the odd beer. When did it all start to go pear-shaped?'

'Why did you tell Emma that Leo was going to be here alone?'

'I don't know.' Grant rubbed his hand over his face. He felt like he'd been up all night. Which partly he had – chatting, very amiably, with Emma's friend Caron. She was a lovely girl and he hoped that he'd see her again. Very soon. He did, however, wish that all of his cylinders were firing. It wasn't a good day to be feeling below par. 'I wasn't really thinking straight. I just didn't want to give too much away about Leo's circumstances. How could I tell her that Isobel was ill? I don't know what she might have done. As it was, I had a horrible feeling that she might be here when we arrived. It looks as if I was stressing unnecessarily.' Which seemed to be happening a lot at the moment.

Leo appeared carrying Isobel in his arms. She was wrapped in a blanket and looked pale and clammy and, frankly, not long for this world. 'We're ready,' he said.

'So are we,' Grant and Lard confirmed.

Leo carried Isobel out of the flat and down to his car, Ethel. Grant and Lard jumped in the back and he laid Isobel down on the front seat. Then he sprinted round to the driver's seat and slid in.

'Jeepers, Leo.' Grant held his nose. 'What the hell have you been eating in here? It smells like a Greek brothel.'

There was the vague odour of stale lamb. 'Kebab,' Leo said, rescuing the crumpled package from underneath his bottom. Though he had no idea when. He couldn't remember leaving it in there, but he was sure that he must have.

'You are such a waste of space,' Grant tutted. And Leo knew that they were back to normal. They were brothers once more.

He wasn't usually a litter lout, but needs must – and he tossed the greasy paper out on to the street, promising to clear it up later if it was still languishing on the pavement when he returned. Leo suddenly gave an involuntary shudder as he wondered when that might be.

'Ready?' he asked everyone. The boys, squashed together in the back, nodded their assent. Lard was chain-eating chocolate already. Isobel moaned softly. Leo squeezed her hand. 'Not long, darling. Hang on.'

Buckling up, he started the car and, with an anxious glance at Isobel, he set off down the street. Leo attempted the style of top racing driver, Ralf Schumacher and instead got demented kangaroo. 'Come on, Ethel,' he urged, patting the steering wheel. 'Do your worst!'

Chapter Sixty-One

Cobblestones feel very bumpy when you're banged up in a cardboard box. My bottom is numb already and I've lost all feeling from my legs before we've hit the end of my street. I'm beginning to regret my rashness.

Tom and Eric career round a corner and my cardboard box slithers to one end of the van. It's like being on the worst possible theme-park ride that you can imagine.

Then suddenly the van comes to an abrupt halt. It's either yet another set of traffic lights or we've arrived at Leo's flat. I sincerely hope that it's the latter. It couldn't come a moment too soon. My courage is leaving me with the speed of rats diving off a sinking ship. I hear Tom and Eric fling open the van doors and my sigh of relief is rapidly replaced by a surge of panic. Leo will find this funny – surely he will. This is the sort of thing he does all the time. It isn't, however, the sort of thing *I* do. Ever.

'You all right in there?' Tom's voice whispers close to my ear, slightly muffled by the cardboard.

'I'm fine,' I mumble back. Which is just as well, because no sooner do I speak than I'm hoisted into the air again. I can feel Tom and Eric struggling up the half a dozen steps to the main door of Leo's flat.

'This will do,' Tom pants. And I'm unceremoniously dumped on the ground.

'Oouff,' I say, and then am gripped by a fit of the giggles as I wonder what it must sound like from outside my box.

'We'll be going now,' Tom says, down by my ear.

'Right.' I hear the doorbell ring, much scuttling of feet, the slam of a Transit van door and then the screech of wheels as it roars away.

Then there's a silence, the like of which I never thought possible to encounter in London. I sit there waiting – excitement and terror mounting in equal measures. What if Leo takes this the wrong way?

225

Then again, how many ways are there to take a woman – an ex-girlfriend – jumping out of a cardboard box on your doorstep dressed only in her underwear and a gift bow?

He should be coming down the stairs by now. I count the steps. Then count them again. Perhaps I've caught him while he's in the loo. I allow for a little time lapse – flush toilet, wash hands, dry hands. Then I count the steps again. Still no Leo. I check my watch, which thankfully, I thought to keep on. Five minutes have passed already. Perhaps he's nipped out to the newsagents at the end of the street to buy a newspaper or some chocolate or something. Or there's probably a beer shortage – that's the usual thing that lures Leo into the great outdoors. Whatever it is, I just wish he'd hurry up. Thankfully the weather is reasonably warm so I'm not likely to freeze to death, sitting here in my skimpies – cardboard is surprisingly cosy – but I'm getting mightily uncomfortable.

After twenty minutes the first shadow of doubt crosses my mind. Clearly Leo has gone out and, quite possibly, he's staying out. Leo doesn't indulge in any unnecessary movement, so he won't have gone jogging and he doesn't have a dog, so a brisk walk is pretty much out of the question. If he'd simply gone to the local shop, then he would have hurried back as quickly as possible to make acquaintance with his sofa once more. Perhaps Grant was wrong. What if Leo isn't at home at all?

I wish that I'd thought to put my mobile phone in the box with me. What was I thinking of? No self-respecting contemporary woman can operate without her phone. I could have at least called Grant again or Lard, or tried to track down Leo – although that was a mission impossible even Tom Cruise might shrink away from. Leo never usually manages to hold onto a phone for more than a few days at a time and, on the rare occasion that he does, he invariably forgets to turn it on. There's nothing else for me to do other than sit it out.

After an hour and still no sign of Leo – or anyone else for that matter – I'm now starting to panic. It's Tom's anxious words about oxygen consumption that have started to play on my mind. And, to be honest, there's nothing else to do whilst passing time in a cardboard box, other than to panic. And worry. And chew your own fingernails down to the quick. I can barely move now and I wonder if my muscles have started to waste away already. No wonder Hollywood features it so often in films – put people in a sweatbox for any length of time and they come out like gibbering idiots, too helpless to walk and weak with hunger. My stomach rumbles. It's been a long time since lunch. Is it just my imagination that I'm starting to feel faint? Perhaps my oxygen really is starting to run out. I wish that I hadn't sealed the seams with Superglue quite so lavishly now. If I hadn't, there might be more air gaps. Anxiety is prickling over my skin. This is ridiculous. I can't sit here all night on Leo's doorstep. Wherever Grant had got his information from, it was wrong and I'll have words with him at some future juncture. Assuming that I live to tell the tale.

That's it. I can't contain my fear any longer. I have to get out of here. I don't want to die in a box on Leo's doorstep in my undies – I still have so much living to do!

Outside the box there's the sound of a cat meowing at the front door. Surely someone will come down and let it in. The nice couple in the flat next to Leo have a cat – a white fluffy thing with a bad attitude – I hope it's theirs. I can hear it rubbing against the side of the box. 'Here, kitty, kitty,' I murmur sweetly. I've never been a catlover, but talking to anything is preferable to letting my mind race wildly over my predicament.

Dutifully, the cat meows back.

'Here, kitty, kitty.'

I can hear the cat scratching at my box now. Where's the wretched owner? Don't they know that their cat is out here begging to be let in? I should report them to the RSPCA. The cat meows again, rather pitifully. It's a very endearing sound. But the next sound isn't. It's the sound of the cat weeing on my box. The acrid stench of cat urine fills my airspace. 'Bloody hell!' I shout at it. 'Clear off, you mangy animal!'

The cat meows again. That's it. Now I'm being used as a toilet for the wildlife of the area. I've had enough. Scratching frantically at my box, I bang on the lid. There's no way I can even get a fingernail under a corner to lift it, let alone rip my way out. I'm so squashed in that there's no room to try to kick my way out. This cardboard is tougher than it looks. I should have thought to bring a knife or some scissors or some way of getting out of here. In fact, I should have thought the whole mad idea through a lot more carefully. There's only one thing for it.

'Help!' I shout feebly. 'Somebody help me!'

Chapter Sixty-Two

'I can't believe you drive like this even when you're not drunk,' Grant complained loudly from the back seat.

'Sorry,' Leo offered.

'There are creatures in the Australian outback that kangaroo less than this.'

Leo had his own particular lurching style of motoring. He blamed it on the fact that it was a very long time ago since he'd learned to drive and he didn't do it very often and he wasn't very good at it when he did. However, this was an emergency.

Leo hated driving in London and the route had, so far, been torturous – out towards the motorway and their ultimate destination. They were heading away from the smoke of the city to the gateway to the Land of Light which, according to the internet, was slap-bang in the middle of the ancient circle of stones that formed Stonehenge. Leo hoped that their source was reliable. Quite frankly, he didn't trust the internet at all. He'd bought three CDs on eBay once; two of them never appeared even though his credit card was debited and the final one, which did turn up, was supposed to be *The Best of Motörhead* but instead he received a copy of *The Nolan Sisters' Greatest Hits*. To be fair, it was in very good condition. Hardly played. It was slightly unsettling though, that they were relying on this rather erratic tool to help repatriate Isobel to her own home, time, land, whatever.

'Jeez, Leo,' Grant moaned again. 'I can't sit here while you take for ever to jump us all the way there. Pull over. Go on.'

Leo pulled Ethel into the nearest lay-by. Well, hopped, skipped and jumped into it really.

'Get out and let me drive,' Grant snapped.

'You're not insured to drive my car,' Leo objected.

'Does it matter at this point?' his friend wanted to know.

'No,' Leo said, too tired and anxious to argue.

'Not unless we're stopped by the police,' Lard pointed out from the back seat.

They both glared at him. Cars whizzed by.

'When was the last time you saw a policeman?' Grant asked.

Lard quietly conceded that police patrols were somewhat scarce on the ground in this, the age of the speed camera.

'Leo, you can get in the back with Isobel,' Grant said. 'Lard, come in the front and navigate.'

Leo bounded out of the car and went round to the passenger side, lifting the listless frame of Isobel into his arms. Grant squeezed out of the back and slipped into the driver's seat. Lard also climbed out, relinquishing the back seat. He helped Leo to settle Isobel across his lap, so that he could cradle her. If Grant employed his usual driving style they'd be going at warp speed to Stonehenge.

'Quick, Lard,' Grant said impatiently. 'Don't dolly about. Get in.'

Lard made the most sprightly move Leo had ever seen and positively sprang into the passenger seat.

'Are we quite ready?' the driver asked.

'Yes,' Leo said.

Isobel stirred. 'We're running out of time,' she whispered.

Leo stroked her face. 'Not long now,' he murmured. 'Not long now.'

Grant swung out into the traffic once more. Leo was happier now that he'd relinquished control to someone that he trusted with his life – with Isobel's life. He sagged back into the seat. 'Step on it, Grant,' he instructed. 'And don't spare the horses.'

Grant was driving as if he had a starring role in *The Italian Job*. He was hunched over the steering wheel, concentration etched between his eyebrows. The party had inched their way through the rush hour, but now the flow of traffic had picked up again and they were making good progress. Leo was sure that if Isobel had been stronger she could have magicked them all to Stonehenge in a trice – but then if she'd been stronger, they wouldn't have been going there at all.

Leo's heart was heavy and his head ached from his fitful night. Conversation in the car had died and they all sat in an uncomfortable silence. How different from their usual boys' road-trips, where the banter flowed as easily as the beer. They were weaving in and out of the traffic on the motorway, eating up the miles as they headed nearer towards Stonehenge. Grant normally drove a TVR Tuscan and Leo thought that he'd probably forgotten that most people had cars that don't go that fast. He hadn't thought that Ethel was capable of going over forty, but now under Grant's tutelage she was doing a ton and smoking. And Leo didn't mean 'smoking' in a trendy, street way – he meant that there was smoke coming out from under her engine and it was pouring out of the exhaust pipe in a great black plume. He now wished that he'd had her serviced more often – or at all.

Isobel was asleep in his arms. Sleep had slackened the lines of pain on her face and she seemed comfortable at least. Dusk was gathering, the cobwebs of clouds thickening in the sky. The sun was falling out of view and Leo hoped that there wasn't some sort of unseen, unknown deadline on this escapade and that their best really would be good enough.

Then, in the rear window, he caught a glimpse of a flashing blue light at the same time as the siren on the police car started.

'Oh bugger,' Grant, Lard and Leo said together.

The police car came alongside of them, so that they were in no doubt that they'd been clocked. Leo thought that 'it's a fair cop' would be an appropriate phrase at the moment.

Without further ado, Grant pulled over onto the hard shoulder. It would be futile trying to outrun a souped-up police Volvo in a decrepit Beetle, but it crossed Leo's mind to urge Grant to do so.

They sat anxiously awaiting their fate. Grant rubbed at his eyes, which must have been tired. The policemen got out of their patrol car, put on their peaked caps and ambled up to the side of Ethel – who they viewed with more disdain than was necessary in Leo's opinion.

Grant wound down the window. One policeman leaned on the roof. He was considerably younger than Leo. He gave them all a supercilious smile. 'In a rush, sir?'

'Yes,' Grant said, and took a deep breath. 'We have a sick fairy in the back of the car and we're trying to get her to Stonehenge.'

'A sick fairy?'

'Yes,' Grant confirmed. 'I believe in this situation that honesty might be the best policy.'

The policeman didn't look as if he agreed. He peered into the car and ran his frosty gaze over Leo and Isobel.

'Isobel,' Leo urged her. 'Get your wand out. Zap him. Zap him now.'

She managed to rouse herself, but said weakly, 'I can't, Leo.' She shook her head sadly. 'I can't.'

Then, he felt, they were doomed.

The policeman sighed. The word 'clowns' was written all over his face. He turned to Grant. 'Would you mind stepping out of the car, sir?'

Chapter Sixty-Three

'Hello?' the man says. 'Hello? Is there anybody in there?'
I sag with relief at the sound of a human voice outside my box.

'Yes there is. Help,' I say urgently. 'Help me. Please.'

'Are you okay?'

'I'm fine,' I say. Panic-stricken, stiff, hungry and getting cold, but other than that, fine. 'Can you just get me out, please?'

There's some tugging and pulling at my box and I brace myself against the sides. Then all goes still again.

'I need to go back up to the flat and get some scissors,' the man tells me with a disgruntled puff. 'I'll be back in a minute. I'm Dominic, by the way.'

'Hi, Dominic,' I say. 'I'm Emma. We've met on the stairs a couple of times before. I'm Leo's girlfriend. I *was* Leo's girlfriend.'

'Oh,' Dominic responds as if that explains everything. 'Won't be long.'

I know exactly who Dominic is. He's the dreamboat who lives next door to Leo with his equally gorgeous girlfriend, Lydia. Leo and I always used to row about Dominic and Lydia. Dominic cuddles his other half to death even when they're just going down the stairs. Leo isn't even that keen on holding hands in public. Dominic and Lydia were always very friendly when they passed in the hallway and, as couples, we always said that we'd get together and have a drink or dinner some time, but never did. Now I wish we had. It isn't a good idea to be formally introduced in this way. Maybe if we'd made time to have a quick pizza with Dominic and his girlfriend, I wouldn't be so mortified now. Why can't the person who witnesses my shame be one of the other folks from the apartments – the forty-two-year-old divorcée or one of the gay blokes or, preferably, a visiting relative who is less attractive than Dominic and also blind. I sigh and try to cheer myself up. Not long now and it will all be over.

I hear Dominic go back up the steps to the flats. 'Come on, Chloe,' he says pleasantly to the cat. 'Get down from the top of the box. There's a good girl.'

Wait till I get my hands on bloody Chloe – although to be fair the cat did come to my rescue in a roundabout way. I lean back in my box, looking forward to escaping my self-inflicted prison, but not relishing the next part. Exposing my folly to the world. That will teach me to try to be spontaneous and fun.

'I'm back,' Dominic says a few minutes later. 'Had to search for the scissors. Hold still. Have you out in a jiffy.'

Leo's neighbour gets to work with the scissors. I duck out of the way as the sharp points slice through the box. 'I knocked at Leo's door to let him know that you were here,' Dominic says. 'But he's out.'

I'd managed to work out that much.

'Good job that I came home early from the office,' he says cheerfully as he works away.

He's nearly got the lid off. I cover myself as best I can. This is going to take some explaining away. After a few more snips, Dominic flips open the top.

'Aargh!' I shout.

Oh no. My hair is stuck to the Superglue on the lid. 'My hair. My hair.'

Dominic quickly lowers the lid again and peers under it, before recoiling. 'Oh!'

So he's noticed the underwear then.

'I'm sorry about my appearance,' I say quickly. 'This is a prank that's gone very wrong.'

'I think you're right there,' he agrees and then peers in again.

I shrink away from him. This is supposed to be for Leo's eyes only. Perhaps Dominic will lend me some clothes to go home in. All I want to do is get away from here with some shred of dignity intact, climb into a steaming hot bath and consume some very strong drink.

'You've stuck your hair to the lid,' he says, tsking loudly. 'I think I'm going to have to snip some off.'

'Cut my hair?'

'There's quite a lot of it plastered to the box.'

I want to cry. This has been a hare-brained scheme from start to finish. Exactly the sort of thing that Leo would do. And I'm beginning

233

to have some empathy with his more idiotic pranks. I was so well-intentioned and this has gone so horribly wrong. There's no way though, that I deserve this humiliation. 'Cut it,' I instruct. 'Just be careful.'

Dominic gingerly slips his scissors inside and slices at great hunks of my hair. It feels like a re-run of *Edward Scissorhands*. Erratic snip, snip, snipping echoes in my ears. I just hope that Leo doesn't turn up now in the middle of all this. The only thing I want to do now is hide myself and run for the hills.

My rescuer flips the lid again and I gulp in the fresh air, glad that the overpowering smell of cat wee is out of my nostrils.

'There you are.' Dominic smiles at his handiwork.

'Thank you,' I say gratefully. 'Thank you.' I go to stand up but can't move.

'Easy there,' Dominic advises. 'I expect you're a bit numb. Been here long?'

'Yes,' I admit. 'Hours.' Hours and hours and hours and hours. For most of my adult life. At least, it feels like that.

'Do you mind me asking,' he says. I know the question before he asks it. 'Why exactly are you in a box on our doorstep?'

'It was a prank,' I explain. 'A silly joke. Leo and I have split up. I thought this would be a fun way to get his attention again.'

Dominic looks as if he doubts my sanity.

'I realise now,' I say, before he decides I'm a complete headcase, 'that I have made a terrible mistake.'

'Here.' Dominic offers me his hand. 'Let me help you out. I'll avert my eyes,' he continues, doing anything but. He has a good ogle at my MISS FUNNY FANNY thong.

Reluctantly, I let go of the gift bow covering my breasts and reach out my hand. The skin on the back of my arm rips painfully. 'Arghh!' I cry out and withdraw my hand. What the hell is that?

I try to move it again. But it's stuck fast. 'Oh no,' I say, panic returning. 'Please no.'

I try to move my legs, but the bottom of my feet are firmly attached to the seam of the box where I so fervently applied a liberal coating of Superglue. I try moving my bottom, but I can't budge an inch. I thought it was merely the confines of my cardboard box that were restricting my movements. Once again, I'm wrong. The glue must still have been wet when I settled myself in. How could I be so stupid? 'I can't move,' I say tearfully. 'I can't move at all.'

'Oh dear,' Dominic comments, frowning worriedly.

'I Superglued the seams of the box before I got in it,' I admit. 'I think it was a bad idea.' One in a long line of bad ideas.

'It does look like you're rather stuck.'

I feel that's something of an understatement. 'What am I going to do? How am I going to get out, Dominic?' I turn my eyes to plead with him.

'Er . . .' He nibbles his lip. 'It's dastardly stuff, this Superglue,' he informs me.

'I know. I know.'

'This isn't going to come off with a bit of Fairy Liquid and a nail-brush. If I try to prise this off, it could seriously damage your skin.'

'*Seriously* damage?'

'I reckon it needs specialist treatment.'

A cold shiver runs over me. 'What sort of specialist treatment?'

'I think there's only one thing for it,' he says, shaking his head. 'I need to call the Fire Brigade.'

Chapter Sixty-Four

Ten minutes later, two bright red fire engines arrive, sirens blaring, and block Leo's street. As no cars are able to pass, the drivers waiting in the resulting traffic jam simply get an eyeful. To add even more discomfort to my predicament, a small and very curious crowd of neighbours start to gather. Even the guys from the greasy kebab take-away wander up the road to take a peek.

By this time too, Dominic has managed to cut away some of the box. It means that I'm not feeling quite so encased or claustrophobic, but it also means that the entire street has a great view of my under-wear. So I'm now sitting on Leo's doorstep, in gift wrapping and my smalls, framed by a cardboard cut-out sculpture. The rubber-neckers all crane to get a better view. The only person who isn't anywhere in sight is, of course, Leo.

Half a dozen fire-fighters – all male, all built like brick outhouses and all smirking – make their way up the steps to the flat. They come armed with a selection of axes and cutting tools and other things that look like instruments of torture which I really hope they won't need. I wonder if any of them are friends of Caron's brother. I sincerely hope not. All those hunky men to hand and look at the state of me. Why can't I have something dignified wrong with me that needs a sensible, life-threatening rescue, instead of having Superglued myself into a box? I huddle into myself and pretend that I'm somewhere else, while Dominic kindly explains what has happened.

A couple of the burliest fire-fighters grab hold of the box and start trying to prise me from it.

'Aargh!' I cry out again. I shrink away from them and somehow the button on my MISS FUNNY FANNY thong gets pressed and my underwear starts to giggle maniacally.

The fire-fighters join in. So does Dominic. I want to die. I wish I'd just given up and suffocated in my box.

When the thong has ceased giggling, the laughter finally dies down and the fire-fighters stop rolling about on the ground. The men try to compose their faces into suitably serious expressions and turn their attention back to me.

'I think we need to call for an ambulance, miss,' one of the fire-fighters informs me.

'I don't think that will be necessary,' I say.

'That Superglue is terrible stuff.' He rubs his chin in a considered fashion. I think he might be trying to wipe the smile off his face. 'They'll be able to get it off in Accident and Emergency without you having to part with your skin.'

'Please, please,' I beg. 'Don't take me to hospital. Just get one of your axes and cut my arms and legs off instead. I'll be fine.'

'What you need is a little bit of solvent and it will be all over.'

'I don't . . .' I start to protest. My eyes fill with tears. 'I don't think I could bear it.'

'Trust me,' the fire-fighter says, holding up a hand to quiet me. 'It'll be for the best. A lot less painful. Your boyfriend can ride in the ambulance with you,' he goes on, nodding towards Dominic.

'That's not my boyfriend,' I say, and then give up. They're much more interested in my taste in underwear to bother themselves with my taste in men.

The fire-fighter wanders off, presumably to call for an ambulance – which is a shame because a ride in a fire engine might have offered some sort of compensation for my suffering.

'Do you want me to go and make you a cup of tea?' Dominic asks.

'I'm fine, thanks.' I'm desperate for a cup of tea, but I'm even more desperate to go to the loo and I'm not sure how I'm going to manage that with my knickers glued to my backside.

My rescuer sits down on the step next to me and I notice that he angles himself between me and the crowd, so that not all of the neighbours can get an eyeful of my lingerie. Which is very thoughtful. He's been really nice to me even though he hasn't been able to fully liberate me. 'I'm quite happy to come with you in the ambulance,' Dominic says.

'Won't Lydia be worried about where you are?'

Dominic shakes his head. 'She left me,' he explains with a shrug. 'A few weeks ago. Went off with someone from work.'

Suddenly, I notice that he looks tired and pale. 'I'm sorry to hear that,' I say. 'It happens.'

'I didn't think of posting myself to her in a box,' Dominic confesses. 'I've just been at home trying to drown my sorrows with passable red wine. This shows great ingenuity.'

'It shows great stupidity.'

Dominic laughs. 'This is more the sort of thing that I can imagine Leo doing,' he says. 'You always seemed more – well . . . reserved.'

'I wanted to break out of my box.' We both smile ruefully at my choice of metaphor. 'I thought Leo would like this. Instead, I'm sitting here covered in Superglue while he is off somewhere – who knows where – probably having a great time.'

'Leo's a lot of fun,' Dominic says. 'I wish I could be more like him. While the rest of us are burdened by responsibility, Leo has always managed to remain childlike.'

'Childish,' I correct.

At that moment, the crowd parts and the ambulance arrives. I let out a weary exhalation. 'Let the next part of the fun commence,' I state.

'I will come with you. If you want me to.'

'I'd like that,' I say. 'You're very kind.'

'I was going to watch the football this evening,' Dominic admits. 'This is much more interesting.'

Oh, I'm so happy that I've been able to provide him with an entertaining distraction.

Two paramedics get out of the ambulance and go over to talk to the fire-fighters who, with a cheery wave to me, then jump back into their fire engines and drive away. I can imagine that I'll be the talk of the station room for some time to come

'I'll go and get you some clothes for later,' Dominic says. He nips up the stairs and disappears into the flats.

The paramedics come over to me and, after taking in my underwear, also fall about in a fit of giggles. Just wait until they move me and set off my chuckling knickers again, I think miserably.

Dominic returns with a small holdall.

'We'll lift you and what remains of the box into the ambulance,' one of the paramedics says.

Dominic smiles at me and, putting his hand on my shoulder, says, 'Nearly over.'

He really is very sweet. I let my head fall back against the remains of the box. Just then, a truck with *LONDON LIVE* emblazoned on the side pulls up and a television crew leap out. Nearly over, it seems, but not quite. It looks as if I'm going to be on the evening news in my underwear. Oh good.

The reporter sprints over to me. Hot on her heels is a burly cameraman and a sound engineer with one of those big, furry boom things. 'How are you feeling?' She pushes her microphone into my face. 'Why are you doing this? Is it a protest against something? Who glued you into the box?'

'No comment,' I say. If I could get one of my arms free, I might punch her.

Dominic does his best to shield me from their attention.

'Just relax,' one of the paramedics advises me. And then they both hoist me into the air with a chorus of inelegant grunts and edge their way through the crowd, with the reporter in tow. Whereupon my under-wear sees fit to burst into life once more and giggles hysterically all the way to the ambulance.

Chapter Sixty-Five

Grant was standing on the hard shoulder. The youngest and strop-piest policeman was making him blow into a breathalyser bag. Thankfully, Grant hadn't touched a drop of booze today – yet. But no doubt they would make up for that omission later on tonight.

Lard and Leo were looking sheepish in the car. They had no idea what to do and time was marching on. Isobel's eyes flickered open.

'We are in big trouble,' Leo told her, whispering urgently. 'The police have stopped us. Isn't there anything you can do?'

Her eyes were dilated black circles. She looked as if she'd been doing some heavy drugs.

'Where's your wand?' he asked. 'What about if I wave and you tell me what to say?'

She opened her mouth, but she hadn't the energy to speak. This was not a good place to be.

'Isobel, please try,' Leo urged. 'Please try. Otherwise we're stuffed.'

The policeman came back towards Ethel, and Grant followed him. The young man leaned into the car and took in the sight of Isobel draped across Leo's lap. 'Is she all right?' he asked.

'No,' Leo said. 'She's very ill. We're trying to save her.'

'Miss?' the policeman said. 'Miss?'

Isobel's eyes struggled open once more. 'Help me,' she mouthed and as she did, she opened her hand – a tiny unfurling of her fingers – and a silver butterfly fluttered out towards the policeman. It landed on his hand and stayed there opening and closing its wings. 'Help me,' she whispered again.

Leo looked over to Lard and saw that he had tears in his eyes too.

The policeman gazed in awe at the butterfly which fluttered slowly away, disappearing into thin air within an arm's length. Then the officer stood up and adjusted his hat. 'Right,' he said, twitching his neck. 'We'll give you a high-speed escort.'

'Thank you,' Leo breathed, hardly daring to speak in case he did something to break the spell. With Isobel so weak, he didn't know how tenuous this might be.

'Where did you say you were going?'

'Stonehenge,' Grant answered.

'Then you'd better get a move on, sir,' the policeman said. 'We'll take you as far as we can. That'll speed things up a bit.'

Lard and Leo nearly passed out with shock. Grant looked as if he couldn't believe his ears, but jumped back into the car and gunned it into life once more. The policeman returned to his car and, with lights flashing and sirens wailing, pulled back into the stream of traffic.

'You did it, Isobel.' Leo hugged her to him. But she had slipped away from them again.

'What happened there?' Grant said as he tried to keep up with the racing police car.

'I don't know,' Leo admitted.

'I had to say this heap was mine, Leo.' His friend was clearly affronted that he had to pretend to have such bad taste. 'And I still got a tug for speeding.'

'I'll pay the fine,' Leo said.

Grant shook his head. 'That doesn't matter,' he said. 'All that matters is that we get Isobel there in time.'

They were all quiet in the car as they continued their journey, zooming along the motorway after the police car. Ethel ate up the miles, complaining little at the breakneck speed. As they came off the motorway the police officers waved them a cheery goodbye and peeled away. They continued their journey alone, following the signs for Stonehenge. Leo was holding his breath as they rushed past fields, fields and more fields, endless swathes of golden hay gleaming in the last vestiges of late-evening sun. Grant sped along the narrow, unlit dual carriageway lined with mile after mile of dark, claustrophobic trees until, eventually, they burst out onto a stark, open plain. Ahead of them, standing proud on the horizon, were the towering black silhouettes of the monoliths of Stonehenge.

Relief flooded through Leo. He leaned over and kissed Isobel. 'We're nearly there, baby. Hang on.'

The night was now drawing in, darkening slowly, and the clouds had huddled together. The sun was on its downward path towards the horizon and the space between the earth and sky was spattered with splotches of pink and apricot and fire red. Leo hoped this was a good omen. Coming closer into view was the huge circle of stones – great monoliths outlined against the vastness of the sky. Leo wasn't a man prone to this sort of thing, but he could feel the strong pull of ancient powers. Isobel shifted in his arms and he clung to her. Inside, Leo had a horrible empty sensation and he wondered how much longer their time together would last.

Even though they'd made it this far, Grant and Lard were looking decidedly worried. And Leo got the feeling that as one part of the journey was ending, another more terrifying part was about to begin.

Chapter Sixty-Six

It took two very patient nurses, two very long hours to peel away all the Superglue from my tender skin with some sort of foul-smelling solvent. My skin feels bruised and raw, but there'll be no permanent scarring – just a painful memory that I'd really rather forget.

Prior to this, there'd been another two-hour wait in a cubicle in the Accident and Emergency department – where they'd left me, still in the remains of my cardboard box, perched on top of a trolley, screened from too many prying eyes by nothing more than a pair of flimsy, ragged curtains.

Dominic has been fantastic. The nurses gave him some scissors while we waited and he quietly and methodically cut away at some more of my firmly adhered box, until I could actually straighten my legs. He endured, stoically – as I did – the parade of junior doctors who had clearly felt moved to come along to offer their vital medical opinion and not simply to have a gawp at me in my sleazy underwear. Eventually, one of the nurses brought me a surgical gown which Dominic tied round me to cover as much as he could. While we waited for the de-gluing to commence, we'd talked about Leo and Lydia and agreed what idiots they both were. It helped me to avoid thinking about what an idiot I am.

This is not how I envisaged the day would end. By now I should have been in Leo's arms, quite possibly in Leo's bed – he would have found it hard to resist me, I'm sure, in red giggling knickers. Instead, Leo's poor neighbour has been roped in to perform the role of knight in shining armour. I look over at Dominic, and my new friend smiles crookedly at me. I have to admit that he's done a very good job.

Now we're in a cab on the way back to my flat. Dominic had brought me some clothes in his holdall – clearly ones that the recently departed Lydia had left behind. They're a bit tight – maybe Lydia doesn't have my attachment to all things calorific – but they're certainly a lot more suitable than my previous ensemble.

I lean back on the seat of the taxi. I'm absolutely knackered. Being stuck in a cardboard box for the best part of the day has been an emotionally draining experience. Particularly when I've got nothing but a collection of red and very sore patches of skin to show for it. I glance over at my companion. Dominic looks completely done in too. For once it's quite nice to be the stupid one, while someone else takes control. I can now appreciate Leo's addiction to it. What on earth is making me act like this? What on earth is making me act exactly like Leo? My mind drifts to my ex-boyfriend and I wonder where he is now. Has he returned home to his flat completely oblivious to the fuss that has been created outside it all afternoon?

The cab pulls up outside my place. Dominic pays the driver and we get out.

The bars and restaurants on Shad Thames are still bustling. I want to crawl into my bed and sleep for ever. I limp towards the flat, all of my bones aching. It would have served me right if I'd never walked again or had spent the rest of my life in that hideous red thong. My bottom will bear the marks of it for weeks.

'I want to make sure that you're okay,' Dominic says into my moping. 'I hope you don't mind.'

'I'm fine now, really,' I insist stoically, when inside I don't feel fine at all. 'But I should give you Lydia's clothes back. Just in case she turns up for them.'

'I think that's unlikely,' Dominic admits.

'It might be better if I give you them back straight away. It would be easier than trying to explain to her why I borrowed them.'

Dominic laughs. He's a great-looking guy. Relaxed, tousled. Laid back, but with a good deal more commonsense than some I could mention. Someone like Dominic might well be able to turn my head. A lightness comes over my spirit – something that I haven't experienced in weeks. Perhaps my 'in-the-box' experience might have a worthwhile outcome after all. The thought makes me smile, even though my jaw aches with tension.

I open the door to my flat and let us both in. The red light on my answerphone is blinking away at me. Hopefully, it will be Leo having found out that I've suffered a cruel indignity on his doorstep and begging my forgiveness. If it is, I don't want to listen to the message while Dominic is here.

'Shall I put some coffee on while I go and get changed?' I ask.

He must be starving too, as neither of us has eaten during our ordeal.

'I should be going,' Dominic says with a shrug. 'I've got work to do before tomorrow.'

I realise that I don't even know what work Dominic does and that, apart from a brief session of slagging off Lydia, I don't know much about his personal life either. 'Maybe I could take you out to dinner one evening soon,' I offer. 'As my way of saying thanks.'

'You don't have to do that.'

'But I'd like to.' And I realise that it's true.

'Then I'd like that too,' Dominic replies shyly.

'Scribble down your number while I change.' I indicate a pad by the phone.

'You've got a message.'

'Yes.' I feel myself flushing scarlet for the seventeen-hundredth time today. 'I'll listen to it later.'

Dominic doesn't question my motives.

'Make yourself comfy,' I tell him. 'I won't be a minute.'

My friend turns to write down his number and I slip into the bedroom. Pulling off Lydia's clothes, glad to be free of yet another constriction, I then yank on my comfiest tracksuit bottoms. All I want to do is sink onto my bed and never get up again. Instead, I root in my wardrobe, find a carrier bag for Lydia's loaned clothes and pop them inside.

Dominic still waits patiently as I emerge from the bedroom. He hasn't made himself comfortable, he's sort of hovering about the flat, and when I go towards him, I can see that he's looking at a picture of me and Leo together. I could kick myself that they're still displayed all over the place – masses of photos of me and Leo in giggling, romantic poses. We did have our moments. Rather a lot of them, actually.

'Here are Lydia's clothes.' I hand the bag over and he stuffs it into his holdall. 'Thanks again. That was very thoughtful of you.'

'You're welcome,' Dominic says. 'I'd better be off now.'

'Shall I call you a cab?'

'I'll walk,' he shrugs. 'It's a nice night. It might help me sleep.' My heart goes out to him. I know all about sleepless nights.

'I'll give you a call,' I say. 'Soon. And thanks again for everything. I don't know what I'd have done without you.'

'It was certainly an interesting experience,' Dominic agrees. 'Even from my point of view.'

'I promise to wear more clothes when we go out for dinner.'

'No need to on my behalf,' Dominic replies with a smile.

I kiss him on the cheek. Oh, it would be so easy to turn my head and kiss his lips. Quickly, I pull away. Perhaps I've got some Superglue on the brain.

'I'll speak to you soon.' And with that, Dominic leaves. I think about watching him walk down the street from my balcony, but wonder if he'd misconstrue it. I wonder if he *should* misconstrue it!

I pick up Leo's photograph. Will it be possible to replace Leo in my affections? Who knows. It's too late and I'm too tired to think about it. Still, I'd better listen to his message – see what he's got to say for himself.

Flicking on the answerphone, I listen in. But it isn't Leo. My father's wavering voice rings out into the flat.

My father never rings me. Ever. That's my mother's job.

'Darling,' he says shakily. 'It's Daddy. And I've got some terrible news.'

Chapter Sixty-Seven

The towering circle of stones were so distinct on the horizon. An unmistakable monument to long-departed ancestors. Though to this day, no one really has any idea what Stonehenge is all about or how the gigantic slabs of blue Welsh stone came to be here. It looked like a great place for sacrifice and rituals and pagan worship and magic. Those Druids – or whoever built it – certainly knew how to pick their spot.

Leo and his friends turned down a small, dark country lane and bumped along towards the monument. As Grant pulled into the gravel car park at the Visitor Centre, Ethel's wheels made an intrusive crunch in the overwhelming silence.

Leaning down, Leo whispered to Isobel, 'We're here.' She managed a weak smile. And not a moment too soon, Leo could have added.

The area was absolutely deserted – theirs was the only car around. The snack bars were all closed up, the ice-cream vans and the tourists' coaches long gone. In the distance, Leo could see that the stones were surrounded by a high wire fence; he was sure that when he last came here as a boy, he'd walked right up to them.

Without talking, they all climbed out of the car. Lard helped Leo to lift Isobel into his arms. An officious sign announced that the Visitor Centre closed at 7.00 p.m. and went on to give a long list of rules for 'enjoying' the stones. The row of turnstiles were locked, clamped with padlocks, for the night. The pay booths were shuttered against them. Racks of audio commentaries stood idle. Even if they'd wanted to, the tiny group couldn't have parted with the extortionate entrance fee.

'Oh flip,' Leo said with a heartfelt sigh. 'It's shut.' In his haste to get there, he hadn't even considered that they might not be able to get access to the stones. He hoped that Isobel had one last wave left in her wand as they might well need it. 'What now?'

Lard picked up his holdall. With a flourish like a sword, their dark little friend produced a crowbar from inside. 'We go and find fairies,' he said.

Grant and Leo looked on in amazement as Lard marched up to the turnstiles and jumped over with a surprising degree of athleticism. They followed him, speechless, and Grant jumped over too and then took Isobel from Leo's arms while he did the same.

By the time they'd sorted themselves out, Lard was already at the door of the Visitor Centre. In fact, they were so surprised that they followed him, unspeaking, until they were all huddled round the door – Lard with his crowbar in hand.

'We have to go through here to get to the stones,' he told them.

'Isn't there another way?'

'No.' Lard shook his head firmly.

'We can't break in,' Leo said.

'We can,' Lard insisted, exhibiting an assertiveness previously unseen in his character and outside of *Terminator* films.

Leo looked to Grant as the voice of reason. 'Let's do it,' his friend said.

And, with a minimal amount of effort, Lard leaned on his crowbar and eased his way in. The front door gave amazingly quickly – they really needed to look at their security arrangements here. Grant and Leo exchanged a stunned look. They never knew that Lard had this in him.

'Have you ever done this professionally?' Leo asked.

'Leo,' he answered, 'if we get caught, I might not have any choice.'

Leo could see how having form for breaking and entering might not sit well with an accelerated career path in the City. But that was the least of their worries tonight.

They eased their way in and tiptoed past the waiting rack of books, DVDs and videos selling the story of Stonehenge from every possible angle. Leo would have thought that there might have been a burglar alarm in the shop, but then again, who on earth would hear it ringing out here in the middle of nowhere? The nearest police station must be miles away.

'Do we need anything from in here to help us in our quest?' he asked.

'What good is a Stonehenge thimble to us?' Grant said. 'Or Stonehenge playing cards?'

'I don't know,' Leo admitted. 'But I thought I'd check.'

They jemmied the door at the other end of the gift shop and slipped out into the tunnel which went under the road and linked them to the site of the stones.

The tunnel was lit with psychedelic spotlights in pink and green, picking out naive paintings of bare-chested Anglo-Saxons heaving stones on wooden rollers. They hurried along it – Leo panting with the weight of Isobel in his arms – until they came out onto the vast open plain. Leo's shirt was sticking to his back with sweat.

Despite the night being hot and clammy, there was a cool, steady breeze blowing. Leo turned his face to it, thankful for a moment's respite. Just ahead, there was a sentry box, but thankfully there was no security guard on duty. Instead, a huge metal gate barred the way.

'It's terrible that they have to go to so much trouble to protect the stones from vandalism,' Leo said with a sigh.

Grant and Lard turned to look at him.

'What?'

Lard opened his holdall once more and pulled out some bolt cutters.

'Why have you got all these things?' Leo wanted to know. All he owned was a Black & Decker drill – unused. And . . . no, that was it. Just the drill. And Emma probably bought him that one Christmas in an attempt to domesticate him. What previous use had Lard had for a range of tools like this? Obviously, there was much that they didn't know about their little chocolate-eating friend.

Lard cut through the gate with his bolt cutters like a warm knife slicing through butter. They all slipped inside.

Once in the middle of the hallowed circle, they gazed in awe at the massive stones, humbled by the sheer audacity of their size. Leo felt as if they'd been standing waiting for them all this time.

'Wow!' Lard intoned breathlessly. Leo thought that his friend was quite taken aback by his own skill at skulduggery.

'Isobel's fading fast,' Leo told them. 'What do we have to do?'

'Lay her on the ground in the centre of the stones,' Grant instructed.

Leo kissed Isobel and held her to him tenderly, before gently laying her on the lush grass, thick with springy clumps of clover and a sprinkling of buttercups and daisies. The circle was no longer complete and some of the great slabs of stone lay higgledy-piggledy on the ground. Leo wondered what this place might have been – a temple to a Sun God, a prehistoric observatory or some sort of calculator for celestial activity? All of these things had been mooted by experts in the past.

He'd never heard anyone say that it was a kind of underground station for fairies who needed to get home. Which worried him.

Grant and Lard exchanged a glance. 'Is this a bad time to mention that we're all supposed to be virgins?' Grant said sheepishly.

'Oh great!' Leo paced the ground. 'You've been shagging everything that moves for years.'

'Thanks.'

'None of us are exactly,' Lard interjected, 'well, pure. What's the opposite of virgins?'

'Slappers,' Leo said. 'We're all slappers.'

'Apart from Isobel,' Lard noted respectfully.

Leo gazed down at her on the grass and wondered how it could have come to this – that she'd had to put her trust in three City slappers and Google. He covered his eyes with his hands. 'What are we going to do?'

'I don't know,' Grant admitted. 'Perhaps we should all think clean thoughts while we do the rest of it.'

'What "rest of it"?'

His friends exchanged another dodgy look. They really were getting more and more like an old married couple every day, Leo thought.

Lard delved into his holdall once more and pulled out a ghetto-blaster which he placed, with some reverence, on the ground between them.

'I put new batteries in it,' he said proudly.

'Good.' Leo stood open-mouthed still awaiting some explanation. There was very little light left now and they were peering at each other in the dark.

Grant cleared his throat. 'We do a fairy dance.'

'What the hell's a fairy dance?'

'How should I know,' Grant snapped. 'That's all it said on the internet. It didn't give me the steps.'

'Marvellous.'

'Try to enter into the spirit of this, Leo,' he shouted. 'We are doing it for you, after all.'

'We're doing it for Isobel,' Leo said quietly. 'Come on. Let's get on with it instead of doing our Marx Brothers routine.'

Lard produced another packet from his seemingly bottomless holdall and with great solemnity handed out sparklers.

'Sparklers?' Leo asked, trying not to sound cynical.

'Sparklers,' Lard shrugged in response.

'Look, Leo,' Grant snapped again. 'Just accept that we do not understand the great unfathomable mysteries of the universe and go with the flow.'

Leo examined his sparkler. He hadn't had one of these for a long time – Bonfire Night circa 1980 would be his guess. It was rogue one and had burned a hole in his glove. He turned his attention to the ghetto-blaster. Leo hardly dared ask this question. 'What's that for?'

'Fairy music,' Grant said.

'Of course.'

Lard flicked the switch and a blast of tinkly piano music filled the air. Leo could feel a frown coming on.

'What on earth's that?' Grant demanded.

Lard looked offended. 'Liberace.'

Grant and Leo in unison. 'Liberace?'

'Fairy music,' Lard explained. 'I didn't have any Elton John so I borrowed this from my mum. It's just the job.'

Grant huffed with exasperation. 'It said to play some music *for* a fairy, you clot – not *by* a fairy!'

Liberace's latest fan shrugged. 'What's the difference?'

'Turn it off! Turn it off!' Grant shouted.

Lard clicked off the ghetto-blaster and the eerie sound of silence returned once more to the vast landscape. 'What else have you got?'

Rooting around in the bottom of his holdall, Lard muttered mutinously under his breath.

Leo could have wept. He could have wept for his beautiful girl, who was having to suffer this indignity.

Chapter Sixty-Eight

My father seems to have shrunk. The proud, bad-tempered curmudgeon has disappeared to be replaced by a small, frightened man who looks older than his years.

The man who is so meticulous about his appearance has dishevelled hair and a mismatched jacket over his trousers. I fly straight to him and hug him.

'Where is she?'

'Through there,' he says, indicating double swing doors. 'I just came out for some air.'

The reception of the private clinic my mother has been taken to is a far cry from the tatty Accident and Emergency department I've just left. It's decorated in soothing blues and is filled with sumptuous sofas and vases of delicate flowers. Tasteful modern artworks hang on the walls. Catherine would hate them.

'How is she?'

'Asleep,' my father tells me. 'She's comfortable.'

'Is she going to be all right?'

He shakes his head. 'It's hard to tell at this stage,' he says, his voice hoarse with tiredness. 'It seems to be a minor stroke, thank goodness, but she's lost her speech and the movement down one side. That might take some time to come back.'

'But it *will* come back?'

Daddy puts his arm around me. 'We don't know, darling. We simply don't know.'

I burst into tears and cling to my father. 'Mummy can't be ill,' I say. 'She's never ill.' It's my father who's been swallowing pills for his angina the best part of ten years, not my mother. She never takes so much as a headache tablet. She never even has a common cold. Catherine Chambers is the picture of health.

'We're going to have to do things differently from now on,' my father says. 'Your mother has always run the family. She's the powerhouse. We're going to have to take the pressure off her. We need to look after her now.'

'I don't want to see her like this,' I say.

'Come on, now.' My father rubs his thumb over my face, smudging my tears, and I think that it's probably the first time he has touched me like that in years. 'My big strong girl. You can cope. You always do. Catherine doesn't look any different. Just more vulnerable.'

And that's exactly how I feel. More vulnerable than I've ever felt in my life.

My mother lies on the hospital bed attached to an array of machines and drips. Something beeps methodically. She looks pale against the starched white sheets. I go over to her and kiss her on the forehead, which feels too cold and dry, but my mother doesn't stir.

My father pulls up two armchairs and we both sit down. He holds my hand, too tightly. I rest my head back. I'm so unbelievably tired.

'How did it happen?'

'Catherine was out shopping with Henrietta Gooding,' my father explains. 'She collapsed in Harrods. They were marvellous. Thank goodness she didn't keel over in a lower-class establishment,' he says with a shake of his head. 'She might not be here to tell the tale.'

I hide a smile. Even in this state, my father still manages to be a pompous snob.

'Henrietta is normally so feeble-brained,' he continues, 'but the woman came good this time, phoned me immediately. I pulled a few strings and we brought your mother straight here.' He pats his wife's hand and fusses with her bedclothes. 'Much better than that terrible general hospital. I called you as soon as I could, but they said you hadn't been into work today.'

I sigh. 'I had a small emergency of my own.'

My father raises an eyebrow in question. Thankfully, he hasn't been watching the television news.

'All sorted now,' I say quickly. 'I'm sorry it took me so long. Do Clara and Arabelle know?'

My father nods. 'They'll be here tomorrow. They both needed to make arrangements for the children to be cared for.'

'Will Mummy be in here for long?'

'We don't know yet, sweetheart,' my father admits. 'We'll have to see what the doctor says.'

253

We both settle back into our armchairs. I feel so helpless just sitting here, watching my mother; there's nothing I can do for her, except wait and be here. I close my eyes. It would be unbearable if anything happens to her. It seems as if my entire support network is being kicked away from me at the moment: first Leo, now my mother. Both people I've taken hideously for granted. Maybe it's God's perverse way of making me realise that I should have appreciated them both more.

'I do love your mother,' my father says into my thoughts. 'I don't think I ever showed it enough.'

'Of course you did, Daddy,' I insist.

'I should have told her more often. I should have taken her out more. She's a very beautiful woman.' His voice is laden with tears. 'I should have said so every day.'

'She knows you love her,' I tell him. She knows, but I realise that I've never heard my father say it to his wife. That suddenly seems too sad.

'You plan for the future,' my father continues heavily, 'but none of us knows how long we've got. We never understand the frailty of human life until it hits us in the face. We really are a very arrogant race. We always think we've got for ever.' My father fiddles with his watch. 'I'm going to take her on a cruise. She'll like that. A long one. Round the Caribbean. As soon as she's well. We must do the things we've always said that we'd do.'

He doesn't say 'before it's too late' but I know that's exactly what's on his mind.

'I'll work shorter hours,' he goes on. 'Maybe take early retirement.'

'But your work is your life, Daddy.'

'Your mother must be my life from now on. She's always been there for me – for all of us. Now I must do the same.' He turns bleak eyes to me. 'I don't want her to leave me. I don't know what I'd do.'

I hold my father to me. It surprises me to realise that this is the longest conversation I've had with him in many years. Normally, it's a few brisk exchanged words, before each of us rush off to do something more important. Why is it that sometimes the people you love the most, you know the least? Why do we build barriers around our feelings for our closest relations? Maybe I have some thinking to do too.

'She won't leave us,' I say determinedly. 'Mummy won't give up without a fight. She's an old battleaxe. That's why you love her.'

'I do love her,' my father says. 'I do.'

Suddenly I need Leo. I need to talk to him. Just to hear his voice. 'I'll be back in a minute, Daddy,' I say and slip out of the hospital room.

Outside the front door there's a tranquil Japanese garden. Rich burgundy acers flutter in the breeze. A fountain splashes lazily over a beach of smooth, grey cobbles. I find a small bench and sit on it, flipping out my mobile phone now that I'm out of the confines of the clinic. Slowly, I push the digits of Leo's number. I feel so alone without him. Like my father, I think I should have told Leo more often that I love him. I should have shown him more. It's only now that I've become aware that all the stupid, insane, irritating things he did filled the space that's inside me. Leo is the sun in my sky, the rain in my desert and, sometimes, the fly in my ointment too. But I should have loved him for it. All of him. Leo sees the magic in the world – in the small things – whereas I'm far too uptight to even imagine it. I love looking at Leo when he doesn't know I'm watching him. When he's relaxing, he has the face of a child – without guile and accepting. I'd lost my appreciation of his qualities and had become so concerned with what other people thought of my relationship with him that I'd forgotten what it meant to me.

His mobile phone rings and rings. Then there's a strange humming noise on the line and I can't tell whether Leo has picked up or not. 'Leo,' I say, choking back the emotion in my voice. 'Is that you? Where are you? I need to talk to you.' I speak quietly. No jumping out of a box in my underwear, no gimmicks, no coercion, no shouting, no emotional blackmail. 'Please call me. I need you, Leo. I really need you.'

There's no reply. So I hang up. All I can do now is wait.

Chapter Sixty-Nine

L ard lit their sparklers which burst into life, showering silver sparks into the sky and illuminating their pale, tired faces. Finally, Leo thought, they were ready.

They stood in a circle round the inert form of Isobel and Leo prayed silently to a God that he didn't really believe in, but he hoped existed and took pity on this poor sinner below. Because he was desperate, truly desperate. If this place did mean anything, he hoped fervently that it meant something good.

The last trace of the sun had now gone and the moon was full and high in the sky. The stones cast grotesquely eerie shadows on the ground. Lard clicked on the ghetto-blaster again. Liberace had been replaced by the rather more contemporary B52s, and the funky notes of 'Love Shack' kicked out into the night.

They danced vigorously in a way that Leo hadn't done since the night of the Thornton Jones annual ball and his John Travolta imper-sonation. Leo's heart squeezed at the thought of it. That was also the last night that Isobel was well and he hoped that this ridiculous ritual they were performing would have some effect. He couldn't bear to see her like this – so weak and so fragile, so lifeless. She was completely still, prostrate in the middle of their ragged, disco-dancing circle.

Leo looked across at his friends strutting their stuff, sparklers in hand, whooping and hollering against the ancient powers of Stonehenge, and it all just seemed too far-fetched, too silly, too hopeful to work. Tears filled his eyes. 'Love Shack' was a great song, a classic, but he couldn't believe that it would open for them the gateway to the Land of Light. What they needed was a miracle. A bloody, bastardy 24-carat miracle. Leo sank to his knees. He'd failed. They'd all failed. They'd failed Isobel. And he had never felt so wretched in his life.

Lard and Grant stopped dancing too and stood in the great circle of stones, breathing heavily. They had been true and valiant friends and they had tried their best. Really they had.

Grant looked off into the distance and the inky black sky. 'Oh. My. God,' he breathed.

Leo followed his gaze. Mysterious pinpricks of light appeared in the sky, brighter than stars, multi-coloured, and they were swooping about, almost playfully. He stood up and joined his friends and they all stared in slack-jawed amazement.

'It's working,' he said, hardly daring to voice his thoughts. 'I don't believe it, but it's working!'

The lights came closer. They rushed about the sky like the Northern Lights on speed – bright kernels of illumination trailing shimmering gossamer strands – threading themselves in and out of the giant standing stones. The lights circled closer to the three friends, brushing against their arms and their hair, teasing them. They felt like warm breath.

The lads all started to cheer, indulging in some very unseemly American-style whooping and hollering. 'Woo! Hoo!' they all shouted. 'Woo bloody hoo!'

Isobel was still inert on the ground. A myriad of colours played over her body. The light intensified until it was almost blinding them. Leo turned away, covering his eyes. All at once, a million pinpricks of light rushed into the centre of Stonehenge with the ferocity of a raging waterfall. He did hope that this was what was supposed to happen. Leo felt a mixture of elation and downright fear as sparks showered over him. Those fairies, he thought, certainly knew their pyrotechnics.

'It's beautiful!' Grant cried out and started spinning, arms held out to the sky, letting the lights twine round him.

Leo laughed out loud and he felt lighter than he'd done in years. Lard was dancing again, kicking his legs in the air like a man possessed. The lights started moving faster and faster, blurring together in front of them, as if they were on a high-speed fairground ride. Faster. Faster. Faster in an insane frenzy. Leo couldn't make out Grant or Lard now. They were lost to him, gone in a kaleidoscope of colours.

And then the ground started to shake. Gently at first, then with more intensity. Leo couldn't keep his balance and he fell to the grass, landing near to Isobel. Crawling towards her, he pulled her close and lay over her, trying to protect her with his body. Leo hoped that they hadn't mistakenly called on some malevolent spirits in their attempts to get Isobel home, that they hadn't enticed forth some eight-headed beast with bad breath and a bad attitude. Perhaps it was more important than they thought for them all to be virgins. Flip.

The ground shuddered and shook again. Leo had never previously been involved in an earthquake, but he was pretty sure that this was one. Great cracks appeared in the ground and even the huge immovable stones seemed to shake to their core. Maybe it was too hard for them to cross time zones or astral planes or whatever the hell it was that they were trying to do. It seemed as if the whole place might split apart or implode. Leo cast his mind back to all the episodes of *Star Trek* he'd ever watched – their transporter equipment always used to get them into trouble. And, unlike Captain Kirk, Leo was there without the aid of a bad toupee and a corset.

He heard Grant and Lard shout out. 'Whoa! Whoa!'

Out of the whirling lights, they crawled across to Leo and Isobel on their hands and knees. They all huddled together.

'I have no idea what we've started,' Grant panted. 'Forgive me, my friend, if this all goes horribly, horribly wrong.'

'I'm really beginning to wish we'd gone to the pub instead,' Lard cried.

Leo would second that. Then his mobile phone rang.

'Bloody hell, Leo. Talk about inappropriate timing,' Grant shouted above the growing noise of the wind.

'It's Emma,' Leo said, checking his caller display. 'Emma, can you hear me? *Emma!*'

'I need you, Leo. I really need you.' Emma's voice was faint, barely audible, and there was a load of extraneous noise on the line as if she were phoning from inside a washing machine.

They were the only words he heard before the line went dead. As if he didn't have enough cold shards in his heart, another one pierced him to the core. Emma needed him. And Emma never needed him. Something must be very wrong. He shouted back into the phone, 'Emma. Emma!'

The ground shuddered beneath them, the wind reached screaming pitch. As he tried to cling to the ground, Leo's mobile phone fell from his grasp, bouncing out of his reach.

And then, as suddenly as it had all started, everything simply stopped.

Chapter Seventy

It's way past midnight when I tear myself away from the hospital, leaving my father sleeping in the chair next to my mother.

When I finally get home, I'm crushed to find that there's no message on my phone from Leo and he hasn't tried my mobile either. Wherever he is, it seems that he hasn't picked up my call. More than at any other time, I need to hear a friendly voice. I need Leo to tell me that everything will be all right, that I can manage and, preferably, for him to rush round and take me in his arms. This time I need him to come through for *me* in a crisis, but it looks as if I'm going to be disappointed. Perhaps he simply doesn't care enough any more.

I look at Dominic's number on the telephone pad and briefly consider calling him as a substitute, but decide that he's really done enough for me for one day and, even though he told me that he rarely slept well at the moment, it really is very late.

With nothing much else to do, I fall into my bed, unwashed, unloved and still fully clothed to endure a night of fitful sleep filled with fragmented nightmares – Leo floating across the sky on a rapidly deflating balloon, my mother in a wheelchair bouncing out of control down endless flights of steps, my father as small as a child holding tightly to my hand, Dominic Superglueing me back into a cardboard box. Dawn didn't come soon enough.

Now I'm pretending to eat a bowl of low fat, low sugar, low taste cereal while I decide how to approach the day.

First of all, I call my father at the hospital to check on my mother. There's no change, apparently, but she's still sleeping which is deemed to be a good sign. The more my mother can rest, the quicker her recuperation will be, seems to be the general opinion. I've discovered that you can easily spend your life worrying about nothing of any great importance, when family is all that really matters. I'll go to the hospital later, but as my next port of call I go into work.

When I enter the gallery, Caron looks at me aghast. I must look as bad as I feel.

'I saw the news,' Caron says.

'Oh.'

'They were loading you into an ambulance in nothing but red knickers and a bow.' Caron looks as if she can't believe what she's recounting. 'What on earth has happened? What were you thinking of? Have you gone mad?' my friend wants to know. 'You look terrible.'

Starting with my initial bright idea for the cardboard-box fiasco, I regale her with the whole story – the Superglue, the cat wee, the Fire Brigade, the television crew – paying particular attention to the part that Dominic had played in my rescue and rendering my friend suitably impressed by his prowess with scissors. Then I end by tearfully telling Caron about my mother's stroke.

'I called Leo,' I admit, nibbling at a fingernail. 'I didn't know what else to do.'

'Was that wise?'

'I don't care, Caron. I miss him. I want him back.' I must look suitably distraught as she doesn't even try to convince me otherwise. 'I don't know what he was up to all day yesterday but he should be in the office now.' My glance strays to the clock. 'I'll give him another ring.'

'I'll put some coffee on. You look like you need some.' Caron disappears into the back room.

I sigh as I slowly dial Leo's number, clasping the telephone receiver to my shoulder. What do I really want to say to him? Do I simply want to tell him about my mother's illness, or do I want to go for it and tell him that because of this, I've really and truly had a wake-up call? Having realised how easy it is for loved ones to slip away from you when you aren't looking, I've come to appreciate how much he means to me. Life without Leo would be inconceivable. I have an irrational fear that unless I tell him so right now, I may not get another chance.

Leo's office telephone rings and after a few moments is answered by a female voice that I don't recognise.

'Can I speak to Leo Harper, please?'

'I'm afraid that Leo isn't in work today.'

'Oh.' A pin bursts my bubble. 'Could you transfer me to Grant Fielding, please.'

260

'Unfortunately, he's not here either,' the woman says. 'Anything I can help with?'

'No,' I reply. 'It's a personal matter. It's his girlfriend. Ex-girlfriend. Is their other friend, Lard, around?' I have no idea what Lard's proper name is.

'He hasn't turned up today either.'

The hairs on the back of my neck stand up. Call it feminine intuition, but I don't like the sound of this. 'Isn't that a little unusual?'

'We've got used to those guys acting off the wall,' the woman answers me with a brief accompanying laugh. 'But, yes, it is strange that we haven't heard from any of them.'

'Not at all?'

'No. Not a thing.'

'Thanks.'

'If you do hear from them,' the woman says in a quieter voice, 'tell them that Old Baldy is gunning for them.'

I hang up. He isn't the only one. I rub my hands over my red-rimmed, gritty eyes. Here I am in my hour of need, ready to forgive and forget, and now I've learned that Leo and his chums have bunked off somewhere without telling anyone – no doubt on a jaunt, or pulling some sort of stupid stunt. They are, probably at this very moment, teeing off somewhere in Ireland or Spain, clad in bad-taste shorts, golf club in one hand, beer in the other. Why did I ever think that Leo and I could get back together again? We're different kinds of people and always will be. I am sensible and responsible. Leo is not. I push away any thoughts of my recent cardboard-box escapade.

Caron comes back with my coffee and I sip it gratefully.

'Well?' my friend says.

'Leo and Grant have gone AWOL, it seems,' I tell her. 'They're all missing in action. Lard too.'

Caron frowns. 'I'm supposed to be having dinner with Grant . . .' Then she stops.

I raise my eyebrows. 'Oh really?'

'He called in to see you and you'd gone out with whatsisname, the boring one.'

'Atrocious Alec.' I shudder at the memory of my dire dating experience. 'Did you tell him that?'

'No, of course I didn't,' Caron says. 'We decided not to waste the evening and went out for a drink together. And something to eat. Then he came back to my place. For coffee. That's all. We got on very well,' she adds sheepishly.

'I see.'

'Is it okay with you?' Caron asks. 'I know he liked you, but you said you wouldn't touch him with a barge-pole.'

'Grant's lovely.' I shake my head. 'But he's too close to Leo. It would be like dating his brother. At least you know exactly what you can expect with Grant.'

'Maybe he'll be different with me.'

I raise an eyebrow. 'And maybe he'll turn up in time for your date from wherever he is.'

Caron pulls out her mobile phone. 'I'll ring him.'

But, sure enough, there's no answer from Grant's phone either. 'It sounds like it's been disconnected.' Caron's forehead creases with concern. 'There's just a weird static on the line.'

'If he is anything like Leo,' I warn, 'he'll have forgotten to pay his bill and he'll have been cut off. When are you supposed to be seeing him?'

'Tomorrow,' Caron says.

I give her a rueful glance. 'Then let's see if they've all turned up by then.'

Chapter Seventy-One

They were no longer in the middle of Stonehenge with a war of lights waging around them. The ground was still, as ground should be. But it was a lot softer than the ground they'd left behind.

Grant was the first to speak. 'Oh my word,' was all he said.

Leo was still lying over Isobel, protecting her body, and she still wasn't moving. They had, however – by some strange and perplexing miracle – arrived in the middle of a small wooded glade. Leo wasn't big on fairy folklore, but if he had to guess, he'd say that they'd somehow managed to turn up in the right place. He was prepared, however, to have that illusion dashed.

They all appeared to have landed unscathed – helped, no doubt, by the lush cushion of moss beneath them.

'Are you okay?' Leo asked the guys.

They both nodded at him.

The colours were so clear that they hurt the eyes. The sky was the hue of sapphires, the leaves like emeralds. Clear water rushed by in a small, tumbling stream which sparkled like diamonds. Leo wished that he had his sunglasses with him. Butter-coloured sunlight streamed through the trees, bringing the most perfect dappled shade. Even the air tasted like champagne and it was heavy, soporific and scented with jasmine. Leo's body was warm and he felt a buzz of euphoria inside. He'd once had a rush like this after smoking a joint and listening to Jimi Hendrix music. It wasn't an unpleasant experience then either.

The clearing was covered with tiny red toadstools – yes, exactly like the ones you saw in fairy stories. Sweet music that sounded like a flute was dancing gently on the breeze and mysterious flashes of light swooped around them. And Leo knew, instinctively, that this indeed was a magical place. He wondered what Isobel must have thought of dreary old, polluted South London in comparison with this. It made him realise how much she'd given up to come and spend time with the poor, bedraggled specimens of the human race.

She lay next to him now and he turned anxiously to her. 'Isobel,' he said, touching her cheek. 'We're here. I think we're here. Wake up.'

As Leo kissed her forehead, Isobel opened her eyes. 'The Land of Light,' she breathed. Tears rolled silently down her face. Colour flooded into her face, tingeing her once pale cheeks with a soft pink glow. She took his hand and squeezed it. 'You brought me home.'

'We did,' Grant said, brushing his arm across his eyes. Leo saw a tear escape. 'We bloody well did.'

Leo could hear the emotion choking his voice and he tore himself away from Isobel for a moment to go over and put his arms round his friend – in the most manly way he could manage. Grant had saved her. His friend had saved his love. Leo hugged him to his chest. 'Thank you,' he said, and they cried in each other's arms.

'Bloody hell,' Grant sniffed copiously, 'we'd better not tell them about this back at the office.'

They let go of each other self-consciously. 'No,' Leo agreed. 'You're probably right.'

Leo and Grant both wiped their eyes on their sleeves. Lard was sitting there looking shell-shocked and they went to hug him too – now that they'd got this emotion thing sorted.

'I need chocolate,' was all that Lard could manage to say. 'A Mars Bar.'

Isobel sat up and looked around her. The pinpricks of light became bolder, darting closer to them, and as they did Leo could see that they were tiny, iridescent fairies and silver butterflies no bigger than his thumbnail.

'How are you feeling?' he asked Isobel.

'Fine, Leo,' she said. Her skin was changing from flesh tones, taking on a more translucent quality. She seemed so serene. Happy. And, Leo supposed, relieved. If Leo had been her he would have been very worried about placing her survival in the hands of three fairly useless City types. But they'd made it. And no one was more amazed than Leo.

He patted his pockets but he hadn't got his mobile phone. Shame, but then two miracles in a day might be asking too much. 'Give me your phone,' Leo said to Grant. 'I have to call Emma.'

'Leo, this is the Land of Light. Remember? I'm not sure that the Vodaphone network stretches that far.'

His friend handed over his phone anyway and, sure enough, modern technology once again had met its limitations. Why was it that you could never get a signal when you most needed one?

'Then we have to go back,' Leo said.

'What?' Grant and Lard looked aghast.

'We have to go back.'

'But we've only just got here.'

'Emma needs me,' he said starkly. 'She's never ever needed me. Something must be terribly wrong.'

Chapter Seventy-Two

I never imagined that my mother could look so frail. Suddenly it's like looking at an old woman. Catherine has always been so regal in her bearing, now she seems so tiny in the hospital bed. Her hair, always so meticulously styled, appears thin and lank on the pillow. One side of her face is slack and there is a fine line of drool coming from her mouth. She'd be mortified to see herself like this and for me, and the rest of the family, it's frightening to see her so incapacitated.

Daddy is still being extraordinarily solicitous to his wife and, for once, I can tell why his patients love him so much. It's the first glimpse I've had of my father's legendary bedside manner. At home all we see is his gruff, complaining side and I rather like the softer father I've discovered. He's slept in the armchair next to Mummy all night and is now beginning to look as if he has. I've urged him to go home and, at least, shower and change. He's barely eaten either. Finally, he's agreed, but I know that he won't be away for long, so I've given him a list of useful things to bring in for my mother – toiletries and clean night-gowns being at the top.

My sisters Arabelle and Clara have arrived – their children having been despatched into the temporary care of various reliable friends. They won't be able to stay for too long, and I know that I wouldn't want to look after any of my nephews and nieces for any length of time; between them they can trash the most immaculate home within half an hour.

Arabelle is white-faced and dry-eyed. Clara, usually as constrained as me, has gone completely to pot and sobbed in my arms, terrified that our mother might never wake up. But around mid-morning Mummy rallies and we're all immensely relieved. My mother tries to speak, but it's impossible to understand what she's saying. It sounds as if she's been at the gin bottle for half of the night and I pray fervently that it will only be a short-lived loss for her.

Catherine currently has no movement down one side of her body too, but the doctor has reassured my father that this too could return with enough rest, enough physiotherapy and enough good luck. The private room is hot and crowded with equipment, and my sisters and I are squashed together. Already flowers are starting to arrive – great bouquets of lilies, carnations and gerberas. It seems that Henrietta Gooding has been straight onto the Kensington and Chelsea bush telegraph to transmit news of her friend's misfortune. I smile to myself. All my mother's cronies love a good crisis – Catherine herself is no exception. And I so hope that she will be up and about and gossiping soon.

I kiss my mother on her forehead. 'I'll be back later,' I say. My sisters will have to leave shortly to be at home for their children and I become acutely aware that I have no one to rush home for. I'm the only one of my siblings without commitments and that's more painful than I had imagined. The hospital is only a short Tube ride from my flat, and the plus side of my unshackled lifestyle is that I can call in any time. My sisters aren't so lucky. I hug Arabelle and Clara and say goodbye, then I go out from the stifling heat of the hospital to the stifling heat of the London streets.

Caron is going to cover for me at the gallery again today and I know that if I want to take extended compassionate leave then I'll need to talk to Gregory, the gallery owner. I feel that if there's little that I can do for my mother while she's in hospital, then I'll probably be better occupying my mind with work. She might well need me more when she's allowed to come home.

I walk along aimlessly. There are things I know I should be doing, but I can't make my brain function clearly. A jumble of thoughts are swirling round my brain. And it isn't long before I find myself outside Leo's flat. I didn't mean to come here, but I don't know what else to do with myself.

Pressing the doorbell, I'm disconcerted to find that there's still no answer and I stand here not knowing quite what to do. It seems as if another lifetime has passed since I was here, trussed up in a box like a turkey. I rest my finger on the bell and lean against it, as if dogged insistence might make my missing ex-boyfriend materialise. When nothing happens, I sit down on the doorstep and begin to cry. I should write Leo a note or something, but I can't find the energy to search in my handbag for a pen or a piece of scrap paper.

'This is becoming a habit,' a voice says next to me.

Wiping my eyes, I look up. 'Dominic.'

He sits down next to me. 'I haven't seen Leo for a couple of days.'

'He seems to have disappeared off the face of the earth,' I tell him. 'He wasn't in work today.'

'Perhaps he's just taking a breather from the stresses and strains,' Dominic suggests. 'He might be having a great time somewhere and here you are pining away. You didn't do anything else silly with Superglue?'

'No.' I smile through my tears.

'Is he worth all this angst?' Dominic asks. 'It seems as if he's treated you very shabbily.'

'It's stupid, I know,' I say with a sniff. 'This isn't all about Leo though. My mother's ill.' My voice cracks. 'And I don't have anyone else to turn to.'

Dominic puts his arm round me. 'You have me,' he says, hugging me to him. 'Come with me and let's see if we can find you some medicine.'

So, not having a better idea, I take Dominic's hand and follow him down the hall.

Chapter Seventy-Three

R ed wine, I agree, is very good medicine. After three large glasses
of a particularly good Bordeaux, I'm feeling relatively little pain.
My symptoms, whatever they were, have cleared up nicely.

Dominic grins in my direction. He's standing at the cooker, stirring
an impromptu sauce to go with the pasta that's bubbling away in the
other pan. This is a man who has a supply of fresh vegetables in his
fridge. Courgettes, peppers, mushrooms, onions – a whole selection.
There are three different types of yoghurt. The only thing that Leo has
three different types of in his fridge is beer.

I look at Dominic over my glass of wine. It would be easy to fall
in love with a man like this. It sort of helps that he's really rather handsome too. Dominic has a lived-in air. He wears fairly battered jeans,
scuffed trainers and a black T-shirt that has seen better days. However,
he looks as if he means to be scruffy, whereas Leo can wear a Paul
Smith suit and still appear as if he's fallen straight out of bed.

'This is nice,' Dominic says. 'Cooking for one is infinitely more
boring.'

'Did you do the cooking when Lydia was here?'

He nods. 'One of my many talents.'

'Rescuing damsels in distress being another?'

'I'm afraid that skill has only recently been added to my repertoire.'

'I'm very glad of it,' I say sincerely. I'm becoming too comfortable in
Dominic's sofa. 'I feel very lazy sitting here. Can I do anything to help?'

Dominic shrugs. 'No,' he says. 'I can manage. Besides, I think you're
in need of a bit of pampering, don't you? You've had a very traumatic
few days. The pasta won't be long.'

I take the time to look around the flat, noticing that photographs
of Lydia still grace most of the surfaces – as do photos of Leo in my
flat. Whether you are male or female, it still takes a long time to let go
of loved ones, it seems.

Dominic's cat, Chloe, eyes me with deep suspicion. I return the gaze and, knowing when she's beaten in the staring-out stakes, she slinks out of the room. This place isn't a bachelor flat – the décor definitely holds a female touch. The sofas are cream brocade, scattered with beige embroidered cushions – a dead giveaway. What man would ever think to buy embroidered cushions? I bet the bedroom will be decorated in a pastel shade – lilac or aqua, maybe even pink with highlights of teal. Each of the flats in Leo's block seemed to have a different layout – probably because it's a converted house. Here, the living area is one big room with a small dining-table in front of French doors that overlooks the garden. I wonder if this flat has a roof terrace like Leo's.

'This is a great place,' I say.

Dominic pulls a face. 'All Lydia's design,' he replies, only confirming what I thought. 'I have nothing whatsoever to do with anything that might smack of good taste. Unfortunately, I may well have to move out. Lydia's the biggest earner between us and I won't be able to afford to stay here on my own. I guess she'll want her share out of it too. At the moment, she's dossing down on her sister's couch.'

'Do you miss her?'

'Oh yes,' he says sadly. 'Very much.'

'Perhaps you can find a way to stay here?'

He turns away from me to stir the sauce. 'I'd take a lodger but we've only got one bedroom. And I'm afraid that my line of work isn't likely to earn me a quick million. Unfortunately, they don't dish out huge salaries to youth workers.'

'Is that what you do?'

My genial host nods. 'I manage a centre for delinquent teenagers. The Little Bastards as we fondly call them.'

'Very noble,' I say.

'And very badly paid.'

'But rewarding?'

Dominic nods again. 'Amid the paperwork there are rare occasions when we manage to get one of the kids off drugs or off the street or off the "At Risk" register. Then it's rewarding.'

'I work in an art gallery,' I say flatly. 'There's no merit in that.'

'People need beauty in their lives,' Dominic says. And for some reason that makes me cry again.

Dominic comes over to me and kisses my hair gently. 'It will get better. Just give yourself time.'

'It hurts,' I say. '*I* hurt. In places I never knew possible.'

'Pasta with Dominic's special sauce is a very good anaesthetic,' he tells me. 'Plus it feeds the soul. And if we're not very careful, it's going to be burned. Ready to eat?'

I nod, but even though a delicious smell of garlic scents the air, I have very little appetite.

'I thought we'd go out onto the roof,' he says. 'It's a warm night.'

'You have a terrace?'

'All Lydia's doing again,' he confesses. 'But it looks great up there. You'll see.'

He leaves me and is going back towards the kitchen area when a familiar pitter-pattering starts on the windows. Dominic lets out an exasperated sigh. 'Rain. How typical,' he complains. 'The British weather thwarting my best-laid plans. Sorry, but it looks like I'm going to have to set the table inside.'

'Do you mind if I go upstairs to have a look?'

'Help yourself.' Dominic nods towards a corridor at the other side of the room. 'Just don't be too long.'

'I'll be two minutes,' I promise. I walk through the corridor, past the bedroom – which is, much as I'd predicated, a shade of pale lilac with cerise pink highlights. Chloe lies curled up on the bed. She steadfastly ignores my approach and continues going through some sort of grooming ritual, probably sharpening her claws. Beyond the bedroom is a short, steep flight of stairs that leads to a heavy door. The key is in the lock and, turning it, I let myself out onto the roof.

The rain is coming in distinct, weighty splots, splashing rhythmically on the terracotta tiles of Dominic's terrace and spotting them darkly like a Dalmatian dog. It's cooling on my head, which seems to be thumping with the start of a headache. Which I suppose isn't surprising after the events of the last few days.

Like the flat, the roof terrace is a tasteful affair. Steel tubs hold exotic-looking plants and help to screen the small wrought-iron table and chairs in the middle of the patio. A Chinese-style water feature trickles delicately in the corner, holding its own against the faint hum of traffic noise. Nets of fairy lights are strung out on the back wall of the flat and, even in the rain, it has an intimate, magical air. Definitely Lydia's touch again.

I gaze across to Leo's flat. His roof terrace isn't quite as attractive. There's a rusting bike, a few old plastic sacks held down by bricks.

Some scattered weeds in lieu of sophisticated planting. And very little else. No intimate little dinner setting. No magic. The lack of a woman's touch is evident. Also, there are no lights on in the flat. Definitely deserted. It's worrying. Where on earth is he? He can't have simply upped sticks and moved in with this Isobel woman. That just isn't the sort of thing Leo would do. But then, even I'd be the first to admit that Leo hasn't been acting like his normal self recently. I will, however, kill him if I find out that he's whisked his new girlfriend off to some tropical paradise for a holiday, as he would never have dreamed of doing that for me.

From the bottom of the stair, Dominic's voice comes, 'Dinner's ready!'

I take one final look over the rooftops of London. It would have been very romantic to have eaten dinner out here, under the stars. My eyes fill with hot tears. Out there somewhere is Leo, just beyond my reach.

Dominic pokes his head through the door. 'It's wonderful up here, isn't it?'

'Yes,' I say as brightly as I can manage. 'What a shame it's raining.'

We smile at each other rather sadly and I wonder if we're both wishing that we were with someone else.

Chapter Seventy-Four

'Maybe you could come to visit us some time,' Leo suggested. 'You know that I can't go back,' Isobel said quietly.

Tiny wings fluttered over her shoulders and she looked as if she might disappear at any moment, popping into the atmosphere like a soapy bubble. Even in this guise – full fairy mode – she really was extraordinarily beautiful. All trace of the contemporary young woman had gone, to be replaced by an ethereal, shimmering being. It was quite a transformation. In contrast, Leo felt too solid here, too substantial, too inextricably linked to reality. Truly the proverbial bull in the china shop. Being here was like climbing inside a Disney movie. Too cosy, too colourful, too cheery. Rather nice, but not quite real.

This was the moment he had been dreading and he had to force the question from his lips. 'Never?'

'No.' She looked up into his eyes. 'Not in human form. My powers are too weak.'

'Can't you take advanced fairying? At night school, or something? Upgrade yourself a bit.'

Isobel laughed, but at the same time she shook her head. 'The world is too harsh a place for me.'

'It is for me too,' he protested. 'I'm a sensitive soul on the quiet.'

'You're meant to be there, Leo. I'm not. You're stronger than you think.'

Leo traced his fingers over the palm of her tiny hand. 'Maybe one day there'll be a way. Maybe we miserable mortals will find the magic in our lives again. Maybe we'll believe in fairies once more.'

This time Isobel stayed silent.

His heart sank. 'That bad, hey?'

Leo's fairy friend nodded.

'I don't want to leave you,' he said. 'But you understand that I have to go back. Emma needs me.'

Isobel nodded.

The thought of Emma made Leo's heart contract. If she knew where he was, she'd be worried. She always worried about him. But how could she know? How could she know the things that Leo knew? Even though she thought she had the measure of him, she really had no idea what had been going on in his life.

And Leo was a very different person now from the one he once was.

Chapter Seventy-Five

I sit at my mother's bedside, her chill, frail hand clasped between mine. We're watching some terrible daytime television show together. I don't think that my mother has ever before seen daytime television. *The Paul O'Grady Show* would make her want to spill blood.

On the screen, women confront their boyfriends in high-pitched, shrieking voices about a series of misdemeanours real or imagined but often involving their best friends while a bouffant-haired presenter with long acrylic fingernails tries to keep them from punching each other. It's banal beyond explanation. Is this the best that modern-day relationships have to offer? Feckless men shacked up with tattooed harpies.

My mother is propped up in the bed, surrounded by piles of pillows. 'This is not fun,' she says, her speech still slurred by her stroke. 'Whatever happened to chivalry?' But now she sounds as if she's had three glasses of gin, not three bottles. 'I do worry about you.'

I laugh. 'What – that I'll end up on one of those shows?'

'Men don't want to settle down now,' my mother says. 'And I want you to be happy and married.'

'I don't know that the two go hand-in-hand now, Mummy.'

'It's lying here.' She sighs wearily and worries at the bedclothes with her fingers. 'It gives me too much time to think.'

Catherine has been in hospital for a week now and has made remarkable progress. Due to her sheer dogged determination, she's regained some movement already in her right arm. She uses it now to flick through the channels on the television.

Over on the QVC shopping channel a stiff-haired woman is in raptures over a real cubic zirconia pendant. On the next channel, yet another house makeover programme is in full-flight – the presenter going giddy over some poorly constructed MDF wardrobe that will, no doubt, fall to bits a week after the camera crew departs. On another, a perma-tanned newsreader is recounting in sombre tones the story of a break-in by vandals at the ancient site of Stonehenge.

'What a bunch of idiots.' I tut at the screen. 'Haven't they got anything better to do?'

My mother clicks off the television. 'This is too depressing,' she says. 'What is the world coming to?'

'I'll bring you some more books in.'

'That would be nice, darling. I'm so bored.'

'It won't be for much longer. You'll be out soon,' I assure her. 'Giving us all hell.'

'Yes.' My mother sinks back into her pillow. 'Just you wait.'

'I have to go soon,' I say. 'I'm due at work.' Caron has been great, covering for my shifts this week but I don't want to take advantage of her, so I come in first thing in the morning to relieve my father for a few hours while he goes home and performs a few perfunctory household chores – the ones that previously he was so unused to having to do. He has become a dab hand with a duster. My father has been fantastic, rallying around Mummy to make her as comfortable as possible. I didn't expect my father to have a nurturing side to him, but now it's full on.

'Daddy's been marvellous,' I say to my mother. 'I thought he'd go to pot without you.'

'Your daddy is a tough old boot,' my mother tells me. She turns towards me, her lop-sided face serious. 'You know that he's given in his notice at the hospital?'

'I didn't,' I admit. 'He talked about it, but I never thought he'd do it.'

'Me neither,' Catherine says, struggling to raise an eyebrow. 'They're letting him take early retirement. In three months' time, he'll be a free man. Apparently we're going to spend the rest of our lives travelling and having fun. Before it's too late.' My mother indicates a pile of holiday brochures on her bedside table. 'I see Charles flicking through them in the wee small hours.'

'That sounds great. I'm pleased for you both.'

'We don't know how long we'll have together, Emma,' my mother says. 'We want to make the most of it. You can make all the plans you want for the future, but you never know when the future can be snatched away from you. At least we've had a warning. It means that we can get our priorities right from now on.'

'You'll be up on your feet before long,' I pat her arm. 'They can't keep a good one down.'

'Have you heard anything from Leo yet?'

I shake my head. 'Not a thing. There's no sign of him at his flat.' I've walked past often enough to know that. 'His mobile phone sounds as if it's been disconnected. It's just making strange crackling noises. Neither he nor his ditzy friends have turned up to work for a week now.'

'I'm sure there'll be a perfectly plausible explanation.'

'There never is with Leo,' I say. 'It's always something hare-brained. He'll probably try to convince me he was abducted by aliens.'

'Leo's a lot of fun.'

He *is* fun. There's no disputing that. 'I've been seeing someone else.'

'Really?'

I'm not sure that one almost romantic candlelit dinner for two is enough to be classed as 'seeing' someone, but I feel there's a spark of attraction there between Dominic and me that could be encouraged to grow. And he's normal. He's useful in an emergency.

'Is he nice?'

'Yes,' I say.

'You could sound a little more enthusiastic.'

'He's nice. He's normal. He's . . .'

'Not Leo?'

'No.'

'Everyone deserves a second chance, darling. I hope that you and Leo have one.'

I hope so too. If only I could find him.

Chapter Seventy-Six

Isobel led him away from Grant and Lard and they sat on the ground beneath the shade of a tree. She wrapped her arms around Leo and said, 'It'll soon be time for you to go.'

'Oh.' Leo knew that his place was back on earth with Emma, but it didn't mean that he was finding it any easier to leave. He seemed to have spent all of his life being detached from his most important relationships. Leo never saw his parents or his brother, he'd taken Emma completely for granted and yet with this small, mischievous fairy he'd finally found out how to connect on a deep emotional level. How to love unconditionally. Leo sighed into Isobel's hair and held her tighter. 'This is the hardest thing I've ever had to do. Are you sure you'll be okay now?'

Isobel met his eyes. '*We'll* be fine.'

'We?'

Isobel took his hand and placed it on her tummy. 'A part of you will always be with me.'

Leo's throat closed with emotion and tears rushed to his eyes. 'I'm going to be a daddy?'

Isobel nodded. 'A male child.'

Resting his head against her, Leo let the tears fall. 'A boy.' He imagined that he could see the new life growing inside her. Then a thought went through his mind and he sat up sharply, brushing away the tears. 'Wait. Wait. A boy? He's not going to be a gnome or anything?'

Isobel laughed. 'Our child will be an air spirit, Leo. Free and unfettered.'

'So your trip to London wasn't entirely wasted?'

'I met you, Leo. How could you think that it was anything other than wonderful?'

'But if I go back, I'll never see him. How will I know what he's like?'

'We'll be on the breeze as it blows in your hair. On your cheeks in the falling rain. In the sun as it warms your face,' she said. 'You'll know, Leo. You'll know.'

Leo didn't want to let her go. It was even harder now than before. Before, it was just about the two of them – now the equation was so much more difficult. 'You know that I have loved you,' he said. 'In my own stupid earthbound way.'

'Our love could only ever be a passing thing. There is someone for everyone, Leo. You have already found your love on earth.'

'Emma?'

Isobel nodded. 'She's your soulmate.' Then she lowered her eyelashes and looked coy. 'I have a confession to make.'

'Will I like it?

'Emma wished me into your lives,' she said.

Leo's eyes widened. That was a revelation.

'The alignment was right in the universe. That enabled me to respond.'

Rather like playing on the slot machines and coming up with three cherries in a row. Big payola. Emma, instead, got Isobel.

'She doesn't know it though,' Isobel admitted.

'It will certainly help to explain my behaviour over the last few weeks.'

'But you mustn't tell her.'

'There's always a catch with you fairies, isn't there?'

'Yes,' she said, and took his hand. 'Don't let her slip through your fingers, Leo. I have done as much as I can. Now it's up to you. Cherish her. Love her fully, as you know you can.'

'I'm going to try,' he said sincerely. 'I'm going to try my very best.'

'Then it's time for you to leave.'

'Can I kiss you one last time?' Cupping her face in his hands, he let himself drink in the taste of her lips.

Isobel stood up and led him by the hand back into the centre of the glade where Grant and Lard waited for him.

'Okay?' Grant wanted to know.

Leo nodded. And then Isobel handed each of them a gold chalice. 'Drink this,' she said.

Grant, Lard and Leo eyed the cups suspiciously. They were brimming with golden liquid that sparkled in the sunlight. They looked at each other in reluctant agreement and then each one took a cautious sip. Disappointingly, it tasted rather like Diet Pepsi.

They stood there for a moment until Leo said, 'Now what happens?'
Then everything went very, very black.

Chapter Seventy-Seven

I'm lurking outside Leo's flat again and now I'm getting seriously worried. A week has gone by and there's still no sign of him. Dusk is falling and there should be a light on inside by now. I sit on the wall outside and wonder what to do.

A few minutes later, while I'm still gripped by indecision, Dominic arrives home from work.

'Hey,' he says with a gentle smile. 'We must stop meeting like this.'

'Hi, Dominic.' My spirits lift on seeing him even though I didn't exactly expect to bump into him.

'At least you're waiting for me on the doorstep fully-clothed.'

'And not glued in a box.'

He laughs. 'It was very amusing,' he says. 'With hindsight.'

'And from your perspective,' I add wryly.

My rescuer laughs again and then says, 'What are you doing here?'

'I . . . er . . .' It doesn't seem polite to say that I've been hanging around waiting to see if Leo turns up. I've been meaning to call Dominic since our dinner together, but somehow I haven't got round to it. With visiting my mother in the hospital and fitting in work and all the other things I have to do . . . Suddenly they all sound like feeble excuses. I've found time to walk past here every day in search of my missing ex — so I could have dropped in to see Dominic any time, and it occurs to me that it's strange that I haven't. But then Dominic has my telephone number and he hasn't called me either when he said he would. I frown.

'I've been meaning to call,' he says as if reading my mind.

'That's okay.'

'No,' he says. 'I want to talk to you about something. I think you'd better come in.'

Wearily, I follow him up the stairs and into his flat, trying not to stare too much at Leo's door. Would one little ring on the bell hurt?

'Coffee?' Dominic says once we're inside.

'Please.' I'm suddenly overcome by exhaustion. Why is life always such a struggle? Do people ever manage to escape from the dreaded rat race and carve out a quieter, more peaceful existence for themselves?

Sitting down on the sofa, I look around me. This place is far too tidy for a guy who lives on his own. There isn't so much as a CD out of place and they look suspiciously like they're all in alphabetical order. Isn't that a bit spooky? Will someone so controlled be any good in bed? Then it occurs to me that all *my* CDs are arranged that way too. Suddenly that seems to be a bad idea. What does it say about me? Am I changing? Is it a positive step that I can now consider having my CDs arranged randomly? Perhaps I too have always been too uptight to be a good lover. What would it be like if two control freaks went to bed together? Think of the fights to be on top. I'm not even sure why I'm thinking along those lines. It's years and years since I've slept with anyone other than Leo and, somehow, I still don't feel in a rush to. While I grapple with my inner turmoil, Dominic chatters pleasantly about nothing while he makes the coffee and I let the conversation flow over me.

He comes and hands me my coffee. Then, instead of sitting next to me on the sofa, he deliberately crosses the room and takes up position in one of the armchairs.

'Thank you for a lovely dinner the other night,' I say. 'It was very kind. You must let me reciprocate soon.'

Dominic stares down at his mug. 'I don't think that's going to be possible.'

My friend sighs and looks at me from across the expanse of laminate flooring that separates us. 'Lydia came back,' he says. 'A few days ago.'

'It didn't work out with . . .'

'Gerry,' he supplies. 'No. Apparently he had too many bad habits. Lydia's managed to knock them out of me over the years. I'm almost perfectly house-trained now.' There's a slightly bitter edge to his voice. He too takes in the neatly-arranged cushions and the meticulously-spaced row of church candles. 'I don't think she could face going through that all over again.'

'She probably just realised she'd been a complete idiot,' I offer gently. 'You're a great guy.'

'She's out at the gym tonight.' He glances nervously at the clock. 'It won't be long before she's home.'

282

'Then I'd better be going.' I put my untouched coffee on the table beside me and stand up.

'I thought that maybe you and I could have . . .' His voice tails off. 'Well, you know what I mean.'

'I thought so too.'

'Put it down to terrible timing,' Dominic says with a shrug. 'But I've got to give this another go.'

'I hope she begged.'

'She did.' He gives me a tired smile. 'I've forgiven her. Life seems a lot better with her than without her. I decided that I wasn't ready to move on with someone else. Perhaps unwisely, I still love her.'

We kiss awkwardly on the cheek. I point at the door. 'I'm out of here,' I say with forced cheerfulness. 'I might just give your errant neighbour a knock on the way out.'

'I still love Lydia,' Dominic repeats. 'And you still love Leo.'

'That obvious?'

''Fraid so.'

'I hope it works out with Lydia,' I say. 'Tell her she's a very lucky woman.'

Dominic closes the door behind me and I stand in the darkened hall, gazing at Leo's door. Resting my finger on the bell, I let it ring and ring until the tip goes numb. Of course, there's no one there. Leo has disappeared into thin air. He's gone. Vamoosed. Has been spirited away. Where on earth can he be? And is he there with that other damn woman? I plod unhappily down the stairs to the front door. All I need now is my own happy ending.

Chapter Seventy-Eight

Everything was still very, very black. Leo could hear birds tweeting and there was a rasping sound by his ear.

Opening his eyes, Leo found that it made it too, too light again. He was lying on his back in a field. The rasping noise was a sheep chewing at the grass; on seeing Leo, it decided to lick his face instead. Pushing away the slobbering sheep, he forced himself upright. His legs, his arms, his everything, felt as weak as a kitten's. Blinking against the strong light, he looked around. They were back in the middle of the great circle of standing stones at Stonehenge, surrounded by sheep, and Leo was relieved that he hadn't ended up somewhere else in the wrong time and the wrong place like that unfortunate time-travelling bloke did every week on *Quantum Leap*.

Grant and Lard were lying on their backs beside him and they too were slowly coming back down to earth. Their hair was standing on end and Leo didn't suppose his was an exception. They had stupid grins on their faces and, of course, they were all covered in glitter.

His friends opened their eyes and took in their surroundings.

'We made it back,' Grant said with a grateful sigh. 'Thank goodness.' 'Are you okay, Lard?'

Lard checked his limbs. They all appeared to be intact. 'Fine,' he said. 'Never better.'

The sun was coming up, picking its way between the stones to reach its pinnacle, and the sky was aglow with a rich pink wash. Their green and pleasant land had never looked more beautiful.

'I was worried,' Grant admitted. He rubbed his hair, causing a glitter shower, and they all exchanged a knowing look. 'I thought we might get ourselves into some sort of trouble.'

Then, out of the exquisite silence, there was the sound of sirens. Two police cars pulled up by the perimeter fence and four rather burly policemen jumped out and ran towards them at full pelt, riot

284

batons drawn. And Leo felt that their troubles might be just about to start.

He sighed, lay down on his back again and waited for the onslaught of officialdom. Had he really chosen to come back to this life over paradise? Leo heard Grant and Lard groan behind him. The policemen were still thundering their way across the field towards them.

Leo put his hands behind his head, crossed his ankles and said, 'Welcome home, boys.'

Chapter Seventy-Nine

It isn't something that I particularly want to do, but I can't help it, like some sad old moth to a particularly troublesome flame. I sit on my bed, surrounded by mementos of my relationship with Leo. A battered biscuit tin lies open next to me, overflowing with photos of us together and silly tokens of love.

I open a small tin can. A lurid green plastic snake shoots out and blows a raspberry. It makes me smile. I'm not sure that it did at the time. Perhaps I haven't always been fully appreciative of Leo's line in presents. Now they're my most cherished possessions.

The doorbell rings and I put the lid back on the biscuit tin, pushing it under my bed, before going to answer the door. We're having another girls' night in. Three lonely spinsters, too much Chardonnay, a DVD featuring Orlando Bloom and hours of discussing men without any of us currently having a relationship with one. Is this what I have to look forward to for the rest of my life?

Caron breezes in first, Jo following in her wake. I join the procession and we go through to the kitchen where Caron proceeds to pull cartons out of a carrier bag from Antonio's deli – a fine, expensive establishment just further down the street from my flat in Shad Thames. As well as being fine and expensive, it's also far too convenient and is the main reason why my oven has seen so little action during the time I've lived here and my bank account has seen so much.

Jo kisses me on the cheek. 'Okay?'

I nod bravely.

'Caron told me about Dominic.'

'Another one bites the dust.' I force a laugh. 'I'm beginning to think that I wear the wrong brand of deodorant.'

'So,' Caron says expectantly. 'Have you heard from the three missing reprobates yet?'

I shake my head. 'No. Not a thing.'

My friend's face falls. 'Bastards,' she says vehemently, before turning her attention to the food. 'For our delectation, I got tuna wraps, three sorts of salad, smelly cheese and . . .' she holds up her *pièce de résistance* like a trophy, 'coffee cake. Lots of it. Particularly good in times of crisis. Have you got any chocolate ice-cream?'

'Is that a stupid question?'

'Fabulous.' Caron claps her hands together, then scrunches up all the paper wrappers and throws them in the wastepaper bin. 'Where do you suppose they are?'

'Who knows,' I say. 'Aren't men always a law unto themselves? No doubt they'll turn up again one day as if nothing's happened.'

'Plates?' Caron demands.

'Plates.' I pull them out of the cupboard and put them down on the work surface.

My friend dishes out with a professional hand. 'I liked Grant.' Caron arranges the lettuce with the eye of an artist. '*Really* liked him. I had high hopes for him.' We all pick up our plates and go back through to the lounge, plonking ourselves down at the table by the window. 'I'm fed up of dating lame men. I should have realised that he'd be flawed because he's a friend of Leo's.' She lays a hand on my arm. 'No offence.'

'None taken,' I say.

'It's not difficult to find men. I could pick up a different guy every night of the week.' Jo is never one to mince words. 'But all they want to do is come home with you for casual sex. No one is interested in a serious relationship. How do you find a good man without wasting too much time on the losers?'

'I've never been very good at that scene.' I've always been too uptight about my own body to consider sharing it with a stranger, and the thought of going through all that again fills me with dread.

'That's all there seems to be. Women grow out of it, but these days men don't seem to. They're all babymen now,' Jo says. 'Thirty-year-old toddlers. Grown men who behave like petulant infants and who have the same sense of responsibility. They're an embarrassment to their own gender.'

'Do you think it's our fault?' I say. 'Whenever Leo attempted to do anything remotely manly I always used to make fun of him. I guess it's no wonder he stopped trying. Perhaps they've no idea what their role is supposed to be any more.'

'I wonder if men judge us as harshly.' Caron pours out wine for us all. 'Let's face it, we want nothing less than perfection now in a partner. No baldies, no one with a beer belly rather than a six-pack, nothing less than a six-figure salary and definitely no kids from previous wives in tow. We want them to look all sporty and athletic, but not to spend hours away from us playing sports. We want them to have great careers without spending too much time at the office.'

'Whatever happened to unconditional love?' Jo wants to know.

'It sucks,' Caron says. 'Particularly if you're the one dishing it out.' She slugs back her wine. 'We are the generation of women who want it all.'

I sigh. 'And end up with nothing.'

'Bugger,' Jo says miserably. 'Now we're going to have to get seriously drunk.'

We raise our glasses and clink them together.

'We have become our own cliché,' Caron declares.

When Leo comes back – *if* he comes back – I'm going to win him again. I'm going to be soft and floaty and feminine. I'm going to bake him homemade cakes and start doing roast dinners. I'm going to turn the clock back thirty years and love him like my mother loves my father. I'm going to love him unconditionally. And there's no way that anyone – no matter how cute – will stand in my way. I smile sadly. 'I'll drink to that.'

Chapter Eighty

So, that was the end of the Great Stonehenge Escapade. Grant, Lard and Leo were bundled into the back of one of the police cars and were driven to the nearest nick.

Apparently their downfall was that they'd startled some Druids who were performing ancient rituals at dawn. Grant, Lard and Leo had dropped out of the sky about three feet in front of them, scaring them all to death. You would have thought Druids were made of sterner stuff. But no. They'd rushed off, gowns hitched up around their knees and had raised the alarm. Flying in the face of convention in this country, the police arrived pretty soon afterwards. If it had taken them the normal three days to turn up to an 'incident', then the three of them could have had it away on their toes and no one would have been any the wiser.

Except, of course, Grant, Lard and Leo were all captured in full glory on the gift shop's closed-circuit television system during their breaking and entering phase. And, of course, they'd left Ethel in the car park for all to see. Not marvellous at covering their tracks then. Somehow Leo didn't think they were cut out to be career burglars.

Now they were all in individual interview rooms, being 'interviewed'. There was no good cop, bad cop thing going on; the officers were just all pretty grumpy with them. This was mainly because Leo and his compatriots had decided that they would stick to the truth. And in this case, the truth was decidedly stranger than any fiction.

Leo's policeman, as he'd fondly come to think of him, was red and sweating in the face. He folded his arms. 'Run this past me one more time.'

'We were trying to get a sick fairy home.'

'To the . . .' the officer consulted his notes '. . . *Land of Light*.' This was said with a degree of cynicism often found in members of the constabulary.

'Yes.' The policemen were struggling with this because although Leo, Grant and Lard had forced their way into the gift shop, they hadn't actually stolen anything. Quite frankly, there wasn't anything worth stealing – unless your heart's desire was a *Welcome to Stonehenge* tea towel.

'Have you recently taken any illegal substances?'

Leo sighed. 'Not unless you count lavender poteen.'

'Don't get funny with me, sonny,' the policeman warned.

Leo felt as if he had the worst possible case of jet lag. All he wanted to do was lie down and sleep for a fortnight.

'The Druids said that you fell out of the sky.'

'Then perhaps you should ask them if they've been taking illegal substances too.'

'You're in very serious trouble, you know.' The policeman was looking exceptionally cross now.

'I'll pay for any damage we've caused,' Leo said. 'I'm very sorry about it, but it was an emergency.'

'What I want to know is, what were you doing there in the first place?'

'Trying to get a sick fairy home,' Leo and the policeman said in unison.

After three hours of interrogation and several cups of tea, the policemen decided that they had no option but to let them go. But not before exploring the possibility of getting them sectioned under the Mental Health Act for insanity and being a danger to the public at large. When they realised that wouldn't stick, they charged them all with criminal damage and let them go.

Such was the British justice system that when their case eventually came to court – shortly before they were old and grey and this was all a distant memory that they'd laugh about from time to time – they'd probably get a few hours of community service and a fine, which, of course, they could all pay with ease because they were relatively rich. And they'd all have a criminal record to add to their CVs, which far from hindering their career prospects as Leo had first feared, the City being what it was, it would quite probably enhance them. In the meantime, Leo would send a large cheque to the powers-that-be at Stonehenge, so that they could repair the damage to their tacky gift shop. In all honesty, the three lads would probably have done them a

290

favour if they'd smashed the lot up. Who in their right mind would want to take home a Stonehenge fridge magnet as a souvenir, or a life-like plastic replica of the magnificent stones? Although there were some rather nice Stonehenge shot glasses that Leo wouldn't have minded . . .

Then, he guessed, life would go on and the authorities would remain blissfully unaware of a fantastic opportunity to discover just how powerful the ancient monument in their keeping really was.

Grant, Lard and Leo met up by the front desk. They all looked as dishevelled as each other and just as exhausted. The police were already losing interest in them; it must have been time for their lunch-break. In step, the three miscreants plodded out into the car park.

'Did they rough you up?' Leo asked his partners in crime.

'You watch too many cop shows, Leo,' Grant told him with a world-weary huff.

'You're both okay though?' Leo's friends nodded at him. 'Apart from a slight tug from the long arm of the law,' he told them, 'I think we could class that as a successful mission.'

Grant put his hand on Leo's shoulder. 'At least Isobel is safe now.'

Suddenly it was all too much. Leo sagged to his knees on the dirty grit of the car park and, for the first time in his life, cried openly and loudly while Grant and Lard held him. And Leo started to realise just how awful he really felt.

Chapter Eighty-One

My father and I have bought a fold-down single bed from eBay – a revelation of virtual shopping for my mystified parent, whose retail outlet of choice is either Harvey Nicks or Harrods. My brother-in-law, Awful Austin, collected it in his Transit van and delivered it to the house yesterday. Between us we wrestled the bed into the downstairs study for my mother. It's still only a relatively short time after her stroke, but Catherine is making marvellous progress. Her balance still isn't great, however, and we know that when she's allowed to come home, the stairs might well be a problem for her to manoeuvre.

My father has cleared his study, packing away files and case studies with an air of finality. It's the first time in my life that I have ever seen his desk completely free of paperwork. Having made the decision to take early retirement, it's obvious to all that he now can't wait to leave. He's hired a cleaner too – a good one, it seems, as the place shines like a new pin.

My father sits down on the single bed which seems to take up much of the study.

'I'm sure we could have squeezed a double in here,' he says, rather optimistically.

'Nonsense,' I tell him. 'You and Mummy would have had to climb over each other to get out. The idea is to make it easier for her.'

'I know.' My father's voice wavers. 'But we've spent so few nights apart during our marriage. It seems wrong to be sleeping in separate beds under the same roof.'

Sitting down next to him, I give him a hug. 'I didn't know you were such a soppy old thing.' And it's true, my mother's illness has brought out a caring side to my father that I've rarely seen and it makes me realise that I don't really know my parents as people. My relationship with them has been entirely based on how they've interacted with me. But then how many people are best friends with their parents?

My father smiles self-consciously. I never knew that the love between them was so tender and it makes me feel proud to be their daughter.

'This won't be for long.' I cast a glance at the temporary bed. 'You know what Mummy's like. She'll be defying medical science by running marathons next year.'

'I do so hope that you're right, darling.' My father rubs the bridge of his nose. He's barely slept since my mother has been in hospital and he hasn't shaved as meticulously as he normally does – rushing home to perform small domestic tasks as quickly as possible, anxious not to be away from his wife's bedside for too long – white bristles push through his pink skin and he's nicked himself too many times. 'I do miss her,' he says, eyes brimming with tears.

I've never seen my father cry and that seems strange after thirty years in his company. I guess that he's from the generation of men who perceive crying as a weakness. But he cries now, dabbing awkwardly at his tears with a cotton lawn handkerchief. 'I have spent the latter part of my life trying to make already beautiful women even more perfect. And I wonder what the point of it all was. You mother is very proud of her looks; she was always asking me to do little nips and tucks, but I never would. I never thought she needed them. Now I look at her, with her face all slack down one side, dribble coming from her mouth and her clumsy movements, and do you know, Emma . . .' He takes my hand. 'Catherine has never looked more beautiful to me.'

I feel the tears come to my eyes too.

'Find someone to love like that, darling,' he says with a sniff. 'Even if it is that damn Leo.'

Chapter Eighty-Two

Leo called Emma as soon as he got home. Butterflies circled in his stomach and his mouth was dry. But on her home number, the wretched answerphone clicked in and Leo couldn't bring himself to leave a message as he didn't know what to say. He tried her mobile.

'Hello.'

'Emma. It's Leo.'

The phone went dead. He pressed redial and tried again. 'Emma?'

She hung up again. So he tried again and again and again, and every time he said, 'Hello,' Emma hung up. Though he didn't actually know what he would have said if she had been willing to engage in conversation, come to think of it. Leo, having raided his stock of mobiles, put his phone back into his pocket and slumped onto the sofa.

The flat seemed weird. Empty. Having Isobel there had definitely left some sort of imprint on it. Everything had stopped looking so perky and had gone back to being normal furniture and fittings. Even the cushions seemed to have lost their oomph. He suspected that his mirrors wouldn't talk to him any more. Maybe he'd up sticks and move. This place was starting to hold too many memories.

Grant came out of the kitchen bearing two mugs of tea. 'Mate,' he said, 'you look wrecked.'

'I've been calling Emma,' Leo told him, 'but she keeps hanging up on me.' All he wanted to do was lie in a nice, long, hot bath and make the world go away, but this was important. Emma's message had sounded urgent. He'd only been gone overnight, so hopefully he'd still be back in the nick of time to help out.

'Why don't you hit the sack for a while,' his friend suggested. 'After all that you've been through, you could do with a rest.'

Leo couldn't argue with that. 'I could try phoning her again.' He ferreted for his phone.

'You don't look in any fit state to speak to her now.'

'But she said she needed me.'

'It seems that perhaps our dear Emma has already changed her mind about needing you,' Grant pointed out. 'You'd be no use to her in this state, anyway.'

'I should go down to the gallery. See if she's there.'

'Hitting the sack would be your best idea. You look like you haven't slept for a week.'

'I need to see Emma,' Leo insisted.

'You're hardly in a condition to present a rational argument,' Grant said. 'If you want her back, Leo, crashing in there looking like one of our homeless friends isn't the best recipe for success. Let me go down there on my way into the office and see how the land lies. If she's hanging up on you then she must have her reasons. I've got to talk to Caron too. I'm due to take her out for a wild night on the town. I'd hate to think that she'd been calling me while we were away for the night.'

Leo yawned, his eyelids grew heavy and his eyes rolled as sleep washed over him. He laid his head down on one of his subdued cushions. 'I don't want her to think that I don't care,' he mumbled. Because he did care, and Emma had to know that as soon as possible.

Chapter Eighty-Three

At Art For Art's Sake I've just taken delivery of the work for our latest exhibition. I'm busy unpacking cases and cases of delicate pottery painted with cartoon figures in strange sexual positions and scenes of mass torture in lurid colours. Truly the produce of a warped mind and I wonder which of our fabulously wealthy clients will be snapping these up. The ones with a total taste by-pass, I conclude. It's making my eyes ache to look at them. Just the sort of thing I can imagine my parents having in their lounge. If they suddenly went insane, that is.

The majority of the wire-mesh torso sculptures have found new homes and have been shipped out by my ever-efficient friend, Caron, over the course of the last week. The rest are being packed and sent back to the artist, along with a cheque for his share of the loot. I think back to Rodin's statue of *The Kiss* in the Tate Gallery. My mother's right – that *is* art. Real proper art, with real proper people in it. Perhaps I should consider looking for a new job. Maybe I should consider a new life. Pack it all in and go to work in a scuba-diving centre in the Cayman Islands. I'm just arranging the new gallery layout and my new lifestyle when the door opens.

Grant stands there, looking sheepish.

I put down the pot I'm holding in case I'm tempted to throw it. A ten thousand pound temper tantrum is way beyond my meagre means – even to make a point. Then I'd be heading for the Cayman Islands out of necessity. Instead, for safety's sake, I place my hands on my hips out of harm's way. 'Look who's back from the dead,' I say sarcastically.

'Long time, no see.' He gives me a small, uncertain wave and inches his way further into the gallery.

'I take it that if you've turned up again – like the proverbial bad penny – then it means that Leo is back in circulation too.'

'Yes,' Grant says. 'That might be a correct assessment of the situation.'

'So? I think an explanation is required. I did consider going to the police to report you all missing.'

I think I see Grant flinch. 'Missing?'

'I've been calling Leo for over a week now and nothing, *nada*. His flat was empty. None of you were in work. Where on earth did you get to?'

'A *week*?' I'll swear that Grant blanches. He looks as if his knees have turned to jelly as he grabs hold of the nearest display case. 'We've been gone for a *week*?'

'Yes, you have. Are you going to tell me where you've been?'

He snorts as if he's surprised and says, 'A week?' once more.

'Well?'

'We just took a few days off together.' Grant tries – and fails – to look innocent.

'So? Did you have fun?' I ask.

'Not in the traditional sense of the word.'

'Where did you go?'

'Er . . . away.'

'Probably Ibiza or Las Vegas or Amsterdam.' I narrow my eyes. 'Anywhere that boys can behave badly would be my guess.'

Grant says nothing.

'Didn't you think to tell anyone where you were going?'

'It was a spur of the moment decision. Very last minute. We only thought we'd been . . . er, we only thought we'd *be* away overnight.'

'You are so irresponsible,' I chide. 'When normal people go on holiday, Grant, they tell friends and loved ones. They tell the people that they work with and work for. They don't just disappear off the face of the earth for days on end.'

'In Leo's defence, he has a lot on his mind.'

'And I don't?' I say. 'I've been pacing anxiously for days while Leo has been gadding about and has been just too busy to be bothered to call?' It's so typical of him and I wonder why I'd ever considered that I might want a relationship with him again.

'He's been trying to call you since the minute we got back, Emma. You keep hanging up on him.'

'I don't want to hear his feeble explanations.' What I actually want to do is hit him over the head with a frying pan.

'We did have our reasons,' Grant insists.

'And they were?'

'I can't tell you about them,' he says. 'But one day you'll understand.'

I sigh. 'If I ever start to understand anything Leo does, please shoot me.'

Grant stands there looking pathetic, hands in pockets, down-turned mouth.

'Caron has been worried about you,' I tell him gruffly. 'Fool that she is, she likes you. You had a date arranged and you never turned up.'

'Oh shit.' Grant looks crestfallen. 'I didn't do it on purpose, I swear.'

I put on my disbelieving face.

'I'll call her.'

I keep my face impassive.

'I will,' Grant promises me earnestly. 'I will. She's great. I hoped she might be here today. I'd love to take her out again.'

'Get in the queue, then,' I snap. 'In fact, go to the back of the queue.'

Grant hangs his head.

I sigh again – a relenting sigh rather than an exasperated one. 'You look like you need coffee.'

Grant nods and his smile reappears. He risks coming into the gallery fully and even sits on the chair at my desk. I go out to the kitchen, busy myself pouring some rather stewed coffee – if he thinks I'm making fresh coffee for him then he'd better think again – and take it out to Grant.

We sit for a moment sipping our bitter, too strong coffee quietly. 'Okay,' I say. 'I give in. Where is he now?'

'At home,' Grant tells me. 'He wanted to come down here, but I made him go to bed. He hasn't slept in a few days.'

Now I'm alert. 'He's not been sleeping?' Leo could sleep through an earthquake. 'What's wrong with him?'

'He's feeling pretty awful, Emma,' Grant replies, not meeting my eyes. 'You know that she . . . that Isobel's gone.'

'No.' I don't even try to hide my surprise. 'I didn't know. What happened?'

'You need to talk to Leo about that.'

My eyes turn to slits again. 'Is this all tied up with your disappearing act?'

'Yes.' Grant seems tired and there are dark shadows under his eyes. He looks terrible. A month's sleep and a few vitamin injections wouldn't go amiss here either. 'We're worried about Leo, Emma. He's had a tough time. In the past few weeks he's had a lot of growing up to do.'

298

'That would be hard for him.'

'Go easy on him when you speak to him.'

'What makes you think I'm going to speak to him? My mother's been ill, Grant. Seriously ill. Where was Leo when I needed him?'

'He needs you, Emma. More than he realises. More than you realise.'

One of my father's 'pahs!' comes out of my mouth before I can stop it. Sometimes I'm too much my father's daughter. 'Every time I go all soft and squishy on him again, he does something stupid. I can't keep going on like this, Grant. My mind feels as if it's being tossed about in a tumble dryer. I can't think straight any more.'

'He still loves you, Emma. I think you feel the same. Would you ever consider taking him back?'

'Is hell ever likely to freeze over?'

Grant smiles sadly. 'So you do still love him?'

'What's that got to do with anything?' I say crossly. 'I'm immune to Leo's charms. I've moved on. I've met someone else.' I don't tell Grant that my particular someone else has just been reunited with his girl-friend. Instead, I flick back my hair and declare, 'I am *completely* over him.'

And, perhaps if I say it enough, one day it will be true.

Chapter Eighty-Four

'Here.' Leo beckoned the schoolboy towards him. 'Will you go into that shop and get me a bunch of flowers?'

The kid nodded. 'It'll cost you.'

'A fiver,' Leo said. 'On delivery.'

'Done,' the kid said. And Leo knew that he had been.

He handed over the money, including the purchasing fee, and moments later the kid came out of the florist's clutching a bouquet of pink-coloured flowers wrapped in cellophane. 'Great,' Leo said. 'Nice choice.'

He put the flowers behind his back and walked the ten minutes to Emma's parents' home, hideously self-conscious of the blooms he was bearing. He rang the doorbell and waited. Emma's father, Charles, opened the door. He was wearing an apron and rubber gloves.

Leo cleared his throat. 'Mr Chambers,' he said. 'Hi. Hello. I understand that Emma's mother has been unwell. I thought I'd pop in to give her my best wishes.'

Leo had never popped in to see Emma's parents before. They were not 'popping in' sort of people. The expression on Emma's father's face said that nothing had changed on that front.

'Come in, Leo,' Charles Chambers said, finding his manners. 'Come in.'

Leo followed Charles into the hall and then stood fidgeting uncomfortably.

'We've just finished lunch. Come through to the kitchen. I'm washing the dishes and having a tidy up. You can join us for a cup of tea.'

Leo followed him. Emma's mother, Catherine, sat at the table. She looked as if she had aged and was thinner and paler than when Leo had last seen her on the fateful night of her daughter's thirtieth birthday party.

'Leo,' she said warmly. His only fan in the Chambers household was clearly pleased to see him. 'To what do I owe this pleasure?'

'I wanted to come and see how you were.' Leo kissed her on the cheek. 'I'm sorry I didn't come sooner.' He handed over the flowers, grateful to be rid of them.

'Very nice,' Catherine said. 'My favourites. How thoughtful. Isn't Leo thoughtful, Charles?'

Charles didn't look entirely convinced.

'You're looking well.' That wasn't exactly true, but Catherine didn't look as awful as he'd expected. Or perhaps after his recent experience with Isobel, he was marginally better at dealing with illness than he had been.

'I'll be back to my old self before too long,' she assured him, patting his hand gently.

Leo realised that he'd taken his role in this family for granted too and he wanted to do anything he could to make amends. It was terrible to see Catherine looking a shadow of her former self and it made him think of his own mother and how little he'd seen of his parents in recent years. As soon as he left here, he'd call them and arrange to go to see them. But then, that alone could make them die of shock.

Charles switched on the kettle and then returned to his washing up. Leo joined him at the sink and picked up the tea towel. He dried the dishes as Charles washed.

'I've also come here with an ulterior motive,' Leo admitted to them. 'Emma isn't speaking to me. She won't return my phone calls.'

'And you want us to put in a good word for you?' Catherine said.

'Then you must be very desperate, Leo. When did my daughter ever listen to me? Or to anyone else for that matter.' Charles Chambers stripped off his rubber gloves.

'I'd like to become part of this family once again. If you'll have me.'

Catherine slowly shook her head. 'We'd love that, Leo. But there's nothing we can do for you. You're going to have to convince her all by yourself.'

'I know that we haven't always seen eye to eye, Mr Chambers, but I do love your daughter.'

'I don't doubt that, Leo,' Charles said. 'She loves you too. But do you make each other happy?'

'I'd like to think that we could, given another chance.'

'Well, there's one thing for certain,' Charles said with a heavy sigh. 'She's been damn miserable without you.'

Chapter Eighty-Five

The alarm clock went off yet again and Leo knocked it to the floor. Flipping onto his back, he stared at the ceiling. He kept hoping that, like Bobby Ewing on *Dallas*, he'd wake up in the shower and it would all have been a terrible nightmare and that none of it had really happened. But every morning he was in his bed facing harsh reality with no hope of a cop-out ending.

He'd been back in the real world now for over a week and it wasn't all that it was cracked up to be. Getting up and struggling through the day wasn't proving any easier. Leo wondered how long he could carry on with this feeling – or lack of it. He wasn't sure that numb and sick were classed as emotions.

Forcing himself out of bed, he padded through to the kitchen. Leo was looking too scary to go near a mirror – even he fully appreciated that. His hair was a disaster zone and he hadn't shaved at all over the weekend – somehow there didn't seem to be any point. His time was spent entirely alone, watching as many Disney films as he could find in the local video shop featuring fairies, while partaking liberally of red wine. How he missed Isobel and her mischievous little ways. She would know how to sort this out for him. She'd have made Emma return his calls with a wave of that wicked wand of hers. Instead he'd lost two great women – and he wondered how he could have made such a mess of his life.

The sink was piled high with dirty dishes and Leo stood and surveyed the mess with disgust.

'Not so keen to spruce yourselves up now, eh?'

His dishes remained silent.

Leo sighed. 'Me neither.'

Going to the sink, he picked out the least dirty dish and then took a box of Kellogg's Frosties from the cupboard. There was no milk in the fridge – he already knew that as he had run out yesterday and

302

couldn't be bothered to nip out to the shop. Leo quite liked black coffee anyway. Except that coffee was the other thing he'd run out of.

Sitting at the table with his dish, he went to tip out some cereal, but alas there was nothing in the box. Still, he hadn't much of an appetite anyway. Leo put his head on the table and, mercifully, sleep overtook him once more.

When Leo finally got to the office, Grant and Lard were already at their desks. They exchanged one of their glances as he entered.

'Leo!' Grant said. 'Where have you been?' He glanced at the clock. It was nearly eleven o'clock.

'I know. I know. Sorry. Sorry.' Leo slid into his chair and tried to busy himself with turning on his computer and other stuff that he really didn't care about.

Old Baldy came out of his office and glared at him. Their boss had been like a bear with a sore arse since Isobel had gone too. The fact that she'd been replaced by some pinch-faced temp with a tweed suit and librarian's bun couldn't be helping.

'On the late shift again, Mr Harper?'

'I know. I know. Sorry. Sorry. I'll be here on time tomorrow.'

'Nine o'clock, Mr Harper. Sharp. Or the number of your tomorrows will be severely curtailed.' And Old Baldy flounced back into his office.

'Bugger,' Leo muttered under his breath.

Grant and Lard waited until Old Baldy was engrossed in something else and then sidled over to Leo's desk. Lard put a Danish pastry down next to their friend.

'Breakfast,' Grant said. 'Eat it.'

Leo shook his head. No glitter. 'Cheers, mate,' he said, 'but I've already eaten.' He patted his stomach just to prove how full he was.

'You haven't,' Grant said.

'No.'

'Not for days.'

'I'm on a diet.'

'Yeah?' Grant said. 'And so is Lard.'

Grant and Leo looked up at Lard who was eating his customary Mars Bar with relish.

'I've got work to do, boys.' Leo tried to look interested in his computer while inside it felt as if his world was crashing.

303

Grant sat next to him and pulled his chair up close. 'This can't go on, Leo,' he told him softly. 'We are all in deep, deep doo-doo after our week's little unauthorised holiday, even though we only thought we'd been gone for one night. I'm not sure how we've managed to keep our jobs, but we have. If you don't buck up – and quick – Baldy will give you the bullet.'

Something inside Leo snapped. 'Do you think I care? Do you really think I care about whether stocks go up or down or bloody sideways?' He knew that he was shouting. People in the office were looking at him. 'What does it matter? *Why* does any of it matter?'

Grant lowered his voice further, the voice of calm in his storm. 'Leo. I'm your friend. Your best friend. I know what you've been through. I know what you're *going* through. I know the things you've seen. But, mate, you've got to get your act together.'

Leo turned and faced his friend. 'Why?'

Grant was clearly taken aback. 'Why?'

'Yes. Why?'

Grant looked at a loss for an answer. 'It's what we do,' he said. 'We carry on.'

'Grant,' Lard interjected, 'you know what she was like. You of all people know. You must be able to understand why he's so gutted.'

Leo raked his fingers through his hair.

'This isn't about Isobel though, is it?' Grant asked candidly.

Leo sighed and it wavered sadly on the air. 'Losing Isobel was bad enough, but I can rationalise that in some small part of my brain. She was a *fairy*, for goodness sake.' He lowered his voice. 'We were different beings from different places – it was never destined to last. I can cope with that. Sort of. But with Emma it's not the same. She's here. She's flesh and blood. There's no reason for us not to be together. We're *meant* to be together. She's the sensible one. I thought she'd see that. I thought she'd want us to carry on just as we were. I miss her so much that even my fingernails hurt from the pain of it.'

'I wish I could wave a magic wand for you and make it all better.'

'But you can't,' Leo said. 'No one can. There's suddenly a bit of a wand shortage round here. I lost Emma, then I lost Isobel and now I've lost Emma again.' He felt like wailing out loud. How careless could one man be? 'I have to get through this on my own.'

'You have us,' Lard told Leo. 'You have your friends. We'll always be here for you.' He put his hand on his heart.

Leo and Grant raised their eyebrows at this.

'You said you were going to win Emma back, you prawn,' Grant said with more than a hint of exasperation. 'What have you done so far? Made a few whingey phone calls. Hung around outside the gallery and her flat when you know she's not there.'

'I went to see her parents.'

'That's it? The sum total of your effort?'

'Emma has made it very clear that I've blown it.'

'I know you're in the depths of despair and I hate to see you like this, but now you know exactly how Emma feels, mate. She's gone through all of this crap for you. Her fingernails have been hurting too. Why should she trust you again?'

'I've changed.'

'How does she know that?'

'I don't know. It's rather difficult to show her how when she won't see me or speak to me.'

'So let's get back to basics. Why did you break up in the first place?'

'Because Emma felt we'd lost "the magic".'

'Then show her it, you idiot. For heaven's sake, Leo, you should by now know more about magic than most. Think about that.'

Leo's friend clapped him on the shoulder and he and Lard walked away. Leo sat and stared at his computer, utterly speechless. He stuffed the Danish pastry into his mouth and made himself chew even though he couldn't taste anything at all and might as well be eating a beer mat or his own underpants.

Grant's words reverberated round his brain. Leo had no idea that he could feel – or cause – this amount of pain. He was shocked to the core. Why was he never capable of showing Emma how much he loved her? Leo felt sick. Sick to his stomach. Sick to his heart. If it wasn't for the fact that Old Baldy would sack him if he even moved from this desk before nightfall, Leo would have gone to the bathroom and would have spilled his guts.

Chapter Eighty-Six

L eo was sitting alone in the dark, which he appreciated was a sad
    sack thing to do. Even worse, he was listening to Whitney Houston,
but he did have a can of beer in his hand, which to Leo's mind sort
of evened things out. He had got stuff to do, but he wasn't sure what,
and he didn't know if he could be bothered with it anyway. He should
probably iron a shirt for work tomorrow, but if he kept his jacket on
then no one would see the creases.

The doorbell rang and he considered ignoring it, but it was ringing
in a particularly persistent manner and whoever it was didn't seem to
be in a rush to go away. Leo padded out to the hall.

When he opened the door, Grant and Lard were standing there grinning inanely.

'We have curry,' Grant announced cheerily. 'We have beer. We have
a DVD of Manchester United's golden moments. We have all that is
required for a good time.'

'Nearly all,' Leo said miserably.

'The lap dancer said she'd be along later,' Lard told him with a wink.

'Oh good.' Leo smiled at them tiredly. 'Come on in.'

In the lounge, Grant threw him a worried look. 'Whitney Houston?'

'It's a temporary phase.'

'I'm glad to hear it, mate.' Grant cut Whitney off in mid-warble and
replaced her with the White Stripes.

'How are you feeling?' Lard asked sincerely. '*Really* feeling?'

'Fantastic,' Leo replied. 'I'm *really* feeling *really* fantastic.'

'You will,' Grant said, clapping him so heartily on the back that he
nearly fell over.

They went through to the kitchen and Leo stood there being as useless
as a chocolate teapot while Grant and Lard washed some plates and dished
out heaps of biriani and onion bhajis and piles of poppadoms. Neither
of them mentioned what a state his kitchen or, indeed his life, was in.

Grant sang while he ladled out the vegetable curry and, call Leo slow on the uptake, but he then twigged that this forced *bonhomie* was all for his benefit. Part of the Rehabilitate Leo Plan. Even though he was still a miserable old git and he was absolutely sure that it wouldn't work, he was touched that they had gone to so much trouble on his behalf.

Succulent pieces of chicken tikka steamed gently in a silver-foil tray. No refined Indian gentleman popping up to serve it this time though. But for the first time in weeks, the smell of the spices pricked at Leo's appetite. He wasn't sure whether he'd eaten at all today, but suddenly he realised that he was starving.

'Can't you do something to help, you lazy bastard?' his dear friend Grant said over his shoulder.

'I'll get us some more beers,' Leo said, and turned his attention to the fridge to hide the fact that he felt like crying again.

Two hours later. Curry gone. And beer. All merry. Happy times. Happy times. Drink. Drink. Lots of drink. Sat in row on sofa. Watched football. With mates. Leo loved Grant. Loved Lard too. Great mates. The best. David Beckham. Also best. Loved Dave too. Loved Emma most of all. *Manchester United Golden Moments.* Top DVD. Much scoring. Naff off, Whitney Houston. Sloppy, sloppy, terrible music. All bollocks. Sorry, Emma.

'Goal! Goal! Goal!'

Mexican wave on sofa. Leo stood up. Wobble. Cheering. Cheering. Hoorah!

Leo. 'Boys. Boys. Sing-song. Sing-song.'

Grant and Lard stood up. Wobble. Wobble.

Leo. 'There's only one David Beckham!'

All. 'There's only one David Beckham! One David Beckham! There's only one David Beckham!'

Not so pissed. Saw Grant and Lard exchange relieved glance. Top mates. Ha! Old Leo was back. David Beckham saviour of all mankind. Emma sexiest bird on planet. Hurrah! Fell over. Ouff!

Seventeen cups of coffee and a little doze later and they were all a bit more sober and righteous. And who knew what it was, maybe the curry, the booze or the fact that Manchester United *were* the top team in the universe, but something had shifted inside of Leo and he knew that from now on, things could only get better.

Grant and Lard were at the kitchen sink and they were washing Leo's dishes. They were also wearing aprons which they had found who knows where. They must surely have been something to do with Isobel. Leo's heart squeezed at the thought of her and the fact that he was never likely to see her again – no bumping into her down at the shops or the pub, no catching a glimpse of her on a passing bus – but he didn't feel quite the amount of hopelessness that he previously had. Isobel had been an important part of his life and he'd never forget her, but he saw that it would be possible to let go. He'd learned a lot from her and he should put all this new knowledge to good use and not squander it as he'd squandered everything else in his life.

Before he was berated for his lack of domesticity, he started to cram the empty foil cartons and remnants of the curry into a black bin bag.

'You need a dishwasher,' Grant said.

'I do not.'

'You do.'

'You need to get out more,' Lard said.

'I do not.'

'You do.'

Now they were all sober and they realised that Leo wasn't about to top himself, they clearly thought they were safe to nag him again. He thought Grant and Lard would make a wonderful couple.

'You need a woman to look after you,' Grant said.

'I definitely do not!'

'You do!' Grant and Lard insisted in unison.

'Yeah?' Leo sat down at the table, resisting the temptation to open another beer. 'Look at the state of me. Miserable. Morose.'

'Manky,' Grant added. 'You might be crap at relationships, Leo, but you don't do great single either.'

'I'm not ready for another relationship.' He shook his head. 'I wouldn't want me. Who else would?'

Grant and Lard exchanged a demonic grin. 'Emma,' they said.

'No. No. No. Many times no.' Leo held up his hands. 'I have hurt that woman enough.'

'True,' they agreed.

'Anyway. What about you?' Leo frowned at Grant. 'I thought you and Emma were getting . . .' He rubbed his arms up and down himself in a seductive manner.

'Oh, Leo.' Grant sighed at him. 'When are you going to learn? If you could ever get your two brain cells to collide it would be a cataclysmic event.'

'Perhaps I should stand aside and let you get on with it.'

'She happens to be in love with someone else.'

Leo was horrified. 'Who?'

Grant turned to Lard. 'You hold him down while I knock some sense into that stupid thick skull of his.'

Leo gazed at them incredulously. 'She's still in love with me?'

They both rolled their eyes.

'She can't be,' he said. 'I'm such a pain in the arse. She has told me many times and in many different ways. She won't even take my calls.'

Grant and Lard gave him one of their special looks.

'I'm not saying it would be easy,' Grant said. 'You'd need a very cunning plan.'

'Emma wouldn't want me back with a bow tied round me.' A rush of warmth flooded into his body. Suddenly there was hope in his wounded heart. 'Would she?'

Chapter Eighty-Seven

I'm meeting Jo and Caron for lunch at their favourite haunt down by the River Thames, but I've got some time to kill and am stocking up on a few bits and pieces to see me through the weekend at my other favourite haunt – the Hay's Galleria. I've bought my friends a few little trinkets too, for being so fabulous over the last few weeks. I don't know how I would have managed without them.

The weekdays aren't too bad – when I'm busy at work and I often stay late researching and planning new exhibitions just to avoid going home – but the weekends loom large ahead of me and they're sheer torture. Friends are great, but they're not the same as having a partner waiting for you to slob around with.

I'm going to see Caron again tonight, but we aren't going out on the town. There's only so much enforced partying that I can stand and I've pretty much reached my limit. Instead, I'm planning to regroup and conserve my energies. Which essentially means that Caron and I are going to sit in and watch yet another DVD featuring an unattainable man. Jo, despite her disgust at men who want only casual sex, doesn't seem to be able to manage without it either for any longer than a week or two either – so she's hitting the clubs with the intention of getting soundly laid. No doubt we'll hear about her tawdry escapades during the week.

This morning, I've been to see my mother who is now, thankfully, back at home, ensconced in her downstairs makeshift bedroom. I think that she still looks frail, but there's no doubt she's making a good recovery. My father is running round, catering to Mummy's every whim, like a teenager in love. It's both wonderful and heartbreaking to see. My mother has never been incapacitated in her entire life and it's strange to see her so dependent on other people. It's even stranger to see my father coping so well. If ever there's a silver lining on a cloud it's the fact that Daddy has somehow broken down his own emotional barriers and is now openly affectionate to his wife – and, even more bizarrely – to everyone else around him. He even smiled at the spotty teenager who delivered his newspaper today. There's no doubting that my parents are still deeply in love despite all that life has thrown at them. They have magic in their lives and there aren't many people who can count themselves so lucky. It gives me hope for the future. Even a future without Leo.

Leo has been home for weeks now and has given up calling me. And even though I kept hanging up on him when he did, I do really want to talk to him now. I could call him, but I haven't managed to summon up the courage to do that yet. Perhaps we're both too stubborn for our own good. It could also be that Leo has moved on, has found someone new, and this really is the end for us. I shift the weight of my carrier bags in my hands. We had such great potential and I still find it hard to believe that we managed to fritter it away so easily. We have both been stupid in taking each other for granted. But, when all is said and done, Leo is still probably more stupid than me.

Leo came out of the novelty gifts store, clutching at his bulging carrier bags. This was a complete trial for him as he wasn't a natural shopper. He was a man for a start and men just didn't have the right genes for it. This, however, was important shopping. So important that Leo had even scribbled down a list for himself. And he hadn't lost it. He wanted to get everything perfect, so nothing would be left to chance – or to his two cohorts. He must accomplish this feat alone. The amount he'd spent was making him feel dizzy and he decided he must consume some strong alcohol before he'd be capable of moving on to attempt phase two.

Leo headed towards the nearest bar in search of some medicinal Budweiser and as he did, he saw Emma coming out of one of the other shops. His heart nearly stopped beating. She was swinging down the middle of the arcade, smiling. He thought she'd lost some weight – which she'd like. But he had to say, she looked great. Happy and perky. Without him. And Leo wondered whether Lard and Grant had read this whole situation wrong. They were convinced that Emma still held a torch for him, but Leo didn't know if that was the case. She didn't exactly look miserable. He had to conclude that she'd usually looked an awful lot more miserable when he was with her. Was it insane to place his trust in two men who were just as clueless as he was when it came to reading what women want? Leo thought it might well be so. But they had helped him to get Isobel home and he supposed he could do worse than rely on their instincts again.

Emma was heading straight towards him. He felt like a rabbit trapped in the headlights, standing there with his arms chock-full of carrier bags. This was dastardly timing, indeed. He didn't want to bump into her now when he wasn't prepared. It reminded him of the day they saw each other here when he was shopping with Isobel and how it felt to see Emma with another man – a man he'd thought she was planning to marry. That left him more than breathless. He could never let that happen again. Leo felt panicky. Was this plan madness? Should he just shout out to Emma now and take his chances? They could maybe have lunch, a coffee – break the ice that had developed between them that way. Leo looked down at his carrier bags; he felt he'd come too far to veer from his chosen route now, although his courage nearly deserted him. She was a few metres away from him. Any second now they'd be face to face. A group of American students pushed their way past him, laughing and giggling, chattering in high-pitched East Coast accents. Leo lost sight of her in the tide of people, even though he stood on tiptoe and looked over their heads. By the time they'd passed by, he looked up and saw that Emma was walking away from him. And he thought that, for the moment, it was probably a good thing.

Chapter Eighty-Eight

L eo could do this. He could do this. He was pacing up and down outside the very smart florist's shop in the Galleria. It was true that he'd had a drink, but he was trying to curb his dependence on all things alcoholic. It had brought him nothing but trouble and was, obviously, along with money, the root of all evil. This situation, however, counted as exceptional circumstances and had required a few swift glasses of beer for courage. Leo made no excuses for his weakness.

There was a very lovely lady standing inside behind the counter in the florist's and she was looking at Leo as if he was a stalker. This was primarily because this wasn't his first time of pacing up and down outside. For half an hour now he'd been hoping that a suitably bribable child would pop up – but he was out of luck. This particular mission, it seemed, was going to be down to himself entirely. He chewed at his fingernails and he could feel sweat peppering his brow. Now he was making her look nervous. Leo knew what it felt like to suffer agonies of indecision.

With a deep breath he dived inside the shop. The woman looked suitably terrified and he was sure he could see her hand hovering over a panic button. This was possibly worse than buying underwear. 'I . . . I . . . I . . .' My goodness, he'd developed a stammer! 'I . . . I . . .'

'Yes?' She tried to give him an encouraging look.

'I . . . I . . .' Leo's hands had gone clammy and he was feeling faint. He wished he hadn't had a drink now. Leo was sure she could smell it on his breath. 'I . . . I . . .'

'You'd like to buy some flowers?'

'Yes.' A sigh of relief rushed out of his mouth. 'I'd like to buy some flowers.'

'Roses?'

Leo wiped his damp palms on his trousers. 'Roses would be lovely.'

She smiled at him and went over to a stand that had a display of a

313

dozen different colours of roses in stainless steel vases. 'Is it for a romantic occasion?' she asked.

'Yes,' he said, with an over-enthusiastic nod. 'A romantic occasion.'

'Then I think red roses, don't you?'

'Yes,' he said. 'Red. Red is good.'

The florist smiled at him again. 'There,' she said. 'That wasn't so bad, was it?'

'No,' Leo said. 'That wasn't so bad.'

'And how many would you like?'

'About two hundred, I think.'

The florist went pale. 'Two hundred?'

'Yes. More if you have them.'

'Do you have any idea how much that's going to cost?'

'No,' he said. 'Whatever it is, it will be worth it. But I need them today.'

'I . . . I . . . I'll have to ring round our other shops,' she said. Now she'd developed a stammer. 'But I'm sure we can do that.'

'I'll take what you have now,' Leo told her. 'Can you have the rest of them delivered as soon as possible? I have things to do.'

'Yes,' she answered in a vaguely stunned way. 'I'm sure we can do that.'

Now she was looking terrified whereas Leo was gaining confidence by the minute. He handed over his address and an awful lot of plastic money. Then he took his leave of this lovely lady and strode outside the shop with a carrier bag filled with roses, heads peeping out. Leo had no idea why he had avoided this flower-buying lark for so long. It felt great.

Half an hour later and he was nearing home. Leo shifted his shopping against his chest. He was sure his arms were considerably longer than they were when he had set out, but he didn't care. Leo had worked his way through the greatest hits of Queen on his way home and was now on to 'It's a Kind of Magic' at the top of his voice. He even tried a few dance steps. It had worked for Gene Kelly, it could work for Leo. The sun was out. The birds were singing. Strangers smiled at his one-man concert rather than avoiding him. Old and faithful Ethel was parked patiently outside awaiting his return. Leo went over to her and kissed her roof. 'You and I are going to look irresistible,' he said. 'You just wait and see.'

Leo sprinted up the stairs – even though he was weighed down with a dozen different carrier bags – and just as he went to open the door, his lovely neighbour Dominic came out. 'Hello, lovely neighbour,' Leo said brightly. 'How the hell are you?'

'Fine,' Dominic said, looking decidedly shifty. 'I'm fine.'

'Good. Bloody hell, you look miserable, mate.'

'I'm fine,' he repeated. Then he shrugged. 'Lydia and I have had a bit of a tiff.'

'Bugger,' Leo said. 'Women. Thought she'd left you?'

'She's back,' Dominic said tightly.

Leo grimaced apologetically. 'Behind with the news. Haven't seen you in ages.'

'No,' Dominic said. 'But I understand you've been away.'

'And now I'm back,' Leo told him. 'Da! Da!'

'Good.'

Leo pulled a beautiful red rose out of his carrier bag with a flourish. 'Give this to Lydia,' he said. 'Tell her you love her.' And, just to show what a nice guy he was, Leo gave Dominic a big kiss on the cheek. He was sure he saw his neighbour flinch.

'How's Emma?' he asked croakily.

'Wonderful,' Leo said. 'Very wonderful. And very soon she's going to think I am too!'

'Give Emma my love,' Dominic said quietly. He clutched the rose to him. 'Tell her I send my love.'

Leo managed to stop himself from frowning.

'I will,' he said, and continued bounding on his way. 'I definitely will.'

And then his neighbour was gone, rushing away down the street as if his life depended on it, leaving Leo to wonder why Dominic would be sending Emma his love?

Chapter Eighty-Nine

It would be polite to change out of my tatty old T-shirt and sweats that have seen better days, but it's only Caron who's coming round for the evening and my friend has seen me in a worse state than this on many occasions. At least I'm clean. I languished in the bath, indulging myself in some of the lavender de-stressing bath oil that Caron bought me for my birthday. It's wonderful stuff, so I'm feeling very chill. All my make-up has been scrubbed off, along with a few layers of London grime, and I promise myself that I will do something wonderful with my hair tomorrow. For tonight, it can stay swept up in my scrunchy.

Padding barefoot through to the kitchen, I make myself a cup of green tea. A new health regime. No chocolate. No booze. I'm going to detox my body. Except, for tonight, I've bought in a box of chocolate Celebrations and a nice bottle of Rioja – so, apart from the green tea, I will start in earnest tomorrow. Honestly. *The X-Factor* is playing away to itself on the television.

The intercom buzzes. 'Hi,' I say. 'Come up.' And I buzz the door open. Turning off the television, I select a CD and click that on instead. Caron is bringing a soppy DVD which we'll watch later with a box of Kleenex to hand. Then I go to open the door to the flat.

'Hi.'

The last person I expect to see standing there is Leo. But he is.

He's wearing a dinner suit with a red rose in his lapel and looks breathtakingly handsome. Leo smiles at me and holds out an enormous bouquet of red roses wrapped in purple tissue paper. He leans jauntily on my doorframe turning up his smile, but something in his expression makes him seem surprisingly vulnerable and his eyes hold a worried look that I haven't seen before.

I examine the roses. They're exquisite. 'Thank you.'

'You're welcome,' Leo says.

I have wondered what this moment would feel like. I imagined that

I'd fall into Leo's arms, all the hurt and pain forgotten – but it isn't like that. I feel tense, affronted and Leo looks like a stranger to me. Perhaps I'm in shock. 'What are you doing here?'

'I've come to take you out,' he says brightly.

'Take me out?'

'If you'll let me.'

'I'm seeing someone else.'

'You're not,' Leo says. 'My spies have reliably informed me that you're still an unfettered, single woman.'

'Well, I could have been,' I sigh.

'But you're not.' Leo fiddles with the rose in his lapel. 'I saw Dominic today.'

'Oh.' I feel myself flush. 'Did he tell you what happened?'

'Er . . . yes. Of course he did. Man to man.'

'It was an experience.' I try very hard not to recall a vivid image of it. 'A dreadful experience. I'm going to have a life-long aversion to cardboard and Superglue. And red underwear.'

Leo raises a puzzled eyebrow and I wonder how much Dominic has really told him.

'He said to send you his . . . regards.' Leo nods thoughtfully. 'His regards. He and Lydia seem very happy together. Very happy.'

'I'm sure they are.' I'm glad it's working out for the man who was briefly a good and caring friend to me. Dominic has forgiven his straying girlfriend and has taken her back. Am I willing to do the same?

I rake my hair and then realise what I must look like. Why couldn't Leo have warned me that he was going to drop back into my life un-announced? 'You'd better come in,' I say.

Leo comes into the lounge and sits down next to me on the sofa. It could so easily feel like old times, but something has changed in both of us. I can feel that there has been an unidentifiable shift somewhere and wonder whether it's in me or whether it's in Leo. And I also wonder whether it's for better or for worse. Would it ever be possible to get the old times back?

'You can't just turn up like this,' I tell Leo. 'Out of the blue. Couldn't you have phoned me? It's been weeks since I've heard anything from you.'

'I know, and I'm sorry. I thought you'd hang up on me again.'

'I can't just drop everything,' I say. 'I am expecting someone, as it happens.'

'Caron.'

'Yes.'

'She isn't coming,' Leo tells me.

A frown crosses my face. 'How do you know?'

Leo has the grace to look sheepish.

'Oh,' I say, penny dropping. 'You organised this with her? Caron who used to be my best friend, but the situation is currently under review.'

'Caron *and* Grant.' Leo checks his watch. 'They are currently enjoying a convivial meal together at a lovely Italian restaurant. I think they'll make a nice couple.'

'And what would you know about that, Leo? You've suddenly become a relationship expert?'

'Everyone thought that you'd missed me.'

'Oh, did they?' I fold my arms. 'Well . . . well, you can even miss toothache once it stops.'

Leo grins at me. He can read me like a book. 'Caron told Grant that you couldn't stop thinking about me.'

'Caron, who is now looking for a new best friend, said that?'

Leo reaches out and takes my hand. It's warm and familiar and sends a weakness to my knees that I hadn't expected. It's just like the first time I met Leo. His face is suddenly serious. 'I want to try again.'

'Oh.'

'You said that the magic had gone out of our relationship and I had no idea what you meant. Really I didn't. But I do now and I want to see if we can get the magic back,' he says.

'Oh. Oh.' My heart is pounding. 'And what about Ms Incredibly Gorgeous Isobel?'

'She's . . . er . . .' Leo looks sad. 'She's gone. For good. And she won't be coming back. You don't have to worry about that.'

'I can't be second choice, Leo.'

'It isn't like that,' he says. 'It was never like that.'

'Do you want to tell me what happened?'

'No.' Leo shakes his head. 'I'm not sure what happened myself. It's a very bizarre story. You wouldn't believe me.'

'I never believe you anyway, Leo.'

'I'll tell you when we've grown old and grey together.' He strokes my hand tenderly. 'Then you'll trust me.'

'If I agree to go out with you again, I'll be old and grey within two weeks.'

Leo grins at me. 'So you are considering it?'

In some ways it feels so good, so right for us to be here together again. Can I forgive and forget all that has gone on between us and start over with a clean slate? In striving for perfection, I've been less than perfect too and it looks as if Leo can forgive me. Aren't the strongest relationships made by people who are prepared to work through the bad times together?

Then I shake my head sadly. 'I can't do this, Leo.' I can't risk getting hurt again. Even though I'm hurting without Leo, it's a constant pain – not the rollercoaster ride that I was on before. 'I'm not sure that I can trust you with my emotions again.'

'You can.' Tears fill Leo's eyes. 'I promise you.'

'I can't risk it,' I say.

'Then it's really over?'

'I'm sorry.' My throat has closed, so I can't say anything else. I don't want to cry but I can't help it. Tears roll slowly down my face.

Leo stands up and I follow suit. He takes my hands in his warm ones. 'It's a terrible shame, Emma,' he tells me, 'because the new, improved Leo is a really great bloke.'

He holds me tight and kisses me like I've never been kissed before. Then he turns and walks out of the door while I stand and wonder what the hell I've done.

Chapter Ninety

L eo's car, Ethel, is parked on the road outside my flat under the spotlight of a nearby lamp post. She's decorated with a garland of tiny
white lights and has swags of tinsel round the outside. Ethel is also
wearing huge black false eyelashes on her headlights. Leo is already
climbing into the driver's seat.

'Leo!'

He stops and looks back at me. I suddenly realised I couldn't let him
go, so now I'm standing on the pavement feeling ridiculous. My eyes
fill with tears and my throat is still constricted. Leo comes over to me.

'That looks pathetic,' I manage to say gruffly.

'Come on,' he says, tugging gently at my hand. 'Get in.'

'Where are we going? I can't go out looking like this.' Skanky sweats
and scrunchy are not a good look. 'You're in your dinner suit.'

Brushing my cheek softly with his thumb, Leo says, 'You look beautiful just as you are.'

Leo opens the passenger door for me. The back seat of the car is
filled with hundreds of red roses.

'Have you bought these all by yourself?' I whisper.

Leo nods. This is not the man I know and have loved. Someone must
have taken him and waved a magic wand over him. By some divine
intervention or top-rate miracle, Leo has turned into a proper boyfriend.

The perfume in the car is intoxicating. My head is reeling. I slide
inside.

'I feel very silly,' I say without conviction. 'Can anyone see us? Where
are we going?'

'Sit back and relax,' Leo instructs. 'Leave everything to me.'

He gets in the car next to me. Then we sit and look at each other
for a moment, still in the silence, and I can see that Leo's eyes are full
of love. Love for me. 'I have missed you,' I say tearfully. 'I've missed you
a lot.'

My favourite Whitney Houston CD starts playing on the car stereo. Which is very strange because Ethel doesn't have a CD player. The stereo doesn't even appear to be switched on. Even Leo looks taken aback.

'How did you do that?'

'I didn't,' Leo says, bemused. 'It must be magic.'

He guns Ethel into life.

'Is all this magic going to make your driving any better?' I ask.

'No.' He shakes his head. 'It's magic. Not a miracle.'

'So some things never change?'

'No. I guess not.' He leans over and kisses me on the cheek. 'But some things do. You wait and see.'

Leo pulls out into the street and, in his usual style, kangaroos off down the road, shouting out of the window, 'Tally ho!'

We drive past a cyclist, way too close, causing him to swerve.

'I know you!' Leo shouts and gives the cyclist a friendly wave. 'Yoo hoo!'

He turns to me. 'I made him fall off his bike the night of your birthday party,' he confesses. 'Doesn't that seem like another lifetime ago?'

'Yes.' Another lifetime ago. In the past. Behind us.

In the rearview mirror I notice that the cyclist has fallen off his bike once more. He jumps up cursing and gives Leo the finger.

We both burst out laughing.

'Sorry!' Leo yells back at him. 'Sorry! Awfully sorry.'

Chapter Ninety-One

Lard pulled uncomfortably at his shirt cuffs. 'I've never been on a blind date before,' he complained.

'Shut up moaning,' Grant said, as they entered the restaurant. 'And be pleased that I care enough about you to arrange this.' He nudged Lard in the ribs and whispered, 'They're here.'

Caron and Jo were already seated at the table that Grant had booked. They both looked lovely. Not shimmery and sparkly, but grounded, substantial and beautiful women.

'Oh my word,' Lard said. 'I wish I'd worn my best undies now.'

Grant put his arm round Lard and hugged him. He'd developed a much stronger need for human contact and warmth since coming home. It was as if all his senses had been scrubbed out and were shiny and raw. His bond with Leo and Lard had strengthened from their experience and he knew that whatever happened to them in the future, it would never be broken. 'I told you I wouldn't let you down, my lovely little friend.'

The conversation in the restaurant babbled like the brook in the Land of Light, and Grant wondered if he would ever stop getting flashbacks to their visit there. It was like suffering from Post Traumatic Stress Disorder – little images could be triggered by such trivia. Except that the vision didn't frighten him or give him nightmares, but filled him with a powerful sense of love, loss and longing. When he saw flickering lights, would it always take him back to their weird and wonderful night at Stonehenge? Would these images always be imprinted so sharply on his brain, or would his memories fade with time? How much worse must it have been for Leo, to have loved and lost a being from another world? All he and Lard could do was try to support Leo and, when he felt alone and overwhelmed, let him know that, for a brief time, they had shared an earth-shatteringly surreal experience with him that had changed them all. Grant could see a kernel of compassion and humanity in the three of them that had never existed before.

Grant kissed Caron as he sat down. He was eternally grateful that she'd been able to forgive him for standing her up on their first official date and had agreed to give their stalled, fledgeling relationship another try. 'Hello again.'

Caron smiled shyly. Lard hovered nervously in the background and Grant pulled him into the nearest chair. 'Meet Lard,' he said by way of introduction.

'Why are you called Lard?' Jo wanted to know.

'I used to be chubby,' Lard confessed. He looked down at his new slim-line stomach – one of the bonuses of having persuaded a giggling Isobel to cast a spell on him. Now when Lard ate chocolate in vast quantities it only helped him to lose weight. The more Mars Bars he consumed, the more the pounds dropped off. It was a shame they couldn't bottle it and sell it.

'And now you're not,' Jo said. 'So what's your real name?'

'Tim,' Lard answered. 'My name's Tim.'

Grant looked at him in surprise. He was sure that he must have once known what Lard's real name was, but no one had called him that for years.

'So Tim,' Jo continued, 'if I let you buy me dinner, are you going to expect to sleep with me tonight?'

'No,' Lard said, faintly aghast.

'Shame,' she said. 'Let's eat. You can reconsider your answer later.'

Grant sighed with relief. They were going to be okay. Lard wouldn't stand a chance if Jo decided they were going to be an item. Which was good, because it meant that he could forget about keeping an eye on his friend and concentrate on his own date.

'It's good to see you.' Grant took hold of Caron's hand.

Caron filled his glass for him and they touched them together. 'To us,' she said.

'To us,' he echoed.

She sipped her wine and then said, 'I wonder how Emma and Leo are getting on? Do you think they'll still be talking to us?'

'I don't know,' Grant admitted. 'We've done all that we can to try to bring them together again. The rest of it is up to Leo and Emma.'

'I hope it's going well for them,' Caron said.

'Me too.'

'Leo's lucky to have a friend like you,' she said.

'No.' Grant shook his head. 'We're all lucky to know Leo. He's a very special guy. I have a lot to thank him for.'

It had been a strange few weeks, but life was gradually getting back to normal again and he was looking forward to settling down to more mundane pursuits once more. No fairies, no spells, no magic. He looked over at Caron; her eyes were shining in the candlelight. Perhaps it wasn't fair to class someone so stunning as a mundane pursuit. He smiled at Caron and felt a rush of warmth to his heart. And as for magic, well, maybe it was a bit rash to say no to magic. He hoped that he was always going to remain open to a bit of that.

Chapter Ninety-Two

It was a marvellous starry, moonlit night. Leo couldn't have asked for anything more perfect. And he'd seen some pretty amazing things in the past few weeks. They could hear nothing but the sound of the lapping waves on the beach, the rush of water over shingle. Leo didn't know what had really happened in the Land of Light or with the whole Isobel thing, but he did know that he felt more calm than he had in his entire life. There was a contentment at his core that had been missing before, and instead of charging aimlessly and foolishly through his life, he was going to start to appreciate the things he had. Leo Harper was going to stop and smell the roses.

Emma and Leo were sitting on a tartan blanket that he'd set out on the beach. Leo had whisked her down to Brighton – snuggled together in the beautifully-scented Ethel, eating up the miles with ease. This had always been one of their favourite weekend haunts and somewhere they hadn't visited in a long time. Now it was dark and the day-trippers were long gone, heading for the bars and restaurants, the renowned nightlife. The lights of the town sparkled in the distance and the huge framework of Brighton Pier provided their backdrop. They were alone, looking out over the vast sweep of ocean.

Leo had taken a lot of trouble in packing the picnic, trawling his brain to remember all of Emma's favourite foods. He realised that it felt great to do nice things for the person you love the most on earth.

The night was warm, but Leo had gathered some firewood and lit a fire on the beach. Cuddled up together, they were watching the sparks dance in the air. They'd both rolled up their trousers to their knees and had stripped off their socks so that they could toast their toes by the fire.

'Warm enough?' Leo asked.

Emma nodded, but he took off his jacket anyway and draped it around her shoulders. She didn't complain, just leaned against him, eyes closed. Leo undid his bow tie and let it hang. Tonight he had managed to tie it all by himself without the aid of a fairy and her magic wand. Isobel was right, he was perfectly capable of managing without her, and that thought somehow made him smile.

'What's wrong?' Emma squeezed his hand.

'Nothing,' he said. 'Nothing at all.'

'This is wonderful, Leo. Magical. Thank you.'

Reaching over to the picnic basket, he pulled out a bottle of champagne. He unwound the wire carefully and then let the cork fly – for once not having to worry about denting someone's ceiling or taking someone's eye out. As he did, a shooting star rushed across the sky.

'Did you see that?'

'Yes,' Emma said. 'That's the first time I've ever seen a shooting star. Aren't they supposed to be a good omen?'

'Make a wish.'

Emma's eyes met his. 'It already came true.'

Leo wondered if he would ever be able to tell Emma about Isobel. About why she'd been here. And how you should be very careful what you wish for. Maybe some time, but not now.

'Here . . .' Leo handed her two glasses and the champagne frothed over into them.

He took the wire fixer from the cork and twisted it around. Taking Emma's hand in his, Leo said, 'Emma, will you do me the very great honour of marrying me?'

Emma's eyes filled up with tears. 'Yes,' she breathed.

Leo slipped the champagne wire ring onto her finger. His fiancée admired it in the moonlight. 'It's beautiful.'

They stood up and wrapped their arms around each other.

'We need to make a toast,' Leo said.

Emma and Leo clinked their glasses together. 'To the moonlight, the madness and the magic. To us.'

They toasted each other, savouring the taste of the champagne. The wind picked up gently and lifted Emma's hair in the breeze. Lights sparkled in the sky, tiny pinpricks of colour that Leo knew instinctively he'd seen somewhere before. He turned to the fire; the flames flickered, showering sparks into the air. In the flames Leo saw an image of Isobel and she was smiling out at him. A tiny silver butterfly broke free of the flames and, as his eyes followed it, it fluttered away high into the sky until soon it was out of sight, vanished in the darkness. But he knew that Isobel was happy and Leo was happy too. She'd always be with him in spirit, but he had Emma – always his one true love – here on earth. And he was glad that he'd had the chance to know Isobel. He was glad that she had come along to open his heart, to blow it apart and to show him just how much he could love. She had managed to teach Leo a lesson that was well worth learning.

Punching his arm into the air, he cried out at the top of his lungs, 'Hoo! Hoo!'

Leo swept Emma up into his arms and twirled her around. She shrieked with delight. Then he ran down the beach, loving the crunch of the pebbles beneath his feet and the wind in his hair. They reached the sea and he carried Emma into the waves, letting the icy water rush over them both, gasping as the foam hit them.

'I love you,' Emma said, her mouth against his neck.

'I love you too.' Leo held her to him. 'We'll get it right this time. I promise you.'

'I'll hold you to it,' she warned. Then she jumped down and ducked him into the water, splashing and laughing. And Leo had never felt happier or more alive in all his life.

Chapter Ninety-Three

Everything is pitch black. Only the dying embers of the fire remain. The beach is completely deserted. Everyone sane is tucked up in their beds by now. But I never want this night to end. I'm loved. And I'm in love.

'I'm bloody soaked through,' I say, doing my best to sound cross.

'Sorry. Sorry. It was fun though.'

'It was *not* fun,' the future Mrs Leo Harper insists.

'Sorry. Sorry.'

'Just look at me.'

'I am.'

'I'm going to have to take *all* of my clothes off,' I say.

It may be dark but I can still make out the smile on Leo's lips – so I know he can see the smile on mine. '*All* of them?'

'Every last thing.'

'I could help you,' my husband-to-be suggests.

'Don't you come anywhere near me, Leo Harper. You are nothing but trouble.'

'Do I have to take all of my clothes off too?'

'Yes. Unless you want to catch your death of cold.'

'I'd rather take your clothes off first.'

'Ahh! Leo. Get off! That tickles. I'm serious.'

We help each other undress, laughing, loving. I'm still not sure what has happened between Leo and me, but it's finished now and behind us. We've learned from it and will move on. Leo covers my body with kisses. Tender, butterfly kisses. I have Leo back. The new, improved Leo. And I will cherish him as he deserves to be cherished.

'Come here, wifey,' Leo says. 'I want to show you what a thoroughly wonderful husband I'm going to be.'

I laugh and, holding each other tightly, we sink onto the brand new picnic blanket Leo has splashed out on. Another shooting star crosses

328